S. R. Smith

# The Wyoming Valley in the nineteenth century

Art edition Volume I.

S. R. Smith

**The Wyoming Valley in the nineteenth century**
*Art edition Volume I.*

ISBN/EAN: 9783742840394

Manufactured in Europe, USA, Canada, Australia, Japa

Cover: Foto ©Andreas Hilbeck / pixelio.de

Manufactured and distributed by brebook publishing software
(www.brebook.com)

S. R. Smith

**The Wyoming Valley in the nineteenth century**

# The
# WYOMING VALLEY

### IN THE

## NINETEENTH CENTURY.

---

### BY S. R. SMITH,

AUTHOR OF

"THE WYOMING VALLEY IN 1892" AND OF "THE LACKAWANNA VALLEY FOR A
QUARTER OF A CENTURY."

---

## *ART EDITION.*

### V. 1
### VOLUME I.

---

WILKES-BARRE LEADER PRINT.
1894.

# A REVIEW.

BY S. R. SMITH.

———

THIS VALLEY is the fairest in all the earth; it is a page on which we are writing an epic; it is a field wherein we are turning daring furrows from which we hope to grow a better moral, intellectual and spiritual life.

Our history is a sad tale, and the giving it immortality was the accident of circumstance and position. Its weakness and misfortune in that one supreme summer of '78 give it a claim to the sympathy of humanity. It is an act of devotion to bring back the past from the many vanished years, and to remember with affection those who are waiting for us in the dust and silence of the cemetery.

It is something in the nature of a crime against human nature and our progenitors to idly disregard the past. On the contrary, we should say grace when we start to read the history of the early settlers of this Valley, and the descendants of those early settlers, with many new-comers as well, are not to be blamed for the jealous solicitude with which they seek for and take down the narratives that fall from the trembling lips of the aged. Their words are gathered up as a precious legacy which they will preserve and hand down to posterity, that their own descendants will not some day have to seek in vain for memorials of their ancestry.

Our forefathers were Puritans; and all we are and all we possess we owe to them. They were the boldest and bravest men that ever lived; they made that which had been for centuries the nightmare of kings and the dream of the common people, prevail; they plucked the fairest jewel from the British crown, and made this nation the world's ideal; they created a new world on the foundation of civil and religious liberty; they gave us a country without a dominant church, an inquisition or king; they gave us a new life from out the eternal dust-heap of the waste of centuries. These men had a spirit of unconquerable resistance, and were cast in heroic mold. Their mission was to pluck the mantle of authority from the shoulders of royalty, and place it on the back of the unjustly oppressed. Moreover, these forefathers of ours were a homogeneous people; they spoke but one language, had but one form of religious worship, recognized no social barriers, had been religious rebels at home, and, above all, had, under Cromwell, overthrown royalty in the Civil War.

And although they were iconoclasts, image-smashers, idealists, yet with all their cruelty and fanaticism their memory comes down to us with the perfume of poetry as if blown over hills of roses.

The Indian and the Puritan had little in common; one represented a wild democracy, the other was the incarnation of individualism. The Puritan loved the Indian because he had so little skill in driving bargains, but after that had for them nothing but degradation and annihilation. In return, the only satisfaction the Indian had was to creep up to the settler's door and utter that never-to-be-forgotten, soul-appalling yell which he loved so much. The tawny brave was the embodiment of physical courage, for while his tormentors were lopping his ears, splitting his nose, swearing his wounds with hot ashes, while all the time his naked body was roasting in the flames, even then he shouted his death-song with a steady voice until his tormentors plucked out his tongue or dashed out his brains.

As Indian names often sounded harsh in the original tongue, which we changed into melodious accent, so it is to a great extent true that much of the poetry and romance with which we invest the forest denizens are of our own invention. The truth is, their lives were too hard to be romantic, and while their women were faithful as wives, they spent their youth in unrestrained licentiousness, and in their old age were vindictive hags. The stoicism of the Indian had its foundation in pride, for his delight was to boast of his deeds in the presence of the unblushing squaw. He was the only American aristocrat, the tribe composed the only American aristocracy.

We have attempted to establish an aristocracy on the basis of ancestry, but the source from which we come is too near. An aristocracy of wealth has proven impossible, for wealth gathers all kind of fish into its net; and an aristocracy of talent is equally impossible, for talent cares not for the lauble.

Our forefathers in this Valley were poor. They were obliged to subsist on what the soil could be made to produce. Indeed, in the year 1784, after the great flood had swept the Valley from mountain to mountain, had it not been for the shad coming up the river in the spring, all the settlers would have perished.

Before they gained their independence, they dare not make so much as a tooth for a rake, or wear a home-made garment, without being rebels in the eyes of the home government. They were not allowed to manufacture the most common necessities for domestic uses, without paying a heavy tax; and what they needed the most was taxed the highest. But the colonists put a tariff cob in the Lion's mouth, and George Washington pulled down the flag of George the Third; they refused to let England convert this country into a royal hunting-park, or to pay their bills.

The Puritans had a licentious soldiery saddled upon them. In this Valley, they also had the Pennamites, who, like so many in Virginia and the Carolinas, inclined to Toryism, to torment them. These Tories, while their patriotic neighbors were away with the Continental army, were selling stock to the Hessians, and faring sumptuously on their substance. Our Connecticut ancestors were therefore never lacking a foe, either at home or abroad. And to-day, there is no royal family in Europe but would openly or secretly rejoice at any evidence of our decay and approaching downfall, for a republic is a menace and a reproach to monarchy.

The every-day life of one hundred years ago presents much to us that is wholesome and attractive. The people knew little of luxury, and simple piety, kindliness and good sense were the foundation of their lives. They were isolated, and consequently provincial; their

lives were narrow, hard, and commonplace; and were spent mostly in the kitchen. Their houses were without paint, the floors were white sand sprinkled on the earth; the only piece of furniture of any importance was a chest of drawers where the family linens were kept, and in which the matron invariably rummaged while entertaining her guests. Their eating was out of wooden trenchers, and their seat was a straight-backed wooden "setter." Their hair they wore tied back in a cue, and lace hanging down over their hands gave them an air of unmistakable gentility. The test of a well-made man was to keep his breeches above his hips, without suspenders, and his garterless stockings above the calf of his leg. The poorer people wore petticoat breeches that came to the knee, and no farther; when the seat became prematurely worn out they made front and rear reverse situations.

The houses were scattered loosely about the Valley, and for protection they would hurry to the fort when the signal-gun warned them of danger. The roads were not much more than lanes, except the stage route. The arrival of the stage, by the way, was the event of the week. An entire family would simultaneously drop all work and rush to the doors when the old lumbering box swept by with two or three passengers. The front yard was a medley of dog-kennel, grindstone, beehive, blue-flag, marigold, bachelor-button, sweet-william, caraway and tansy. The front gate was a pair of bars: one of the windows was usually adorned in some quarter by an old hat.

The old people were much attached to the church; they revered the house of God, and their religions meant much to them; they were as familiar with the passages of God's Word as with the blue sky above them. The old hymns were engraved on their hearts. The women took their knitting to meeting, and worked and worshipped at the same time. The minister was loved and venerated. He dared to be bold. He would mention the individual sins of each member of his congregation, as well as the collective sins of the community. He would make very pointed remarks, during a political campaign, to the candidates of each opposing party. On the other hand, he himself could get drunk, if not too drunk, without affecting his prospects in this world or the next.

The young people had no amusements except balls and parties. The old people believed that the young were dancing on the edge of perdition, and that a pack of cards and a fiddle were the devil's kit. Children were taught to obey; they did not get much book-learning, because "toeing the mark" was more important than correct spelling. The poor little things would strain their necks to sit up stiffly in church, like their elders, and they probably wondered if the lower regions were paved with infants' skulls. At public gatherings the old men would be extravagantly polite, and would endeavor to outdo nobility in point of punctilio. The host would fill the guest's plate many times, and it was bad form for the guest to refuse to eat if his stomach could accommodate another grain. When repletion was complete, he put his knife across the plate and his spoon across the tea-cup, as a sign that he could eat no more. Many of these old customs come down to within fifty years ago. Even then flint and tallow-candles were in vogue.

We are filled with amazement when we think of what these men accomplished, and are led to exclaim that surely humor and caprice do not determine human destiny. These Yankees were the men who gave us, their descendants, "letters-patent of nobility." We are proud of the distinction because to be without ancestry is a serious thing in this Valley.

To come down, now, to a much later period. The Civil War resulted in a great revolution of our social and public life. Old conditions were overthrown and new ones created, and the result has been to direct the public mind to the studying of economic questions. Suddenly the nation's thought found new and deeper channels in which to flow. We may say that we are in a way to realize the Puritan dream of government. We have a higher type of civilization and a quickened intellectual growth; a warmer, and more earnest, moral sentiment; a stronger sense of national patriotism; more contentment among the masses; more purity and seriousness among all people.

We owe much to the English nation. Britain boasts that three-fourths of our population are of their flesh and blood, and thereby hangs our greatness. This strictly speaking, is a vast error. However, had the British written that the British Isles furnished us with three-fourths of our population the statement would then be nearer correct. They have given us a host during the last forty years who came here vicious and illiterate, without the first conception of civil liberty. They assumed to control the government and capital of our institutions by violence. They have planted a saloon on nearly every street in the Valley. Unprincipled men have become more or less supreme, and have left the public helpless. The demagogue has inflamed, for his own ends, the working man against capital, and raised a barrier between them that has resulted in the loss of millions in this section. We have an ultra-English element, who, when England flung over the ocean during the Civil War the cry that the United States was a bursted bubble, and that slavery was the irremovable corner-stone of the republic, echoed the lie.

At the present time, we have between these mountains the most varied population ever gathered in common citizenship; but, fortunately, we will not allow foreign intermeddling, and all citizens must become Americanized in spirit and in speech.

No power can perpetuate in this country European tongue, institutions, or sentiments. The foreign element has had full swing. They have played the statesman and legislator. While we have not altogether held this element in check, we have civilized it, and in the rising generation the distinctions of nationality show signs of disappearing. The host of emigrants on our heels impose a great responsibility and task upon us. The melting pot of the common schools has a great part of that task, and the church worker the rest, of fusing this heterogeneous multitude of many languages into one English-speaking people. We must produce public men with inspiring policies that dare speak of the divine mission of America. Let us realize that it is the want of knowledge that causes mankind to perish; let us learn that ignorance is more a barrier to business and social success than poverty,—infinitely more. Let us hope that there even now is a great revolution taking place, and that something splendidly American is beginning to make itself dominant. Certainly one favorable sign is that so much money is being given to institutions that aim to improve the social, religious and intellectual status of man. This is the crowning glory of the nineteenth century.

Another gratifying aspect is the fact that among the young men of to-day, more so than at any previous time, there is a sentiment which tends to prevent them from frequenting saloons. The cause is undoubtedly that men are increasing in self-respect.

Those who come after us, it is hoped, will live a freer and higher life, and will make our towns and cities centres of morality and culture; that they will have different and better ideals than ours, where wealth will be less centralized; that reforms will be less

confined; and that knowledge of every university and college will be brought to every door for the asking; when the coloring element of life will not be of the ancestral type; when the divided segments of our life will be gathered together and find harmonious expression. We are of the faith that what is right must triumph; what is evil must perish. The most striking feature of our life is its many woven threads of infinitely diverse elements that hold each other in check and prevail together.

The power of an enlightened public opinion is fast becoming the power that will cure vice and punish crime. It is like the golden smithy of Aaron, where the high priest throws the jewels and pounded ornaments of the people which are fused into objects of public adoration. The nineteen century has been a period of struggle, of trials, and of victories. The irrepressible conflict of light with darkness, of truth with error, of superstition with demonstration, through these years, has brought the dawn of a brighter day which steadily grows more roseate, and we are about to see the full glory of a day in which ideals shall become actualities, and America shall exhibit to the world manhood in its highest development.

## THE FAMILIES OF THE VALLEY FIFTY YEARS AGO.

All the facts used in these annals were obtained from the score or more of old white-haired men who still occupy the old arm-chair in the shadow of the porch, with life's battle all fought and their part acted to admiration, waiting, justified and fully contented, for the last summons.

The people of the valley fifty and sixty years ago were mostly Anglo Saxon. They have divided their possessions among the Celts and other foreign people and given place to this mongrel, sharp and restless generation.

In the changes that the years have wrought we have lost much, but we have gained more. The old neighborly feeling has passed away, yet in our cosmopolitan population we have conditions that make the best kind of a community for the development of all classes and the general good.

The thrush has been silenced and the blue-jay has fled to the grove of odorous pine. We still have the old-fashioned daisies blooming on the hillside and old-fashioned birds singing old-fashioned songs in the hedges, and in the garrets are broken spindles, shad seines and pigeon nets, rotting with the rusting accoutrements of war—their occupation gone. All the wild beasts have fled, but will return again in a few centuries to undisturbed possession of their ancestral haunts in these hills and plains.

These records are but little more than gossip about our progenitors, yet we all love gossip better than all the classical literature of the past.

The writer believes that this little history will prove a lasting contribution to the historical literature of the Valley and bring the past to the remembrance of this forgetful generation, so that the past and the present may be an unbroken thread.

Wilkes Barre became a borough in 1806. Lord Butler was the first President of the Town Council. It was incorporated into a city in 1871, and Charles Parrish served as the first President of the City Council. The position has been filled by Charles A. Miner, Herman C. Fry, G. M. Reynolds, D. A. Frantz, E. W. Sturdevant, E. L. Dana, H. H. Derr, William J. Harvey, and the present officer, W. H. McCartney. The first Mayor was

Ira M. Kirkendall, who was followed by M. A. Kearney, W. W. Loomis, Thomas Brodrick, C. B. Sutton and F. M. Nichols.

Sixty years ago there were no paved streets nor sewers; now we have over twenty miles of the former and thirty of the latter.

Beginning at the corner of West Market street and Public Square, where the Long block stands, was originally a frame house, occupied fifty years ago by Rev. Rufus Lane, who preached in the old church on the Square. The late Isaac Osterhout bought the property and built a store that was burned down in a fire which swept that side of the Square to the Luzerne House. Adjoining he built a brick block. Where the bank building of the Wyoming Valley Trust Company, formerly the Rockafellow bank, stands, was a frame house, the residence of Anthony Brower; Mrs. Squire Parson was his daughter. Barnet Ulp lived in a frame house adjoining. Next to the alley stood a small house, the occupant not known. Across the alley lived Daniel Collings, who was postmaster; he kept a jewelry store also, J. B. Collings, Esq., of Scranton, and Samuel, who married a daughter of Andrew Beaumont. Mrs. A. J. Baldwin, Mrs. Charles Dougherty are his children. James Sutton had a store for many years where Isaac Livingston has his store; formerly the lot was occupied by a frame house used by William Carey for a cigar store. Beyond him was the store and house of Jonathan Bulkeley; he was Sheriff of the county; Dr. Bulkeley and Charles, the Alderman, Mrs. A. R. Brundage, are his children. The property where the Luzerne House stands was owned by him. George P. Steel built a hotel, one of the famous hotels in those days. Later the property became apart of the Ziba Bennett estate.

On the corner of the east side of the Square lived Lord Butler, the father of E. G. Butler, Esq., and Mrs. William Hillard. Lord and John Butler built and occupied the first steam grist mill in this town; it stood on the spot where the Hillard grocery store now stands. The next property was the currier shop of Wm. Bowman and Josiah Lewis. The next property was where Judge Kidder and Lawyer Nicholson had their offices. Dr. Boyd came next. Then Mrs. Overton. Where the Exchange Hotel stands there was a tavern kept by John D. Shafer. The old building was burned in one of the many fires that were so common in this city before we had a paid fire department. Then the present structure was erected. The corner property was where Judge Scott lived for many years; Mrs. Judge Kidder was his daughter. On the south side of the Square, on the corner where the Osterhout block stands, was a tavern famous in its day as the resort for the public and professional men of the county; it was kept by Archippus Parrish; Charles, Archibald, George, Gould, Bradley, Mrs. F. W. Hunt and Mrs. Hugh Fell are his children. Joseph Slocum lived in the building now occupied by S. L. Brown; he was the brother of Francis Slocum. James Helme carried on the cabinet business on the next lot; he was the son of Oliver Helme. Next to him was the tin-shop of Samuel Howe. Next, on the corner, was the blacksmith shop of Laning & Drake.

On the opposite side, where Robert Baur has his printing office, was a store kept by Whitney Smith. On the next property stood a foundry and blacksmith shop of Mr. Laning. Where the Welles Building stands were a few frame buildings called Rag Row, in one of which lived Conrad Teeter, the proprietor of the semi-weekly stage from Wilkes-Barre to Painted Post, N. Y. Then came the Anhaeuser house. On the corner General Isaac Bowman lived; Miss Mary is a daughter; Monroe, Horatio, Frank and Samuel were his sons.

Main and Market street crossed each other in the centre of the Square. On Market street, west of Main were four brick pillars, two on each side of the street, covered with a roof, but open on the sides. This was the market house. On the east plot was the fire-proof, on the southern plot the court house, on the western plot the old Ship Zion, on the northern plot the Academy.

North Main, on the east side, next to the corner, was where Alderman Gilbert Burrows had his office. Here was a number of offices called Buzzard Row. Above was Benjamin Drake, a blacksmith; his children were Rev. George, C., Thomas, and the first wife of W. W. Loomis, Mrs. Miner Blackman, Mrs. Polly Marcy and Sarah Helme. The adjoining lots were occupied by a number of old buildings, tenant houses.

There was a cabinet shop near where Adam Behee built his brick block. Mr. Behee is still alive; he was a blacksmith. Where the Forrest House stands Dr. Jones lived. James, of the Wyoming bank, William and three daughters were his children. On the corner of Union street was a log house. Near the canal were a few old wooden buildings, owned by Joseph Slocum. Oliver Hillard's property adjoined; Mrs. Samuel Lynch, Mrs. W. L. Conyngham, Mrs. Rufus Bell are his daughters.

John Myers, the father of Lawrence, Henry, William, Charles and three daughters lived in the next house. Then came the shop of William Hodman. This was Gabtown. On the north side of Main street from Public Square, the first buildings were two stores and next was the residence, still standing, of Ziba Bennett, the father of Mrs. John C. Phelps and George S. Bennett. Mr. Bennett was an influential man in his day. Where James Laird's harness shop stands was the office of Lawyer Winchester. Above this was the Methodist class room. Above that was the law office of George Dennison, and his residence was adjoining. Then came the office of Dr. Jackson. Beyond him was Job Gibbs. Z. Grey's bakery stood next. Then came the residence of Sharp D. Lewis. Later Byron Nicholson, Esq., erected a building on the lot, after the old one had burned down. Gilbert Barnes lived next. On the corner was a log house. Across Union street, on the corner, Dr. Thomas W. Miner lived. Over the canal lived a Mr. Phillips and Jake Sauber. Beyond them was a wheelwright shop. Then a tavern kept by Paul Dunn. Then came the shop of Mr. Gilchrist. Above Jackson street was a log house, still standing.

West Market street, from Public Square, on the north side: Next to what is now the Long block was the Ebenezer Bowman property, extending to the property of Henry F. Lamb, a druggist. The Bowman residence was on this property. Mr. Bowman was a prominent man. Mrs. Thomas W. Miner was his daughter. Then came the Lamb property on the corner of what is now North Franklin street. There was a drug store near the corner. The property at an earlier date belonged to Edward McShane; his widow married H. F. Lamb. The property came into the possession of the youngest daughter, Mary, who sold it to Robert Pettebone, the son of the late Payne Pettebone, of Wyoming. Where the Second National Bank stands was owned by Jacob J. Dennis, who kept a tavern. Gilbert Laird kept the first drug store, on the corner, afterward used as a tavern. The next property belonged to Abram Thomas. On this property was a double house. His daughter, Emily, married Washington Lee. There were four daughters. Next was Thomas Hutchings, who traded the property to Charles Terwilliger. Mrs. Nancy S. Drake owned the next property. She subsequently sold it to William Wood. A two-story frame stood on the ground, where Mrs. Drake carried on the millinery business. Mrs. Drake was a large owner of real estate and

was a woman of great force of character as well as possessing great business qualities.
Mrs. W. W. Loomis and Mrs. Blackman were daughters and W. D. Loomis is her grandson,
who inherited her property. The next property belonged to Mathias Hollenback and
extended to River street. On it was a building occupied by a refugee from San Domingo.
The next building was the tin-shop of Samuel Howe. The next building was occupied by
William A. Merrit, a hatter, and later by Mr. Van Fleet. The corner house had a wing that
was used as a bar-room; William Johnson kept a bar-room in a part of the building at a
later day.

The south side of West Market street from River: Next to the Hollenback store and
residence on the corner was the office of Col. H. B. Wright. Where C. E. Butler now
has his book store, stood the dwelling-house of Jacob Sinton; Mrs. Sidney Tracey
was his daughter. Next was his residence and next lived Sidney Tracey. On the corner
where the Wyoming Bank stands was a store conducted by Sinton & Tracey. There was
a high board fence fronting on Market street and some large Lombardy poplars.

West Market street, between Franklin street and Public Square: Where the Rutter
block stands there stood a house a little way from the street, where ex-Sheriff Jonathan
Bulkeley lived in 1828. Mr. Bulkeley was a merchant. On the next property stood a building occupied by Andrew Beaumont with the post-office; John C., his son, was a Commodore
in the U. S. Navy. Henry lived and died in this city; Andrew was in the United States
service; Eugene was an officer in the United States Army; he retired and is living in this
city. There were four daughters, all now deceased. Then came Edmund Taylor, Z. Gray
and Charles B. Drake's store.

East Market street, from the Public Square: Beyond the Parrish house was the old
stone jail, a two-story, eight room building, with kitchen attached, with an old porch in
front. On the opposite side was an old house, the occupant forgotten. There was an
old log house occupied by George Tucker.

East Market street: On the hill lived Christian Gruver, a farmer. Near him lived
Abram Marks.

North River street, from Market: Where Music Hall stands was a tavern, kept by
Mrs. Johnson, and later a building in which Samuel Nicholson, Thomas Blake and Andrew
Beaumont, Jr., kept stores at different times. George H. Resett, a nephew of George Hollenback, also had a store there. Fred. McAlpine, the father of Andrew McAlpine, used the
building for a tin-shop. Where William S. Wells lives was a small building. Then was
the cabinet shop of James C. Helme. Later was a building built by Wm. Willetts, now occupied by Nathaniel Rutter. Next, where Anthony Emily lived, was a large residence built
and occupied by Lewis Worrel; adjoining was a large building in which he had a pottery;
on this lot Captain John Urquhart, the father of Dr. George, built and subsequently occupied the house now occupied by Arnold Bertels. There was a log house occupied by
William Russell next. Isaac A. Chapman, the historian, lived where Jonas Long's
sons built their residence. Squire Eleazer Carey married Mr. Chapman's widow and lived
there. B. F. Dorrance and Caleb Wright lived in the house at a later day. Above was
the Ingham brewery; it was finally purchased by John Reichard; it stood near where
what was the home of F. V. Rockafellow. Mr. Reichard built the Rockafellow house
and lived there until he sold the property to Mr. Rockafellow. Across Union street
was the Griswold house, occupied by Harris and Henry Colt, and their sister, Mrs. Gris-

wald; Andrew Beaumont, Pierce Butler and Sharpe D. Lewis married the daughters of Arnold Colt; one son, Harris, was in the United States Army; Harry was a prominent surveyor; Chester was in a department at Washington. Dr. Charles F. Ingham lived there and built the residence where his family now resides. On the bank of the canal was a house where the young men of Wilkes-Barre conducted a theatre, the talent being entirely local.

South River street, from Market : On the corner was the old Geo. M. Hollenback dwelling and store. This was a brick building, one of the four brick buildings in the borough. The ground floor on Market street was a store, this was the leading store in this part of the State. Where the Valley House stands was occupied by the Phoenix tavern; from it the stages started up and down the river and across the mountain by the old turnpike. South River street and Northampton were important streets. The tavern was kept by Orlando Porter, the father of George Porter, the artist and preacher, and the author of a volume entitled "From Infidelity to Christianity." Mrs. John M. Burtes was his daughter. Later W. H. Alexander became the proprietor; he is the father of John, Charles, Emily. He was followed by McGilchrist. The building was torn down. The next house below was built by Judge Charles D. Shoemaker, the father of Fred. W. M. and Robert, of this city; it became the property of Amzi Fuller, who was a very prominent man; Henry A. Fuller, Esq. of this city, is his grandson. The next residence was built by Andrew T. McClintock, Esq. On the next property, where Misses Caroline and Emily Alexander live, was the old stone residence of Jacob Cist; he was postmaster in 1821; after his death Chester Butler married his widow, who was a sister of George Hollenback, and lived in the house. Where Irving A. Stearns lives was built by Judge John N. Conyngham; formerly the site was occupied by a small frame house where Samuel Wright, a darkey, kept a confectionery and bakery; Sam was a bachelor who was highly esteemed. The ladies of the village came to his place once a year and made him quilts and overhauled his belongings; he in return prepared an elegant repast for their entertainment. Judge Conyngham, who came into possession of the property, came to the town as attorney for the Philadelphia bank; after the bank was discontinued he became a member of the Luzerne Bar and finally President Judge, filling the position with great honor for thirty years: Mrs. Charles Parrish, the wife of Bishop Stevens, Charles M. and W. L. are his children. Where Col. R. B. Ricketts and Benjamin Reynolds built their double block is on the site of the Philadelphia bank. Below it stood a century box, in the yard, where a watchman kept guard at night. The door of the vault in the bank was of sheet iron fastened by an old-fashion lock; the cashier was John Bettle. When the bank was closed Judge Conyngham moved into the building and here most of his family were born. Hendrick B. Wright afterward lived there. Where Sheldon Reynolds lives was occupied by his father, William C. Reynolds. On the corner, where S. L. Brown built his residence, was a vacant lot. On the opposite corner, across Northampton street, where Judge Stanley Woodward lives, was the residence of Lord Butler, the father of Mrs. Judge Conyngham, Mrs. D. Donnelson, Charles, John, Lord and Zebulon. After the Pennamite War the building was used for county offices. After Lord Butler's death it was occupied by John L. Butler; it was torn down by Judge Stanley Woodward and his present residence erected in its place. Where the elegant residence of Charles Parrish stands were two buildings, one a one-story building occupied by a carpet weaver named Overholtz, the other was a frame house; in

front of these houses was a stone supposed to have been used by the Indians to pound corn in as there was a shallow basin hollowed out of the top. Where Dr. Edward R. Mayer lived so many years was built by John W. Robbinson, father-in-law of Col. H. B. Wright. Where Col. Wright's house stands was a little unfinished house occupied by John C. Snow. Next to him lived Joseph Backinstow, a tailor. This man deserves special mention as the carrier of the gossip mail bag. The town was so infested with gossips that the men in self-defense employed this tailor to go and stand each morning for ten minutes under the window of each gossip with a leather bag to catch the gossip. On the next property was the house of John P. Arndt, who brought to this town old Michael, the sexton of the old ship Zion, and the constable of the village. Later Thomas H. Morgan occupied it and used it for a stage house; Mrs. David Wilmot was his daughter. The boys of the village used the barn and the garret for a circus. There are only four survivors of the troop—N. S. Rutter, Charles E. Lathrop and C. E. Butler and T. N. Smith. John P. Arndt had a store house on the river bank that was used for an ark depot. Old Michael lived there after his benefactor died. Here he had a pound where he locked up pigs, cattle and drunkards all together. The boys formed a juvenile military organization, in imitation of their elders, who loved to wear brass buttons and on holidays would move up in line in front of old Michael's house and salute him. To show his appreciation of the honor done him he would come out and give each officer two pence and the privates one. In those days the bell of the old ship Zion, on the Square, would be rung by the old sexton for all the lights of the village to be extinguished.

Where Mrs. Emery's house stands was the old homestead of Moses Wood, the father of John, William, Isaac, Matthew and Moses and four daughters. The next place was that of John P. Shott, one of the first houses built in this section; it stood where E. H. Chase now lives. On the site occupied by the R. J. Flick residence was the home of Roswell Welles, who was one of the ablest lawyers of this section ; he dates back to 1805. He married a daughter of Col. Zebulon Butler. In front of where the William M. Conyngham residence stands, on the river bank, was a large double house built and occupied by Jabez Fish. This was a handsome residence, beautifully located. Mr. Fish farmed the island, which was called Fish Island. The old stage route from Northumberland came by the house. Here one of the many forts built along the river had been located, as it commanded a view of the river in each direction. This locality had been a favorite camping place of the Indians for the same reason. Here stood a beautiful grove. Below there was a wide beach where the shad seines would be hauled in. The only house on Academy street was that of John Davis. Some distance below, on Carey avenue lived Henry Keck, whose son Henry deliberately shot his father with a rifle because he was coming home intoxicated. The young man was pardoned by the Governor, much to the disgust of the people of the town, who held a mock execution on the Public Square and hanged the Governor in effigy. Cuff Hick read the death sentence. Back in the early days in the Valley there stood a log cabin built by the settlers for an Indian chief who had been converted to Christianity by the Moravian missionaries. This chief was esteemed by the settlers. The six nations became jealous of his popularity and as the Indians in the Valley were simply a tributary tribe, they sent a committee down here who fastened him in his cabin and burned the building. His name was Teedyuscung. He was intoxicated at the time. In front of the Fish residence was an old Indian burying ground.

Union, from River street: On the corner was the Ingham house, built by James C. Helme. Next was a small house occupied by the widow Wilson. Next lived Patrick Gorman. There was a house where the Loomis residence stands, the occupant not known. On the corner of what is now Franklin street lived a family by the name of Bowman. On the opposite side lived Mr. Vernet; Mrs. Dr. Ingham is a daughter. Across the street Mrs. Tracy kept a boarding house. On the lower side lived Thomas Patterson. Next lived a man by the name of Kirkoff. On the upper side lived Job Barton; his son Samuel was one of the postmasters of Wilkes-Barre. Near Canal street was the house of Conrad Picket, one of the first Germans who settled in this city. On the upper side of the street was Patrick McGuigan. Beyond him lived George Dickover, the father of William Dickover, of this city.

Northampton street, from River street: Steuben Butler had a printing office on the southwest corner of Franklin and Northampton where he with Charles Miner published the *Gleaner* and afterward the *Wyoming Herald*. On the northeast corner was a one-story house occupied by Mr. Dupuy, a refugee from the island of San Domingo, the father-in-law of Ralph Laco. Next to Dupuy came the Gibson house, built by Chief Justice Gibson, afterward occupied by Judge Jones, then by Judge Woodward; Stanley Woodward was born there. Near him lived Doctor Streater, in the old Gildersleeve house, father of W. C. Gildersleeve. Beyond Main street, on the left-hand side, Lord Butler lived, where he began housekeeping. Next to him was Hart Alkins. On the opposite side of the street lived William Hart, the father of Port Hart. Jesse Feil lived in a house, a part of which is now standing on the corner of Washington street. This house is where the first anthracite coal is said to have been burned in a grate by Jesse Fell. This place was a tavern. Mrs. Joseph Slocum and Mrs. J. J. Dennis were his daughters. Beyond the canal lived John Connor, father of John, David, William and Mrs. John Dickover. On the next lot was a colored family by the name of Brown. Many fugitive slaves escaping from bondage found shelter in this house. When the many citizens of our city who were in sympathy with the South rode Mr. Gildersleeve on a rail through the streets of the town this house was blockaded for defense; a shot was fired in the yelling crowd; a man was killed. This was followed by the house being raided. This house was a station of the under-ground railroad.

Hazle street, from South Main: On the top of the hill was the McCarragher farmhouse; his son, Samuel, was a lawyer. Below lived farmer Sharpe, the father of Richard Sharpe, of this city; William and two daughters are his children. On the left side lived Joseph Davis, a farmer; he shot a neighbor by the name of Divel. Near Blackman street was the gun-smith shop of Henry Young. Below, on the right-hand side lived David Williams, a blacksmith. There were two other houses below, the occupants forgotten.

Canal street sixty years ago had a house in which old Granny Young lived, one of the oldest houses in the Valley. The cemetery was on the corner of East Market street, and the sexton lived on the corner of the grounds.

What is now Scott street was the Parsons road. Judge David Scott lived on the hill; he was President Judge; William, his son, was a lawyer, and E. Greenough Scott, Esq., of this city, is a grandson; Mrs. Judge Kidder was his daughter. Beyond Laurel Run lived Johida Johnson, a farmer and distiller; his son Ovid F. became Attorney General of Pennsylvania; Johida, William, Priestly R., father of Henry E., of Kingston; Wesley, father of Fred. C., one of the proprietors of the Wilkes-Barre *Record of the Times*; Miles,

the father of Wells Bowman Johnson ; Mrs. Charles Reel and Mrs. Henry Wilson are the children.

What is now Parsons was Laurel Run. Here lived Hezekiah Parsons, the father of Calvin Parsons; he had a large carding mill and a broom handle factory located there; Mrs Benager Baily, Mrs. Hiram McAlpin were his daughters.

The old Miner's Mill road from Parsons is one of the old streets. John Albright, a farmer, lived near Laurel Run. Charles Miner, the historian; William Penn, the founder of the *Record of the Times*, Mrs. Jesse Thomas; mother of Isaac M. Thomas; Mrs. Fuller Abbott, the mother of Rev. William Abbott ; Sarah, the blind poet ; Mrs. Stout, Mrs. David Thomas were the children. The Miner homestead is still standing. The next place was that of Asher Miner, a miller and farmer, the grandfather of Charles A. Miner, of this city, Dr. Thomas W., Samuel and Joseph Miner. Thomas Stocker lived above Miner's Mills. Then came the tannery of Mr. Bailey and a tavern kept by Mr. Elisha Blackman.

North Main street, above Union : Col. A. H. Bowman, an officer in the United States Army, lived on the hill on the left-hand side. The house is still standing and was a beautiful place in the past. Ebenezer Bowman, one of the first lawyers at the bar, lived in a small house adjoining.

The next place was that of Peter Alabach, on the same side. One son was a civil engineer and the other was an officer in the United States Army; was in the Mexican war; Col. in the late war, and died in Washington captain of the police in charge of the Capital; his name was Peter. The next place was called the Rodgers place; one of the sons was a Baptist preacher. Above, on the left side, was a log house owned by Harris Colt; William Dickover was born in this house. Matthias Hollenback's grist mill and dwelling was at Mill Creek; he was a cousin of Matthias of Wilkes-Barre; his grandson was J. M. Hollenback. He owned a large farm and North Wilkes-Barre plot is located on it. Nearly a mile above was the house and farm of John Abbott, on the right-hand side, the son of Steve. Robert and the two Misses Abbott, of Wilkes-Barre, are his children. Robert Miner lived above on the other side of the street, a son of Asher and father of Charles A. Miner, of Wilkes-Barre. William, was on the south side of the street; he was a son of Steve. Above came Steve Abbott, the father of John, William and Stephen F., the father of the Rev. William Penn Abbott, and one daughter, Mrs. Robert Miner.* On the left-hand side was Thomas Williams, the father of George, Ezra, Thomas, Moses, Mrs. John Carey, Mrs. Matthias Hollenback, of Mill Creek, Mrs. David Blanchard. George Williams, who was County Treasurer at one time, lived across the street below; his sons were Thomas, Edwin, Charles, Frank, and one daughter. Edwin is a prominent man in one of the cities of Ohio. A man named James Canedy lived above.

John Carey occupied the next place on the hill, on the right-hand side; he was one of the old families. The red school-house stood on the top of the hill. Crandel Wilcox lived next on a large farm, one of the finest in the county; his large family of children went west. On the same side of the street was a house where John Myers lived and in this house Lawrence Myers, of this city, was born. He was the father of Henry, Lawrence and some other children. On the right-hand side was Hiram Stark. The next place was that of Henry Hay, a blacksmith. James Stark came next; he was a farmer, merchant, Justice of the Peace and a prominent man; his sons were Henry, John M., now of Wyoming, James, Hiram, Scott, a banker in Pittston, William, now of Plains,

Mrs. D. Ben, of Pittston, and two or three other daughters. Fredrick Wagner lived above on the same side of the street; Peter and William, Mrs. James Stark, Mrs. William Apple were the children. Then came Benjamin Courtright, on the left-hand side, the father of Hamilton and James, who kept the White Horse Hotel in this city; one son was County Treasurer; there was one daughter. William Apple lived next, a farmer. On the opposite side was the Half-way House, a hotel kept by Henry Shiffer. John Clark lived on the opposite side of the street. The next place was owned by a farmer and brick-maker by the name of Wilcox, the father of Bowen, the brick-maker in Plymouth, and the grandfather of Chester Wilcox, of Kingston; James, the gate keeper over in Luzerne, is a son. Moses Williams lived on the left-hand side of the street; his children are Henry, Rev. John C; Charles C. is a hotel keeper at Plainsville. Above lived Samuel Sailor, who kept a tavern and postoffice; here was where the mail was exchanged, which was done while the horses were being watered and the passengers were taking a drink of whiskey. Here the stage road branched off from the main road. We will continue up the main road: Above the forks was Joseph Swallow, the father of Rev. Miner Swallow, of Kingston, George, Benjamin and some other sons; Mrs. Rev. William Keatley is one of his three daughters. On the other side was William LaBarr, a tailor, an uncle of Rev. John LaBarr, of Wyoming.

Peter Winters came next; he was a farmer and for many years Justice of the Peace. Joseph Armstrong, a farmer, lived adjoining. James Thompson came next. John LaBarr, a wagon-maker and farmer, lived on the left-hand side of the street; his sons were Charles and the Rev. John LaBarr, and two or three daughters. There was a house on the right-hand side, the occupant was probably an Armstrong. Then came William Tompkins; Able, of Pittston, is his son. This brings us to Pittston.

To go back to the forks on the main road: Above was Cornelius Courtright, the father of Benjamin Courtright, of Plains, and Mrs. John Abbott; the rest of the children's names are not remembered; he was County Commissioner, and a prominent man.

The next property was that of John Blanchard, of the old Revolutionary stock. Then came a few houses, the occupants not known. Then came Pittston.

The main road to Hanover from South Wilkes-Barre: First came Thomas Quick, the father of Thomas, of South Wilkes-Barre; Mrs. Avny, Holbert and Mrs. William Beyer were children. Next to him lived Frederick Naugle, a farmer. Auditor Jacob Rymer is his grandson. John Inman lived below. Then came Henry Fisher. Below lived Bakeman Downing; Reuben Downing, late of Wilkes-Barre, was a son. Lorenzo Ruggles lived on the adjoining farm; he had a large family. Mrs. Rev. John LaBarr is a daughter. This is down to the cross-roads.

On the river road at Buttonwood lived the Lazarus family (see H. B. Plumb's sketch). Near them lived Oscar Blodgett. Below was the old John Inman, the old Revolutionary Inman.

Then came the Dilley farm-house; William, Richard and other children were of the family. Below came the Red Tavern, still standing; Sullivan Horton kept it sixty years ago. Farther down was the Garringer house. Then Peter Mills. A Fairchilds lived in the vicinity, of whom we have no information. This brings us to Nanticoke. Col. Andrew Lee owned a mill and residence. He owned a thousand acres of land in that section, and

was a prominent man He was an officer in the War of 1812. He divided his property among his relations, not having any family. Mrs. Zilia Bennett and Andrew Lee were of his heirs. There were a few houses back at Newport, of which we have no definite knowledge.

South Main street, west side: Below the corner were some two-story frame buildings. One was occupied by the father of W. R. Maffett as a printing office. Here he published the *Susquehanna Democrat.* Beyond was the house of Judge Henry Pettibone; afterwards the building was occupied by General Ross and in it he had the postoffice. Then came Allen Jack, a merchant; his store was a brick building, one of the first four in the borough. Adjoining Thomas Davidge had a shoe manufactory. Beyond was the Crystal tavern; here for a long time the stage stopped. Henry Cady, the father of Mrs. Augusta Laning, lived on the next property. Then came the Jermain house. In 1830 this building was used both as a store and residence. The next place was the old residence and store of Matthias Hollenback. The building is still standing—a long, low frame structure. Mr. Hollenback's trade extended as far north as the lakes and reached nearly every settlement and Indian village for hundreds of miles in every direction. He was the owner of many thousands of acres of land. Undoubtedly he was the most astute man that has lived in the Valley. He was in the Massacre, escaping by swimming down the river. It is said that he tied his belongings to his cue and put the gold coins he had in his possession in his mouth, one of which he lost when a bullet from the rifle of an Indian splashed water in his face. This store was at a later day removed to the corner of West Market and River streets and conducted by his son George. Below it was open country, with a post and rail fence next to the road.

Opposite where Lewis LeGrand's wagon-shop and residence now stands was a large frame house occupied by Frank and Lee Stewart. This house, like most of the houses in the borough, was built a little back from the street. Most of the dwellings were farm-houses and were of the old colonial order of architecture. Where the residence of the late Judge Edmund L. Dana stands was a small building supposed to have been occupied by the Judge's ancestors. Below was a farmer named Moore; some of his children live in the city. This section was only partly reclaimed for agricultural purposes. Edward S. Loop relates that he has seen deer feeding with the cattle in the fields near the road. An old gentleman, who has not been dead very many years, related that, when a boy, his parents, who lived near Hanover, would send him out to keep the deer out of the corn and the wild turkeys from the grain. The farmers very often would have their hogs killed by bears. The mother of Calvin Parsons had the experience, one night shortly after she was married, of having her house, at Laurel Run, during the absence of her husband, surrounded by wolves and panthers that filled the woods with their terrible discord.

South Main, east side: Next to the corner lived Thomas Dyer. Then came Dr. Edward Covell; his daughter, Eliza R., resides in this city. Beyond was the cabinet-shop of Captain Jacob J. Dennis. On the corner of Northampton street was the Perry house, still standing. Opposite the Hollenback house was a log house where General William Ross lived. Where Dr. Harvey lives was the old Ross homestead; it is still known by that name. Down to the Hazleton turnpike was farm land. Where Lewis LeGrand lives was occupied by the sister of General Ross.

South Franklin street, west side: The first house below the corner was the O. Collins homestead; his law office was in his house. Then came the office of William Wurts and later of Lyman Hakes. Next was the residence of Jasen Greene, now occupied by the Westmoreland Club. Below stood the Episcopal church, a frame building, on the same lot where the present splendid church edifice now stands. Next was a blacksmith shop. Below was a house built by Whitney Smith; in this building E. Lynch lived; he was the father of Samuel Lynch; the front part of the building was occupied by the Wyoming Bank; this is where the Wyoming National Bank began its existence; it was chartered in 1829; later it was moved to River street and then to its present location on the corner of Franklin and West Market streets. Then the barracks of the infantry soldier during the war of 1812. Joshua Miner built on this lot, and next to him was the Presbyterian church; the first building was wood and was built in 1831. Across Northampton street was the printing office of the *Wyoming Herald*, edited by Steuben Butler. Some distance below was a small house in which lived the father of Jerusha Whitney. Below was a small house occupied by Mrs. Jacobs.

South Franklin, north side, from Market street: Samuel Howe had a tin-shop near where John Laning lives. Next was the residence of Steuben Butler, and where the Female Seminary stands was the office of Judge Mallery, and adjoining was his residence. Then came a little house on the corner occupied by Dupuy. There was no building below this. Some of the old men of this city remember dropping corn on the ground facing Franklin and West Market streets, and stoning frogs in the pond on Public Square.

North Franklin, from Market street, east side: Above the Lamb property there was a frame building occupied by Captain Morse, a tailor. A one-story school-house came next, in which Josiah L. Arms presided, teaching painting out of school hours. Then came the Gilder-leeve property; he was a noted abolitionist; in 1837 he was ridden on a rail, after having his face colored with hatters' blacking; he was the father of Mrs. Rev. N. G. Parke. Next was a house occupied by Charles and John Davis. Where the First M. E. church stands was a vacant lot. The adjoining property was owned by Ziba Bennett. Then came Anthony Brower, the grandfather of Edith, of Wilkes-Barre, and father of Mrs. W. S. Parsons. Beyond lived Sharp D. Lewis. Then came the Yarrington house. On the corner of Union lived Charles Vernet.

North Franklin from Market, west side: Above the corner lived Edmund Taylor. Then came the old Bowman property, occupied by Anning O. Cahoon. The school-house of Mrs. Ruth Elsworth, where many children of that generation received their education, came next. Beyond lived Gilbert Laird, the father of James Laird and Mrs. Easterline. Next lived John P. Babb. Where General Osborne lives was the Andrew Beaumont homestead. Then came the house of Amos Parker and next the Claxton school-house. Then came the Methodist Parsonage, and the last house was built by Andrew Beaumont.

Down River street from South Wilkes-Barre: The first house was where General Sturdevant lived. The Richards family lived near. In that neighborhood was the Weeks property; the three sons of the elder Weeks were killed at the Massacre, Philip, Jonathan and Bartholomew; a daughter of Philip was the wife of Silas Benedict, who was killed in the Massacre; Hulda afterwards married Comfort Carey, and lived on the back road in Hanover, almost the southern line of Ashley; the family all went west. Between the Sturdevant place and the Hanover line were a number of other houses not now remembered.

On the Hanover line lived Miller Horton; one son, N. Miller Horton, lately died in Wilkes-Barre. Miller Horton was a stage proprietor and ran a number of lines of stages.

Then came the house of Jonas Hartzell, who married Sarepta Downing. Alexander Jamison's house came next; he married a daughter of Capt. Lazarus Stewart and through her came into possession of that property. The Stewart block house stood about half way between the river and river road. There was a road that went from the Stewart block house to the outlet of Solomon's creek. The Inmans lived on that road. The old man was Elijah; his son, Richard, was the one who became intoxicated on the way to the Massacre and laid down by the side of the road and went to sleep, but after the fight woke up in time to shoot one of the Indians who were chasing Rufus Bennett. Every one remembers how Bennett, seeing Inman sitting with his gun, halloed to him and asked him if it was loaded, and being informed that it was told him to shoot the Indian, which he did. The Indians hunted people here afterwards as they hunted turkey or other game. Fourteen were killed in Hanover by these hunters. After the settlers returned to possess their plundered farms many were killed or taken prisoners. A number were killed in the fall of 1778. The Valley was largely made up at this time of widows and orphans, who were dependent upon the public. The history of the murders and the captures and the rescues is not made public to any great extent. The Spencers, Inmans, Hibbards, Stewarts and others lived on this old road; fifty years ago George Lazarus lived there and some of his children since. George Learn lived in the large house beside the canal, belonging to Alexander Jamison. His son George lived there until about 1866. One of the Wades lived near there. There were several log houses that stood along there off from the road, apparently without any road leading to them, as the old road had been abandoned from near where the Buttonwood now is down to the outlet or mouth of Solomon's creek.

On the present river road: Below where the railroad crosses was the house of George Sively; Mrs. Plouts is his daughter. Below was a property owned by old Matthias Hollenback; this was the first land he ever owned; Thomas Lazarus lived on the property; his father bought it of Mr. Hollenback in 1818. On the same lot, on the east side of the creek, Ashel Blodgett lived; his wife was a daughter of old George Lazarus. Below was the old George Lazarus house. Next below lived Coble Spencer. There was an old log house in that neighborhood that belonged to George Sively. Below lived a Jacobs family. Edward Inman lived still further south; he married a Dilley; one of his daughters was the wife of John Espy and another was the wife of John Turner, of Plymouth.

Across the road lived Dr. Crystal, the grandfather of John Laning, of Wilkes-Barre. There were several houses there that have been gone for many years. The next house was on the top of the hill, where James Dilley lived. John Greenawalt, a tailor, lived on the left-hand side below. On the right was the old log house that belonged to the Dilley heirs, where lived the two old maids, the children of Richard Dilley, Jr.

There was a frame house below, on the left, where a blacksmith lived. Adjoining the Green was a beautiful little cottage; this was where Cyprian Hibbard lived before the Battle of Wyoming, 1778; his wife was Sarah Barrett; he was killed in the Massacre; ten years later she married Matthias Hollenback, of Wilkes-Barre. The next was the cemetery lot, known as the Hanover Green. The church was built as a German Reformed

church in 1825 ; the attendance has not been large enough for thirty years to keep it in repairs. Adjoining lived Stephen Burrett, then came the Red Tavern, which Frederick Christian built as early as 1789; previously he had a distillery : the town meetings and the elections were held there for many years. On the next lot on the hill, on the left, lived Rebecca Thomas. There was a house down by the river where the father of George Palmer Steel, of Wilkes-Barre, had a ferry. There was a distillery there. Below, on the river road, was a house where John Garringer lived : he came about 1810 ; Charles, his son, lived there after him ; the Hurlbuts originally lived there. Beyond, on the right, lived Henry Minnich. Beyond was the old Henry Sively house ; George Kocher lived in the house at a later day. The next place beyond that belonged to Barnet Milier ; on that lot Roswell Franklin lived before the Revolution, and after till 1796; his son was murdered, his house burned and his stock driven off by the Indians : he is supposed to have built a block house there. Next was the farm-house of Samuel Pell. Below was a log house, then across the Nanticoke creek was the house of James S. Lee, on the right ; then came Samuel Jamison, on the left, the son of John Jamison, who was killed with Asa Chapman while riding to Wilkes-Barre on the road at the Green ; Stewart Pierce erected a stone there to mark the place and a monument in the cemetery over the men ; Dr. Hakes married a granddaughter of Samuel Janison, and at her death he came into possession of the property ; Samuel Jamison's aunt married Elisha Harvey ; Samuel Jamison married a Hunlock and his sister married a Hunlock.

Below on the left, was a place that belonged to Capt. Lazarus Stewart ; James Campbell married his daughter and lived on the place afterwards ; his daughter married James Dilley, on Dilley's Hill ; another married James S. Lee and was the mother of Mrs. Zilba Bennett, who is still living. Peter Mill owned the place later. This brings us into Nanticoke.

The Middle Road from South Wilkes-Barre to Newport : On the hill below the Vulcan Works stood a farm-house that belonged to William Ross; Jacob Rummage lived there in 1839. On the same side of the road, near Solomon's creek, high up on the bank, stood a little log house that looked as if it was about ten feet square and twenty feet high, in which lived William Askam, the tailor and peddler, who when his wife sent him after oven wood took seven months and three days to gather it.

Across the creek on the right-hand side lived the father of the late Thomas Quick and Mrs. Avery Hurlbut. Fifty years ago Fritz Deitrick, the father of Miller H. Deitrick, so long the Kingston street-car conductor, lived on the hill ; Fritz's wife was a Lazarus. In sight, on the crossroad, lived Mrs. Stroh ; her husband and son were drowned near the head of the Island, in the river below Wilkes-Barre. Down the hill in an old house Christian Naugle lived ; he had a distillery where he made cider into cider brandy ; in front of his place was a watering trough, and the cup put there for the accommodation of the public would never be disturbed; this was some time ago; it isn't so now. In 1833 the Deerhamer house stood on the left, south, up the hill ; this property is now the Hanover Catholic cemetery. Further up the hill John Inman lived ; he had a coal mine opposite the Deerhamer house and supplied the people in that section with coal. About half way up the hill from the Inman house in an old house lived Mrs. Stroh ; Amos, her son, lives in Pittston ; the property belonged to William Shoemaker, who afterwards built a brick house there. On the top of the hill lived Joseph George, a tailor; later Simon Rinehamer lived in the house. Across the road rocks crop out above the soil, on which

can be plainly seen the action of glaciers. Below, south, on the left-hand side, on the corner of the road going over to Sugar Notch, lived Samuel Burrier. On the right-hand side, farther down, was the Jacob Fisher house; formerly, back in the field from this, there was a house in which his father lived; his mother was 105 years old when she died. The next place was the old Benjamin Carey house; Mrs. Bateman Downing and Mrs. Harvey Holcomb were daughters. Lorenzo Ruggles lived on the right-hand side; his wife was Polly Bennett; here was the creek that comes down from Sugar Notch. Across the creek lived a Mr. Wright in a house that is still standing. Nathan Bennett lived on the right-hand side of the street, forty rods further south. On the top of the hill Henry Hoover lived, on the left. Opposite was the Hoover-Hill school-house which Avery Marcy built in 1838. Back of the school-house was a road back to where Edward Edgerton lived; his wife was Prudence Dilley. There were some old houses in this locality of which I can obtain no information, except that in one of them for many years lived a woman who, when a girl, worked for the father of Frances Slocum, and was the girl who, when the Indians carried off little Frances, caught up one of the children and ran to the fort over on Public Square; the Slocum house stood across the street from where is now Conrad Lee's planing mill; the fort on the Square was the second one built there, as the first one was partly destroyed by the Indians by fire.

South of the Hoover house lived an iron maker by the name of Wiggins, who worked in the forge at Nanticoke; Mrs. Cornelius Robbins, of Kingston, was a daughter.

At Askam was the Metcalf house. Near was the house where old John Hyde lived; he planted the orchard that is still standing; he died in 1804; his daughters were Mrs. Eleazer Blackman, Mrs. Rev. S. Phinney, Mrs. Boaz Stearns; one son married Catharine Hurlbut; there were several children; the Hydes were of the family of Lord Clarendon; the Hanover branch were intelligent, prosperous and influential. Richard Metcalf moved on the place and is still alive. On the right-hand side across the street was a private road that led to the house of Rufus Bennett, by Bennett's creek; Rufus Bennett was the grandfather of the progenitors of the Marcy family in this section; one of his daughters married George Gledhill. Next was a stone house built by William Hyde; the house is still standing and must be a hundred years old. Next came William Askam. Here Speck Miller's house stood; his name was John, but he was called Speck because he went one night to a neighbor's and stole what he supposed was a shoat lately butchered and left there to cool off, but when he reached home and unwound his load he found that it was the corpse of a negro child; the people nicknamed him Speck, which is the German for pork.

This section has not furnished much material for the historian, but from Wilkes-Barre to Nanticoke nearly every house has an interesting history. It might be added that if some of this history was published it would make a sensation.

On the left-hand side, some eighty rods beyond the Askam house, was where the Shafer family lived when they came to the Valley; Harvey Holcomb owned the place and lived there at a later day; there had been, across the Nanticoke creek, on the right, a log house, afterwards belonging to the Rummage family. On a rise of ground was a house where John Babb lived; it formerly belonged to the Sorber family. On the other side of the road, and forty or more rods beyond the Babb house, on the side of the hill, which, by the way, was named Hog-Back, which leads us to infer that the Hanoverians paid more

attention to pork than poetry, was the residence of Conrad Rinehimer, the father of all of that name now living in this section. Opposite Rinehimer's was Mrs. Ash's house, afterwards owned by John Sorber. Below lived John Keithline on the corner of the cross-road that goes over to Nanticoke. On the right was a house belonging to James Stewart, the son of Captain Lazarus Stewart, who was killed in the Massacre. John Espy, who was the grandfather of B. M. Espy, Esq., of Wilkes-Barre, lived in the next house on the left. Beyond this place lived Henry Lines, down in the hollow to the left, back from the road; he was the father of Abram and Samuel. On the line of Hanover and Newport townships lived Conrad Lines, the father of the late John R. Lines. Nearly a half mile below lived Abram Lines; his wife was an Espy; his daughters are Mrs. Rev. W. S. Smyth, Mrs. Charles Wells and Mrs. Augusta Hollenback.

ASHLEY, and the Back Road: Beyond the McCarragher house on the top of the hill, on the left, many years ago, there was a house in which a Dow family lived. Beyond, also on the left, were two houses, in one of which Joseph Davis lived; this man was a miser and died in an insane asylum; he shot a man by the name of Dively or some such name, a neighbor, who tormented the old man. Below, at Blackman street, on the lower side, was the gun-shop of Henry Young, on the left, where Hart's house now is. On the left, further on and back in the field, on the bank of the creek, in 1845, a brother of Judge Kidder lived. On the right, on the high bank, lived the Bergolds. Below was the wooden bridge across the creek, where a railroad has long run to the Blackman mines. Back in the field, on the right, was a log house, of the tenants of which no one has given me any information. Up the hill on the left Joseph Frederick lived. On the top of the hill the father of S. V. Ritter, of Wilkes-Barre, lived. Here was the Hanover line, the place now called Newtown. Here, across the Hanover line, on the left, was the house of Thomas Brown, who married Askam's daughter, Maria, in 1815. Across the road from Brown's lived Jacob Deitrick, and there were other houses here whose owners are not now remembered. Here the road branches, the left going toward Ashley. In the triangle at the point was the log cabin of Phebe Williams and her mother. A little beyond, on the left, was Luman Gilbert's house, and on the right Daniel Frederick, who still lives, 87 years old. On the right-hand side of the street was another log house and beyond was still another, where the father of Louis Landmesser lived. There were many log houses in this section sixty years ago, a number of which were tenantless and given over to the elements.

Daniel Hartzell lived where the wagon road goes under the railroad toward the Blackman mines, and the house of Samuel Pease came next, on the right. On the top of the hill, on the right, Fritz Deitrick kept a tavern. Down on the flat was a store known as the "Scrabble Town Store." On the left, where the road turns up the mountain, old Valentine Keizer lived, and near him some other Keizers. Up the mountain was a green house that belonged to the Cook estate. Up the creek at Solomon's Falls was the old William Ross mill, or the old Red mill; this was a beautiful and picturesque place; for many years the mill was rented to tenants, and finally burned down.

Going up the mountain you came to a stage house that, previous to 1840, was kept by Israel Inman. So many places, like this one, that were well known in the past have not only disappeared but also every trace of their tenants, or even a memory of their lives. Like a sealed book, these old taverns, mills and cabins awaken an interest and also declare in a humble but impressive manner the brevity of human life.

From the foot of the plane: On the main road, across the bridge, over the foot of the inclined plane, and across Solomon's creek, on the right, lived Daniel Kreidler; he had a trip-hammer and carried on quite a business there. On the right was one of three green houses that was a part of the Cook estate; the next house on the left was one of three green houses; opposite was a house that George W. Bennett built in 1846. On the right lived Comfort Carey; he had formerly lived in a house that stood back from the road. On the lower side of Ashley there was a house on the land of William Ross. Here is the south line of Ashley. Beyond, on the right, was a house with a high stoop and a basement, that belonged to John Saum. On the left below was Darius Preston, afterward Williston Preston. There were no buildings until you came to the Knock house. On the top of the hill at Sugar Notch borough was a little log house belonging to Andrew Shoemaker, on the right, where the road crossed over to the middle road at Samuel Burnier's. On the cross-road lived Cornelius Garrison; he was thrown from a wagon and killed; he came here from Alsace, France, during the Revolution as a French soldier and settled here. On the main road below lived Rachel Garrison, by herself, for many years. Over the creek lived Jacob Rimer. On the left-hand side of the street was the residence of Ashabel Ruggles. On the right was a small log cabin where Peggy Sterling lived. Down by the creek Ishmael Bennett, who was one of the early settlers, built a log house. Later his son, Josiah Bennett, lived in it, and his father, Ishmael, built a log house that is still standing on the south side of the creek. The next house was that of Henry Bunny. On the right, the next was a house belonging to Speck Miller; Abram Smith lived there at one time. Across the road a little below was the house of Josiah Bennett, the grandfather of the writer; this was built about 1816. Below lived John Garrison, in a two-story log house. On the cross-road on the right-hand side was the residence and property of Elisha Blackman, the grandfather of H. B. Plumb, Esq., the historian, to whom the writer is greatly indebted for information. Elisha came here in 1791 and made the first clearing south of Ashley.

On the back road below this cross-road Harry Blackman lived; the house is standing. The next house was on the left and at one time belonged to Henry Mack. The Rummage property was in this vicinity; there were four houses on the property in which four branches of the family lived. Here the back road ended now, but formerly it ran on. A mile and a half beyond there were some houses. George Koker lived in this neighborhood. Below him lived Polly Pell. Half a mile below at the end of this road was the old homestead of Christian Lueder, who owned a good farm and raised a family of children that were a credit to him.

KINGSTON. The old road to Wilkes-Barre went from the ferry opposite Northampton street across the flats and was, as it is now, the dividing line between Kingston and Plymouth townships. This street ran across the mountain in a straight line. The ferry was kept by Major Helme. What is now Wyoming avenue joined it down on the flats where an old barn now stands. The place was called the Kingston corners. There was no bridge across the river. The present road to Wilkes-Barre was laid out at a later day. Market street only extended back to what is now Seminary street. At the end of Market street stood the old Methodist church; this was moved to the lower side; it was destroyed by fire and the present structure erected. Where the Seminary stands was an orchard, which extended to Main street, as the avenue was called. Market street from the

corner back was opened by Thomas Myers about 1840. Lawrence Myers owned a tract of land that extended from the Curtis lane up to where Benjamin Tubbs now lives, and from Wyoming avenue back to the first hill; his residence stood where the shoe-shop of Joel Walp stands. There was only a lane going back to his house and barn; the old well is covered by the sidewalk in front of the shoe-shop.

Plymouth street ran across Ross Hill to Shawneytown, the old name of Plymouth. Curtis's lane extended back to the farm house of Lawrence Myers, past the old Kingston graveyard. Many of the old families of Kingston and vicinity were buried there; most of the remains were removed some years ago. William Gallup gave the land for a graveyard. He received a grant of land extending from the river to the mountain, as did Lawrence Myers a similar strip adjoining. All the land was divided up in these grants. Mrs. Curtis retains a few acres of the original grant to her grandfather, F. B. Myers also retains some of the grant to his great-grandfather. Pringle's lane was the same as now; above was called Sharpe's lane.

The old stone house on the corner of Plymouth and Market streets was built by James Barnes, and antedates the recollection of the oldest resident. It was built for a residence and store, probably being one of the finest houses in the Valley; there was a foundry in the back part at one time. Barnes was a wealthy Quaker; part of Ross hill belonged to him. A strip of land over Ross hill was owned by Levi Hoyt, an uncle of John D. Hoyt. The house where James Franck lives was built by him and was for one year the residence of Judge George W. Woodward. In its day this homestead was an elegant place. The daughter of Judge Woodward, with two of her young lady friends, was drowned. They attempted to cross the flats on the ice; the water had flooded the flats and frozen over. On the old road crossing Ross hill was an old long farm-house with a porch the entire length, that remained until a short time ago. Here Ross lived, after whom the hill was named. The stone house on the corner was at a later day the home of Thomas Myers; later it was used as a store. On the north corner, where the hotel stands, was owned by Lawrence Myers, who had a store there. Near where George Lazarus has his market was the store of William Reynolds; where Mrs. Abram Reynolds lives was his home. This grant was originally occupied by a store and dwelling built and occupied by Henry Buckingham. The Exchange Hotel was formerly owned by James Wheeler, who was Sheriff of the county; later Major Helme was the proprietor; the building is still standing; here the county conventions were held. Next was Dr. Parker; later George Reese built a house and a hat store there; Sharp D. Lewis published his paper there. Where Dr. Tubbs' family lives was the old Elijah Loveland homestead; William Loveland is his son; he built this house.

What is now Pringle's store was the store of Elias Hoyt, and where Dr. L. L. Rogers lives was his residence. Benjamin Bidlack, the old Revolutionary soldier, lived on the next lot, in a house that was taken over to Seminary street and was the Roat homestead. Bidlack became famous for singing the Swaggering Man, when he was a prisoner of the Pennamites at Sunbury, and being given too much liberty to act his song he sprang over the enclosure and escaped. Dr. Wright, a surgeon of the United States Army, lived in a house that stood where is now the residence of Mrs. Samuel Hoyt. Dr. John Little, who was also a cabinet-maker, had a shop and house up near the next corner. The old yellow house that is now standing on the northwest corner of Wyoming avenue and Hoyt

street was the Daniel Hoyt homestead, the father of Elias, Ziba, Levi and Abel, Mrs. Benjamin Reynolds, the mother of Mrs. Dr. Tubbs, Mrs. Lois Hoyt. He owned the land from the Myers grant up to what is now Hoyt street, from Main street over the hill.

Plymouth street, Kingston: The first house below the stone house on the corner stood where the residence of A. J. Roat now stands, and was the residence of Anson Martin. James Gallop lived on what is known as the Slocum property, below the school house. Next below lived the father of John Gates; John Gates lived there for many years; the house is still standing. Near where Plymouth street turns to go to the hill was the farm of Aaron Roberts; this property now belongs to William Loveland, who inherited it from his father, Elijah Loveland. Across the street lived Adoniram Covert; there were two houses on this place, one near the road and the other at the lower end of the lot. Near where the L. & B. R. R. passes lived Bester Payne, the father of the late H. B. Payne, Esq.; at an earlier day a Mr. Moore lived in the house; the old homestead is standing, occupied by Hungarians. On the lower side of the street (the right hand side), near the creek Major Helme had a turning works. Albert Skeer lived near the creek for many years.

Below the lane going back to the Myers property the father of Thomas Macfarlane, of Kingston, lived; later the place was owned by Dr. Tubbs, of Kingston. On the hill lived the grandmother of the late Isaac Rice; Mrs. Dr. Rogers, of Huntsville, was one of her grandchildren. In Blindtown lived John Covert. Down the old road the first house was on the upper side, where a Mr. Jacquish lived, and owned by John Covert. Beyond him was Lenard Devans, father of Benjamin. Ezra Howard lived below, then came Joseph Kellar, the father of John and Peter, late of Larksville. Next lived George Snyder, father of Gardner; opposite was Peter Snyder, the father of George, well known in Larksville. In Poke Hollow Joseph Morgan and a man by the name of Cool lived.

Wyoming avenue, south side, from the corner: There was a little red house near the corner, the occupant not known. Albert Skeer had his blacksmith shop and residence adjoining, and later James Barnum lived on the premises. Above was the house and harness shop of Arnold Taylor, a brother of Judge Taylor. Joel Linn now lives in this house; Stephen Vaughn was born there. Then came the house and store of David Baldwin, who was a son-in-law of General Thomas. Where Thomas Macfarlane lives was the old homestead of Ezra Hoyt. The next building was the old Kingston academy; it was located above what is now the home of John B. Reynolds. A large farm extending back to the river and from the Dorrance estate down to what is now the Rutter annex was owned by Pierce and Chester Butler; Pierce lived on the ridge by the creek. Benjamin Dorrance, father of the late Charles Dorrance, owned the land adjoining this property.

Down Pringle's lane lived Thomas Pringle, the father of Alexander, Samuel, George, Mrs. Elias Culver, Caroline and three other daughters; Peter Sharp was the original owner. The next property extended to Sharp's lane and was owned by Anson and James Atherton. John Sharp owned the next property; Peter, William, Jacob and John were some of his children. Ziba Hoyt, the father of the late ex-Governor Henry M. Hoyt, lived where the railroad crosses Wyoming avenue, and it was here where the Governor was born. The other children were John D., of Kingston, the wife of Rev. Charles Corss, Mrs. Abram Reynolds. Noah Pettibone owned the property above on both sides of the street.

On the right-hand side, above the stone bridge was an old house where Anning Owen, a blacksmith and a local preacher, lived. The last family that lived in the house was Robert

Sealey, the father of the late Mrs. Alfred Darte. The Benjamin Dorrance tract extended from the river back of the first hill to the foot of the mountain; in the division of the land, that on the east side went to Col. Charles and that on the west side to the Rev. John Dorrance.

A large barn stood on the corner of the street going down to Mill Hollow. There was an old cider mill next to the barn.

Goose Island: Gilbert Lewis lived here. There were two buildings on the lower side, a tannery and a house in which Joshua Belding, a broom-maker lived; he owned some property there. Below the tannery was one of the old Hoyt houses.

FORTY FORT, north from Vaughn's corner: Where Stephen B. Vaughn lives was the home of John Bennet, a prominent man in his day. The old house was built about 1819. John Gore lived where Jacob Ely lives; he had four sons; Mrs. John B. Wood, the mother of John G. Wood, of Wilkes-Barre, and Mrs. Moses Wood were daughters. Thomas Slocum built a brick house between J. Bennet's and I. Tripp's. It burned down and was afterwards built by E. McNeill, who owned the property, and was General Superintendent of the L. & B. R. R. Later it was sold to M. A. Lines and is now the residence of his daughter, Mrs. Augusta Hollenback. The Isaac Tripp property was owned by Anson Atherton; Thomas, Mrs. Michael Laphey, Mrs. David Corey, Mrs. Alice Abbott, Mrs. Needham, James, Thomas, Anson were the children.

Across from the cemetery lived George Shoemaker. On the present site of the Isaac Tripp homestead was a log house where the father of Elisha Buskirk lived. Above was a farm-house. Above was the old frame house where Robert Shoemaker lived many years. Then came the Shoemaker strip, settled upon by Elijah Shoemaker, one of the first settlers in the Valley. There was a large tract of land extending from the river to the mountain and from the Isaac Tripp farm to the Maltby lane belonging to Elijah Shoemaker. That was divided. From Isaac Tripp's to Shoemaker's land was set apart to George; then Robert came in next; then Charles next; then Elijah Shoemaker up to Maltby's lane. The old Shoemaker store stood on the opposite side of the street, on the corner of the cemetery. Above, back from the road, was the house of Pierce Smith, who was a brother of Dr. John Smith, of Wilkes-Barre. The property was sold to Maltby. Next was the house of Joseph Tuttle, who owned a mill opposite. This is Abram's creek and is covered by one of the substantial stone arches that our fathers built.

Up the creek from the bridge was the home of Lazarus Denison; all the late generation of that family were born there. The next house was that of Elisha Atherton, the father of Mrs. William Henry and Mrs. Charles A. Miner; Mrs. Henry is the mother of Thomas H. Atherton, who took the name of Atherton. Above lived Cook Atherton; then came Thomas P. Hunt, the celebrated lecturer and the great temperance reformer. The house belonged formerly to the Willis family. William Swetland, who donated Swetland Hall to the Wyoming Seminary, owned a large estate adjoining. He was a farmer and merchant. The old store house on the opposite side of the street is still standing. Opposite Erastus Hill owned a farm. There was no house until above the monument on that side of the street. Then came Fisher Gay, a farmer, and next an old settler by the name of David Perkins, who owned a large tract of land in that section. Beyond the Perkins property lived John Breese. The next was a house owned by Steuben Jenkins. Where is now the Laycock hotel, was a house. The first building above was that of John

Perkins; he kept a tavern. The next property was a house standing down near the river occupied by Christian Miller. There was a road down to the river where Miller had a ferry. Where the fair-ground is located lived Henry Hice, who owned a farm there. The next property was that of John Schofield. Beyond him was Charles Fuller, on the ridge. S. Larnard lived in the next house. Above was Joseph Schooley. Then came David Goodwin, the father of Mrs. John R. Gates, and brother of Abram Goodwin. Lot Breese, a brother-in-law of James Jenkins, lived next. Across the street lived Peter Sharp, a farmer. This brings us to the forks of the road leading to Pittston.

From Laycock's hotel, going up on the north side of the street: On the corner was a tavern kept by James Jenkins, the father of Steuben Jenkins. Then came the Samuel LaFrantz house. Above were two old houses, the occupants not known. Near them was John Cowder. Then there was no building until you came to the Exeter line. Mrs. Betsy Landon lived at this point.

On the back road below Wyoming were a few old houses. John Gore and the father of David Laphey lived there. The street from Wyoming back to the mountain: There was an old house, of which we have no information, near the corner. James Jenkins lived next. Across lived John Jenkins. Near the creek on the left lived the father of Lot Breese. Beyond was Ezra Breese. Jonathan Moore lived next to him. A watch-maker by the name of Ensign lived on the next lot. Then there was Jacob Shoemaker's tavern; Isaac and William were his sons; Mrs. David Baldwin, the first wife of Isaac Tripp, Mrs. Holden Tripp and Mrs. Ira Tripp were his daughters.

Up the back road was a house where a brother of William Swetland lived. Above lived Abram Goodwin, the father of John Goodwin, and Abram Goodwin, formerly of Kingston. Daniel, the father of Henry VanScoy, of Kingston, lived beyond, on a property that was owned later by Mr. Shaw. There was a tenant house next. Then came the Daniel Jones homestead. Then William Jacobs.

West Pittston, from the forks of the road: On the left-hand side of the street lived Albert Polen. Next was a Mr. Polen. Next to him was a tenement house. Near the site of the West Pittston depot lived William Sharps. Near him were Charles Chapin, and Isaac Carpenter. Then came a family by the name of Slocum. The Carpenter hotel stood up by the river and above was Laton Slocum, the father of William and James.

North from the stone bridge on the right-hand side of the street: The first house above the bridge was that of Noah Pettibone. Near was an old house occupied by the father of Sharp D. Lewis. This was taken down by Noah Pettibone. He was the father of Jacob S., Henry, John S., Stephen H., Mrs. Martha Myers, Noah, Walter G., Harper N., Mrs. S. E. Johnson. The next house was occupied by Mrs. Daniel Marsh. Where the Rev. E. H. Snowden lives, who is alive and well, nearly one hundred years old, was owned by James Jones. Then came the cemetery and the old church. Elijah Shoemaker, the father of the Shoemaker family, came next; it stands next above the residence of the late C. D. Shoemaker. Above was the Shoemaker house on the ridge. Then came the grist-mill of Joseph Tuttle.

Forty Fort, River street, from Wyoming avenue: The first house on the lower side was Gideon Underwood, the father of Dr. Underwood. Philip Jackson lived next, in a house that stood where James Space lives. The famous log house and tavern of Philip Myers stood, until it was burned down a few years ago, in this locality. He was the father

of Henry, Thomas, John, Mary and other children. Where Rev. H. H. Welles lives was a log house. Below was Asa Jackson. Across the street lived Christopher Buskirk. On the cross street was the home of William Church; Almond, Adison, Anson, Jabez and Mrs. Thomas Reese and Eunice were his children. A family by the name of Bigbow lived near and later Oliver Pettibone.

In the early days there was but one street down the Valley on the west side and that followed the creek down back of Forty Fort and ran along the brow of the hill where A. H. Coon lives and bisected the old road to Wilkes-Barre down by the creek at the end of Goose Island. Along the ridge many of the old families originally settled, building log houses and farming the bottom land, which was free from forest but covered with a tall rank grass. When the settlers left the Valley, after the Massacre, most of the houses on this ridge were burned; some of them were rebuilt.

On this old road lived Oliver Pettibone, when he first came from New England. Noah Pettibone, Jr., was killed at the Massacre and his brother Steve was killed on the upper flats near where the motor-house of the electric railroad is located. He with five men came over from the block house on the Redout to thresh grain in a barn located there. There were a few bands of Indians in the vicinity, notwithstanding that General Sullivan had broken up their villages and thoroughly routed them. One of these bands surprised these men at their work and shot five of them; one man fell in fright, then feigned death and was scalped. The men in the block house, hearing the firing and guessing the cause, hurried to the rescue. The Indians had fled, but not before they had headed off a man with a team of oxen who was part of the way across the flats and shot and scalped him. The man that had fallen and had been scalped recovered but was prematurely bald. Many of the Indians remained permanently in the Valley. Some dashes of their blood still remain to testify of Indian ancestry.

Old John Gore, Benjamin Dorrance and the Pettibones lived on the old road. The Butlers lived where the Butler house now stands. Pierce Butler, who lived there, was a man of great intelligence, generosity and force of character. Below lived George Lazarus and later John, his brother. This was the Hollenback property. Where A. H. Coon's house stands was an old house. Mr. William Barker, the father of Abel Barker, had a blacksmith shop there. The Ira Carle house was built by General Samuel Thomas, captain of the company in which James Bird belonged when he was shot at Lake Erie.

What is now Wyoming avenue was opened nearly one hundred years ago. Most of the settlers on the back road had been killed by the Indians, their houses burned and their stock driven off either by the Tories or the Indians. The cemetery at Forty Fort holds the remains of many of the old settlers, some are buried in the little burying plot at West Pittston. There was an old grove of primitive oaks in front of the old church. The old Union church was built in 1808. It is a quaint old structure, with high-back, unpainted pews. The pulpit is twelve feet high, curiously paneled and is approached by a winding stairs. It is now known as the old Forty Fort church. The style of architecture came from Kingston, R. I. Kingston was named after this town. The cemetery was not the first burial ground in the Valley, but it is the oldest now in use. In 1770 this burial place was laid out and contained an acre of land. Where the Shoemaker stone-house stands was a house in which a man named Landon lived. Henry Stroh's father lived where the hotel stood that was burned, below on the river side of River street. Below him lived

Charles Bryant.   Next was the father of David Culver.   Then came the Reel house, next was Abe Jackson.

LUZERNE was originally named Hartzoff, after a German who was one of the first settlers.   Later it was given a post-office and was named Mill Hollow.   Up the creek, between the mountains was a paper mill built by Henry Buckingham, an uncle of Stephen Vaughn.   Where the turnpike begins was the flour mill of John Gore; he was a brother of Jerry.   John and Asa; Harry Pettibone owned the mill afterwards; later John S. Pettibone bought it; then Samuel Raub.   Where what is known as the Wright mill now stands was an iron furnace and foundry owned by Gaylord & Smith, of Plymouth, and afterwards by George W. Little, of Kingston.   The present residence of Andrew Raub, Jr., was at one time a tavern kept by Lambert Bonham; his children are Miller, Lambert, Henderson, of Luzerne, James and Barns.   The next building was the old island school-house.   Where the Schooley mill stands was a mill owned by George M. Hollenback; George Bartholomew bought it; he was a prominent man; one of his sons was a surveyor and another a doctor; Mrs. John Lutz, of Luzerne, is his daughter.   Across Toby's creek was the old Charles Mathers house, located where Waddel's breaker stands; he was a millwright and a prominent man; his wife was a daughter of Andrew Raub; Mrs. James Atherton, Mrs. A. C. Church, Mrs. Fuller Bonham were sisters of Mrs. Mathers; Judson, Andrew, Correy, Samuel and Orlando are his children; John Mathers, a brother of Charles, lives on the hill; Mrs. J. C. Jackson, Mrs. George Boughtin, Stella, Mary, Charles, William Penn, Zilia and Frank are the family.

On the main road lived David Laphey, who was one of the old settlers; Thomas, his son, lives in the old house.   There was but one building from Laphey's until you came to the James Hughes property, except an old barn that stood where the Ross drug store stands; Mr. Hughes was one of the old settlers; Captain James Hughes, who is still living, is his son; Mrs. Hiram Johnson, Mrs. John Denniston, Charles and Edward are the children.   John Bowman lived where the Atherhol building stands; he had a trip-hammer and was a blacksmith; he also had a comb factory; later William Hancock built a dwelling and store on the property; Pierce, Erastus, Luther, Mrs. Oliver Pettibone, Mrs. William Reel, Mrs. Shotels were some of Mr. Bowman's children.   William Hancock lived in a dwelling that was converted into a tavern; it is now the Luzerne House; he owned what is now the Bennet estate and was a prominent man; James, of the Plains, Henry, deceased, Mrs. Fuller Reynolds, Mrs. Dr. Blair and Mary were his children.   Where Mrs. Harris lives was a house where Jerome V. Blakesly, the father of Dr. Blakesly, of Plymouth, lived.   This was the only building from the Hancock house to where E. W. Abbott now lives.   This place was originally a part of the Oliver Pettibone estate; Daniel C. Marsh lived there; he married a daughter of Oliver Pettibone.   After turning the corner was the residence of Morris Cramer; the property was owned by J. F. Snyder; this house was one of the oldest in the Valley; Cramer was a member of Captain Thomas's company that went to Lake Erie in 1812.   There was no building until you came to the residence of William Hancock; he had a tannery below his house; near by was an old house occupied by O. G. Pettibone, a son of Oliver.   From where the Presbyterian church stands to where the railroad now crosses there were no buildings.   Bennet street extended to the mountain.   There was a coal bed that was opened sixty years ago by John Bennet and Joshua Pettibone.   The Sarah S. Bennet estate was originally owned by Isaac Carpenter; it is now

owned by Martha Bennet, of River street, Wilkes-Barre. There was a house in the field down the creek in which Reuben Holgate, a prominent citizen, lived; he owned a carding mill; it is now the mill of Henry Schooley; it was known for many years as the old red mill. The facts for this sketch of Luzerne were furnished by E. W. Abbott, of that borough.

PLYMOUTH, formerly Shawneytown, and then Shawnee: This is an old town. There is no section in the Valley where there are more marks of formerly stately houses than in the lower end of Plymouth. In the deepest humiliation and disgrace, covered with the grime of time and of the culm pile, swarming with Huns and Poles, they are rapidly going back to nature and, like most of their proprietors, to oblivion.

Going down River street, on the right-hand side, the first building was a mill owned by Philip Shupp, the grandfather of Peter. He owned a large farm on the side of the hill; near the mill was his residence; he was Abram Nesbitt's grandfather. Below lived Jacob Gould, a farmer. Where 'Squire Eno lives was the house of Abijah Smith. Where John Shonk lives was owned by one of the Davenports and was called the Bull's Head tavern. Where the old elm stands was the old whipping post; this statement cannot be verified; near by was the house of Horace Morse. Where the railroad crosses lived Abraham Nesbitt, a farmer, the father of James and the grandfather of Abram Nesbitt, of Kingston. Across the creek, on the lower side, lived 'Squire Noah Wadhams. Below was the store of Andrew Gaylord, on the right-hand side.

The next place was a tavern kept by Joseph Worthington. Where the depot stands was a house where Samuel Ochy lived. Farther down on the same side of the street lived Thomas Van Loon, the brother of the late James Van Loon, of Kingston; Mrs. George Evans is a daughter. Next came the Gaylord residence. The old academy was on the upper side of the street. Below, on the other side of the street, was the store and residence of John Turner, father of Frank, James and Samuel. Lower down came Moses Atherton, the father of Caleb, who served as Sheriff. On the opposite side lived a sister of John Turner. Next was the tannery of Caleb Atherton. Below was the store of Chauncey A. Reynolds; afterwards it was owned by Davenport & Smith. Then came the old Reynolds homestead; he was a brother of Judge William C., Elijah, Fuller and Abram, deceased.

On the opposite side of the street lived John Ingham; Mrs. Samuel Davenport was a daughter of Mrs. Ingham by a former husband—Abijah Smith. Henry Gabriel, the blacksmith, lived opposite; he was the father of Mrs. Charles Young and Mrs. A. J. Root, of Kingston. Further down lived Joshua Pewh; Peter was his son. Below was the store of Samuel Davenport, the father of Abijah. The next house was that of Charity Reynolds, the mother of Thomas, Robert, Daniel, Samuel and other children. John Davenport, the father of Mrs. Ira Carle, of Kingston, Mrs. Frank Gregg, Robert, Ira, Daniel, Elijah, Thomas, William, Mary, Anna and Charity, lived next. Below lived Thomas Davenport. Farther down lived Col. George P. Ransom, an old Revolutionary soldier. Near by lived Samuel French. Below him Samuel Ransom. Then came the home of Joseph Wright, the father of Col. Hendrick B., Harrison, Caleb E. and Ellen. The house was formerly occupied by Moses Wadhams, the father of Phebe and Lydia, the wife of Samuel French. On the lower side William Hodge lived, the brother of the Rev. James Hodge. On the upper side of the road lived Freeman Thomas, and next to him was the old stone house of Thomas Pringle, the father of Alexander, George and Samuel, of Kingston; Mrs. Elias

Culver is his daughter. The next place was that of Jamison Harvey, the father of William J. and H. H. Harvey, of Wilkes-Barre. The next house was that of Silas Harvey; this was the last house on the way to Nanticoke.

Shawnee avenue, from the upper end: The first house was that of James Nesbitt, brother of Abram Nesbitt. Across the street on the upper side Hiram Davenport lived. Then came the father of Dr. Rogers, of Huntsville, and the grandfather of Dr. L. L. Rogers, of Kingston. The next house was that of Albert Bangs, father of Martin, Alba and Benjamin. Below lived Thomas Dodson, then Clark Davenport. In the next house Calvin Wadhams lived, the father of Samuel, who was the father of Moses, Elijah and Mrs. L. D. Shoemaker, all deceased. Adjoining Mr. Wadhams lived Benjamin Reynolds, father of Mrs. Dr. Tubbs, William, Charles, Fuller, Elijah. Next was R. Davenport; adjoining lived Oliver Davenport, the father of Edward, the merchant; Mrs. Whitney, Mrs. Andrew F. Levi, A. S. Shaver, Mrs. H. H. Ashley were the children. In the next house lived Daniel Davenport, Jr. John Smith lived near. The next house was that of C. S. Rinus; William, Ebenezer, Lorenzo Dow, John Shonk's second wife were his children. Samuel Lewis lived below. Then came George Puterbaugh, Patrick Cullen, David Pringle, C. Garrahan, the father of Michael Garrahan, of Kingston.

# BIOGRAPHICAL HISTORY.

ALEXANDER H. VANHORN was born in Hunlock township, February 23, 1833; educated at Wyoming Seminary; went to Carbon county in 1855 and worked on a salary; in 1864 became interested in the coal business; came to Wilkes-Barre in 1871 and became identified with the Wyoming Manufacturing Company, now the Vulcan Iron Works; elected director of the Wilkes-Barre Deposit and Savings Bank, and in 1880 elected president; married in 1867 at Summit Hill to Miss Harriet Abbott; in 1885 married Miss Dora L. Reading, of New Jersey; member of the firm of Payne & Co., limited, and is chairman of the company.

WILLIAM HENRY STURDEVANT was born at Braintrim, Luzerne county (now Wyoming county), Pa., in 1838. He began civil engineering (which he has followed ever since) as a rodman on the L. & B. R. R. during its construction, after the completion of which he was with his father for several years in the survey of lands in Wyoming, Sullivan and Lycoming counties. In 1862 he returned to Wilkes-Barre and with his father established an office of civil engineering, land surveying and land agency, which business he has since followed. He was County Surveyor and a member of the Wilkes-Barre borough council for several years, and when the city was incorporated was elected City Engineer, which office he held until 1882. He is related to many of the old families of the Valley. Three of his great-grandfathers were soldiers in the Revolutionary war; one of them, Lieutenant Asa Stevens, was killed at the Wyoming Massacre.

WILLIAM DICKOVER was born in Wilkes-Barre in 1819; was educated in the borough schools; learned the mason trade and with his father began contracting in general masonry and building in 1850; established brick manufacturing in 1870. In 1872 his son became a partner in building and contracting and in 1883 in the manufacturing of brick; the oldest contractor in Wilkes-Barre; Poor Director for three years.

JOHN GORE WOOD was born in Wilkes-Barre January 13, 1838. He is the oldest son of the late John B. Wood and Sarah Gore, his wife. He was educated in Wyoming Seminary and Philadelphia Business College; carried on a dry goods business successfully for ten years; he then became a member of the banking house of J. B. Wood & Co.; the bank closed business after the death of the senior partner, in good financial standing after operating ten years. Since the death of his father he has been trustee of his estate. In 1883 he helped to start the Wilkes-Barre Paper Manufacturing Co., with a capital of $30,000, which has been increased to $50,000; has been secretary and treasurer of the company for eight years; elected councilman-at-large for the city in 1889 and still holds that position; treasurer of the Wilkes-Barre Steam Heating Co., also director of the Wyoming Campmeeting Association; member of the Franklin street M. E. church. He is a careful and considerate business man. He married Emiline Elizabeth Drake, a daughter of the late William Drake, of Old Forge, Pa., November 22, 1871. He has five children John

B., Elmer, Carl, B. D. and Esther I. Wood. Mr. Wood's wife was born October 18, 1848, and died December 24, 1890.

ROBERT MURDOCH, M. D., was born in Scotland in 1847; came to the United States in 1850; educated in Towanda, Pa.; studied medicine with D. S. Pratt, of that place; graduated from the Hahnemann Medical College, Philadelphia, Pa., 1872; located in Ulster, Pa., then in Burling, Pa.; located in Wilkes-Barre in 1883, at No. 160 South Main street; member of the Homeopathic Medical Society of Northeastern Pennsylvania and the State Society.

LEVI IVES SHOEMAKER, M. D., born in Wilkes-Barre, Pa., September, 1859; son of L. D. Shoemaker, Esq.; educated in the Grammar school, New Haven, Conn.; graduated from Yale College 1882; graduated from the Medical Department of the University of Pennsylvania in 1886; served two years in the hospital in Wilkes-Barre and Philadelphia; physician for the Home of the Friendless Children; member of the staff of physicians of the Wilkes-Barre Hospital; a member of the Luzerne Medical Society and the American Academy of Medicine; married Miss Cornelius W. Scranton, daughter of the late J. H. Scranton.

JOHN TITUS HOWELL, M. D., born in Allen township, Pa., in Oct., 1850; educated at Weaversval Academy and Cooperstown Seminary, N. Y.; mechanical draughtsman until 1878; graduated from the Jefferson Medical College, Philadelphia, 1881; located in Wilkes-Barre, where he is now practicing; member of the Luzerne Medical Society and the Lehigh Valley Medical Association, also the State and National Associations; married Miss Minnie Brandow, 1890.

EDMUND G. BUTLER, Esq., son of Lord Butler, who was the son of Lord Butler, was born in Wilkes-Barre in 1845; graduated from Wesleyan College in 1868 with the degree of A. M.; studied law with E. P. Darling, Esq.; admitted to the bar in 1869; married Miss Clara T. Cox, of New York city, 1869; admitted to the Circuit Court of the United States.

JOSEPH R. PERRY was born in Berks county in 1828; after he left school was a teacher; in 1864 began the manufacturing of organs and later of pianos; has taken out a number of patents, one of which was purchased by the Mason & Hamlin Organ Company; is well known locally as a writer on economic questions.

LEWIS LEGRAND was born Providence, R. I., in 1818; learned his trade in Newark, N. J.; came to this city in 1840 and established what has become one of the largest wagon and carriage manufacturing firms in this section; the firm now includes his son Charles.

SIDNEY WILSON, born in New Jersey in 1827; came to this city in 1835; carried on the livery business; in 1860 became proprietor of the Bear Creek Hotel; in 1861 started a stage line between Kingston and Wilkes-Barre; he had a livery stable in the rear of the Bristol House and remained for fourteen years and then moved to North Main street; he died November 14, 1889.

MILLER DEITRICK, born at Bear Creek, Pa., 1828; educated in Wilkes-Barre; worked on his father's farm; with the L. & S. R. R.; in his father's hotel; four years proprietor of American Hotel after his father's death; in 1868 became conductor on the street car line between Kingston and Wilkes-Barre; connected with the Wilkes-Barre & Wyoming Valley Traction Company since 1892.

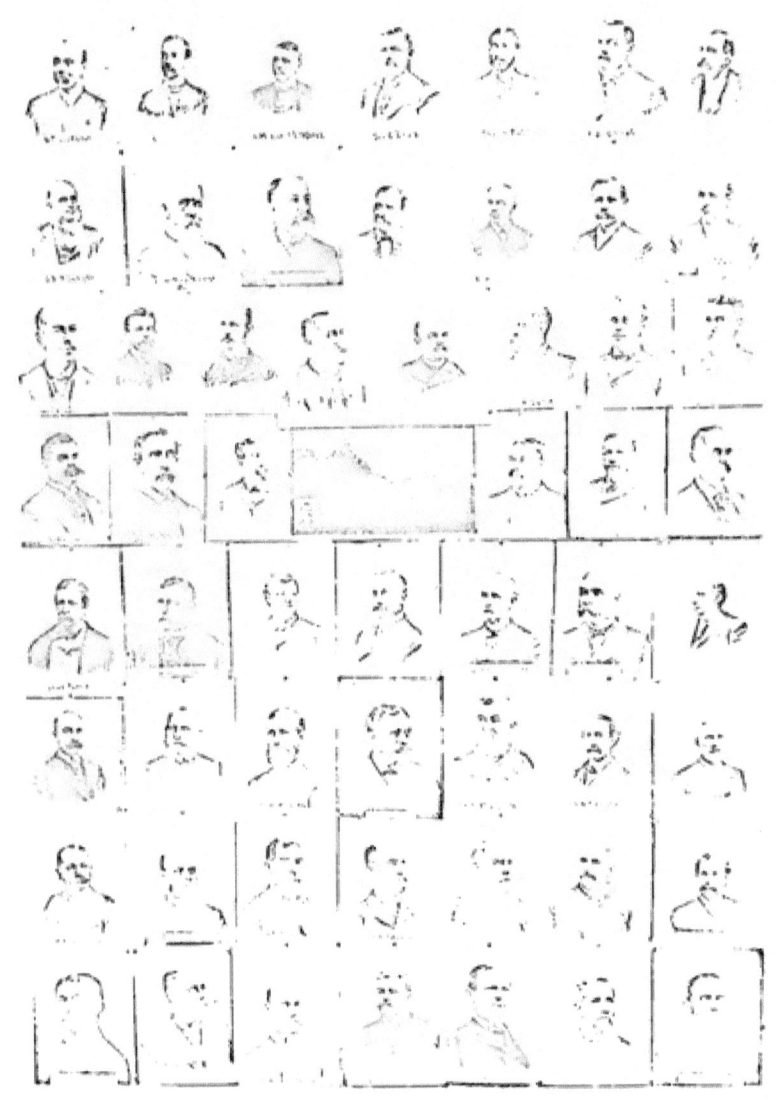

HON. JOHN B. SMITH, born in Plymouth in 1819; son of Abijah; learned the trade of chair and furniture making; entered the store of Samuel Davenport, his brother-in-law; became a partner at twenty-one and at Mr. Davenport's death bought the stock; engaged in the coal business; established the First National Bank of Plymouth in 1864 and is its president; member of the Legislature 1876 to 1880; member of the Farmers' National Congress and Agricultural Society; owns large tracts of land in Colorado and many farms in this section, and has large coal interests.

CHRISTIAN BRAHL, born in Germany in 1815; after his education came to this country; established a grocery, flour and feed business on the corner of Hazle and Main streets, Wilkes-Barre, 1855, and in 1880 retired; was a director in the First National Bank for eight years; vice president and director of the Deposit and Savings Bank; one son a Priest, and one daughter a Sister of Charity; his oldest daughter is the wife of Judge Gunster, of Scranton.

LOUIS PRAETORIUS was born in New Bavaria in 1828; educated for a teacher; studied music under Jacob Vierling, Wendling and later with Nulizer; came to Wilkes-Barre in 1848; began teaching music in the old Dana academy and taught there for seven years; had charge of the musical department of Wyoming Seminary until the beginning of the late war; bandmaster of the Ninth Pennsylvania Cavalry and later captain of Co. D, of the same regiment; was organist in the M. E. and Presbyterian churches and for the last eight years in St. Mary's church. Organized the first brass band in Wilkes-Barre.

NOAH PETTIBONE, born 1838; educated in the Wyoming Seminary and the old Academy; has lived in Forty Fort all his life and farmed; married Miss Jane Renard 1864; is a son of Noah Pettibone.

JOHN SHARPES PETTIBONE, born in Kingston township 1836; went to school at Wyoming Seminary; lived and farmed at Forty Fort all his life; married Miss Rachel Renard 1885; assessor at the present time; son of Noah Pettibone.

GEORGE PETTIBONE, born in Kingston township 1849; educated at the Wyoming Seminary; farmed at Forty Fort all his life; married Miss Helen Space; school director.

IRA CARLE was born at Plymouth in 1812; moved to Kingston in 1837 and bought the house and tannery of General Samuel Thomas, and carried on the tannery business for thirty-five years; served as Burgess for fifteen years and Justice of the Peace for twenty years.

JOHN CONSTINE was born in Bavaree Brehefelt, 1817; came to this country in his youth; established business on Bowman's corner; then built on the south side of the Square. Died February 10, 1882. His son Edward conducts the business.

EDWARD CONSTINE, born in Wilkes-Barre, March 4, 1848; educated in the public schools; succeeded his father after his death; is a member of the Board of Trade. The business was established by the father on the south side of the square and was one of the first in the city.

CHARLES JAMES COOPER, born at Waymart, Pa. Jan. 5, 1847; educated in the Normal School in that place; taught school; engaged in building; in 1891 was elected superintendent of the Wilkes-Barre Heat and Light and Water Co.

WILLIAM CLOUGH ALLAN, born May 6, 1866, at Brotton-in-Cleveland, Yorkshire, England; eldest son of John and Dorothy Ann Allan; educated in the public schools; was one year in a blacksmith shop connected with ironstone mines; then went into the employ of the Northeastern R. R. Co. for six years as operator, ticket and express clerk; came to this country in April, 1887; worked in the Sheldon Axle Works about two years, then graduated from the Wilkes-Barre Business College; entered the office of Charles Parrish in July, 1889; now secretary of the Annora and West End Coal Companies, and private secretary to Charles Parrish; Worshipful Master of Lodge, No. 61, Free and Accepted Masons.

BENJAMIN F. BARNUM was born in Wilkes-Barre in 1851; educated in the public schools and the private school of Squire Parsons; graduated from the Commercial department of Wyoming Seminary; entered in the employment of the D. & H. C. & R. R. Co., then in the employment of the Adams Express Company for fifteen years; for the last five years has filled the position of city ticket agent for the Pennsylvania R. R. Co. in Wilkes-Barre; married Miss Effie Wier, of Wilkes-Barre. He is a son of Judge Charles Barnum, of this city.

DAVID JAMES was born in Dunbar, Pa., 1862; educated in the public schools; studied music for two years in the Peabody Musical Conservatory of Baltimore, Md.; also under Arker Henerik, Henry O. Allen; later under T. J. Davis; located in Wilkes-Barre in 1889; is superintendent of the musical instruction in the public schools of Wilkes-Barre; musical instructor of the Hillman Academy and the Female Institute; choirmaster of St. Stephen's Episcopal church, of this city.

RYLANCE S. SMITH was born in Wilkes-Barre; educated in the public schools; studied music with Miner Austin and Theodore Boettger, of Wilkes-Barre, and at the New England Conservatory of Music, Boston, Mass.; is a teacher of the pianaforte; was organist in the Zion Reformed church of this city and the Roman Catholic church of Plains.

THOMAS WRIGHT, born in Berks county, Pa., 1837; educated in The Friends' school and a seminary; taught school; became a civil engineer; came to the Valley 1868; bought the Samuel Raub mill in 1892; is now following his profession.

ROBERT WILSON was born in England in 1825; emigrated in 1843; engaged in trade in Wilkes-Barre with John B. Wood as partner; was burned out in 1859; engaged in the insurance business; engaged in fruit growing in Delaware. In 1876 he established his present drug business in Wyoming, being the first in the place.

ELMER T. SMITH, born in Forty Fort in 1866; educated at Wyoming Seminary; is engaged in fruit growing and is successful; son of Joseph Smith.

CALVIN PERRIN, born in Wyoming county, Pa., 1844; went to school in that county; taught school; worked in a store at Winton; resides at Forty Fort and carries on a successful mercantile business in Luzerne.

J. FRANK WILSON, born in Pittston, Pa., 1859; educated at Wyoming Seminary; kept books for an insurance company; graduated from the Dental and Medical college in Philadelphia in 1881; associated with his father, S. D. Wilson, in the livery business; established his present business of dealer in carriages, sleighs, etc., 208 South Main street, 1886. Mr. Wilson carries the largest stock of any dealer in Northeastern Pennsylvania.

CHARLES DRAKE LeGRAND, born in Wilkes-Barr, Pa., 1857; educated at the Wyoming Seminary; for fifteen years has had charge of the carriage and wagon manufacturing business established by his father, Lewis LeGrand, on South Main street; became a partner in 1888; married Isadore M. Johnson, of Wilkes-Barre, 1877.

ANDREW E. WATT was born in Kingston Pa., 1851; educated in Wyoming Seminary; established, with Andrew Murray, the firm of Watt & Murray, Public Square, Wilkes-Barre; sold his interest to Murray, 1874; connected with a wholesale drug house of Philadelphia; has a half interest in the Wilkes-Barre Supply Company; a member of Landmark Lodge, No. 442, F. & A. M.

SOL. HIRSCH, born in Germany, 1847; educated in that country; came to this country in 1866; became a salesman; 1874 removed to Plymouth and established a dry goods and millinery business and later general merchandise; opened branch stores at Luzerne, East and West Nanticoke and other towns; in 1888 he opened a wholesale liquor business in Wilkes-Barre; bought out the Australian Red Weed Company; in 1893 went in the commission and real estate business.

LEWIS THEODORE HARVEY, born in Wilkes-Barre in 1853; educated in the public schools; established his present livery business in 1878; member of 704, Odd Fellows; is a Degree of Pocahontas; No. 12, Susquehanna Chieftain's League; Meneto Tribe, 257, and Lozer Circle, 188.

REV. JOHN WHITE was born in Wilkes-Barre in 1823; educated in Wilkes-Barre; is a wagon-maker; lived in Ashley since 1852; licensed as a local preacher; Mr. and Mrs. White have been active in church work.

HORACE S. CHAMBERLAIN, born in Chenango county, N. Y., 1842; educated at the Delaware Literary Institute, Franklin, N. Y.; in the mercantile business for fifteen years in New York State; became associated with the firm of B. G. Carpenter & Co., of this city, in 1875, where he is still employed.

EUGENE K. FRY was born in Wilkes-Barre, in 1865; educated in the public schools; established with E. O. Richards the firm of Richards & Fry, dealers in wall paper and stationery, 45 South Main street; son of Herman C. Fry.

R. B. ALBERTSON was born in Greenwood, Pa., in 1854; went to school at that place; established his present carriage works, No. 258 South Main street, in 1880, where he has erected a large building.

JAMES GARRISON SECOR, born in Orange county, N. Y., in 1856; graduated from the Bloomsburg Normal School in 1883; studied at the Wyoming Seminary; principal of the Parrish street school, was principal of the Custer street school, and is now principal of the Carey avenue school, Wilkes-Barre.

MORGAN WELLER, D. D. S., was born at Richmondville, N. Y., 1857; studied dentistry at Binghamton and attended the Cincinnati College; located in Binghamton for six years and in Wilkes-Barre for ten years; has been successful, and built a handsome residence and office at No. 22 North Franklin street.

WILLIAM HOOVER, born in Dallas, Pa., August 31, 1833; farmer and butcher for many years; large owner of real estate; residence in Wilkes-Barre.

WILLIAM M. McCULLOUGH, born in Scotland, 1838; came to this country in 1853; under John Mitchell at the Dundee shaft; mine boss at Buttonwood; sunk the Henry shaft, Plainsville, No. 2, Plymouth, and several others; mine superintendent for A. Langdon & Co., Grassy Island and Buttonwood colliery, Carbondale; has resided on the Plains for forty years.

JOSEPH A. ANZMAN, born in Baltimore, Md., 1839; educated at St. Vincent College, Pa.; came to Wilkes-Barre 1871 and established his present business—harness and awning —on east Market street, in 1880.

HON. WILLIAM HALL BRODHEAD, born in Philadelphia in 1857; moved to Mauch Chunk and later to the Wyoming Valley; educated in the public schools; has been engaged about the mines; delegate to the Luzerne Democratic County Convention; elected to the Legislature on the Democratic ticket in 1892 for the First District of Luzerne county, which comprises the city of Wilkes-Barre; senior captain in the Ninth Regiment.

JOHN HUGHES, born in Wales; resided in London, and came to this country in 1867; a machinist; then learned the tailor trade, went into business in Wilkes-Barre in 1876, and is now at 45 West Market street; is well known as a musician and has given considerable service gratuitously to charitable entertainments; played the cornet in the M. E. Sunday school for ten years; is a Mason, Knight Templar and an Elk; deals considerably in real estate.

ALBERT HAMILTON KIPP was born November 14, 1850, in New York city; educated in Tarrytown, N. Y., where he spent his youth; studied his profession of architecture in New York city under well known men in the profession; came to Wilkes-Barre in the year 1886 and has practiced his profession ever since; is a Fellow of the American Institute of Architects—made a member in 1887; appointed architect to the Wilkes-Barre & Eastern R. R.; is the architect for the City Hospital and many private residences; Mr. Kipp stands high in his profession.

WILSON J. SMITH, born in Black Creek township, Pa., 1854; educated in the public schools and by a private tutor; established himself as a carpenter, builder and architect in Wilkes-Barre in 1873; built the mechanical art building of the State College, and many other buildings in this section.

JOHN C. KAUFER, born at Wilkes-Barre in 1857; educated in the public schools; a printer; is now serving his second term as Alderman of the Tenth Ward; Financial Secretary of Zion Reformed Church.

EDMUND NELSON CARPENTER, son of B. G. Carpenter, was born in Wilkes-Barre in 1865; educated at the Wilkes-Barre public schools and Wyoming Seminary, Kingston; member of the firm of B. G. Carpenter & Co. since 1889; member of the Board of Trade for four years; First Lieutenant and Inspector of Rifle Practice of Ninth Regiment, Third Brigade, N. G. P.

ELMER V. SCOTT was born at Rockam, Pa.; attended winter school; served three years in the late war in Co. D, Third Heavy Artillery; was with Grant in the campaign of '64 on the Savannah, and with his battery in the battle of Gettysburg; was in twenty-two engagements; an engineer for sixteen years on the Bloomsburg division of the D., L. & W. R. R.; member of Eureka Lodge, No. 104.

C. H. Chamberlin, born at Catskill, N. Y., 1848; educated in the district schools and Schoharie Academy; learned the printing trade; came to Pittston in 1869, was a partner in establishing the *Luzerne Leader*; when the paper was removed to Wilkes-Barre was foreman of the composing room; city editor of the *Evening Leader* from 1879 to 1890; spent three months in Florida to regain his health; from that time to the present associate editor of the *Leader* staff; married Miss Mira A., daughter of Rev. J. M. Howell, of Green Ridge, Scranton; has three children and resides in Kingston.

F. W. Tyrrell, born at Forty Fort in 1861; graduated from the Commercial College of Wyoming Seminary in 1876; clerk for the D., L. & W. R. R. freight department at Kingston; mine clerk at Maltby; weighmaster for W. G. Payne & Co., at Peckville; bookkeeper for Scranton Beef Co., Scranton; bookkeeper for A. Ryman & Son, at Dallas; now bookkeeper for Sturdevant, Fogel & Co., wholesale house.

Henry F. Mooney, born in Hanover township, Pa., 1859; went to the public schools; established his present business of undertaking on Northampton street in 1882; City Auditor, and is now serving his third term; member of the St. Aloysius Society.

Thomas Hunt Rippard, born in Wilkes-Barre, June 14, 1866; attended State Normal School at Baltimore, Md.; received a musical education at Peabody Institute, Baltimore, Md.; at the present time in the Wilkes-Barre Deposit and Savings Bank.

George W. Lewis, born in Hoover, Ohio, June 25, 1870; educated in the public schools and graduated from the Wyoming Commercial College in 1888; accepted the position of bookkeeper with F. A. Phelps & Co., 1888, and became a member of the firm February 1, 1893.

Marion H. Frantz, born at Carverton, Pa., 1860; graduated from the Commercial Department of Wyoming Seminary in 1880; since that time has been bookkeeper for Smith & Frantz, of Wilkes-Barre; he has received a copyright for an "Economic Ready Balance Ledger."

Emmett D. Nichols, Esq., born at Ulster, Pa., in 1855; educated at Wyoming Seminary; admitted to the Luzerne Bar in 1879; studied law with Kidder and Nichols; is known as the father of the present Prohibition party in Luzerne county; chairman of the Prohibition party, one year excepted, since 1880.

John A. Opp, Esq., born at Muncy, Pa., July 16th, 1847; graduated at Dickinson Seminary; studied law with E. H. Little, of Bloomsburg, Pa.; admitted to the Luzerne Bar February 24th, 1873, and located in Plymouth. He has held the position of Judge Advocate in the National Guard with the rank of Major. He served in the Civil War in the Seventh Pa. Cavalry; a member of the Plymouth Borough School Board for twelve years.

Frederick Schwartz, born in New York city January 15th, 1849; educated in the New York public schools and College of the City of New York; embarked in business in Plymouth, Pa., in 1870, continuing the same for twenty three years, being now the senior member of the firm of Fred. Schwartz & Bro.

Max Reese was born in Germany in 1866; educated in the Royal Gymnasium (as German academies are named); came to Plymouth, Pa., in 1882; entered the business of his brother, Abram Reese, and succeeded him after his retiring from active business in April, 1892.

JOHN MUGINES, JR., was born at Wilkes-Barre in 1846; graduated from the Commercial Department of Wyoming Seminary in 1866; for twenty years has been employed by the Kingston Coal Co.; member of the Odd Fellows and the Improved Order of Red Men.

GEORGE PRIDE LINDSAY was born at Plains, Luzerne county, Pa., September 23, 1853; educated at the Wyoming Seminary; began as a clerk; at present time is secretary of the Parrish Coal Co.

GEORGE HELLER, born 1849 in Allentown, Pa.; educated in the public schools and Allentown Academy; manager for the Adams Express Company from 1873 to 1884; then became ticket agent for the L. V. R. R. at Wilkes-Barre.

MINATE COLUMBUS ANDREAS, born at Mifflinville, Pa., in 1858; established the Mifflinville *Record;* merged it into the Nanticoke *Tribune,* and in 1885 sold it to W. H. Capwell; in 1887 with the Genesee Oil Co., of Buffalo, located at Chicago and Williamsport; bookkeeper for the Wilkes-Barre *News-Dealer* for two years; with L. & W.-B. Coal Co. and the Crystal Spring Water Co.; 1889 with the File and Tool Co.; at the present time with the *Wilkes-Barre Evening Times.*

RICHARD CLARK, born at Rock Ferry, Ireland, 1855; came in his youth to Schuylkill county; attended school; worked in a breaker; was a bookkeeper; 1888 entered the office of John W. Haddock, Black Diamond store, Luzerne; general manager 1889; secretary of the School Board of Luzerne Borough.

A. DUNCAN THOMAS, M. D., born at Llewellyn, Pa., 1858; son of Margaret and Duncan Thomas, of Glasgow, Scotland, who came to this country 1842; educated under a private tutor; graduated from Hahnemann Medical College 1881; located at Shamokin, Pa.; two years later located at Forty Fort; largely interested in the real estate business; treasurer of the borough; member of the Board of Trade; active in church work; interested in promoting the development of the west side.

BENJAMIN DAVEY, JR., born in Marquette, Mich.; educated in the public schools of Plymouth and Wilkes-Barre; in 1879 entered the office of Willis Hawkins, architect, in Wilkes-Barre; 1888 established himself in the office formerly occupied by W. W. Neuer, corner of Canal and Market streets, his present location; many of the finest buildings in this section were designed in his office.

JOSEPH P. BURNS, born in Cork, Ireland; educated in England; came to this country in 1882; studied music under Karl Formes and Dr. D. J. J. Mason; composed the following pieces: "Ave Maria," "Ecce Panis," "O Salutaris," "The Yankee Tar," "Love's Devotion," "Dear Friends of Old," "Love Will Live Always," "Deep in My Heart," "Her Little Ivied Cottage," "O Winsome Bessy," and carried away the first prize at the World's Fair September 7th, 1893, for baritone singing, and has won every contest he has entered in solo work previous to that time.

EDWARD JAMES ANTHONY, born in Victoria, Wales, 1844; educated there and came to this country in 1863; a pattern maker; followed building in Schuylkill county, Scranton, Danville; in the passenger department of the L. & B. shops, Kingston, and was general foreman from 1870 to 1875; established with his father the wrought-iron fence and house decorative manufactory; member of the Cambro Americans and was the first commander of Phil Sheridan Castle, No. 145, A. O. K. of M. C.

JACOB I. SHOEMAKER, born in Wyoming 1839, where he now resides; educated in Wyoming; has lived an active business life; farmer, manufacturer, builder, dealing largely in flour and feed; served in Co. E, 43rd P. V. F.; married Miss Mary Margaret Sharp 1863; President of the Borough Council; Trustee of the M. E. church; Trustee of the Wyoming Seminary; President of the Cemetery Association; Director of the People's Savings Bank of Pittston, and several other associations.

GEORGE B. DILLEY, born in 1850 at Ashley, Pa.; moved to Illinois and went to school in that State; came to Kingston in 1870, followed carpentering; insurance agent; moved to Forty Fort in 1883; elected Justice of the Peace, and in 1887 Burgess; re-elected 1891.

ADAM HEISZ, born at Bowman's Creek, Pa., 1846; began farming for himself 1870; in 1873 bought the farm that he now occupies at Forty Fort and built his present residence; Town Councilman for three years; married Mrs. Eliza Jackson, at Forty Fort, 1866.

REV. DAVID L. DAVIS was born in Wales 1849; finished his education in Bangor Seminary, Mar; came to this country 1863; located at Pittston; Carbondale; in 1890 at Edwardsville, Pa., his present charge; President of the Edwardsville School Board 1892; its first Secretary.

SYLVESTER PAUKSZTIS was born 1859; came to this country 1871; was a farmer; 1889 built his present large business block in Edwardsville; is a merchant; President and Treasurer of a lodge of men of his nationality.

HENRY GEORGE JENKINS was born in South Wales 1836; came to this country 1868; educated in Wales; traveled in Spain, France and England putting up machinery; was foreman in the D., L. & W. shop in 1878; opened a store in Edwardsville where he has lived for twenty-six years; Mrs. Mary Jane Edwards was his daughter; Dr. D. H. and George B. are his sons.

JAMES D. EDWARDS was born in Scranton, Pa., 1862; lived in Plymouth and later in Kingston; educated in the public schools; entered the office of the Kingston Coal Co. 1879 and is now paymaster; has been school director and filled other public offices in Edwardsville.

FREDERICK WILLIAMS was born in England 1848; educated in the Parochial schools; lived in Williamstown, Pa., and followed music as a profession; worked as a miner in Plymouth, Pa.; Justice of the Peace of Edwardsville since 1884; is a writer of verse; "Ingratitude, or Old Sport and His Master," appeared in the *Boston Pilot*.

REV. MINER SWALLOW, born at Plainsville, Pa., 1815; educated in the public schools; joined the Wyoming Conference 1834; after serving many circuits was superannuated for one year; the tract agent for two years, then returned to the work; supernumerary relations in 1873; lives in Kingston; Mrs. Swallow, nee Mary Elizabeth Dodson, a prominent Christian woman, died 1893.

ALONZO WINFIELD HOUSER, born at Huntsville, Pa., 1851; educated in Wilkes-Barre; learned the trade of blacksmithing; employed by Buck Mountain Coal Co., and at Chester, and later at Kingston; is now at the Pettibone mines at Dorranceton, with the Delaware, Lackawanna and Western Coal Co.; patented a double-box slate-picker, also a safety block; is Councilman of Edwardsville; was an Elder in the Bennet Presbyterian church at Luzerne in 1875.

HARRY LAMON GROVER, born at Beach Grove, Pa., 1863; graduated from the Commercial Department of Wyoming Seminary 1888; baggage master and express agent for the D., L. & W. R. R. at Kingston since 1889; member of the P. O. S. of A., 709; married Miss Maggie Culver, of Kingston, 1888.

GEORGE W. CARR, born in England 1848; went to school; came to this country 1870; located in Kingston; is a professional gardener; has the only hothouse in Kingston; has been a Mason for fifteen years.

GEORGE NESBITT, born in Jackson township, Pa., 1860; farmed and went to school until 1884; then established a mercantile business in Kingston with Mr. Rogers; two years later bought out his partner; member of the Town Council.

WILLIAM F. CHURCH, born in Kingston, Pa.; son of Addison, one of the old merchants of Kingston; educated in the Wyoming Seminary; 1867 went in the drug store of Abram Goodwin; purchased the business 1883; 1889 removed across the street; married Miss Annie H. Corss 1876; postmaster of Kingston 1878 to '82; Ruling Elder in the Presbyterian church; and a Mason.

STEPHEN H. PETTIBONE, born in Forty Fort; educated at Wyoming Seminary; lived and farmed in Columbia county for five years; returned 1871; moved in his present residence on Wyoming avenue, Forty Fort, 1881; married Lucinda C. Pettibone 1854; they have six children.

HARVEY YEAGER, born in Columbia county 1847; educated in Danville, Pa.; in business in that town for three years; in 1875 came to Plymouth, and established the Opera House store; 1889 purchased the Valley Co. store at Forty Fort, where he is at the present time; married Margaret E. R. Smith, daughter of John B. Smith, 1871; School Director of Forty Fort for three Years.

REV. WILLIAM T. GIBBONS, born in Chester county, Pa., 1859; educated at Bucknell University and graduated from Princeton Theological Seminary 1890; pastor of the Stella Presbyterian chapel, Forty Fort, Pa.

SAMUEL T. SMITH, born at Forty Fort, 1858; graduated from the Commercial Department of Wyoming Seminary, 1877; Auditor by appointment 1882; U. S. Deputy Clerk of Internal Revenue, Twelfth District of Pennsylvania, for three years; traveling salesman for Garney Bros., Scranton; member of many lodges. The old homestead stands on or near the site of the old fort at Forty Fort.

REV. EBENEZER JOSEPH MORRIS was born in Wales in 1845; graduated from New College, London, in 1870; came to this country the same year; located at Neath, Pa., 1870 to 1884; Welsh Congregational church in New York city, 1884 to 1889; pastor of the Puritan Congregational church, Wilkes-Barre, 1889, his present charge; author of "Prejudiced Inquiries" and "Prayer Meeting Theology."

JOHN C. BOUND, born in Broome county, N. Y.; went to school; worked on a farm; then went in the employment of the N. Y. & Erie R. R.; then with the D., L. & W. R. R.; came to the Bloomsburg division 1860; resigned and went with the Wyoming Valley Traction Company 1892; married Miss Elizabeth A. Clark 1853, who died 1859; then married Miss Fanny Hunbock.

JACOB SHARP PETTIBONE, born on the old farm at Forty Fort 1821; educated in the Kingston Academy; is a farmer; Councilman and Treasurer ever since the borough was organized.

JOHN BIERMAN, born in Narrowsburg, N. Y., 1849; went to school in that place; went with the L. V. and E. & W. R. R. 1860; in 1866 with the D., L. & W. R. R., Bloomsburg division; served in several positions, and was passenger conductor for four years; accepted a position with the West Side Electric Road 1891, where he is now employed.

P. A. A. REAVES, born in the Mohawk Valley July 4, 1825; educated at the Amsterdam Academy; came to Carbondale in his sixteenth year; with the D. & H. Co. in the machine shop for five years; 1850 took charge of pumps and mine machinery force of the Pennsylvania Coal Co.; a shaft sunk then one hundred feet was the first shaft in the valley; changed the chain for hoisting to wire rope; 1852 made iron safety carriages; made the plans and drawings for the Pennsylvania Coal Co. for fifteen years; his health failed and he went south; on his return went to work for the D., L. & W. R. R., in the mine machinery department at Kingston.

CHRISTOPHER HIMMLER was born August 7th, 1844, in Cumberland city, Md.; went to school in that city; on his father's farm; in 1865 went with the D., L. & W. R. R., and with the exception of three years spent farming has been with that company until the present time; an engineer for twenty years; was in the late war; a Mason and a member of the Brotherhood of Locomotive Engineers; married Miss Ada Lozo 1873.

CHARLES WESLEY McALARNEY, Esq., born at Mifflinburg, Pa., 1847; educated at the Mifflinburg Academy; read law with his brother, J. C., at Harrisburg; admitted to the Dauphin County Bar 1873; to the Luzerne Bar 1876; located in Plymouth, where he is practicing his profession.

WILLIAM DAVIS, born in Schuylkill county, Pa.; educated in that county; kept books in Scranton for Conly & McAndrews and Thomas Egnan & Co.; served in the late war, first in Schooley's Battery from Pittston, then in the 9th, 18th and 22d Army Corps; Captain Co. C, 112th Regiment, 9th Army Corps; removed to Plymouth, Pa., 1868; established his present business of general merchandise; member of the School Board for twelve continuous years and has been re-elected; member of Plymouth Lodge, 332, A. Y. M., since 1870.

ERASTUS MARION SMITH, born at Old Forge, Pa., 1839; educated at the Wyoming Seminary; farmed until his twenty-fourth year and then went to Janesville, Wis., and conducted the European Hotel; removed to Scranton and was Street Commissioner for four years; went to Florida; was one of the largest growers of fruit in the State; in the real estate business in Scranton; conducts the Frantz House at Plymouth.

JOHN E. MILLER, born in Newark, N. J., 1856; came to Wilkes-Barre 1865 and attended school; a marble cutter; established a marble yard in Kingston 1884; removed to Wilkes-Barre to his present location, 133 S. Main street, 1889; Mr. A. C. Laycock became his partner 1891; this firm does the largest business of any in the valley in its line.

JOHN SCHNEIDER, born in Wilkes-Barre, Pa., 1865; went to the German Catholic school; worked in the mines; clerk for Jacob Reuffer; in 1891 became proprietor of the hotel 52 South Main street; member of the Sængerbund.

PHILIP WEISS, born in Prussia 1851; educated in that country and graduated from one of the seminaries; came to this country 1870; kept books in Syracuse, N. Y.; 1876 clerked for A. G. Hall; solicitor and collector for Robert Baur; 1891 passenger and freight agent for the C. R. R. of N. J., office on Public Square; member of the Sængerbund.

FRANK JACOBS, born in Germany 1856; educated in that country; came to this country 1880; Financial Secretary of the Sængerbund of Pennsylvania, and Schuetzen Verein, B. A., Washington B. A., Constatter Volksfest Verein, Liedertafel, Sængerbund societies; is now located at 112 South Washington street.

H. S. CARKHUFF, born in New York 1864; educated in the Clinton Academy; learned the art of ladies' hair dressing in New York city, where he spent five years; established his present business in Wilkes-Barre 1888; he has elegant rooms in the Welles Building; has made a special study of scalp diseases.

JAMES P. HUSTEAD was born in Ross township, Pa., 1862; educated at Huntington Academy; taught since 1881; in Plymouth three years, eight years at Edwardsdale; in 1888 elected principal; now principal for Plymouth township; married Miss Nellie Davenport 1885; his father was in the late war and died in the hospital at Philadelphia.

ALFRED J. RINGSTRON was born in Sweden 1853; came to this country 1872; in the public school until his sixteenth year; learned telegraphing in the government school; farmed in Lehigh county; moved to Pittston and was employed as an engineer; with the Electric road at the present time; school director in Edwardsville.

DAVID J. THOMAS was born in Carmarthanshire, South Wales, 1852; came to Olyphant, Pa., in his youth; educated in the public schools; came to Kingston 1870 and since that time has been employed as agent for Jones Brothers and Grand Union Tea Company. Active in the Welsh Congregational church; has been School Director for two terms of Edwardsville Borough; Sunday School superintendent; deacon of his church; was active in the erection of the fine school building in that borough; active in the Knights of Pythias as Past Chancellor.

DANIEL S. EDWARDS was born in Pottsville, Pa., 1857; moved to Scranton 1858; to Plymouth 1866; to Edwardsville 1873; educated in the public schools; followed carpentering for nineteen years and in that capacity is now employed by the Kingston Coal Co.; Chief of the Edwardsville Fire Department for the last three years; member of the Odd Fellows and other societies.

THOMAS JEROME CHASE, born at Benton, Luzerne, now Lackawanna county, Pa., May 26, 1844; brought up on a farm; educated in common schools and Madison Academy at Waverly, Pa.; served nine months as a soldier in 1862 and 1863, in the 132d Regiment, Pa. Vols.; studied law in the office of Winton and Chase at Scranton; admitted to the Luzerne Bar in November, 1866.

HENRY CLAY PERRY was born in Berks county, Pa., 1830; went to school in Schuylkill county; has been a builder in Wilkes-Barre from 1851 to 1886; has retired from active business. Mr. Perry is a connoisseur in violins; has made many valuable instruments.

GEORGE W. COOLBAUGH, born in Wyoming County, Pa., 1854; educated in public schools; has served on the staff of several papers in this section; editor and proprietor of the *Telegram*; is in the real estate business.

GEORGE H. KIRWAN, M. D., born of Irish parents in Hawley, Wayne county, Pa.; was educated in the public schools of Wilkes-Barre, and Wyoming Seminary, from which he graduated with a thorough English and a rudimentary classical education. He began the study of medicine in 1878 and graduated with honors from the College of Physicians and Surgeons, medical department, Columbia College, New York, May 16th, 1882, since which time he has very successfully practiced his profession in Wilkes-Barre. Doctor Kirwan is a gentleman of liberal views and refined manners, and possesses recognized ability in his profession, especially as a surgeon, and has attained some distinction as an expert witness in court. He is a Catholic in religion and a Democrat in politics, and is a member of Luzerne County Medical Society, Pennsylvania Medical Society, Lehigh Valley Medical Society, American Medical Association; attending physician and surgeon Luzerne county prison, &c.

GRANVILLE T. MATLACK, M. D., born at Downingtown, Chester county, Pa., February 5, 1862; graduated at Chester Valley Academy, at Downingtown, Pa., spring of 1879; graduated in medicine at Jefferson Medical College, Philadelphia, spring of 1884; appointed resident physician of Wilkes-Barre City Hospital during 1884-'85; afterwards located at Miner's Mills, Pa., and practiced medicine there until the summer of 1891, when he moved to 133 South Washington street, Wilkes-Barre, where he is at present a practicing physician; a member of the Luzerne County Medical Society, also a member of the Lehigh Valley Medical Society; married Clara R. Courtright, of Clark's Green, Pa., April 5, 1888.

LOUISE M. STOECKEL, M. D., was born in Bath, Northampton county, Pa. In early childhood her parents removed to Wilkes-Barre, and later on to Dallas, Pa. She taught Gen. Paul Oliver's private school at Laurel Run for several years, and in 1886 entered the Woman's Medical College of Pa., graduating in 1890. For a short time practiced her profession in Dallas, and in the fall of '90 opened an office in Wilkes-Barre, where she is at present located at 26 North Franklin street. Dr. Stoeckel is a member of Luzerne County Medical Society, of the Lehigh Valley Medical Association, of the State Medical Society and of the American Medical Association.

DR. MARIS GIBSON, M. D., born October 31, 1841, at Buckingham, Bucks county, Pa. Education finished at Madison University, New York State. Graduate of University of Pennsylvania in medicine, 1883. Located in Wilkes-Barre, Pa., at 185 South Washington street, January, 1884. Member of the Luzerne County Medical Society; Secretary of same now and for the last four years. Member of American Medical Association.

J. FRANKLIN HILL, M. D., was born in Salem township, this State, February 13th, 1856; educated at Wyoming Seminary, State Normal School and New Columbus; read medicine with Dr. R. H. Little, of Berwick, Pa.; graduated from the Jefferson Medical College in the class of '85; located in Nanticoke, Pa., where he is now practicing his profession; is also engaged in the drug business; married Miss Millie F. Hoover, Wilkes-Barre, Pa., October 5, 1892.

DOUGLAS S. KISTLER, M. D., born July 19, 1870, in Lynn township, Lehigh county, Pa.; graduate of Hahnemann Medical College, Philadelphia, May 12th, 1893; located at 213 South Main street, Wilkes-Barre; member of Wyoming Homoeopathic Medical Society; diseases of women and children a specialty; hospital experience at the Hahnemann Hospital, Philadelphia.

CHARLES LONG, M. D., born May 21st, 1861; educated in the public schools of Philadelphia; medical degree from Jefferson Medical College of Philadelphia, 1882; resident physician of Wilkes-Barre City Hospital, 1882-'83; visited European hospitals 1883-'84; located at 21 South Washington street.

WILLIAM PETTY, M. D., was born in Hanover township in 1861; educated in the New Columbus Normal School; graduate of Long Island College Hospital, Brooklyn, N. Y., 1886; located in Wilkes-Barre, where he has been in continuous practice ever since; bought out Stark's drug store 1887 and removed to his present location, Hanover street.

D. W. DODSON, M. D., was born in Luzerne county, 1852; received his preliminary education at the New Columbus Academy; graduated from the Jefferson College, Philadelphia, in the class of 1888; located in Nanticoke, Pa., where he is now practicing his profession; married Miss Anna Vincent, of Ashley, 1890.

J. ANSON SINGER, M. D., was born April 12, 1858, at Stroudsburg, Pa.; attended public schools and Collegiate Institute of above named place, also Orangeville Academy; graduated from the University of the City of New York on the 13th day of March, 1883; began the practice of his profession at Brodheadsville, Pa., the same year and continued there until July 1st, 1891, when he moved to Forty Fort, Pa., his present home.

SARAH J. COE, M. D., born of New England parents in Genesee county, New York State; educated and graduated at Genesee Wesleyan Seminary, Lima, N. Y., after which she studied art in its various branches. For five years she was a teacher of Art and Modern Languages in Seminaries in Wisconsin and Michigan. By invitation of the Art Committee of Wisconsin she and her pupils had pictures on exhibition at the Centennial in Philadelphia. She graduated in medicine from Michigan University and after a year in Hospital and Dispensary work located in Wilkes-Barre in September, 1879. Besides having held the several offices connected with the Homœopathic Medical Society of Northern Pennsylvania, Dr. Coe has been greatly honored in the State Homœopathic Medical Society, since 1883 having been called to serve as Censor for three years, Chairman of Bureau twice, Second Vice President and now First Vice President. She is also State Secretary of the Medical Department of the Queen Isabella Association in connection with the World's Fair. Besides medical work she finds some time for religious work in Sunday School and the Young Women's Christian Association, holding the position of President of this society.

T. W. THOMAS, Dentist, was born in Carmarthanshire, South Wales, January 20th, 1861; came to this city with his parents in 1869; attended public schools and Wyoming Seminary; employed in shipping coal for L. V. Coal Co.; graduated at Pennsylvania College of Dental Surgery in 1886; has practiced in Wilkes-Barre since that time.

T. AUBREY POWELL, Dentist, was born at Upper Lehigh, Luzerne county, Pa., March 1st, 1867. Engaged in the furniture and carpet trade at Hazleton, Pa. Engaged in the study of dentistry and graduated from the Pennsylvania College of Dental Surgery in Philadelphia 1890; then located in Welles Building, Wilkes-Barre, Pa.

HUGH JONES was born in Wales in 1837; after going to school learned the carpenter trade; came to this country 1872; established his present business in Edwardsville of undertaking; was the first Assessor of the borough; one term as Town Councilman; is Assessor at the present time; Trustee and Treasurer of the Welsh Congregational church of the borough since 1889.

JOSIAH LEWIS, JR., a resident of Wilkes-Barre, was born in Kingston on the 18th day of November, 1845. He was a man of genial disposition, of energy, and of the strictest integrity. He was considered one of the substantial business men of that community. His father, Josiah Lewis, who died in Lackawanna township on the 2nd of May, 1851, was the only son of the Hon William Lewis, one of the most distinguished Philadelphia lawyers of his day, who was appointed by the President, George Washington, a Judge of the United States District Court in 1791. Mrs. Lewis' mother was Margaret, daughter of Colonel Sharp Delaney, one of the early patriotic Irish settlers in Philadelphia. He is a descendant of Ralph Lewis, who emigrated with his wife, Mary, from the Parish of Illam, in Glamorganshire, Wales, in 1683, and settled in Haverford township, Chester county, Pa. Mr. Lewis was married to Arabella D., daughter of George Chahoon, on the 12th day of September, 1843. His death occurred on the 11th of July, 1890. Surviving him his widow, son George, Mary C., wife of L. H. Gross, of Allentown.

ISAAC LIVINGSTON was born at Elsdorf, Prussia, twenty miles from Cologne, in November, 1827; educated in his native town; came to this country in 1848; lived in Norwalk, Conn., until 1853, and was engaged in the building business; lived there when the great railroad accident happened on the bridge; came to Wilkes-Barre 1853; married to the widow of Lewis Reese, who was murdered by Reese Evans in Wilkes-Barre, 1854; carried on the clothing and shoe business; sold out the shoe business in 1888; lost his wife 1888; sold out his clothing business in 1891; lost his oldest son, M. J. Livingston, the same year; administrator and guardian for numerous estates, and has dealt extensively in real estate; assessor for ten years—appointed by the Hon. Judge Harding; has taken great interest in public improvements and in politics; member of the Board of Trade.

WILLIAM N. JENNINGS was born in Kingston 1829, in the old Hoyt house at what was Tuttletown; educated at Wyoming Seminary; worked at nearly every occupation that was available; went across the continent to California in 1850, and came home by way of water; engaged in the business of rafting lumber down the Susquehanna; engaged in manufacturing lumber at Jenningsville, Pa., 1852, and still retains an interest; removed to West Pittston 1857 and engaged in the lumber and grain business; moved to Wilkes-Barre 1865 and conducted his former lines of business; moved to the city of Bradford, McKean county, 1878, and in 1883 removed to Wilkes-Barre; his sons are in the lumbering business; married Miss Sarah Hicks 1853. Mr. Jennings devotes some attention to literary composition.

HON. CHARLES A. MINER was born in Plains township, Pennsylvania, in 1830. Son of Robert Miner; educated in Wilkes-Barre and West Chester. Mr. Miner is widely known in the business and political interests of this section. He served three terms in the Pennsylvania House of Representatives; represented the State as Honorary Commissioner at the World's Exhibition at Vienna, Austria. President of the Street Railway Company, Director of the Wyoming National Bank and People's Bank, member of the City Council, owner of Miner's mills.

RICHARD E. S. MIALL was born in Plymouth, England, in 1839, and emigrated in 1861; carpenter and builder, and taxidermist; served in the British Navy for four years; shipmate with the present Duke of Edinburg; was in Mexico during the War of the Rebellion; has been in nearly all the great harbors of the world.

JOHN BEILBY WOOD was a son of Moses Wood, a farmer, who was also interested in mining and shipping coal. He donated the land on which the Central M. E. church of Woodville was built; he died 1853; his father was Joseph Wood, of England, and his father was Michael Wood; Moses Wood, the grandfather of John G. Wood, owned three hundred acres of land and one-third of Wilkes-Barre is on the tract. Joseph Beilby Wood was born in England 1804; was engaged in the mercantile business in this city for many years; in 1876 he with L. D. Flanagan established the banking house of J. B. Wood, Flanagan & Co., and closed in good standing after successfully operating for ten years. Mr. Wood died April 18, 1872; his wife was Sarah Gore, a daughter of John Gore, youngest sister of Geo. W. Ross, and of Peru and General Ross, who were slain in the battle and Massacre of Wyoming. She was born 1805 and died December 21, 1886.

IRA M. KIRKENDALL was born in Dallas, Luzerne county, 1835; son of William W. Kirkendall, a farmer, of Dallas; educated in the public schools; began life, after reaching his majority, as a clerk at Pittston, where he served for ten years; spent two years in the West; in 1859 had charge of the lumber business at Bear Creek, for Pursel & McKeen for six years; moved to Wilkes-Barre 1865; in the lumber business up to 1871; in 1871 elected Burgess for a term of three years, and was elected the first Mayor of Wilkes-Barre in June, 1871, for a term of three years; from 1875 to 1878 was Deputy Sheriff of Luzerne county under his brother, W. P. Kirkendall; from 1880 to 1883 a member of the firm of Kirkendall & Whiteman, grocers, and since 1883 a member of the firm of Kirkendall Bros., wholesale flour and feed dealers; is a Democrat, and has represented the Fourth ward of Wilkes-Barre in Council since 1883.

HON. C. D. FOSTER was born in Dallas, Pennsylvania, November 25, 1836. Son of Phineas Nash Foster, a prominent Justice of the Peace. After attending Wyoming Seminary for three years and a school in Illinois, he studied law with Lyman Hakes, Esq., and was admitted to the Luzerne Bar April 23, 1861. Mr. Foster was a member of the Legislature in 1884 and 1885; Delegate to the National Republican Convention at New York in 1888; Delegate to State Convention in 1889 and 1890. Was beaten by General Osborne for nomination to Congress by twenty votes in 1887.

CHARLES L. BULKELY, ESQ., was born in Wilkes-Barre January 15, 1843. Mr. Bulkely traces his ancestors back to Robert Bulkely, Esq., one of the English barons who, in the reign of King John was lord of the manor of Bulkely of county Palstine of Chester, England. After finishing his education he read law with Asa R. Brundage, his brother-in-law, admitted to the Luzerne Bar January 8, 1866; served as Alderman in the Fourth ward of Wilkes-Barre for three different terms and one term by appointment, and is serving in that position at the present time; is a brother of the late Dr. J. E. Bulkely, late surgeon of the U. S. Army, and a cousin of Morgan G. Bulkely, late Governor of Connecticut.

JAMES N. WARNER was born December, 1845, in Huntington, Luzerne county, Pa.; worked on his father's farm; educated at New Columbus; studied dentistry in South Carolina and graduated from Pennsylvania Dental College, Philadelphia, 1873; located in Hazleton; came to Wilkes-Barre in December, 1875, and located on North Franklin street; member of Susquehanna and State Dental Societies; married Miss Jane Stark, of Wyoming; his father was Dr. Sydney H. Warner, who practiced for forty-five years in Huntington.

RICHARD D. WILLIAMS was born in South Wales September, 1853; came to the United States 1886; a carpenter by trade; for three years was tenor singer in the Kingston Presbyterian church and for the past four years in the First Presbyterian church in Wilkes-Barre; in the largest musical competitions in the State, Mr. Williams has taken most of the first prizes as a tenor solo singer; in his youth he took most of the prizes in Wales; the Vicar of Llandilo, in Carmarthen, in Cologne, gave him the name, according to the Welsh custom, of Eos Carmen; took the first prize for a tenor solo at the World's Fair at Chicago, 1893.

WINFIELD LATTIN PARSONS, born in Wilkes-Barre, Pa., April 2, 1857. Educated in his father's (Winfield S. Parsons) school, the city High School, Wyoming Seminary, graduating at Lafayette College, 1879, taking first honors in mathematics. Taught for two years in King's Mountain, N. C., then for three years in the Spencerian Business College, Washington, D. C. Now doing a general collection business throughout Luzerne and Lackawanna counties, and instructing in bookkeeping in Harry Hillman Academy, Wilkes-Barre. While in Washington he had a considerable patronage in "private" instruction, i. e., preparing political aspirants for the Civil Service Examinations. Several of his pupils now hold positions under "Uncle Sam."

SOLOMON S. CHAN, born in Germany 1857; graduated at University of Deisberg on the Rhine; came to the United States 1879; held a leading position with the firm of Jonas Long; assumed the management of the Wilkes-Barre city ticket office of the L. V. R. R. in 1888; also appointed general steamship agent for all Trans-Atlantic steamship lines and represents Thomas Cook & Son, of New York, for the world-famed Tourist Agency; is a well-known amateur singer and belongs to several musical societies; is a member of the Board of Trade.

HARRY GEORGE MERRILL was born at Delaware, Delaware county, New York, April 4th, 1858. In early life his parents removed to Afton, Chenango county, N. Y., where he was permitted to attend the Academy for two years. At the age of 12 years he commenced learning the printers' trade at Binghamton, and followed this avocation until 1876, when, owing to ill health, he was compelled to seek out-door pursuits, and for quite a time was newsboy on various railroads in Central and Northern New York. Returning to the newspaper business after regaining his health, Mr. Merrill has followed his chosen profession continuously, and is to-day editor and publisher of the *Real Estate Intelligencer*, editor and co-publisher with Isaac E. Long of the *Opera Glass* and *Dramatic Herald*, and on the city staff of the *Daily Record*.

JAMES J. RIBBLE was born in Warren county, N. J., August 14, 1851; educated in his native town; lived with his grandfather, after the death of his father, until his seventeenth year; went to learn the trade of harness making in 1869; moved to Wilkes-Barre in 1877 and established his present business, 67 North Main street; member of Washington Camp, No. 408, P. O. S. of A., and Wilkes-Barre Lodge of Odd Fellows, 704.

HARRY M. SEITZINGER was born in Wilkes-Barre, Pa., and is a son of the late W. G. Seitzinger, who was a son of Jacob Seitzinger, of Tamaqua; educated at Harry Hillman Academy and at Lawrenceville, N. J., and also took an advance course in electricity in the Lehigh University; graduated in 1888; established himself in Wilkes-Barre as a consulting and constructing electrical engineer; Mr. Seitzinger is thoroughly trained in his profession.

JOHN J. MALONEY, one of the editors and proprietors of the *News-Dealer*, was born in St. Louis, Missouri, and at an early age removed with his parents to Lancaster, Pa., where he was educated in the public schools. In 1875 he entered the office of the Lancaster *Express*, where he did reportorial work; later he was engaged in a similar capacity on the *Examiner*. In 1880 he came to Wilkes-Barre and accepted the position of night editor on the *Record*, which position he held till 1887, when, in conjunction with S. W. Boyd, he purchased an interest in the *News-Dealer*.

GEORGE CHAHOON LEWIS was born on the 14th day of August, 1844; since the death of his father, Josiah, Jr., he has been engaged in the real estate business; he served in the 30th Pennsylvania Militia during the emergency in 1863; on the 6th of September, 1876, he was united in marriage to Mary Pometa Squires, of Chenango Forks, N. Y., a descendant of John Barker, one of the first settlers of Broome county; they have three daughters—Anna C., Ruth H. and Mary S.

CHRISTOPHER WREN, born at Pottsville, Pa., August 16, 1853; educated in public schools; removed to Plymouth 1869; learned the trade of moulder in his father's foundry and was employed there until he went into the insurance and real estate business in 1880; elected Prothonotary of Luzerne county on the Republican ticket 1888; served three years and ran again in 1891, but was defeated with the entire ticket; was largely instrumental in locating the Pierson Hosiery Mill and the Roxburgh Carpet Mill in Plymouth.

DANIEL J. REESE, of Plymouth, Pa., was born at Mountain-Ash, South Wales, on the 7th of December, 1857; when very young settled at Bull Run, near Tamaqua, Schuylkill county; educated in the public schools and at Wyoming Seminary; came to Plymouth in September, 1873; has worked in and around the mines since he was eight years old and is at present employed as a miner under the L. & W.-B. Coal Co.; a staunch advocate and a true friend of labor; in politics a Republican; he was elected a member of the House of Representatives in November, 1892, by a majority of 763; Mrs. Reese is a native of Tremont, Schuylkill county, and is the daughter of Rev. Edward Jenkins, of Wilkes-Barre; reside on Gardner street, Plymouth; Mr. Reese is a man of fine literary taste, has written many fine verse compositions and is also a popular speaker on economic questions.

REV. FRANCIS ASBURY KING was born at Dauby, N. Y., 1840; educated in the State Academy at Ithaca; served in the late war, 179th regiment; attended the Wyoming Seminary from 1865 to 1867; stationed on the Plains 1868; stationed at Newport, 1870; at Lehman, 1872; at Clark's Green, 1875; at Carverton, 1878; at Nicholson, 1881; at Brooklyn, 1884; at Lackawanna, 1887; at Luzerne, 1889.

JASON MYERS CASE was born in Jackson, Luzerne county, Pa., April 2, 1846; educated in the public schools; completed the trade of carpenter at eighteen years of age; foreman at building breakers; began contracting and building at Plymouth; in 1888 moved to Dorranceton, where he has established a large business; member of the Dorranceton Council; married in 1870 to Miss Anna James.

JOSEPH H. SCHWARTZ, born in the city of New York July 20, 1860; educated in the public schools and the College of the City of New York; became the junior member of the firm of Fred. Schwartz & Bro., in Plymouth; married Miss Stella Janet Keller, daughter of Philip Keller and Ellen Hunter, 1887.

DANIEL EDWARDS, son of William and Mary Edwards, was born in Eglwysilian, Wales, April 28, 1825; came to America in 1851, and finally settled in Danville, Pennsylvania; married January 17, 1862, Margaret, daughter of Thomas and Anna Edwards, a native of Merthyr Tydvil, Wales. Mr. Edwards early in life became associated with the extensive coal and iron concern of Waterman & Beaver, finally merged into the Montour Iron and Steel Company, and the Kingston Coal Company. The Gaylord Coal Company also was one of Mr. Edwards' organizations; this Company, too, was finally absorbed by the Kingston Coal Company, which is to-day the largest individual coal operating Company in the Wyoming Valley. Mr. Edwards, by pluck, energy, tact and perseverance, coupled with sound judgment and economical management, made the wonderful stride that has, in less than thirty years, made out of a sound, practical miner a President and General Manager of one of the largest industrial individual concerns in our State. Mr. Edwards, while avoiding political preferment, has been a strong factor in all the political campaigns of the past ten years, and his influence has been felt in the advancement of political economy. In 1884 Mr. Edwards was one of the Presidential electors, which college carried the Keystone State for James G. Blaine and John A. Logan with over 80,000 majority. At this writing, March, 1894, Mr. Edwards, although in his sixty-ninth year, is general head of the Kingston Coal Company and Edwards & Company, the management of which he controls, leaving only the detail for efficient superintendents. The Kingston Coal Company mines somewhere about a million and a half tons of anthracite coal per year, while Edwards & Company conduct one of the largest mercantile businesses in Eastern Pennsylvania. Mr. Edwards visited his old home in Wales some five years ago, and many of his friends were of the opinion that it portended a removal to end a well-spent life at the place of its beginning; if such a thing was ever thought of by Mr. Edwards, he gave no sign, hence we conclude that the home of his adoption has become his best love.

WILLIAM JOHN LEWIS was born in Glendyris, South Wales, 1858; came to this country 1868; educated in Wyoming Seminary; associated with Morgan Brothers, of Wilkes-Barre, for ten years; conducted mercantile business for himself for three years; at present represents Lauber & Foster, one of the largest shoe houses in the country; was married when he was twenty-three years of age to Mary J. Price, daughter of Rev. J. R. Price; active in church work; lived in Scranton ten years, now resides in Kingston.

JOSEPH D. LLOYD, born April 24, 1867, at Stockton, Pa.; educated at the Bloomsburg State Normal School and the Commercial Department of Wyoming Seminary, graduating in 1883; with Coxe Bros. & Co., at Drifton, as bookkeeper; 1887 in the stock business with his father in Wyoming; in 1890 with Morgan & Co., Planing Mill Co., as assistant manager; 1892 became traveling salesman for the Atlantic Dynamite Co., for Wyoming Valley; member of the Masons at Kingston; married to Carrie Miller December 10, 1890, who died June 14, 1891; married Miss Margaret J. Gray, of Plymouth, October 4, 1893; elected by the Republican party Burgess of Wyoming Borough February 20, 1894; son of John Lloyd, brick contractor.

ARTHUR CHARLES HOWLAND was born December 24, 1869; attended Wyoming Seminary from January, 1886, to June, 1888, when he graduated; graduated from Cornell University, in the course of Arts, June, 1893; became teacher of Rhetoric and Latin in Wyoming Seminary, September, 1893.

ABRAM NESBITT was born in Plymouth township. His great grandfather was one of the forty claimants that came from Connecticut in 1769; his son, Abram, was Mr. Nesbitt's grandfather. Mr. Nesbitt's father's name was James. He served in the Legislature in the winter of 1835–36; served as Judge and District Attorney; was Sheriff of the county. He died in 1840. The subject of this sketch was educated at the Dana Academy, in Wilkes-Barre, and at Wyoming Seminary, Kingston, Pennsylvania. He began life as a surveyor; was one of the organizers of the Second National Bank, in 1863; was elected Vice-President, 1872, and President, 1873. He is Director of the Wyoming Valley Coal Company and Director of the Ireona Coal Company, in Clearfield; Treasurer and Secretary of Forty Fort Cemetery; Director of the Poor for several years; Treasurer of the Sanson Cutlery Company; one of the organizers of the Spring Brook Water Company, one of the largest in the State, and the People's Water Company of Pittston, Pennsylvania.

REV. H. H. WELLES, born at Wyalusing, September 15, 1824. Son of Charles F. and Ellen Hollenback Welles. Graduated at the College of New Jersey at Princeton, class of 1844. Two years' study in Princeton Theological Seminary; licensed to preach by Presbytery of Susquehanna August 29, 1850; began supplying Kingston Presbyterian church December 1, 1850, and was ordained and installed its pastor June 12, 1851; resigned from the pastorate in April, 1871. Has since acted as stated supply for various churches in the Presbytery of Lackawanna, of which he was the first Stated Clerk. Married, October 12, 1849. Ellen S., daughter of General Samuel G. Ladd, of Hallowell. Maine. Has been President of the Alumni Association of Princeton Theological Seminary, and is Trustee of Lincoln University. Resides at Forty Fort.

HENRY GABRIEL ROAT was born in Kingston January 7, 1836; educated in the Wyoming Seminary; associated with his father, A. J. Roat, in the hardware business; Second Lieutenant in the National Guard.

FRED. L. SPACE, born in Forty Fort 1865; Educated at the Wyoming Seminary; entered the Wyoming Valley store 1880 and later the store of Harvey Yeager, where he is at the present time; Treasurer of the M. E. Sunday School; Secretary of the Borough Council; member of the Good Templars; son of James and Lucinda Space, old settlers of the town; married Maud, the daughter of Isaac Tripp, 1888.

CLARENCE B. MILLER was born in Tunkhannock, Pa., September 8, 1860; entered in the Mansfield Soldiers' Orphans' School 1872 and in the State Normal School 1876; graduated 1878; entered the educational work as principal of the Tunkhannock public schools; has been principal at Pine Ridge, Northumberland; in 1883 became superintendent at Nanticoke, where he is principal at the present time; married Miss Gertrude Harder, 1886.

HENRY LEES was born in England in 1842; educated in that country; came to this country in 1862; established his present business in Plymouth twenty-three years ago; President of the Town Council of Plymouth two years, member four years; is a Mason; Superintendent of the M. E. Sunday School.

MORGAN J. REES was born in South Wales, 1851; came to this country 1860; mine foreman at Janesville for the Spring Mountain Coal Company twelve years; established his present business 1887.

DANIEL METZGER was born at Lewisburg, Pa., July 28, 1808; settled in Wilkes-Barre 1847; was the leading man in his business (plasterer) for a number of years; Councilman for eight years for the borough; was a prominent member of Lodge 61, F. and A. M.

SIMON LONG was born in Pretzfeld, Bavaria, 1827; went to school; established his business in 1846 on the north side of Public Square, and later moved to the west side; in 1859 moved; 1872 purchased his present store on South Main street; President of the Jewish Congregation, B'nai Brith.

EPHRAIM L. DIEFENDERFER, M. D., was born at White Deer Cross Roads, Union county, Pa., on the 23d of March, 1829. Educated in the public schools and at the Bloomsburg Academy. Served a number of years in the drug business under the tutorship and in the drug store of E. P. Lutz, of Bloomsburg, Pa. Studied medicine in the same town under the direction of Dr. J. Boyd McKelvy. Entered the medical department of the University of Pennsylvania in 1860, from which institution he graduated in medicine in March, 1862. Located for the practice of his profession in White Haven, Pa., immediately thereafter; remained there six years; removed from there to Ashley, Pa., in the spring of 1868, where he was actively engaged in the practice of medicine till in the winter of 1878, when, on account of failing health, he discontinued business. During the earlier years of his practice there he opened a large drug and prescription store, at that time the first of the kind in the town; was appointed postmaster, and was examining surgeon for a large number of life insurance companies; was among the first members of the Luzerne County Medical Society; one of the incorporators of the Borough of Ashley, Pa., and one of its first councilmen. After quitting the general practice he took a post graduate course in Gynecology and surgery at the New York Polyclinic and Hospital during the winters of 1890-91 and 1891-92, from which faculty he holds two certificates of three months' attendance each; came to Wilkes-Barre, Pa., to practice his specialties in the spring of 1892. The Doctor is one of the oldest practicing physicians in the valley, and at one time accredited as having as large, if not the largest practice in obstetrics of any physician in this section of the country.

HON. GARRICK M. HARDING, ex-Judge, was born in Exeter, Luzerne county, Pennsylvania, July 12, 1830. His great-grandfather commanded Fort Wintermute in the Wyoming Massacre, and his father Judge of the Court in Lee county, Illinois. Mr. Harding was educated in the Franklin Academy, in Susquehanna county, Pennsylvania, and graduated from Dickinson College. Studied law with Hon. Henry M. Fuller, and was admitted to the Luzerne Bar in 1850; in 1858 was elected District Attorney of Luzerne county; in 1870 was elected President Judge of the Eleventh Judicial District, and resigned January 1, 1880. Judge Harding is a man of fine literary taste and is well known as a writer.

GEORGE R. BEDFORD, Esq., born in Abington, Lackawanna county, November 22, 1840. Attended Madison Academy and the Albany Law School. Admitted to the Bar at Albany, New York, May, 1862, and at Wilkes-Barre November, 1862. Been in active practice as a lawyer ever since, on the civil side of the Court, mainly in corporation cases. Studied law in the office of Judge Stanley Woodward. Married, May 19, 1874, to Emily, daughter of Hon. Henry M. Fuller. Trustee of Female Seminary and of the Hillman Academy; one of the organizers of the Anthracite Bank. Served as a soldier in 1863 under the call of Governor Curtin.

HON. STANLEY WOODWARD, Additional Law Judge of Luzerne county, Pennsylvania, was born in Wilkes-Barre in 1833. Son of a former Chief Justice of Pennsylvania. Educated at the Episcopal High School and Wyoming Seminary, graduating with honor from Yale College in 1855. Studied law with the Hon. Warren J. Woodward, of New Haven, Connecticut; admitted to the Luzerne Bar in 1856. Was counsel for the Delaware, Lackawanna and Western Railroad, Delaware and Hudson Canal Company, and Central Railroad of New Jersey. Served in the War of the Rebellion and commanded a company. Was appointed Additional Law Judge of Luzerne county in 1879; elected in 1880 for a term of ten years, and re-elected in 1890 for a further term for the same period.

HON. EDWIN S. OSBORNE was born in Wayne county, Pennsylvania, August 7, 1839. Graduated from the University of Northern Pennsylvania at Bethany, and the Law School at Poughkeepsie, New York, in 1860. Read law with Hon. Charles Denison, and was admitted to the Luzerne Bar in 1861. Served in the late Civil War; Major-General of the Third Division of the National Guard for ten years. Was a candidate for Law Judge of Luzerne county in 1874. Served in Congress from 1884 to 1891.

HON. HENRY W. PALMER, born in Clifford township, Susquehanna county, Pennsylvania, July 10, 1839. Educated at the Wyoming Seminary, and Fort Edward, New York, graduating from the Poughkeepsie Law School in 1860. Studied law under Garrick M. Harding. Served as paymaster's clerk during the war of the Rebellion. Member of the Constitutional Convention in 1872. Attorney-General of Pennsylvania under Governor Henry M. Hoyt's administration.

W. S. McLEAN, ESQ., born at Summit Hill, Pennsylvania, August 27, 1842. Educated at Wilkes-Barre; graduated at Lafayette College, 1865; took the valedictory addresses and delivered the master's oration three years afterward. Admitted to the Luzerne Bar in 1867; City Attorney, 1875, and has continued in that office ever since; candidate for Judge of Luzerne county in 1879. President of the First National Bank.

DR. JOSEPH A. MURPHY was born in York county, Pennsylvania. Worked on his father's farm until he was sixteen years of age, and attended school during the winter; attended Stewart's Town Academy, conducted by his cousin, Professor J. A. Murphy. Studied languages with the Rev. J. L. Menill. Served in the late war. Studied medicine with the celebrated Dr. John L. Atter, of Lancaster, Pennsylvania; graduated in medicine from the University of Pennsylvania in 1868; practiced medicine in Columbia, Pennsylvania, and came to Wilkes-Barre in 1870. A member of the County, State and National Medical Societies; member of the Board of Trade and Historical Society; stockholder in many of our local industries. Married Miss Fannie Parrish, granddaughter of the late Dr. Smith; his children are Louise, Mabel and Kathleen. Dr. Murphy was one of the projectors of the Luzerne Medical Society, also one of the attendant physicians of the Wilkes-Barre Hospital from its establishment. He is one of the leading physicians of this section.

OSCAR OLIVER ESSER was born January 25, 1850, at Mauch Chunk, Pa.; entered railway service 1862, since which time he has been consecutively water boy, messenger, telegraph operator, yard master, train dispatcher and train master of the Lehigh Valley Railroad; was superintendent of the Wyoming Division of the Philadelphia and Reading Railroad; appointed superintendent of the Northern Division of the Lehigh Valley Railroad 1891. Married June 29, 1871, to Miss Mary C. Mott.

HENRY A. FULLER, Esq., born at Wilkes-Barre, January 15, 1853. Educated in public school of that place; entered Princeton College 1871; graduated 1874; read law in the office of Hon. H. W. Palmer, and admitted to the Bar of Luzerne county, January, 1877, where he has since been in active practice. Married November, 1879, to Miss Ruth H. Parrish. Was Assistant District Attorney nine years; Trustee of Osterhout Free Library; Director of Anthracite Savings Bank; Superintendent of St. Stephen's Episcopal Sunday School.

C. M. CONYNGHAM was born in Wilkes-Barre, July 6, 1840. Son of Judge John N. Conyngham. After graduating from College, was admitted to the Luzerne Bar in 1862, went into active business, and is identified with the corporations of the valley. Served in the War of the Rebellion.

CHARLES A. DURANT was born February 14, 1846, in the province of Ontario, Canada; attended school there; came to this State in 1864, and was employed on the Central R. R. of N. J.; established his present business on South Main street, Wilkes-Barre, 1883; member of Landmark Lodge, No. 442, F. and A. M.

THOMAS ENGLISH was born in Susquehanna county, Pa., January 3, 1846; educated in that county; conductor for the Pennsylvania Coal Company on the gravity road, for seventeen years; in 1888, with J. F. Gorman, established their present business on Main street, tinners, plumbers and steam fitters; served in the late war for thirteen months in a Philadelphia regiment; was County Commissioner for six years, from 1884 to 1890, and Chairman of the Democratic County Committee for two years.

S. EDGAR TROUT was born in Lancaster county in 1855, being the eldest son of Franklin Miller Trout, who was foremost in his line of architecture in connection with the Pennsylvania Railroad. His grandfather, Daniel Trout, being many years a retired Lancaster county farmer and his great-grandfather, Adam Trout, was an officer under Stephen Decatur during the war of this country with Tripoli; his family settling in Maryland about the middle of the seventeenth century, the original name being spelled Trost, of French Huguenot descent. S. Edgar married Frances S. Wendell, of Philadelphia, in 1877, and has three promising children, and his business is now permanently located in the Coal Exchange, corner store, in the wall paper business, having been identified with that business since a boy as designer, decorator, etc., and has been doing business in this valley for a good many years.

HENRY GERMAN, the present President of the Saengerbund, the leading German singing society in Wilkes-Barre, was born in Hessen Darmstadt, Germany, on the 3d of September, 1857. After he left school he acquired the art of cooking, and arrived in this country in November, 1879, having left Germany in 1876, the time from 1876 to 1879 having been spent in an adventuresome life through Spain, Cape Colony, Kaffir Land, South Africa, and the South American Republics. He settled in Wilkes-Barre in 1886, in the capacity of chief cook of the Wyoming Valley Hotel, and has lived here ever since. In 1861 he went into the hotel business and started the "Little Delmonico Hotel," corner Hazle and Main streets, where he is doing a good business and prosperity seems to smile upon him. Mr. German takes a great deal of interest in German singing societies and has been President of the Saengerbund two terms.

CHARLES BUELL METZGER was born at Lewisburg, Pa., November 29, 1839; educated at Wilkes-Barre and Wyoming Seminary; moved to Wilkes-Barre in April, 1848; served in the late war, went with the Wyoming Artillery, A. H. Emly, Colonel; served in the 4th N. Y. Artillery from February 22, 1864, until the close of the war; served twenty-five years continuously in the fire department of Wilkes-Barre and was chief engineer 1881. On February 1, 1868, established his present large wholesale confectionery business, the only exclusive wholesale confectionery house in Wilkes-Barre. Married Miss Annie F. Flack, of Lewisburg, Pa., January 1, 1867.

FRANK A. FARRELL, M. D., son of James J. Farrell, of Plains, one of the leading physicians and surgeons of Luzerne county, was born in Wilkes-Barre 1865. His early education was complete and at the age of sixteen expressed the desire for drugs, which business he entered, and soon became an efficient manager and conductor of same, becoming a registered pharmacist, according to the Act of Congress, in 1887. Is also a member of the Pennsylvania Pharmaceutical Association. Tiring of the drug business he took up the study of medicine under Dr. H. M. Neale, of Upper Lehigh, and entered the Jefferson Medical College of Philadelphia for three years, graduating as a physician and surgeon May 2, 1893. Is also a graduate of the Philadelphia Lying-in Charity, an institution embracing practical obstetrics and the treatment of diseases of females. Having finished his studies in Philadelphia he located in Kingston, Pa., where he has built up a lucrative practice. The Doctor is a close observer and an ardent student.

JOHN LOHMANN was born in Germany in 1843; went to school in that country; came to this country 1864; located in Kingston 1865 and established himself in the barbering business; 1872 moved to where he now resides; Town Councilman for two terms; was the first postmaster of Edwardsville; postmaster for four years and three months.

ELMER E. BUCKMAN was born in Taylorsville, Bucks county, Pa., August 11, 1861. He spent his boyhood and early youth on the farm with his father. His education was received in the public schools and the old Capital City Commercial College of Trenton, N. J. After completing his commercial course he entered the employ of a business firm in Trenton, and remained with them four years. In March of 1886 he came to Wilkes-Barre as bookkeeper for the Miners' Savings Bank, and in February, 1888, he was elected teller of the Wyoming National Bank, which position he still holds.

JOHN D. BACHMAN was born January 28, 1854, at Milford, N. J.; educated in the public schools; came to Wilkes-Barre about twenty-seven years ago; clerk for C. Morgan's Sons, hardware, twenty-three years; married, April 5, 1883, to Sarah Hawrecht; P. G. of Centennial Lodge, 927, I. O. O. F.; Secretary for eight years; P. C. Patriarch of Outtillissa Encampment, No. 39; Secretary of Sarah Bennett Rebekah Lodge, No. 2, I. O. O. F.; Past Regent of Royal Arcanum, No. 396.

SEBASTIAN C. MECKEL was born February 7, 1826, in Coblenz on the Rhine, in the Kingdom of Prussia; received an educational training in Europe, and completed the English branches in America, whither he came in the year 1851; was ordained in the year 1856, and served regular charges as pastor until the war broke out, when he enlisted, in 1864, in Company H, 91st New York Veteran Volunteers; he served as a non-commissioned Chaplain; his last charge was Plymouth, Pa., where he has served for fourteen years, and is now located at No. 51 Hollenback avenue, Wilkes-Barre.

WILL S. WILCOX was born at Plains, Pa., October 17, 1866. He commenced the study of music at the age of twelve years, his instructor being Mr. M. B. Austin. One year later he entered the Wilkes-Barre Academy, of which Mr. J. C. MacKenzie was principal, taking a scientific course. In 1882 the instructor of music at the Academy, Mr. Derman, awarded Mr. Wilcox first prize for the best paper on "Theory of Music." He continued his studies until June, 1884, after which time he devoted himself solely to the study of piano and harmony, under Mr. Theodore G. Boettger, for two years. In 1884 his first composition was published, a ballad, "Florence," which is popular at the present time. September 1, 1886, he entered the New England Conservatory of Music, Boston, Mass., completing his course in June, 1888, and at once entered the employ of the Hallet & Davis Piano Company, as ware-room tuner, which position he was obliged to resign one year later on account of poor health, and returned to Wilkes-Barre. While in Boston Mr. Wilcox was employed by the new Old South Church as organist of Hope Chapel, and April 23, 1887, played two numbers at a public Conservatory recital, receiving an enthusiastic recall for his rendition of Mozskowski's "Serenata." Conservatory pupils are seldom allowed to play in public during their first year, so Mr. Wilcox was considered highly honored. May 7, 1888, he was married to Miss Clara L. Becker, of Boston, and after returning to Wilkes-Barre, 1889, was engaged as organist and director of music at Sacred Heart Church, Plains, which position he filled until September, 1890, when it became necessary to put himself under treatment for an eye trouble. After a few months rest he devoted himself assiduously to composition, eighteen of his works being now published, the best known of which are "Silvery Moonlight" Reverie, "Patriots' March," and the National Anthem, "Hail! Banner of the Free." Mr. Wilcox has received flattering offers to locate elsewhere, the most recent of which is from Dickinson Seminary, Williamsport, which institution desired his services as piano teacher, but he prefers his native town, and is at present organist at St. St. Stephen's Episcopal Church, Wilkes-Barre.

REV. HUGH C. McDERMOTT was born in Dublin, Maryland, September 18, 1852. Educated at Fawn Grove Academy and Stewartstown Classical Institute. Prepared for college but was prevented by circumstances from taking a college course except as a non-resident student. Entered the ministry of the Methodist Episcopal Church April, 1875. Has served pastorates in Willett and Apalachin, N. Y., and Auburn, Factoryville, Montrose and Honesdale, Pa. Has been Treasurer of the Wyoming Conference for the past five years. Appointed pastor of the Kingston M. E. Church April 6, 1892. Married Miss Estella L. Gillette, daughter of J. B. Gillette, of Skeshequin, Bradford county, Pa., April 21st, 1874. Mrs. McDermott is a model home-maker and a most efficient help as a pastor's wife. They have four children—the Misses Ethel L. and Ada A., and Hugh La Monte and Robert Bruce.

JOSEPH C. MEIXELL was born in Saylorsburg, Monroe county, Pa., October 10, 1860; educated in the public schools of Luzerne county; moved to the valley when he was six years of age; associated with his father in contracting and building and in the mercantile business; in 1889 went in with the Edison General Electric Company, and later with the Wilkes-Barre and West Side Electric Street Railway, for one year on the road and for three years had charge of the station; when the present company assumed control of the west side lines he became superintendent of that division under the Wilkes-Barre and Wyoming Valley Traction Company.

D. J. M. LOOP was born at Elmira, N. Y., February 11, 1823. Educated at the old Wilkes-Barre Academy, from which he in September, 1841, entered the sophomore class at Dickinson College, where he graduated in July, 1844. Began studying law at Elmira, N. Y., in the fall of 1845, in the office of Hon. E. P. Brooks; emigrated to Belvidere, Ill., in June, 1847; admitted to the Supreme Court of Illinois in June, 1847; located at Fort Winnebago, now known as Portage City, Wisconsin, in April, 1848; elected District Attorney of Columbia county, Wis., in November, 1848; practiced at Portage City from April, 1848, to August, 1864; admitted to Wisconsin Supreme Court in January, 1849; in August, 1864, located at Columbia, and admitted to Lancaster Bar at that time; located at Hazleton in October, 1866, and admitted to the Luzerne Bar in the fall of 1866; removed to Wilkes-Barre in June, 1868, where he practiced until April, 1870, removing thence to Neosho, Mo.; from thence to Joplin, Mo., in 1874, where he practiced and became Judge of the City Court in 1875; practiced in Kansas from 1877 to 1880; removed from Neosho, Mo., to Waverly, N. Y., in July, 1880, and to Nanticoke in June, 1882, where his office is located. Mr. Loop is well known as a member of the Bar wherever he has practiced, and is to-day the oldest lawyer in active practice at the Wilkes-Barre Bar.

GEORGE R. ANDREAS, M. D., was born at Cherryville, Northampton county, Pa. After receiving a common school education at home he was sent for one year to the Keystone State Normal School, Kutztown, Pa.; he afterwards taught school in his native township; in 1889 he entered the spring course of supplementary lectures in Jefferson Medical College, and matriculated in same college the following fall; after a three years' course of study he graduated from said college; is located at No. 153 Park avenue, Wilkes-Barre, Pa.

ROBERT S. MEIXELL, D. D. S., was born April 27, 1854, in Carbon county, Pa.; educated in the New Columbus Academy; taught in the public schools of this county eight years; graduated from the Philadelphia Dental College in February, 1885; located at No. 20 South Main street, Wilkes-Barre, where he is at the present time; active in the Central M. E. Church, class leader and teacher of Bible class.

C. FRANK WHITE was born in Wilkes-Barre January 8, 1865; attended the public schools until his sixteenth year; entered the Leader office 1881, remaining seven years; graduated from the Wilkes-Barre College 1888; established his present business of job printing, on Public Square in 1888.

WESLEY ELWELL LAKE was born at Vincentown, N. J., August 7, 1870; graduated at Pennington Seminary, Pennington, N. J., 1887; 1887-89 taught public school; 1893 graduated at Wesleyan University, Middletown, Conn. Teaching Latin and Greek at Wyoming Seminary, Kingston, Pa.

T. F. LAWLESS was born December 4, 1859, in Tobyhanna, Monroe county, Pa.; educated in Philadelphia; moved to Philadelphia in his sixteenth year and clerked; in his eighteenth year went to White Haven and entered the office of Albert Lewis, where he remained for five years, and then went to Bear Creek and had charge of Mr. Lewis' books, remaining there for five years; came to Kingston in 1886 and with three others formed the Kingston Lumber Company; in April, 1893, established his present furniture and undertaking business on Wyoming avenue, Kingston; January 23, 1889, married Mary E. Caffrey, of White Haven, Pa.

WILLIAM EDWARD HOWLAND was born in 1855 at Fairmount, Pa.; educated at the New Columbus Academy; taught school for several years; clerked for A. F. Levi, of Plymouth, for nearly four years, and in 1885 established his present business of books and stationery, No. 51 Main street, Plymouth. Member of No. 1, Plymouth Fire Department.

SAMUEL K. PANNEBECKER was born at New Hanover, Montgomery county, Pa., 1843; learned photography at Baumstown, Berks county, where he conducted a gallery for ten years; moved to Wilkes-Barre in 1874; opened his gallery in Nanticoke in 1881, where he still resides.

W. A. FENSTERMACHER was born at Wapwallopen, Luzerne county, Pa., September 24, 1869; a Republican; early life on his father's farm; prepared for college at Bloomsburg State Normal School; taught several years; graduated as a prize and honor man at Lafayette College 1893; principal of the public schools of Kingston 1893-'94; at college was a famous half-back, and still ranks among the foremost foot-ball players; is a candidate for the degree leading up to LL. D.

AMOS D. TUCK was born in Wilkes-Barre, February 6, 1866; educated in the public schools and Harry Hillman Academy; son of William Tuck; established in 1885 a livery and boarding stable at 18½ North Franklin street, Wilkes-Barre, where he is now located; member of Centennial Lodge of Odd Fellows, and is Past Grand.

MICHAEL PETZ was born September 25, 1864, in Bavaria; educated in Germany; graduated at the University of Ingolstadt; came to the United States in 1881; graduated from the St. Vincent College, Westmoreland county, Pa.; has been in the insurance business for eight years, and at the present time has his office in the Hollenback Building, and is superintendent of the People's, of Washington county; a member of the Saengerbund.

AUGUSTUS C. LANING was born in Owego, N. Y., in 1808; had an academic education; came to Wilkes-Barre in his fourteenth year; clerked for his uncle, George M. Hollenback, in the old Hollenback store; opened a store in Kingston; conducted a foundry on Bowman's Hill, and later a foundry on Public Square; then he built the large foundry on North Canal street, which he finally sold to the Dickson Manufacturing Company in 1866; died in 1875; Mrs. George C. Smith, Mrs. William J. Harvey and John were the children.

REV. THOMAS CYNONFARDD EDWARDS, D. D., pastor of the Welsh Congregational Church, Edwardsdale, Pa., since January 1, 1878, was born at Landore, Swansea, Wales, December 6, 1848; ordained at Mineral Ridge, Ohio, January 1, 1871; had charge of the First Welsh Congregational Church, of Wilkes-Barre, from 1872 to 1878. Was Professor of Elocution at Wyoming Seminary for ten years; received his D. D. in 1891 from Marietta College, Ohio. Among his own nationality Dr. Edwards has filled the foremost positions in Wales and America, in the colleges, the eisteddfods and the church. He has published a volume of his poetical works and two volumes on "Elocution and Oratory"—one in Welsh and one in English. His church at Edwardsdale is ranked among the foremost in the State among Congregationalists.

THOMAS SOMERS came to Kingston in 1856, and established himself in the merchant tailoring business, and is the oldest man in that business on the west side; one of the original signers of the borough charter; introduced the first sewing machine in this section.

JOSEPH SWEITZER was born in Wurtemburg, Germany, February 29, 1828; educated in his native city; came to the United States in 1847; was a millwright in his youth; learned the cabinet-making trade in Wilkes-Barre; located in business in Huntsville, Pa.; came to Plymouth in 1864 and established the business now conducted by his son; died in 1886.

WILLIAM ALBERT JONES was born in South Wales October 15, 1857; came to this country 1869 and located in Kingston, Pa.; educated in the Scranton Business College and Oberlin College, Ohio; entered the employment of the Kingston Coal Company, and has been with that company for twenty years; is at the present time mine foreman. Mr. Jones is a fine Shakespearean scholar, and gives some attention to the study of oratory; active in church work and in literary societies.

J. C. BRADER was born February 12, 1856, in Beach Haven, Luzerne county, Pa.; educated at Wyoming Seminary; clerk and telegraph operator; Assistant Superintendent of the Susquehanna Coal Company for five years; in the real estate, insurance, steamship and foreign exchange business for seven years; President of the Nanticoke Light Company; Director and Secretary of the First National Bank; Treasurer and Trustee of the M. E. Church.

REV. WILLIAM R. NETHERTON was born in Cornwall, England, April 28, 1854; came to America in early boyhood and located at Rushdale (now Jermyn). In 1873-'74 clerked for John Jermyn; attended Wyoming Seminary 1875; taught school two terms; entered the Wyoming Conference in 1876, and has served the following charges: 1876-'77, Lacka-waxen; 1878-'80, Beach Pond; 1881-'83, Orwell; 1884-'86, Camptown; 1887-'88, Scranton, Hampton street; 1889-'93, Forty Fort.

ADOLPH HANSEN was born December 10, 1859, at Schwerin; educated in the gymnasium of his native place; sang alto five years in the choir of the Court Chapel, from the age of ten to fifteen; studied instrumental and harmony with Constantine Sternberg; studied vocal with Kucken, the famous composer of songs, and with Karl Hill, singer of the Court Opera at Schwerin. Mr. Hansen became the leader of several singing societies. In 1882 he came to America and after living one year in Philadelphia came to Wilkes-Barre; became the leader of the Concordia Society, and Bellman's Broeter, Swedish singing society; organist and choirmaster at the Jewish Temple; plays the viola in the Raff String Quartette, and a member of the Grand Opera House Orchestra.

ISAAC ROSENHEIM was born in Russia in 1858; educated in his native city and graduated in New York city in book-keeping; came to this country when he was six years of age; began book-keeping in Henrietta, Texas; came to Kingston in 1884 and purchased the old Payne homestead and built a business block and established his present mercantile business.

GEORGE H. LAZARUS was born at Wilkes-Barre in 1850; his grandfather was John and father Daniel, an old family at Buttonwood and Wilkes-Barre; went to school in that city; has been in business in Wilkes-Barre and is now in Kingston.

REV. WILLIAM SMITH was born in Durham, England, 1861; studied in England, and in Wyoming Seminary four years; came to the United States 1886; ordained a Congregational minister 1892, and located at Nanticoke.

GEORGE GALLAND was born in the city of Posen, Germany, December 25, 1854; came to America at an early age and settled at Scranton, Pa., about 1858; was educated at the public school in Scranton; from 1873 to 1877 resided in New York city, returning in the latter year to Scranton, being in the employ of B. & A. Galland, manufacturers of ladies' under-garments. In December, 1881, the firm of Galland Bros. & Co. was formed, locating in Wilkes-Barre, on Market street, removing to their present location, South Washington street, in 1884. Married Miss Minnie Strauss, of Wilkes-Barre, January 24, 1893.

RILEY L. IMBODEN was born at Annville, Lebanon county, Pa., October 3, 1852; went to school in that place; learned the trade of butcher at Pittston in 1864; drove the 'bus at the Luzerne House and the Wyoming Valley Hotel, and was fireman on the L. V. R. R.; in 1877 went in the livery business in Kingston and Wilkes-Barre with Townend brothers; Member of Paxinosa Tribe, No. 165, I. O. R. M, Wilkes-Barre; admitted to the Great Council of Pennsylvania; Past Sachem; also First Lieutenant of Susquehanna Chieftains' League, No. 12, and a member of other societies.

RICHARD DENNIS was born July 26, 1850, in Plymouth, Pa; educated in that place; went in the employment of the Nottingham Coal Company in 1864 as fireman; in 1867 was employed at the lower breaker; 1870 went to the Washington breaker as engineer; 1873 went with the D., L. & W., where he is still employed; 1882 went to the Woodward breaker, near Kingston; moved from Plymouth to Dorranceton 1890; member of the Odd Fellows and of the Plymouth Masonic Lodge.

W. H. TERRY was born in Franklin township, Luzerne county, Pa., in 1847; educated in the public schools; from 1884 conductor on the Wilkes-Barre street cars and on the electric cars; 1893 became toll collector at the Wilkes-Barre bridge; member of the Odd Fellows.

ERNEST S. MILLARD was born in 1866 at Willow Springs, Columbia county, Pa.; educated at the Bloomsburg Normal School; clerked in the general store at Orangeville, Columbia county; with J. C. Brader for six years.

CORNELIUS ROBBINS was born in Hanover January 21, 1840; went to school in Hanover; followed blacksmithing; went in the army in 1861; mustered out in 1864; member of the Grand Army.

F. M. NEWELL, a member of one of the oldest families in the State, was born near Canton, Pennsylvania. In 1883 established the Waverly Manufacturing Company, which became the Newell Clothing Company, Waverly, New York. In 1890 the Newell Clothing Company of Wilkes-Barre absorbed the two first corporations, with a capital stock of $20,000. T. L. Newell, of Kingston, was its first President, and Lyddon Flick its first Vice-President. The capital stock has been increased to $40,000, with Colonel G. Murray Reynolds as President.

DR. A. P. O'MALLEY was born in Ireland, August 22, 1853. Son of James O'Malley, of New Haven, Connecticut. Was educated at Seton Hall College, New Jersey, and graduated in medicine at the University Medical College of New York, March, 1875. He is second to none in the county among his brethren in the medical profession. He has been in this county since 1875, and is one of the most successful in his line. He is a member of the Luzerne County Medical Society, and resides at Wilkes-Barre, Pennsylvania.

DR. JOHN BARCLAY CRAWFORD was born in the town of Crawford, Orange county, New York, in 1827. His ancestors were among the pioneers of that region. His great-grandfather, James Crawford, was an officer in the Continental forces in the English and French War, and was with General Wolfe at the capture of Quebec. His grandfather, John Crawford, was a soldier in the War of the Revolution and served through the entire period of the War. His father, John Barclay Crawford, was a soldier in the War of 1812. The subject of this sketch passed the early years of his life in the usual uneventful way of a farmer's boy. When about eight years of age, his father removed to Moreland, Tioga (now Schuyler) county, New York, a short distance from the present town of Watkins. For several years he attended the common school of the district in which he resided. He subsequently was placed under the care of a private tutor, and afterward entered the Academy at Havana, where he remained until he began the study of medicine. He studied medicine with Dr. Wilcox, of Elmira, and at the Medical Department of Columbia College, New York, and began the practice of medicine in 1850. In 1852 he married Sarah Hammond, of Big Flats, New York, a descendant of one of the early settlers of Wyoming Valley. He resided at Wyoming until 1870, when he removed to Wilkes-Barre. Dr. Crawford entered the army in 1861. He was Medical Director at Camp Curtin; was Surgeon in charge of the Military Department of St. Joseph's Hospital in Philadelphia, and was subsequently appointed Surgeon of the Fifty-Second or Old Luzerne Regiment of Pennsylvania Volunteers, then commanded by ex-Governor Henry M. Hoyt. He served in the field through the Chickahominy campaign and the siege of Charleston. In 1864 he resigned on account of sickness contracted in the military service. Dr. Crawford was one of the original members of the Luzerne County Medical Society. He is one of the oldest members of the Medical Society of the State of Pennsylvania and of the American Medical Association. He served as one of the attending physicians of the Wilkes-Barre City Hospital from the time of its organization until 1860, when he resigned. He was then elected Consulting Physician of the Hospital, and still retains that position. In 1872 he was appointed Coroner of Luzerne county by Governor Geary. He has occupied the office of President of the Board of Examining Surgeons for Pensions of the Twelfth Congressional District of Pennsylvania.

DR. REESE DAVIS was born at Warren, Bradford county, Pennsylvania, July 3, 1837. Received a common school education. Prepared for college at Owego Academy and Susquehanna Collegiate Institute, at Towanda, Pennsylvania. Attended Marietta College, Ohio, one year, and graduated at Hamilton College, Clinton, New York, in 1863. Attended the Medical Department of Michigan University one year; graduated at Bellevue Hospital Medical College, New York, in 1867. Located in 1867 in LeRaysville, Bradford county, Pennsylvania. Removed in 1867 to Scranton and practiced there two years (at Providence). Settled in Wilkes-Barre in 1871, where he has practiced his profession ever since. Is a member of the Luzerne County Medical Society, of which he has been President. Is a member of the Pennsylvania State Medical Society, of which he was President in 1887. Is a member of the Lehigh Valley Medical Society, and an honorary member of the Philadelphia Obstetrical Society. He is a son of David Davis and Elizabeth Davis, who were natives of Wales, and settled in Warren, Bradford county, in 1832. Married Maggie E. Williams, daughter of Philip Williams and Harriet Williams of the above place. Have four children—Maude, Walter, Harriet and Bessie.

CHARLES DORRANCE LINSKILL, was born in Lehman, Luzerne county, Pennsylvania, April 10, 1840. He attended the public and select schools of Lehman and Huntsville and also assisted in the labors on the farm until sixteen years of age when he entered a store as a clerk. For sixteen years he was salesman, book-keeper and foreman in stores of Wyoming Valley. Since 1873 he has been constantly engaged in the newspaper business in this county. In the fall of 1880 he started the Wilkes-Barre *Telephone*, which is now a paper of large circulation and considerable influence. In 1887 Mr. Linskill made a pleasant trip through the British Isles and France, and since his return he has published a history of his European trip in a book, entitled "In Lands Beyond the Sea," which has had an excellent sale and is very highly commended by hundreds of worthy people. We understand that he proposes to publish other works.

REV. PETER H. BROOKS was born near the city of Schenectady, New York. At the age of sixteen he united with the Presbyterian Church in that city, under the pastorate of Rev. Trumball Backus, D. D., LL. D. He attended Union College. Graduated at Princeton Theological Seminary, New Jersey, 1864. Was ordained and installed pastor of the Presbyterian Church at West Milton, Saratoga county, New York, July 13, 1865. He has been nineteen years pastor of the Presbyterian Church in Susquehanna, Susquehanna county, Pennsylvania. For fifteen years he has been Clerk in Lackawanna Presbytery. Two of these years he was Temporary Clerk, then five years Permanent Clerk, and eight years Stated Clerk, which position he still holds, in connection with his recent appointment as Presbyterial Missionary in the seven eastern counties of Pennsylvania, having his residence in Wilkes-Barre.

R. B. RICKETTS was educated at Wyoming Seminary. Commanded a battery of light artillery in the late war; promoted to Major and also Colonel of Artillery. Democratic candidate for Lieutenant Governor in 1886. Director of the Osterhout Free Library. Member of the Sons of the American Revolution.

W. P. MORGAN was born in Wilkes-Barre, March 22, 1853. Beginning a business career at the age of twenty-one, has been a successful business man ever since. Was associated with J. T. Morgan, his brother, in the wholesale shoe business. The Morgan Brothers have lately opened up the large tract of land at South Wilkes-Barre known as the Lee Park tract, and have been very successful with it.

EDWARD HENRY CHASE was born at Haverhill, Massachusetts, February 28, 1835. Graduated from Union College, Schenectady, New York, 1855. Taught one year in Wells College. Came to Wilkes-Barre in 1856. Admitted to the Luzerne Bar in 1859. Went to the front with the Wyoming Light Dragoons. In 1863 married Elizabeth, daughter of Hon. Adam Taylor. Appointed Postmaster of Wilkes-Barre in 1865. In 1868 was chosen Secretary and Attorney of the Borough Council; City Clerk and Attorney in 1871-'72-'73. Collector of Internal Revenue from 1873 until 1885.

BENJAMIN FRANKLIN MYERS, Chief-of-Police, Wilkes-Barre, Pennsylvania, was born in that city in 1846. Educated in the public schools. Worked on his grandfather's farm until his seventeenth year. Enlisted in the Eighteenth Pennsylvania Cavalry and served until the close of the war. Was a carpenter until he was appointed on the police force of Wilkes-Barre as patrolman, and served eight years; then was appointed Chief-of-Police, and has filled that position for fourteen years.

THOMAS C. PARKER was born in England, March, 1846. Came to this country during the Civil War and located at Newark, New Jersey. Later came to Wilkes-Barre. He has established one of the largest jewelry businesses in the city. He is a member of many local societies, and is very often chosen orator on public occasions. He is also a fluent writer.

JOHN HARTWELL MULKEY was born at Rush, Susquehanna county, Pennsylvania. Was educated at the Wyoming Seminary. He is in the mercantile business in West Pittston. He has written many descriptive and religious verses.

HENRY BLACKMAN PLUMB, ESQ., was born in Hanover township, Luzerne county, March 13, 1829. Educated in the common schools of Wilkes-Barre, Pennsylvania. Studied law under Bakeny L. Maxwell, and admitted to the Luzerne Bar in 1859. Mr. Plumb is largely interested in real estate. Author of the "History of Hanover Township."

G. TAYLOR GRIFFIN was born at Moscow, Pennsylvania. His school days were passed at Meshoppen, Pennsylvania. Commenced photography at Meshoppen; opened a gallery at Tunkhannock; came from there to Wilkes-Barre, and from there to Pittston, and in May, 1890, established with C. F. Colburn the well-known gallery, 117 Public Square, Wilkes-Barre.

C. B. SUTTON was born in Exeter township, Luzerne county, on the 9th day of July, 1830. Was the son of Samuel Sutton, who was drowned in the Susquehanna river in 1842. Removed from Exeter to Kingston in 1846. Attended school at Wyoming Seminary during the years of 1848-'49-'50. Removed to Wilkes-Barre in 1853. Was clerk in his brother's store on North Main street until 1861, when he enlisted in the band of the Fifty-Second Regiment Pennsylvania Infantry, under Colonel Henry M. Hoyt. After retiring from the army was clerk for his brother for several years. Was elected Alderman of the Twelfth Ward of the city in 1874; re-elected in 1879 and 1884. Was elected Mayor of the city in 1886, against seven other competitors; was re-elected in 1880, running as an independent candidate against ex-Sheriff William O'Malley, Democratic candidate, and Col. B. F. Stark, Republican candidate, and received within seventy-one votes as many as the two other candidates together; at present Alderman of the Twelfth Ward.

D. O. COUGHLIN, ESQ., the subject of this sketch, is a native of Luzerne county. He is what is called a self-educated man; that is, he was not sent to school, but went to school and paid his own way. He was for several years a teacher in both public and private schools. He was principal of the New Columbus Male and Female Academy five years. Subsequently he attended the National School of Oratory in Philadelphia, and later entered as a law student in the office of A. Ricketts. In 1882 he was admitted to the Luzerne County Bar. He completed the course of instruction in the Valparaiso Law School and was graduated with honors in 1884. Married soon after and took up his residence in Luzerne, Pennsylvania. Since that time he has been practicing law in this county. He served as Deputy Revenue Collector four years under Cleveland's administration, and filled the position with credit to himself and satisfaction to his superiors.

FRANCIS M. NICHOLS, ESQ., was born at Smithfield, Pennsylvania. Educated in the State University of Kansas. Admitted to the Luzerne Bar in 1873. Filled the position of District Attorney by appointment, 1879. Mr. Nichols is well known as a man of fine literary taste. Elected Mayor of Wilkes-Barre, Pennsylvania, in 1892.

GEORGE W. GUTHRIE, M. D., was born at Guthrieville, Chester county, Pennsylvania, on the 28th of January, 1855. Educated in the public schools and at Millersville State Normal School. Studied medicine under the care and direction of Dr. Edward R. Mayer and attended lectures at Bellevue Hospital Medical College, New York, and the University of Pennsylvania. Diploma from the latter institution bears date of March 13, 1873. Located for the practice of medicine in Wilkes-Barre June 13, 1873. Member of the Luzerne County Medical Society and of the Medical Society of the State of Pennsylvania. One of the attending physicians of the Wilkes-Barre City Hospital. For thirteen years was a member of the School Board for the Third District; at present a member of the Consolidated Board of Six.

HON. ELIJAH CAYLIN WADHAMS was born at Plymouth, Pennsylvania, July 17, 1823. Was educated at Dana College, Wilkes-Barre, Dickinson College, and the University of the City of New York, graduating from the latter institution in 1847. From this time until 1873 he lived in Plymouth, engaging in commercial pursuits and in mining and shipping coal. He was Justice of the Peace for twenty years and Burgess for seven years. In 1873 he moved to Wilkes-Barre. He was for many years a Director of the Wyoming National Bank, and at the time of his death, January 18, 1889, was President of the First National Bank of Wilkes-Barre. In 1876 he was elected to the Senate of Pennsylvania and was highly praised for the work he did while a member of that body. He was also a prominent Mason, being one of the charter members of Plymouth Lodge. Hon. E. C. Wadhams combined a liberal education and culture with a high standard of manhood, tempered with that essential factor, common sense. He was respected by all for his integrity, his Christian faith and his earnest and successful work in the church with which he was identified.

LEWIS H. TAYLOR, M. D., was born at Taylorsville, Bucks county, Pennsylvania, July 29, 1850. Received preliminary education in the common schools. Graduated at Millersville State Normal School in July, 1871, having previously taught two terms in the school which in boyhood he attended. Began teaching in Wilkes-Barre, as principal of Franklin Grammar School, in September, 1871, which position he held till 1874, when he was elected principal of the High School. Remained in this position till 1877, when he withdrew to begin the study of medicine. Graduated at the University of Pennsylvania in 1880, and took a post graduate course in diseases of the eye and ear. Settled in Wilkes-Barre in 1880, where he has since practiced continuously, with the exception of seven months spent in special study in Europe. Married in June, 1884, to Emily B. Hollenback. Two children. Has been Medical Inspector for the State Board of Health since 1885. One of the attending physicians of the Wilkes-Barre City Hospital since 1884, and now ophthalmologist to the same. Received the honorary degree of A. M. from Lafayette College in 1891. Member of the American Medical Association, Pennsylvania State Medical Society, Lehigh Valley Medical Association, Luzerne County Medical Society, Philadelphia Pathological Society, American Ophthalmological Society. Trustee of Osterhout Library, Wyoming Seminary and of Wyoming Historical and Geological Society.

THOMAS R. MARTIN, ESQ., was educated at Mercersburg, Franklin and Marshall College, and graduated in 1874. Began practicing law in Wilkes-Barre in 1876. He was a candidate for nomination for Congress, and for District Attorney of Luzerne county. Mr. Martin's office is at 14 South Franklin street.

GEORGE LOVELAND, Esq., was born in Kingston, November 5, 1823. Educated at the Dana Academy, Wilkes-Barre, Pennsylvania, and Lafayette College. Studied law with General E. W. Sturdevant and was admitted to Bar of Luzerne county in 1848.

SAMUEL HOYT, son of Elias and Mary Weston Hoyt, was born in Kingston, Luzerne county, Pennsylvania, November 2, 1815, and died October 7, 1875; buried at Forty Fort cemetery. Mr. Hoyt was a cousin of ex-Governor Hoyt. Mr. Hoyt was regarded as one of the solid men of the Wyoming Valley. After completing his studies he assisted his father as county surveyor and continued in this line for many years. This work made him familiar with the properties and industrial interests of Luzerne county, so that he became an authority as to title and ownership, both of surface and coal lands. He became identified with coal interests and railroads, and was intimately associated in these with Mr. Abram Nesbitt. His name and life are interwoven with the history and prosperity of Kingston and the Wyoming Valley. Mr. Hoyt was a man of strong convictions in politics as well as business, but his modesty forbade any proclamation of them.

JOHN B. REYNOLDS was born in Wilkes-Barre, Pennsylvania, August 5, 1850. Educated at Wyoming Seminary and Lafayette College. Admitted to the Luzerne Bar in 1875. Built the North street iron bridge across the Susquehanna above Wilkes-Barre, and opened it in 1878. Organized and built the West Side electric road. Ran for Congress in 1890, but was defeated.

JOHN W. HOLLENBACK, son of Charles F. and Ellen J. Welles, daughter of Matthias Hollenback, of Wilkes-Barre, was born in Wyalusing, Bradford county, Pennsylvania, March 15, 1827. He came to Wilkes-Barre in 1862, and his family moved into the old Hollenback homestead in 1863, on the corner of River and West Market streets, now occupied by one of the finest, if not the finest, blocks in Northeastern Pennsylvania (erected by Mr. Hollenback). He has been associated with many large corporations. One of the principal stockholders of the Bridge Company. A member of the Board of Trustees and a liberal contributor of Lafayette College for many years. He has given liberally to many institutions as well as churches and private benevolences. President of the Hollenback Cemetery Association, President and promoter of the new bridge. President of the People's Bank since the death of R. J. Flick.

HON. ROBERT H. McKUNE was born in Newburgh, New York, August 19, 1823. Attended school until his thirteenth year, and then began active business life as a baker. In 1849 removed to California. Settled at Susquehanna, Pennsylvania; later at Binghamton, New York; removed to Scranton in 1862. Served in the Civil War, having charge of the advance guard on the Williamsport road, and was conspicuous as a member of the Secret Service. Entered on a general insurance business in Scranton after his return. Elected Mayor of Scranton in 1875. At the present time conducting an insurance business in Wilkes-Barre. Secretary Wilkes-Barre Board of Trade.

SELIGMAN J. STRAUSS, Esq., was born in Wilkes-Barre, Pennsylvania. Graduated from the College of New York city. Studied law with H. W. Palmer, Esq., of Wilkes-Barre, and was admitted to the Luzerne Bar in 1875.

CHARLES F. COOK, who was the oldest photographer in Wilkes-Barre, was born in Newburg, New York, 1834. He served in the War of the Rebellion. Died June 24, 1894.

MOSES H. BURGUNDER was born in Wilkes-Barre, Pennsylvania, in 1854. Educated in the public schools and Wyoming Seminary. Manager of the Grand Opera House, Wilkes-Barre; Scranton Academy of Music, and the Opera Houses of Reading, Allentown, Williamsport, Altoona, Johnstown, Pottstown and McKeesport.

FRED. AHLBORN was born in the kingdom of Bavaria. Educated in the Government schools. Came to this country in 1851, and engaged in the manufacturing business in Pottsville, Pennsylvania; came to Wilkes-Barre 1859 and engaged in the manufacture of soap. In 1871 established a meat business that has become the largest in this section. Died April 30, 1893.

JOHN LANING was born in Wilkes-Barre, Pennsylvania, October 7, 1836. His father was A. C. Laning and mother Amanda E. Laning, now deceased. His education was received at the old Academy on the Public Square, Wilkes-Barre, preparatory to his entering Lafayette College in 1854. After a three years' course at that institution he entered Union College at Schenectady, New York, and graduated from the latter in 1858. Immediately following his graduation he was employed as draftsman and afterward as book-keeper for Laning & Marshall at their machine shop on Canal street, now the Dickson Manufacturing Company. He was a member of the Town Council the year Wilkes-Barre became a city. On the 19th of September, 1865, he was married to Helen C. Brower, in New York city. From 1866 to 1879 he was engaged in the lumber business, running a planing mill in connection with his lumber yard. In 1880 he became Superintendent of the Hollenback Coal Company, and held that position until 1887, when he retired from active business life. He has been conspicuous in improving the city of Wilkes-Barre, notably in erecting the Laning Building. He is a Director in the Miners' Saving Bank, and the Wilkes-Barre Bridge Company.

WILLIAM HENRY SPENCER was born in Manchester, England, in 1845; came to this country when a boy; enlisted in the American army and served three years and eleven months, and has lived in the Wyoming Valley ever since. Miner until some years ago when he began the manufacture of bed springs, and is in that business at the present time.

REV. DANIEL WEBSTER COXE, D. D., graduated at Kenyon College, Ohio; A. B., 1885; A. M., 1868. Honorary degree of D. D., Chicago Lit. College, 1884. Ordained Deacon by Rt. Rev. Thomas H. Vail, D. D., LL. D., July 19, 1868; Priest by same 1869. He was rector of various parishes in Kansas, under Bishop Vail, until 1880. Rector at Tremont, Ohio, 1880-85, and West Pittston, Pennsylvania, 1885-89. In 1889 he became assistant minister of St. Stephen's Church, Wilkes-Barre, at Alden and Nanticoke. He is Secretary of the Archdeaconry of Scranton. Is married and has three children. He resides at Alden.

REV. JAMES PORTER WARE, B. D., born in Massachusetts, April 6, 1859. Graduated B. L. from Delaware College, Delaware, 1883; B. D., Episcopal Theological Seminary, Cambridge, Massachusetts, 1886. Ordained Deacon by Rt. Rev. Thomas M. Clark, D. D., LL. D., Rhode Island, June 10, 1886; Priest by the same, 1887. Rector at Woburn, Massachusetts, 1886. Manville, Rhode Island, 1887. He became assistant and minister of St. Stephen's Church, Wilkes-Barre; in charge of St. Peter's, Plymouth, 1888. He married, October 12, 1887, Miss Helen E. Story. He resides in Plymouth.

FATHER McANDREW was educated at the Holy Cross College, Worcester, Massachusetts, and at the Theological Seminary of St. Charles Borromeo, at Overbrook, and ordained by Bishop O'Hara in 1877. Rector in Scranton for ten years, and had charge of St John's Church, that city. Came to Wilkes-Barre in 1889, as pastor of St. Mary's Church.

F. B. HODGE, D. D., was a graduate from Princeton College in 1859, and from Princeton Theological Seminary in 1862. He was ordained May 9, 1863, and installed pastor of the Presbyterian Church of Oxford, Pennsylvania. Called to the First Presbyterian Church, of Wilkes-Barre. In 1863 he received the degree of Doctor of Divinity from Princeton College, of which institution he is a Trustee, having succeeded his brother, the late A. A. Hodge, D. D. Dr. Hodge is one of the leading ministers in the Presbyterian Church.

REV. HORACE EDWIN HAYDEN, M. A., son of Hon. Edwin Parsons Hayden of Maryland; born at Catonsville, Maryland, February 18, 1837. Educated at St. Timothy's Military Academy, Maryland, and Kenyon College, Ohio; honorary degree of M. A., Kenyon College, 1886. His college course was interrupted by the War between the States, during which he served as a private in the Confederate States army, 1861-65. Graduated from the Virginia Theological Seminary in 1867. Ordained Deacon by Rt. Rev. John Johns, D. D., LL. D., who was his cousin, June 26, 1867; Priest by Rt. Rev. F. M. Whittle, D. D., August 7, 1867. Rector of Christ Church, Point Pleasant, Diocese of Virginia, 1867-73; of St. John's Church, West Brownsville, Pennsylvania, 1873-79; assistant minister of St. Stephen's Church, Wilkes-Barre, since November, 1879. Since 1885 Mr. Hayden has been one of the Examining Chaplains of the Diocese of Central Pennsylvania. He is a member of many historical and scientific societies, and has done something in the field of historical research. He is a member of the Board of Managers of the Pennsylvania Sons of the Revolution, which has about fifty members in the Wyoming Valley. He resides in Wilkes-Barre.

REV. JOHN RICHARDS BOYLE, D. D., the present pastor of the First Methodist Episcopal Church of Wilkes-Barre, succeeded to its pulpit in December, 1890. Dr. Boyle is the son of a Methodist minister, the Rev. John A. Boyle, and was born in Philadelphia, June 23, 1844. He was educated in the public schools of that city, and under private instruction. He also learned the printers' trade, and in early life was for several years a newspaper editor. Enlisting in the 111th Regiment Pennsylvania Volunteers, in September, 1861, he served through the Civil War, in several grades, as an officer both of the line and staff. His final military rank was Captain and Assistant Quartermaster, to which he was appointed by President Lincoln, and in it he was attached to the staffs of Generals Logan and Hazen. He was slightly wounded at the battle of Peach Tree Creek, Georgia, July 20, 1864, and was honorably mustered out of service, March 20, 1866. He was prepared for the ministry in 1869 and 1870, and entered the Philadelphia Annual Conference of the Methodist Episcopal Church in March, 1871. Since then he has successively been a member of the Wilmington, Newark, New York and Wyoming Conferences, and has been pastor of several of the leading churches of the denomination. In 1880 the honorary degree of A. M., and in 1885 that of D. D., were conferred upon him by Dickinson College.

REV. HENRY LAWRENCE JONES, M. A., son of the Rev. Lot Jones, for over thirty-three years rector of the Church of the Epiphany, New York city; born May 30, 1839. Was graduated A. B., Columbia College, New York, 1858; A. M., 1861; graduated Virginia

Theological Seminary, 1861. Ordained Deacon by Rt. Rev. Horatio C. Potter, D. D., LL. D., May 24, 1861. Priest by same, 1863. After a year passed as assistant to his father, he became, in 1863, rector of Christ Church, Fitchburg, Massachusetts. In 1874 he resigned from Christ Church and accepted St. Stephen's Church, Wilkes-Barre, where he has been the beloved rector for over nineteen years. He has in that time held the highest positions in the ecclesiastical affairs of the Diocese of Central Pennsylvania, that is Examining Chaplain, 1876-80; President N. W. Convocation (now Archdeaconry of Scranton), and member of the Board of Missions, 1876-87, when he refused re-election; Deputy to the General Convention in 1886-91; member of the Standing Committee continuously since 1876. Mr. Jones is one of the Executive Committee of the American Church Missionary Society, of which Hon. John N. Conyngham, LL.D., of this city, was long the President. He is also a Trustee of Osterhout Free Library and a Vice President of the Wyoming Historical and Geological Society. He married Miss Sarah Eastman Coffin, of Massachusetts. One of the Bishops who has known Mr. Jones intimately, writes thus of him: "The present Bishop of New York once wrote me in a private letter: 'The Rev. Henry L. Jones is a prince among men.'" To those who know Mr. Jones this description does not seem extravagant, for in the composition of his character there is a remarkable combination of strength and beauty. Simple and unostentatious in manner, there is yet something in his looks and speech and action that suggests a large reserve force, and in his administration of parochial affairs this is more than realized, for he is not only wise in counsel, but possesses exceptional executive gifts. Keeping as he always does his mental and moral equipoise, his judgment is asked by many people in and out of church, and being both just and generous, he has the confidence of all that know him. As a preacher he is thoughtful and instructive and has a becoming literary style. As a pastor he is sympathetic, active and unusually self-sacrificing, while as an administrator he has few peers. The work in St. Stephen's parish has been large and exacting, but his success therein has been remarkable. His assistants love him as a brother, and the affection for him shown by his parishioners is as unusual as it is delightful. He receives and deserves the love of all who know him.

HON. JOHN N. CONYNGHAM was born in Philadelphia, Pennsylvania, in 1798. Graduated with high honors at the University of Pennsylvania in 1817. Came to Wilkes-Barre in 1820. He became President Judge of Luzerne county and served for thirty years. Member of the Legislature in 1849. For fifty years vestryman in St. Stephen's Church in Wilkes-Barre. His death on February 23, 1871, resulted from having his limbs crushed under the wheels of a car.

CHARLES PARRISH has resided all his life in Wilkes-Barre. He is one of the leading coal and railroad men in the State and probably has done more for these industries in this section than any other individual. Was President of the Lehigh & Wilkes-Barre Coal Company, one of the organizers and President of the First National Bank, President of the Hazard Manufacturing Company and is connected with many other industries of the valley.

HARRY C. DAVIS was born in Washington, District of Columbia, September 24, 1856. Educated in the public schools of Washington, and graduated at the head of his class in the Columbian University, in 1878. Became adjunct-professor of Greek in the University and held the position for four years. At Present Principal of the Harry Hillman Academy. In conjunction with Mr. J. C. Bridgman, author of "Brief Declamations."

LIDDON FLICK, Esq., was born at Wilkes-Barre, October 29, 1858. He is the eldest son of the late Reuben Jay Flick, who died December 18, 1893. Mr. Flick received his education at the public schools of Wilkes-Barre and at Princeton College, graduating from the latter institution in 1882 with the degree of B. A. He entered the law school of Columbia College, New York, and upon graduation in 1884 received the degree of LL. B. *cum laude.* In 1885 he was admitted to the New York City Bar, and the same year received from Princeton College the degree of M. A. In 1886 he returned to Wilkes-Barre, where he has since been practicing his profession. Mr. Flick is an energetic, painstaking young man, and most actively interested in the industries and improvements of his native city. He holds the responsible position of Director in the Wilkes-Barre Lace Company, Wyoming Valley Ice Company, Newport Coal Company, Wilkes-Barre and Kingston Bridge Company, Treasurer and Director of the Newell Clothing Company, Vice President Wyoming Valley Trust Company, and Treasurer Grand Opera House Company. He is also one of the Trustees of the Wilkes-Barre City Hospital and of the Musical Association. As a connoisseur and collector of books and fine art, Mr. Flick has more than a local reputation. As a man, his character endures close and intimate acquaintance. In every position which business or popularity has called him, by his energy and integrity he has justified public confidence and the expectations of his friends.

W. A. LATHROP was born August 4, 1854, at Springville, Susquehanna county, Pennsylvania. Graduated at Lehigh University in June, 1875, with degree of C. E. Engaged at mine surveying and kindred mining work with Irving A. Stearns at Wilkes-Barre for about two years; principal Assistant Engineer of Lehigh Valley Railroad for about three years, with office at Bethlehem. Superintendent Midvale Ore Company, Prompton, New Jersey, about one year. General Superintendent and Engineer of the Southwest Virginia Improvement Company from the fall of 1881 until the summer of 1884, during which time he opened and developed the Flat Top Coal Field of Virginia; built the town of Pocahontas in what was then a wilderness, and opened the mines and built the coking plant of the Southwest Company at that place. Superintendent of the Bituminous Coal Department of the Lehigh Valley Coal Company, with headquarters at Snow Shoe, Center county, Pennsylvania, from the summer of 1884 until the winter of 1888, when he succeeded Fred. Mercur as General Superintendent of the last named company, with office at Wilkes-Barre.

H. BAKER HILLMAN was born at Manluck, Pennsylvania. Came to Wilkes-Barre in 1841. His father, Colonel H. B. Hillman, was one of the first coal operators of the valley. Mr. Hillman became a coal operator after completing his education, and has been actively engaged ever since. One of the first Directors of the People's Bank; Secretary of the Vulcan Iron Works for many years; was a member of the last Borough and of the first City Council. The Harry Hillman Academy of Wilkes-Barre is a gift to this city and a memorial to his deceased son, Harry Hillman.

EDWARD STERLING LOOP was born in Elmira, New York, February 11, 1823. Attended the school of J. B. Dow, in Wilkes-Barre, Pennsylvania. In 1840 removed to St. Louis, Missouri; returned to Wilkes-Barre and was employed by Ziba Bennett for fifty dollars per annum. Removed to White Haven in 1842. In 1844 went to New York city, and in May, 1853, was made Cashier of the Wyoming Bank, Wilkes-Barre, and remained until 1874.

ALFRED DARTE, Esq., was born in Susquehanna county, Pennsylvania, and is the eldest son of Judge Alfred Darte, now deceased. He was educated at Wyoming Seminary, and was in early years admitted to practice law, a partner with his father. In 1861, at the breaking out of the Rebellion, they closed their law office, both responded to the call for 75,000 men, and served through the first three months of the Rebellion—the father as a Captain and the son as a Lieutenant in the same Regiment. Afterward he entered the Cavalry service, and was a Captain in the Fourth Pennsylvania Cavalry until discharged for disability from wounds received in action at Trevillian Station, Virginia, in 1864. Captain Darte's command was a part of the famous Phil. Sheridan Cavalry. In civil life Captain Darte has filled many positions of honor and trust. He holds a commission as Lieutenant-Colonel of the Veteran Military League, an organization similar but antedating the Grand Army of the Republic. Is a member of the Grand Army of the Republic, and at present Commander of Conyngham Post, No. 97, of Wilkes-Barre, Pennsylvania; was its Delegate to the National Encampment at Detroit. At the last State Encampment he was elected Senior Vice Commander of the Department of Pennsylvania. Was elected District Attorney of Luzerne county for a three year term, in 1879, and re-elected for a second term in 1888, and vigorously represented the Commonwealth, in the enforcement of her laws, with intelligence and integrity. Captain Darte is one of the most active Republicans in his party and a public speaker of repute. He resides at Kingston, Pennsylvania.

HON. CHARLES E. RICE, President Judge of Luzerne county, was born at Fairfield, New York, September 14, 1846. Prepared for college at Fairfield Academy; graduated from Hamilton College in 1867. Taught in the Bloomsburg Library Institute. Read law with John G. Freeze; graduated from the Albany Law School in 1869, admitted to the Bar of the Supreme Court of New York; in 1870 admitted to the Luzerne Bar; elected District Attorney of Luzerne county in 1876; elected Law Judge in 1879; is at present President Judge.

HON. GEORGE W. SHONK was born in Plymouth, Pennsylvania, April 26, 1860. Educated at the Wyoming Seminary; graduated from Wesleyan University in 1883. Studied law with Hon. H. B. Payne; admitted to the Bar of Luzerne county in 1876. Elected to Congress on the Republican ticket in 1890.

S. L. BROWN was born in Wayne county, Pennsylvania. Educated in public schools. At thirteen years of age had charge of a set of books in a store at Mount Pleasant. Entered the mercantile business at Honesdale, and later engaged extensively in the tannery business. Removed to Wilkes-Barre and became a member of the firm of Conyngham & Paine. In 1886 he established the firm of S. L. Brown & Company, that has become one of the largest oil houses in this section. Mr. Brown has an interest in many business enterprises in this section and owns one of the finest residences in the city.

GEORGE H. PARRISH was born in Wilkes-Barre, Pennsylvania, in 1820. Educated in that city, and has been connected with the coal interest of the valley from early life. Was Superintendent of the Lehigh and Wilkes-Barre Coal Company for many years.

THOMAS H. ATHERTON, born at Wyoming, July 14, 1853. Attended school at Wyoming and Wilkes-Barre until 1870. Entered Princeton University in the fall of 1870, and graduated in June, 1874. Entered the law office of Hon. Charles E. Rice in September, 1874, and was admitted to the Bar in September, 1876.

HON. HENRY M. HOYT was born in Kingston, Pennsylvania, June 8, 1830. Worked on his father's farm until the age of fourteen. Educated at the old Wilkes-Barre Academy and Wyoming Seminary; graduated at Williams College in 1849. Taught in the Academy at Towanda; taught mathematics at Wyoming Seminary; also taught in the Graded School at Memphis, Tennessee. Studied law under George W. Woodward, and was admitted to to the Luzerne Bar in 1853. Served his country in the War of the Rebellion and was brevetted Brigadier-General. Elected Additional Law Judge of Luzerne county. Appointed Collector of Revenue for Luzerne and Susquehanna counties in 1869. Inaugurated Governor of Pennsylvania in 1879. Author of much valuable literature. Died December 1, 1892.

DR. W. S. STEWART was born in Centre county, Pennsylvania, in 1855. Educated in the public schools and in the State Normal School; taught school for several years; graduated from the medical department of the University of Pennsylvania in 1885. Located in Wilkes-Barre, Pennsylvania, in 1884. Member of Luzerne county and State Medical Societies and the Lehigh Valley Medical Society.

GEORGE MORTIMER LEWIS, ESQ., was born in Merryal, Bradford county, Pennsylvania. Graduated from Lafayette College in 1873. Studied law with E. P. Darling. Is a member of the Luzerne Bar. Is interested in Electric Railroads.

GEORGE H. FLANAGAN, Cashier of the Wyoming Bank, was born at Lehman Center, Luzerne county, Pennsylvania, February 4, 1854. Educated in the public schools; spent three years at Wyoming Seminary, and graduated from the Commercial College in 1871. Entered the bank of J. B. Wood, Flanagan & Company, Wilkes-Barre, Pennsylvania. In 1876 was elected Cashier of the Ashley Savings Bank, and in 1882 Cashier of the Wyoming Bank, Wilkes-Barre, Pennsylvania, which position he now holds. Served as a member of the Town Council of Kingston borough for three years. Mr. Flanagan resides in Kingston.

ASHER MINER was born in Wilkes-Barre, Pennsylvania, November 4, 1860. Son of Hon. Charles A. Miner. Educated at the Wilkes-Barre Academy and at East Hampton, Massachusetts. Director of the Millers' Fire Insurance Company, and has served as Captain of Company D of the Ninth Regiment of the National Guards.

JAMES L. LENAHAN, ESQ., was born in Plymouth, Pennsylvania. Educated in the public schools; completed his education at the Holy Cross College, Massachusetts. Read law with his brother John T., and was admitted to the Bar of Luzerne county in 1879. Elected District Attorney in 1885.

WILLIAM DRAKE LOOMIS, born in Wilkes-Barre, where Loomis Building now stands, August 18, 1834. Son of ex-Mayor W. W. Loomis. Was educated at the Wyoming Seminary and at the Preparatory School of W. S. Parsons, and is a graduate of Crittenden Commercial College. He is now one of the Directors and Secretary of the Wilkes-Barre Heat, Light and Motor Company. Served during the War on the United States Gunboat "Granite." He has spent a large amount of money in buildings in the city, having built the store at the corner of Northampton and Washington streets, occupied by Conyngham, Schrage & Company, and the Loomis Building on North Main street, and several blocks of tenement houses.

GEORGE A. WELLS, born at Dundaff, Luzerne county, Pennsylvania. Resident of Wilkes-Barre since 1865. Engaged in Real Estate, Collection and Insurance business, residence, 66 South street. Original Secretary of the Wilkes-Barre Board of Trade; also Secretary of Wyoming Building and Loan Association, No. 1 and No. 2, for full term of both. Precentor of the First Methodist Episcopal Church for ten years. Treasurer of Wyoming Camp-Ground Association for ten years.

STEPHEN JENKINS, ESQ., was born in Wyoming, Luzerne county, in 1819. Educated at Oxford Academy and at the Academy at Bethany, Pennsylvania. Studied law with the Hon. Hendrick B. Wright, and admitted to the Bar in 1847. Was a partner with Colonel Wright for eight years. Served two years in a government appointment in Washington. Served two terms in the State Legislature, namely, in 1856 and 1857. In 1863 was chosen Clerk and Counsel to the County Commissioners of Luzerne county, Pennsylvania. Died in 1889. He left a valuable collection of historical data, Indian relics, fossils, minerals. Mr. Jenkins was a poet, historian and antiquarian.

GEORGE A. EDWARDS is a native of Cardiff, Wales, where he was born in 1846. He came to Wilkes-Barre in 1881, and ever since has been one of its most industrious citizens. He founded the Eagle Iron Works in 1882, and it is now an important industry. Although Mr. Edwards has filled no public office, he is a very busy public man, having his hands full of social duties. He is an able platform speaker and wields the pen with equal ability. In business, in the church, and in philanthropic enterprises he is a very active citizen. The Cambro-American Society, an important organization amongst the Welsh residents, owes its present position to Mr. Edwards's zeal and interest in his nationality.

J. B. WOODWARD, ESQ., born at Wilkes-Barre, April 3, 1861. Educated at public schools, St. Paul's School, Wilkes-Barre Academy, and Yale College; graduated from Yale in the class of 1883. Studied law with A. T. McClintock, W. S. McLean and University of Pennsylvania Law School. Admitted to the Bar September 7, 1885. Married June 6. 1888, to Marion Hillard, daughter of T. S. Hillard.

S. M. BARD, born on a farm in Trumbull county, of the old Western Reserve, Ohio. Was educated in the National Normal School at Lebanon, Ohio. Began life as a teacher in home district school. Taught a number of terms in country and town, then spent three years on the road. Entered Young Men's Christian Association work at Harrisburg, as Assistant Secretary. Was General Secretary at Pittston for six months, and has been General Secretary for eight years in Wilkes-Barre.

TORRENCE BERNHART HARRISON was born in Union township, Luzerne county, Pennsylvania, November 1, 1858. Attended the public schools of his native township until seventeen years of age, when he began teaching. Taught first term in Union; for next two years taught during winter and attended a term of school during the fall at New Columbus Academy; in 1877, 1878 and 1879, taught in Plymouth township. Graduated from State Normal School in 1881, taking the highest honors of his class. Taught in public schools of Kingston borough for two years, the last year as Principal; resigned to accept Principalship of High School at Hazleton, a position he held for two years, and then resigned to accept the Principalship of the schools of what was then the Second District of Wilkes-Barre. Mr. Harrison held this position until his election as Superintendent of Schools of Luzerne county in 1890.

JOHN T. LENAHAN, Esq., born at Port Griffith., Educated under the care of the Fathers of St. Augustine, Delaware county, Pennsylvania, graduating in 1870. Studied in the law deparment of the University of Pennsylvania. Admitted to the Luzerne Bar in 1873.

C. W. LAYCOCK was born October 3, 1860. Educated in public schools of Shickshinny and Wyoming Seminary, Kingston. Entered the Second National Bank of Wilkes-Barre as book-keeper, February, 1880. Elected Cashier of the Anthracite Savings Bank of Wilkes-Barre, Pennsylvania, May, 1890.

EDWARD E. CAMP was born in Camptown, Bradford county, Pennsylvania, September 3, 1851. He followed farming until about 1876, when he went to Tunkhannock and engaged in newspaper work, which he has since continued, making advertising a special study. He entered into partnership with his brother, Cyrus, and established Camp Brothers' News and Advertising Bureau in Wilkes-Barre in 1885. Assumed control of the business in 1894.

AUGUSTUS L. LEGRAND, born in Wilkes-Barre, August 16, 1856. Educated in the public schools of Wilkes-Barre. Entered the employ of the Lehigh and Wilkes-Barre Coal Company at Empire Shops, to learn the machinist's trade, in 1870. Accepted a position as machinist with the Dickson Manufacturing Company in Wilkes-Barre in 1875. Returned to the Empire Shops in 1878. Studied mechanical engineering during leisure hours. Accepted a position as Mechanical Draughtsman with the Dickson Manufacturing Company of Wilkes-Barre in 1880, which position he still holds. Ruling Elder of the Grant Street Presbyterian Church and Superintendent of the Sunday School, succeeding the late Dr. J. L. Miner in above position.

C. BOW DOUGHERTY, born in Wilkes-Barre, September, 1860. Educated in the public schools of that city and Emerson Institute, Washington, District of Columbia. Entered the office of the Susquehanna Coal Company in 1879, and is now Chief Clerk of the Coal Companies of Pennsylvania Railroad. Married Anne W. Posten, February 6, 1883. Enlisted in the Ninth Regiment, National Guards of Pennsylvania, August 1, 1881; appointed Regimental Clerk, 1881; Sergeant-Major, 1883; First Lieutenant and Inspector of Rifle Practice, 1887; Major, 1892, and Lieutenant-Colonel, 1894. Secretary Wilkes-Barre Musical Association (Ninth Regiment Band). Member Pennsylvania Society Sons of the Revolution.

JESSE T. MORGAN, the subject of this sketch, was born in Wilkes-Barre in 1843, and was educated in our public schools. His business career commenced when but a boy as a clerk in his father's shoe store on Market street, in the year 1869. When but twenty-one years of age he became a partner with his father, and took the full management of the business, which was conducted with moderate success. In the year 1876, W. P. Morgan, a younger brother, became a partner—his father retiring. A jobbing department was added to the retail business, and later the business was changed to manufacturing and jobbing, Mr. D. Davis, of Worcester, Massachusetts, becoming a member of the firm. The business was run successfully under the firm name of Morgan Bros. & Company for about eight years, when Mr. Davis retired, he having purchased the manufacturing plant. J. T. & W. P. Morgan continued the jobbing business until 1893. Mr. Morgan is also engaged in real estate largely, being connected with his brother, W. P., in developing the Lee Park addition to the city of Wilkes-Barre.

HON. WILLIAM H. HINES was born in Brooklyn, New York, March 16, 1854. Educated in public schools and Wyoming Seminary. Read law with John Lynch and G. M. Harding, and admitted to the Luzerne Bar in 1881. Elected by the Labor Reform Party to the State Legislature in 1878, and to the same office in 1882. Elected to the Senate in 1888 by the Democratic Party, and to Congress in 1892.

CHRISTIAN WALTER was born in the Grand Duchy of Baden, Germany, in 1848. Came to this country in 1854; has lived nearly all that time in Luzerne county. Received very little schooling, only seven terms of four months each in the country districts of Luzerne county. When nineteen years old took clerkship in country store in Conyngham; remained five years, then came to Wilkes-Barre as book-keeper for Baer & Stegmaier; from there to W. Stoddart & Company as salesman, remaining with them five years, when in 1879 entered into partnership with W. M. Bennett, when the firm of Bennett & Walter, Boot and Shoe Merchants, was established.

LUTHER CURRAN DARTE was born in Susquehanna county, Pennsylvania, and was one of four children of the late Judge Alfred Darte of Carbondale, Pennsylvania. He was educated in the common schools at Carbondale and Business College at Poughkeepsie, New York. Served in the late War when but a lad, in the same regiment with his father and brother. Mr. Darte is a resident of Kingston, Pennsylvania, where he has lived since 1865. He was for a number of years the general passenger agent and general accountant of the Lackawanna and Bloomsburg Railroad Company, leaving the employ of the company when the road was merged into the Delaware, Lackawanna and Western Railroad Company. Was cashier of the Ashley Savings Bank at one time. Was elected County Commissioner of Luzerne county on the Republican ticket, and served creditably three years as such. Mr. Darte is an active and influential Republican, and is well known throughout the State. He was a delegate to the Republican National Convention, which nominated President Harrison, and in the Convention warmly espoused the cause of General Russell A. Alger's candidacy for President. He has served both on the Republican State Committee and as one of the chairmen of the Luzerne Republican County Committee a number of times. He is at present largely engaged in the business of Real Estate and Insurance in Wilkes-Barre.

D. P. AYARS was born in Chester county, Pennsylvania. Came to Wilkes-Barre as a book-keeper for Haggerty & O'Donnell, railroad contractors, in 1867; afterwards entered the Collector's office of Internal Revenue under Hon. J. B. Stark, continuing in this service as a Deputy during the consecutive terms of Hon. C. E. Wright and Hon. H. M. Hoyt, till 1873, when he was elected City Clerk and served in that office till December, 1875, when he was offered and accepted the position of Cashier of the Miners' Savings Bank, in place of Mr. J. A. Rippard, resigned, in which position he continues at the present time. He is also a member of the City Council and represents the Eleventh, Thirteenth and Fourteenth Wards and serves on some of the important committees of that body. Of the Finance Committee he is chairman, and is also one of the Sinking Fund Commissioners.

HON. MORGAN B. WILLIAMS was born in Wales, September 17, 1831. Educated in the English branches. Learned mining in England, Australia and in the United States. Is at the present time a coal operator in Wilkes-Barre, Pennsylvania. Elected to the Senate in 1884. Has served as School Director and Councilman-at-Large in Wilkes-Barre. At present Councilman from the Ninth Ward.

BENJ. F. STARK, was born at Spring Brook, (now Moosic), Luzerne county, in the year 1845, on July 15. His father, Cornelius Stark, and mother, Louisa Wagner, were born at Plains, Luzerne county. B. F. Stark came to Wilkes-Barre in the year 1873, where he began the Livery business and conducted the same until his death which occurred in April, 1893. He became identified with the Ninth Regiment in the year 1879, and was Lieutenant-Colonel. He married Mary F. Warner, a daughter of Hon. D. D. Warner, of Montrose, Pennsylvania.

GEORGE P. LOOMIS, ESQ., was born in Wilkes-Barre, May 1, 1860. Graduated at Wyoming Seminary in 1878 and Syracuse University in 1882. He was cashier in John S. Loomis's large Planing Mills, Brooklyn, for two years. Studied law with Agib Ricketts and Henry A. Fuller, and was admitted to the Bar in 1886. Mr. Loomis's practice is that of a Counselor, and his advice and counsel are sought and highly regarded for one so young. It is seldom he appears in Court. Mr. Loomis has been instrumental in establishing many of the industries in our city.

JOHN THOMSON was born in the city of Glasgow, Scotland. Came to America with his parents in 1842, they settling in Carbondale, Pennsylvania, in 1845. He received his education in the public schools of the State. Served apprenticeship to the trade of machinist in the Pennsylvania Coal Company's Shops at Hawley, Pennsylvania. In 1863 entered the employ of the Dickson Manufacturing Company at Scranton, and has remained with them until the present, serving them in the capacity of Journeyman, Foreman and Superintendent of their works in Wilkes-Barre, Pennsylvania.

HENDRICK WRIGHT SEARCH was born in Salem township, Luzerne county, June 30, 1855. He was educated in the public schools at Shickshinny, which is still his home. He has been a prominent man in public affairs, having filled the offices of Deputy Register of Wills, Commissioners' Clerk, and was High Sheriff of Luzerne county during 1887-8-9. He was also a Delegate to the Democratic National Convention that nominated Cleveland for President in 1888.

J. C. BELL, was born in York county in 1850. Attended the public schools a short time and the State Normal School at Millersville, from which place he graduated. He taught in the public schools ten years, and served as City Clerk one year. In 1881 he commenced banking as clerk in the First National Bank of Wilkes-Barre. Was elected to his present position in 1887, Cashier of the Wilkes-Barre Savings and Deposit Bank.

P. A. O'BOYLE, ESQ., born in Ireland, November 10, 1861, and emigrated from there in 1864 with his parents, who settled in Pittston, where they have since lived. Educated in the public schools of Pittston borough. He began the study of law with Alexander Farnham of the city of Wilkes-Barre, and was admitted to the Bar in 1885. Assistant District Attorney in 1892.

WILLIAM GLASSELL ENO, born in Wilkes-Barre, Pennsylvania. Educated at the public schools of Wilkes-Barre. Son of Josiah W. Eno. In 1870, shipping agent at the coal mines of J. C. Fuller at Plymouth; from 1871 to 1874 with South Mountain Mining and Iron Company, in Cumberland county, Pennsylvania; 1874 to 1876 member of the firm of J. W. Eno & Son, Insurance Agents at Plymouth; since 1876 of the insurance firm of Biddle & Eno, Wilkes-Barre.

JAMES M. COUGHLIN was born in Fairmount township, Luzerne county, Pennsylvania, and received his education mainly in the public schools. He has been engaged in educational work for the past twenty years. During this time he taught in every department of school work, first in the public schools, then in select schools, after he was Principal of New Columbus Academy. He was the first Principal of the Bennett Grammar School at Luzerne. While teaching in Kingston he was elected Superintendent of the Schools of Luzerne county, and held the position for four terms (twelve years). During his career as County Superintendent he became recognized as among the leading educators of the State. He placed the schools of the county in excellent shape, and became very popular as an Institute instructor. He has been called to lecture on educational subjects in nearly every city in this State, and has been frequently invited to address educational gatherings in other States. In the fall of 1891 he was elected Vice-Principal of the Bloomsburg State Normal School, and was called from there to take charge of the public schools of Wilkes-Barre city, which position he now holds.

FREDERIC CORSS, M. D., the son of the Rev. Charles C. Corss, who was one "stated preacher" of the Congregational Churches of Kingston, Forty Fort and Exeter in 1836, was born at Athens in Bradford county, January 16, 1842. Attended school one term at Wyoming Seminary and one term at Susquehanna Collegiate Institute. With these exceptions his preparation for college was carried on at home. Entered the sophomore class at Lafayette College in 1859, receiving the degree of A. B. at that institution in 1862 and the degree of A. M. in 1865. Studied medicine at the University of Pennsylvania, receiving the degree of M. D. in 1866, coming immediately to Kingston, where he has since practiced his profession.

ISAAC LONG, the well known Dry Goods and Carpet Merchant, was born in Pretzfeld, Bavaria, in the year 1834. When a boy of fourteen he left his home and came to America to seek his fortune, and arrived in Wilkes-Barre in 1848, where he remained until he was twenty years old; he then went to Philadelphia, and was engaged in the manufacturing business for a number of years. In 1873, Mr. Long returned to Wilkes-Barre and embarked in his present business, which has been a most wonderful success. Starting with a couple of clerks in a small store in 1873, and in 1891 to be the occupant of the mammoth double store-room and two other floors in the Welles Building, where he gives steady employment to forty-three people, is certainly a remarkable business showing, and can only be due to his pluck, energy and business tact. Mr. Long is one of our most popular citizens, and is interested in a number of enterprises; he is also Vice President of the Electric Light Company and President of the Board of Trade.

P. M. CARHART, Cashier of the First National Bank of Wilkes-Barre, Pennsylvania, was born at Belvidere, New Jersey. His father, well known as a merchant, is still living. Mr. Carhart's experience as a banker covers a period of twenty-seven years—thirteen years with Messrs. Bennett, Phelps & Company, five years at the Wyoming National Bank, and nine years with the First National, of which he is now the Cashier. As a banker, Mr. Carhart is enterprising and progressive, yet careful and prudent. Under his management the business of the First National has steadily grown in volume, and its methods in favor with business men. With Mr. Carhart at its head we predict for this good old institution continued growth and increased prosperity.

FREDERICK C. JOHNSON, born at Marquette, Wisconsin, 1853. Son of Wesley Johnson and great-grandson of Rev. Jacob Johnson one of the original settlers of Wilkes-Barre in 1772. F. C. was taught at the public schools of Wilkes-Barre and at Ripon College, Wisconsin. Beginning with 1871, he had a business training of about ten years in the banking-house of Bennett, Phelps & Company, the coal office of F. J. Leavenworth and the Wilkes-Barre Gas Company, meanwhile engaging at odd moments in voluntary contributions to the local papers and doing special correspondence from the coal region for the Chicago *Tribune*. He also spent a year on reportorial work in Chicago for that paper. He studied medicine at the University of Pennsylvania, graduating therefrom in 1883. Instead of engaging in practice he embraced an opportunity for entering journalism and purchased an interest in the Wilkes Barre *Record*, the oldest daily paper in the city. He has conducted every department of the paper in turn—local, editorial and business manager. Mr. Johnson married in 1885, his wife also being a native of Wisconsin. Two children have been born to them. Mr. Johnson has actively identified himself with the local life of the community in the different ways that were congenial to his tastes. He is a member of the Board of Trade, an officer of the Historical Society, a Trustee of the Young Men's Christian Association, a member of the Luzerne County Medical Society and of the State Society, a member of the Masonic fraternity, the American Legion of Honor and the Heptasophs, and is one of the committee appointed by the State Board of Charities to inspect the public institutions of Luzerne county. He is a member of the State Editorial Association and was one of its Vice Presidents.

The *Record* was established in 1853 by William P Miner, who in 1873 began the publication of the daily. In 1883 the plant was sold to C. B. Snyder, F. C. Johnson and J. C. Powell, Mr. Snyder retiring in 1888, the *Record* continuing since under the management of the firm of Johnson & Powell.

J. C. POWELL was born in 1854, at Lansford, Carbon county. Moved to Shenandoah at an early age. Taught in the public schools of Schuylkill county for seven years. Attended the Millersville State Normal School, Chittenden College of Philadelphia, and Bloomsburg State Normal School. Was employed on the Shenandoah *Herald* for eight years, and helped to establish the *Colliery Engineer*, now published in Scranton. Came to Wilkes-Barre in 1883, and ever since has been one of the editors and proprietors of the *Record*.

WILLIAM P. RIEG was born in Wilkes-Barre, Pennsylvania, March 1, 1872. Son of Prof. Jacob Rieg. Educated in public schools of Wilkes-Barre. Began the study of Music in his sixth year, and appeared before the public in his fourteenth year. One of the founders of the Rieg Quartette. In 1892-3, Musical Director of Music Hall Orchestra, and the season of 1893 Musical Director of Humphrey's Comedians. Mr. Rieg is one of the leading violinists of this section.

CHARLES VINCENT EDWARDS was born in Salem township, Luzerne county, Pennsylvania, in 1860. Went to school in Salem township and at Wilkes-Barre; was at home until his twenty-first year. Learned the carpenter trade with E. T. Long, Wilkes-Barre. Was foreman for Contractor Long for four years. In 1889 began as a contractor and now resides in Kingston, and is carrying on the business of carpenter and builder. Married in 1880 to Euphemia Hutchison.

WILLIAM H. DEAN was born in Illinois. Educated at Lehigh University, taking the degrees of Analytical Chemist and Engineer of Mines. Occupation, Analytical and Consulting Chemist; Professor of Physics and Chemistry in the Harry Hillman Academy.

WILLIAM C. SHEPHERD, eldest son of W. H. and Lydia A. Shepherd, was born in the city of Philadelphia, August 16, 1862. He resided in that city until April, 1868, when he with his family removed to Wilkes-Barre. He received all of his general education in the public schools of this city. In April, 1879, he was compelled to leave the High School on account of failing eyesight. He then learned the carpenter trade with his father. After graduating in the Commercial Course of the Wyoming Seminary in June, 1883, he has been successively foreman, book-keeper and assistant superintendent of his father's business. During the past few years he has given his attention also to the study of Architecture. On November 1, 1891, he became a member of the firm of W. H. Shepherd & Sons, which is well established with most favorable auspices for the future. April 24, 1890, he was married to Alice M., eldest daughter of Dr. and Mrs. Maris Gibson of this city. They have two children, Harold and Miriam.

GEORGE HENRY ROSS was born in Schuylkill county, Pennsylvania, August 13, 1862. Educated in the public schools; learned the trade of blacksmith. In 1886, entered the drug business with his brother, E. E. Ross, in Luzerne, Pennsylvania, where he is now employed. President of the Borough Council in 1890. Assessor at the present time.

MARTIN POOLEY, born in Michigan, August, 1863. His parents moved to Buckhorn, Columbia county, two years later, where he received a common school education. In 1881 went to Nanticoke to learn the printing trade. Came to Kingston in 1886, where he has since resided, and at present proprietor of a Job Printing Establishment in that place.

GEORGE A. PEHLE was born at White Haven, Pennsylvania, July 21, 1852. Educated in Wilkes-Barre and took the commercial course at Wyoming Seminary, Kingston, and also one year at the Harry Hillman Academy. In 1871 entered the drug store of Peacock, Lafferty & Company, of Wilkes-Barre, and learned the drug business. In 1874 assumed charge of Dr. Lape's drug store at Nanticoke. In 1874 established his present drug and general merchandise business at Warrior Run. Postmaster in 1880. An Elder in the Nanticoke Presbyterian Church. At the present time a Deacon and Superintendent of the Baptist Church, of Warrior Run. A member of the Good Templars and an active Prohibitionist since 1880. In 1880 married Miss Herda Myers, a niece of Reuben J. Flick. Mrs. Pehle is president of the Young People's Union. Mr. Pehle is a member of the Prohibition County Committee.

CHARLES S. GABEL was born in Philadelphia, Pennsylvania, November 21, 1839. Went to school in that city. Went in the manufacturing of cigars in Wilkes-Barre in 1861. In 1862 enlisted in the 143d Pennsylvania Volunteers and served through the war; was taken prisoner at the battle of Gettysburg in the first day's fight; took parole on the field. Married in 1866 to Mary H. Zaun, of Wilkes-Barre. In 1870 became proprietor of the Old Fell House, corner of Washington and Northampton streets. For six years he kept a cafe on the south side of South Main street and two years on Northampton street. On the first of April, 1893, moved into the Engel Block and opened the Delmar House, on South Main street. He was a prominent man in the secret societies; Brigadier General of the National Chieftians' League of Red Men. Mr. Gabel died July 12, 1894.

W. H. ROTHERMEL, Dentist, was born in Berks county, Pennsylvania, August 16, 1869. Educated in the Philadelphia Dental College. Graduated in 1893. Located at No. 33 West Market street, Wilkes-Barre, Pennsylvania, his present location.

IRA C. GEORGE was born in Nanticoke. Educated in that borough. Assumed at his father's death the management of his business. In 1891 engaged as Book-keeper for W. J. Rees, where he is now employed.

H. C. BRODHEAD, born at Mauch Chunk and educated in Philadelphia. Began his mining career at Wanamie in the early 70's for the Lehigh Coal and Navigation Company. Upon their purchase of the Red Ash collieries in Plymouth, he was made engineer in charge and served in such capacity for several years. When the same collieries were absorbed into the Lehigh & Wilkes-Barre Coal Company, he was made a Division Superintendent of said Company, and after a time was transferred to Sugar Notch, at that time the most difficult division in the company's possession. After several years service there he was in 1883, promoted to the Assistant General Outside Superintendency, which place he held till his resignation in 1888. His large experience obtained in early life he has been able to utilize profitably in the care of his individual interests in several collieries, all of which have been successful.

REV. JONATHAN K. PECK came from New England ancestry. His father, Rev. Luther Hoyt Peck, was born in Connecticut, and his mother, Mary Kinyon, was born in Rhode Island. The subject of this sketch was born in the town of Pitcher, New York, December 31st, 1824. His father was a hard working farmer and mechanic and he was early schooled in both kinds of work. At the age of seventeen he came into Pennsylvania and found a home with relatives and friends in fair Wyoming Valley. He prepared for college in Wyoming Seminary; taught several terms of school and went to Dickinson College in 1849; graduated in 1852. He taught a select school for one year in Maryland and joined the Wyoming Conference in the summer of 1853, and preached in regular charges for thirty years including four years as Presiding Elder of the Honesdale District. He was married to Mary Searle, of Plains, in April, 1857. During two years of superannuation, viz.: 1884-85 he had the post of Librarian of the Assembly of the State of New York. He was once a candidate for the Assembly of Pennsylvania from Wayne and Pike counties, but was not elected. Mr. Peck's ministry covers a period of forty years. His book entitled, "The Seven Wonders of the New World," is pronounced a very fascinating book and is having quite an extensive sale. He is called a preacher of "Original" Sermons and is said to wield a versatile pen. His historical papers are pronounced vivid and reliable. He is happy in his retirement and a friend to the whole people and a lover of God.

GEORGE J. STEGMAIER was born in Wilkes-Barre, 1858. Son of Charles Stegmaier. Educated in the German and English schools of this city and one year at St. Vincent College, Westmoreland county, Pennsylvania. Learned the machinist trade and followed it for several years. Mr. Stegmaier is an athlete, and a great lover of out-door exercise and patron of all field sports. In 1888 was elected to the Legislature, having the largest vote ever given to a candidate for that office in this district. Was defeated for Sheriff in 1889. Is public spirited and is also a member of many societies. Assistant Chief of the Wilkes-Barre Fire Department, has been a member fifteen years. Married May G. Costello, May, 1889. Has three children.

A. GOTTHOLD was born in Frankfort-on-the-Main, Germany, 1844. Educated in his native city. Came to the United States in his seventeenth year, settled in New York City and followed the trade of wig maker and hair dresser. Came to Wilkes-Barre in 1868. Member of the Saengerbund and Liedertafel singing societies, being secretary of the first named. Mr. Gotthold is an honorary member of several singing societies in New York City, and Reading, Pennsylvania.

ISAAC E. ROSS, M. D., was born 1832, in Bradford county, Pennsylvania. Educated in the Lewisburg University. Graduated from the Geneva Medical College 1867. Came to this valley in 1883, and has been in continuous practice in Wilkes-Barre ever since. Joined the Luzerne County Medical Society in 1883. The last male descendant of the name of original Ross family in the valley. There were three Rosses who came here as original settlers. His great grandmother, Mrs. General Ross, carried her son, Jesse Ross, across to Connecticut when driven out by the Pennamites.

MORRIS SULLIVAN was born April, 1847, in Ireland. Came to this country in 1859. Went to school in Wyoming Valley where he has lived most of his life. Went into the United States service on the 19th of April, 1861; served three years and was discharged and enlisted again; was wounded and taken prisoner at Georgetown, South Carolina; made his escape and was recaptured again after nine days, and was released at the close of the war. Chairman of the Master Painters' Association of Pennsylvania, Vice Superior Chieftian of the State League of the Red Men, also Past Sachem; member of the Grand Army and Heptasophs.

ROBERT BAUR, born December 25, 1825, in Ulm, Kingdom Wurtemburg. After passing the high school learned the trade of a book-binder, and after participating in the Revolution in 1848 emigrated to America, arriving in December, '48. After working for three years at his trade in Philadelphia he came to Wilkes-Barre in June, 1851, became proprietor of the *Democratic Wachter* the July following and has edited and published it to date. In 1868 he established the *Samstag Abend* (Saturday Evening), a paper mainly devoted to literature, both papers being alive to-day.

GUSTAVE ADOLPH BAUR, only son of Robert Baur, born December 1, 1860. After passing Wyoming Seminary and Commercial College learned the printing business in his father's office. Worked in New York, Chicago, San Francisco, and returned after a three years' absence from home and entered into partnership with his father under firm name of Robert Baur & Son. To his energy, management and popularity the firm owes the greater part of its success, having grown from three presses to six, and from eight employes to twenty-five. The business is located since 1862 at No. 3 South Main street, Wilkes-Barre.

GEORGE L. WEITZEL was born in Weilenburg, Germany, August 28, 1849. Came to the United States at four years of age. Went to school in Paterson, New Jersey, in the German Academy for three years. Lived in New York until 1859, then moved with his parents to Paterson, New Jersey, and there learned the business of Decorator and Scene Artist. Came to Wilkes-Barre in 1870 and established business on the old Bowman's corner on the south side of Square. In 1884 established his business consisting of paints and wall paper at No. 51 Hazle street. Mr. Weitzel has finished up most of the finest residences in Wilkes-Barre. Was School Director in the Eleventh Ward. Connected with various singing and other societies. Charter member of I. O. F., 704.

PETER SCHAFFERT was born in Bavaria, Germany, October 28, 1840. Came to Wilkes-Barre in 1854. At the present time is proprietor of the Schappert House, South Main street. Is a trustee of the Sængerbund.

B. J. COBLEIGH, M. D., was born near Pottsville, Schuylkill county, January 10, 1863. Educated in the public schools of Plymouth, Luzerne county, and Wilkes-Barre Academy and Bloomsburg Normal School. Studied medicine and graduated from Jefferson Medical College, Philadelphia, class of 1883. Took a special course in eye and ear surgery, which branch of the profession he has practiced since. Married Miss Margaret Edwards, youngest daughter of Daniel Edwards, Kingston, and is now located on Market street in that town.

J. MILTON NICHOLSON was born in Salem, Wayne county, Pennsylvania, August 29, 1828. Remained on the homestead engaged in farming and school teaching until 1860, when he entered the employ of the Delaware, Lackawanna and Western Railroad Company as agent at Hopbottom, Susquehanna county, Pennsylvania, at which place he was Postmaster during Abraham Lincoln's first term, his commission bearing date of April 10, 1861. Came to Kingston June 6, 1865, as telegraph train dispatcher, which position he occupied until January 1, 1881, since which time he has been ticket agent at that station.

CHESTER WILCOX was born in Plymouth, Pennsylvania. Attended the public schools of Pittston. Has followed manufacturing of brick and building all his life, and built many of the brick buildings of Plymouth, where he lived for sixteen years. Has lived for a number of years in Kingston. His father was one of the first brick makers in the valley. Mr. Wilcox is a fine musician and gives his services free for church and local entertainments.

LEWIS LEONIDAS ROGERS, M. D., born at Huntsville, Pennsylvania. Eldest son of Dr. J. J. Rogers. Educated at the public schools, Wyoming Seminary, College of Physicians and Surgeons, Baltimore, Maryland; Philadelphia Lying-in Hospital, and Jefferson Medical College, Philadelphia, from which he graduated March 12, 1881. Took a postgraduate course in Gynæcology under Professors Baer and Goodell at the University of Pennsylvania. Located at Kingston in the fall of 1881, where he has been engaged in general practice ever since. He is a member of the Luzerne County, Lehigh Valley, and Pennsylvania State Medical Societies; an official member of the Methodist Episcopal Church; Lecturer on Physiology and Hygiene at Wyoming Seminary; one of the organizers of the Kingston Young Men's Christian Association and its Vice-President for two years. Dr. Rogers is a self-educated man, having taught in the public and graded schools for six years previous to his studying medicine.

EDWARD E. ROSS, born at Tuscarora, Schuylkill county, Pennsylvania, October 17, 1855. On arriving at legal age, was sent to the public schools; attended regularly until old enough to pick slate in the breaker, after which attended school during idle time and in the coldest part of the winter. Commenced teaching at the age of fifteen years, and followed the profession until 1885, teaching in the counties of Schuylkill, Northumberland, Union and Luzerne. From 1885 to 1887 established a lucrative drug business at Luzerne. Was then appointed Outside Foreman for the Northwest Coal Company, Limited, at Carbondale, Pennsylvania. Resigned this position in 1889; returned to Luzerne county and re-entered the profession of teaching. Was a candidate for the County Superintendency of Public Schools in 1891. Is now Principal of the Public Schools of Luzerne.

ISAAC GERHARD ECKERT, son of George J. Eckert, was born at Reading, Pennsylvania, August 21, 1858. Pennsylvania German descent on both father's and mother's side. Graduate of Reading High School and Reading Business College. Student at Lafayette College in civil engineering course. Graduate of State School of Mines, Golden, Colorado, as an assayer. Married in Denver, Colorado, June, 1879, to Miss Lizzie Ella Smith, daughter of Levi M. Smith, formerly of Kingston. Book-keeper and assistant cashier in the banking-house of L. J. Smith & Co. Secretary Golden City Republican Committee. Member Jefferson county, Colorado, Republican Committee. Assistant Chief Fire Department. Secretary and Treasurer Library and Reading Room Association. Manager of Golden Opera House. Returned East in the fall of 1881. Manager of George J. Eckert's Fire Brick Works, Reading, until the fall of 1883, when he moved to Kingston. Outside Foreman of Harry E. and Forty Fort Collieries; at present book-keeper for both collieries. Secretary Forty Fort School Board. Secretary Second Legislative District Committee. Assistant Chairman Republican County Committee for Second District.

A. J. ROAT was born April 20, 1833, at Light Street, Columbia county, Pennsylvania. Moved to Forty Fort in 1841 and to Kingston in 1845. Learned the Blacksmithing trade in 1856. Married in 1856 to Mary Ann Gabriel. Carried on blacksmith and wagon work until 1878. Started in the hardware business, which he still continues. From a small business it has grown to be one of the largest in the valley, occupying four buildings. Has three sons who assist him in the business, besides employing six assistants. Has served as School Director, Councilman and Chief of Fire Department.

W. H. SHAVER, born in Dallas township, September 20, 1847. Received a common school education. Was mustered into the United States service August 20, 1862, as a member of Battery M, Second Pennsylvania Volunteer Artillery. Followed the fortunes of the Army of the Potomac until May 25, 1865, when he was honorably discharged. Took the occupation of a locomotive engineer from 1867 to March, 1887, when he went into the grocery business, where he is at present employed.

ALFRED H. COON was born in Luzerne county. Educated in the public schools. Lived in Honesdale, Pennsylvania, and became a partner with his father in building public works. Came to Kingston in 1854. Mr. Coon has filled as many contracts for public works as any man in the State, and has never left a contract unfinished. Organized and built the Wilkes-Barre and Kingston street car line, the first T rail used on a street railroad. This was the first street car line in Northeastern Pennsylvania. Mr. Coon and his brother put the first steamboat on the Susquehanna at Wilkes-Barre, and through his influence secured an appropriation to dredge the river below Wilkes-Barre.

D. H. LAKE, M. D., born in England in 1863. Came to Youngstown, Ohio in 1872, and thence to Scranton in 1878. Entered Marietta College, Marietta, Ohio, remaining three years, when he returned to Scranton and took up the study of medicine in connection with teaching. Graduated from Jefferson Medical College, Philadelphia, April, 1885. Entered the Philadelphia (Blockley) Hospital as a resident Physician, where he remained fourteen months; then in November, 1886, located in Kingston and Edwardsville, where he has since practiced his profession. His father, Rev. Lot Lake, was for eight years pastor of the Congregational Church at Scranton. He is now located in Knoxville, Tennessee, as pastor of the Knoxville Congregational Church. Married in December, 1889.

GEORGE M. PACE was born in Kingston, Pennsylvania. Graduated from the Commercial College of Wyoming Seminary in 1881. Entered the mercantile business, dealing exclusively in teas and coffees. Moved to Kingston in 1891. Purchased the Philip Goodwin estate on which he had erected a business block. Mr. Pace deals extensively in real estate.

ANEURIN EVANS was born at Summit Hill, Pennsylvania, in 1855. Son of Rev. D. E. Evans, M. D. Educated in the public schools. Graduated from Wyoming Seminary in 1872, and the Commercial College in 1873. Learned the drug business in Plymouth, Pennsylvania. In 1877 established the present drug firm of Evans & Son, Railroad street, in Kingston.

DAVID S. CLARK was born in Plains township, Luzerne county, Pennsylvania. Attended school at West Pittston. Followed blacksmithing for twenty years. Served in the Rebellion in the Second Pennsylvania Volunteers; was in the service two years. Was Postmaster at Centermoreland, Wyoming county, and appointed Postmaster at Kingston, Pennsylvania, in 1889. Has been Commander of Conygham Post and is Treasurer of the Kingston Fire Department.

GEORGE DANA KINGSLEY was born at Blakely, Lackawanna county, Pennsylvania, January 31, 1858. Was educated in the common schools at Scranton and at Whitestown Seminary, near Utica, New York. Was employed as weighmaster for a number of years, and later as Foreman of Avondale Colliery, which position he now holds. He is a member of Kingston Lodge, Free and Accepted Masons, Shekinah Royal Arch Chapter, and Dieu le Veut Commandery. Now resides in Kingston.

CHARLES J. TURPIN was born in Ohio. Came to Kingston, Pennsylvania, in his youth, and was educated in the public schools and at Wyoming Seminary. Was a Surveyor for five years, and in the mercantile business until he established his harness business on Railroad street, which he still conducts in connection with the real estate business. He served in the Army of the Potomac in Company D, 143d Regiment, for one year.

MICHAEL GARRAHAN, the subject of this sketch, was born in what is now a part of Plymouth borough, July 4, 1848. In 1860, with his father, he removed to what is known as the "Avondale Farm," where the next twenty years of his life were spent. In the year 1869 he married Miss Maggie B. Hutchison, a person of considerable intellectual attainments and more than ordinary spirituality of mind. For the next ten years both were actively engaged in home mission work, as far as other duties would allow. Owing to the failing health of his wife and family, a change of residence became a necessity. Mr. Garrahan removed to Kingston in 1880, where he now resides.

HERMAN C. MILLER was born at Leipsig, Germany. Educated in the schools of that city. Came to this country in 1847, and has been in the Furniture and Undertaking business for forty years. Served in the War of the Rebellion over three years in the Fifty-Second Regiment Pennsylvania Volunteers (Colonel Hoyt's Regiment). He is Secretary and Treasurer of the Pennsylvania Volunteers' Association of the Fifty-Second Regiment, and has served as President of the Tri-County Funeral Directors' Association and Vice-President of the State Association, and as School Director and Town Councilman of Kingston borough.

CHRISTIAN BACH was born in Rhoden, F. Waldack, April 10, 1850. Was educated in his native town. Learned the trade of Tailor at home. Spent several years in Frankfort-on-the-Main and Wiesbaden. Came to the United States in 1871. Came to Kingston in 1875 and established his present business of Merchant Tailoring. Mr. Bach was the originator of the Electric Light, Heat and Power Company of that place and is its President. One of the originators of the Kingston Young Men's Christian Association, and has taken an active interest in all borough and church matters.

W. L. MYLES, the subject of this sketch, is a typical Cambro-American, having first seen the light of day at Merthyr Tydfil, South Wales, April 25, 1848. His father had to toil hard to procure the means of support, but by practicing economy and diligence, the parents were enabled to give their son the benefit of a few years' education in the parish school. At the tender age of eleven years he was apprenticed to the dry-goods business at The Cloth Hall, in his native town, and followed that business until, with his parents, he emigrated to America in the spring of 1867, and settled with them at Johnstown, Pennsylvania. In 1869-70 he was employed by the Morris Run Coal Company as weighmaster, and 1870-74 we find him as book-keeper in the employ of Connell & Company, Meadow Brook Colliery, Scranton, and Co-Operative Store, Hyde Park. He then returned to Johnstown, (having married in 1870 to Miss M. Llewellyn of that ill-fated town,) and opened a grocery establishment. He was afterward employed at "The Checkered Front," Pittsburgh, from which city, in 1877, he came to Wilkes-Barre and entered the employ of D. C. Jeremy, where he remained until 1885, when he accepted a position of trust and great responsibility with Edwards & Company of Kingston, which position he has held up to the present time, where he may be found trusted and respected by his employers. He does not confine himself to the pressing demands of his business, in the discharge of which he is most capable, but delights to aid in the promotion of every good cause that has for its object the elevation of his fellow men. The Young Men's Christian Association elected him as their first President, which position he filled for nearly eighteen months.

JAMES D. EDWARDS was born in Scranton, Pennsylvania, August 6, 1862. Moved to Plymouth and later to Kingston, Pennsylvania. Educated in the public schools of Plymouth. Entered the office of the Kingston Coal Company in 1879, and is now paymaster. Mr. Edwards lives in Edwardsdale. Has been School Director for four years, and takes an active part in local affairs.

CALVIN DYMOND was born in Exeter township, Luzerne county, Pennsylvania. September 17, 1837, and attended the township schools. Became a clerk in Exeter. Engaged in farming, and in 1868 opened with Mr. Lewis of Kingston, Pennsylvania, the meat stand of Dymond & Lewis. Served four terms as Town Councilman and three years as Assessor. In 1887, with Mr. Lewis, built Dymond & Lewis Hall. He deals in and owns considerable real estate, and takes an active part in borough affairs.

HENRY KUNKLE, M. D., was born at New Ringgold, Pennsylvania. Educated in the public schools and State Normal School at Kutztown, Pennsylvania; graduated from Lafayette in 1887. Studied medicine with Dr. Wenger at Reading. Graduated from the College of Physicians and Surgeons of Baltimore in 1889. Practiced in Brooklyn, New York. Removed to Kingston in 1889. Member of the Luzerne and Lehigh and State Medical Societies. Received the degree of A. M. from the Lafayette College in 1890.

CLINTON W. BOONE was born in Huntington township, Luzerne county, Pennsylvania, March 16, 1832. Educated in the public schools. Became a Carpenter and Builder. Moved to Arkansas. Enlisted as a private in September, 1861, and served four years, being promoted a Sergeant, Second Lieutenant. First Lieutenant; in 1864 was promoted Captain, and the last year of the War was commander of a battalion, and was mustered out of service September, 1865. Returned to Bloomsburg, Pennsylvania, and in 1875 moved to Kingston. In 1877 was elected Justice of the Peace of that town.

RALPH B. VAUGHN was born at Wyalusing, Pennsylvania. Educated in the public schools and at Wyoming Seminary. Telegraph Operator for the Lehigh Valley Railroad, and at the present time Freight and Coal Agent for the Delaware, Lackawanna and Western Railroad at Kingston.

C. W. BOUGHTIN was born in Newbury, Orange county, New York. Educated in the public schools. Came to Kingston, Pennsylvania, in 1849, and established his present business of Carriage Making and Blacksmithing. Has served the Borough of Kingston as School Director, Assessor, Town Council, and other offices.

ALANSON B. TYRRELL, born in Watertown, Connecticut, on June 8, 1833. Was educated in the public schools of that place. Learned his trade as carpenter and joiner in Waterbury, Connecticut. Came to Wyoming, Luzerne county, Pennsylvania, in 1855, and began building breakers in 1857 through the Anthracite coal field, and was the most extensive breaker builder in the United States. He moved to Kingston in the year 1874, where he died. Was married in the year 1855 to Miss Susab S. Marks, of Wyoming, Pennsylvania, formerly of Waterbury, Connecticut. Had served his borough as Councilman and School Director. Left four children—Esther M., a graduate from the Woman's Medical College, Philadelphia; Jennie M. (Mrs. C. E. Roats, resident of Kingston; Fred. W., resident of Wilkes-Barre, an accountant and also in the grocery business in Kingston; B. Frank, resident of Kingston, an accountant and grocer in Kingston.

P. BUTLER REYNOLDS was born in Wilkes-Barre, Pennsylvania. Son of C. W. Reynolds, well known in the valley in his day. His mother was a daughter of Pierce Butler, descendant of Zebulon Butler, commander at the Massacre. Mr. Reynolds was educated in public schools of Wilkes-Barre and at Wyoming Seminary at Kingston. Was surveyor of Luzerne county from 1874 to 1875, and is well known as a Mining and Civil Engineer. At the present time is senior member of the insurance firm of Reynolds & Company of Wilkes-Barre.

ELLIOTT R. MORGAN was born in Northumberland county, Pennsylvania. Educated at Sunbury and Danville, Pennsylvania. Assistant postmaster at Danville for seven years. Became Secretary of the Kingston Coal Company in 1882. Has been a member of the Kingston Town Council, and officer in the Masonic Lodge and Knights Templars.

JOHN D. HOYT, born in Kingston, Pennsylvania, August 15, 1819. Son of Ziba Hoyt and Nancy Hurlbut Hoyt. Brother of ex-Governor Henry M. Hoyt, Elizabeth (wife of Abram H. Reynolds), and Anne (wife of Rev. Charles Corss). Lived in Kingston all his life. For many years Trustee and Elder in the Presbyterian Church. Father of Anne Elizabeth (wife of George Shoemaker), Martha (wife of Dr. Frederick Corss), Abram C. Hoyt, Augusta Hoyt, Edward E. Hoyt, Esq., and Henry M. Hoyt, Jr., Esq.

ADAM CLARK LAYCOCK was born in Columbia county, Pennsylvania, December 3, 1826. Entered Wyoming Seminary the first year that institution was opened. Was a wheelwright and followed other employment, and in 1866 moved to Shickshinny and assumed charge of the Salem Coal Company's store for five years. Moved to Kingston in 1876 and was employed in Edwards & Company's store. Traveled for Chapin & Pringle, marble firm. Deputy Warden of Luzerne County Prison for two years and elected Warden in 1887. Established with Mr. Chapin the firm of Laycock & Chapin, marble and granite business, in Kingston. Was a candidate before the Convention of Luzerne county for Sheriff. Mr. Laycock has taken an active part in Luzerne county politics.

FRANK HELME, son of Oliver Helme, was born in Kingston August 7, 1816. Educated in private schools in Wilkes-Barre, Pennsylvania, and graduated from the old Academy in Kingston, Pennsylvania. Moved to Wilkes-Barre in 1823, and removed to Kingston in 1831. Went in the cabinet business with his brother. In 1858 purchased the farm where he now resides.

CHARLES GRAHAM, JR., was born at Scranton, Pennsylvania. Son of Charles Graham, for many years Master Mechanic of Delaware, Lackawanna and Western shops at Kingston. Mr. Graham was educated at Wyoming Seminary and Lehigh University. Became Foreman of the Delaware, Lackawanna and Western shops at Kingston in 1883; General Foreman in 1886; Master Mechanic in 1891. Mr. Graham began working at the trade of machinist in 1876, and at thirty years of age he became Master Mechanic. He is Past Master of Kingston Masonic Lodge.

WILLIAM LOVELAND was born in Kingston, Pennsylvania, August 15, 1821. He was the second son of Elijah and Mary Buckingham Loveland, whose families were among the Puritans who came to Connecticut about 1630. He received his education in the old Academy on Main street, Kingston, and at Dana's Academy in Wilkes-Barre. Mr. Loveland has always been a farmer. At his father's death he assumed control of the family homestead in Kingston. He has aided to develop and sustain the most important local interests. As a business man he has ever been active and prominent. He has been for years an officer and member of the Presbyterian Church. Mr. Loveland identified himself with the Republican party at its organization and has been deeply interested in its progress to the present time, although never an active politician. In 1856 he married Lydia Hurlbut of Arkport, New York, a granddaughter of Christopher Hurlbut, a surveyor well known in the Wyoming Valley in the pioneer days and a native of Connecticut.

REV. L. L. SPRAGUE, A. M., D. D., born December 23, 1844, in the town of Beekman, Dutchess county, New York. Educated at Wyoming Seminary. Completed a college course by private study. Degree of A. M. conferred by Alleghany College and that of D. D. by the Wesleyan University. Was principal of LeRaysville Academy in 1865. In 1868 was elected Principal of Wyoming College of Business and in 1882 President of Wyoming Seminary. Joined the Wyoming Conference in 1874. Has been continuously teaching since 1868.

REV. F. VON KRUG, born in Darmstadt, Germany, 1850. Educated in the schools of the same city. Attended school one year at Heidelberg. Came to this country in 1869. Preached at Bloomingburg, Ohio, seven years. Came to Kingston in December, 1886, as pastor of the Presbyterian Church.

ALEXANDER GRAY FELL, M. D., was born in Wilkes-Barre, Pennsylvania, April 20, 1861. Graduated from Princeton College in 1884, and the University of Pennsylvania in 1887. Member of the medical staff of the Wilkes-Barre City Hospital in 1890. Located at No. 42 North Washington street, Wilkes-Barre, Pennsylvania, where he is now located. Member of the Luzerne Medical Society. Son of D. A. Fell. His grandfather, on the maternal side, was brought here from Scotland to work the old Baltimore mines. He sank the Empire and a number of other shafts.

CHARLES ORION THURSTON, born in Barre, Vermont, February 23, 1857. Graduated, with honor in chemistry, from Dartmouth College in 1884. Principal Colebrook Academy, Colebrook, New Hampshire, 1884. Principal Newport, New Hampshire, High School, 1885-6. Professor of Science and Mathematics Marston's University School for Boys, Baltimore, Maryland, 1887-8. Professor of Science Wyoming Seminary since 1889.

JOHN H. RACE, a native of Pennsylvania, was born March 10, 1862. Being the son of a Methodist minister, his early education was much interrupted by the periodical removals from place to place. When but a lad of fifteen he began earning his own livelihood, being engaged as a clerk in a general dry goods and grocery store. Later he was employed as a clerk in the postoffice at Tunkhannock, the county seat of Wyoming. From this place he entered Wyoming Seminary. During his preparatory school years he supported himself by keeping the books of the institution. Graduating from the Seminary in 1886, he entered the College of New Jersey at Princeton. Took the full classical course, and graduated from College in June, 1890. In March of the same year he was admitted as a probationer to the New Jersey Conference of the Methodist Episcopal Church, and appointed to Island Heights, New Jersey. During the summer of 1890 he was elected to the Department of Rhetoric in Wyoming Seminary.

RUFUS B. HOWLAND was born in Danby, Tompkins county, New York, September 15, 1851. He prepared for college at the Ithaca Academy and at Wyoming Seminary. Entering Cornell University in 1869, he graduated in 1872 with the first class that took the full course at that institution. In 1873 he was elected to the Chair of Mathematics in Wyoming Seminary, which position he still holds. From 1877 to 1881 he also taught the Natural Sciences in the same institution. In 1887 he published a volume entitled "Elements of the Conic Sections."

HUGO V. STADLER was born in Constance, Germany. Educated at his native place and Berlin. Studied music under prominent masters and finished at Berlin. Taught music in that city. Came to the United States in 1867, and taught music in New York for three years. Came to Kingston in 1871; became Musical Director of the musical department of Wyoming Seminary at Kingston, and has filled that position successfully for twenty-three years. Under his direction the musical department of Wyoming Seminary has become one of the largest in this part of the State.

WILLIS L. DEAN, born in Waverly, Pennsylvania, February, 1857. Educated at Madison Academy and the Wyoming Seminary. Taught in Lowell's Commercial College, Binghamton, New York, from 1873 to 1875. Elected Professor of Penmanship in Wyoming Seminary and Commercial College in 1875, and when Dr. Sprague was elected President of the Seminary, in 1883, he was promoted to the Principalship of the Commercial College, which position he still holds.

E. I. WOLFE was born at Muhlenburg, Pennsylvania, and was educated in the public schools and at Huntington Mills Academy. He has held various positions in the public schools of the valley, including principalships at Plymouth, Beach Haven and Nanticoke, and is now in charge of the Teachers' Preparatory Department of Wyoming Seminary. In addition to his duties there, he has published four annual issues of the *Luzerne Institute*, a paper circulating largely among the educators of the State; and the "Practical Speller," an advanced work in orthography. He is quite popular as a lecturer at local Institutes, and has established a very successful summer school for teachers at Wyoming Seminary.

FRED. M. DAVENPORT was born August 27, 1866, in Salem, Massachusetts. Seventeen years ago he moved with his parents to New Milford, Susquehanna county, Pennsylvania, and has since been a resident of this State. His course preparatory to admission to college was taken at Wyoming Seminary, from which institution he was graduated in 1885. The succeeding four years were spent in study at Wesleyan University, Middletown, Connecticut. In 1889 he was engaged as instructor in Greek and Latin at Wyoming Seminary. In addition to his work as teacher, he did considerable lecturing and preaching, and was the Wyoming Conference Secretary of Epworth Leagues. The family to which he belongs is a branch of the old English Davenport stock, whence come likewise the Davenports of Plymouth. Pastor of the Methodist Episcopal Church at Yonkers, New York.

REV. MANLEY S. HARD, D. D., is fifty years old. He was born in New York. Was graduated from Syracuse University and was President of the Alumni Association for two or three terms. He has been Pastor of the Methodist Episcopal Churches in New York State, as follows: First Church, of Ilion; Centenary Church, Syracuse; First Church, Ithaca; Presiding Elder of Elmira District; Hedding Church, Elmira; First Church, Canandaigua, Centenary Church, Binghamton, and later Presiding Elder of Wyoming District. He was a member of the General Conference in 1884 and 1888, and one of the Secretaries of both bodies. He is also a Trustee of Syracuse University; Wyoming Conference Seminary, and a Manager of the New York State Custodial Asylum for Feeble Minded Women. His present residence is Kingston, his first living in Pennsylvania. Now one of the Secretaries of the Church Extension Society of the Methodist Episcopal Church.

THOMAS F. HEFFERNAN was born in Plymouth Township in 1871. Educated in Wyoming Seminary. Teacher in the Plymouth Township schools, and in January, 1892, became Assistant West Side Correspondent for the *Wilkes Barre Record* and the *Times*. In May of that year assumed the entire charge of that department.

GEORGE HOLLENBACK BUTLER, born in Kingston Township, Luzerne county, Pennsylvania, September 2, 1857. Is second son of James M. Butler. Was educated at private schools. Read law with E. P. and J. V. Darling. Was admitted to the bar of Luzerne county in 1881, and is now engaged in the profession. He is a Republican in politics. Has been elected Burgess of Dorranceton Borough a number of times and also a Justice of the Peace. Is married and has one son, John Lord Butler.

THOMAS DAVENPORT CARLE, son of Ira, of Kingston, was born in Kingston, Pennsylvania, April 7, 1846. Educated in the public schools. Spent eight years in the West with an engineer corps and finally returned to Kingston in 1878. Now resides in Dorranceton where he has a store and is contracting in stone work and excavations. Married Mary Gervey, of Memphis, Missouri. Has six children.

Dr. Charles Paxton Knapp, of Wyoming, Pennsylvania, was born at No. 24 North Franklin Street, Wilkes-Barre, Pennsylvania, August 13th, 1853, and is the son of George and Ellen Eliza (Hurlbut) Knapp. The doctor's ancestors are of Anglo-Saxon origin, and came early to this country—the Knapps in 1630, the Hurlburts in 1635, and both took part in the early Indian wars and were soldiers of the Revolution and war of 1812. Dr. Knapp is a graduate of Lafayette College, Easton, Pennsylvania, and of Bellevue Hospital Medical College, New York City. He began the practice of medicine in Wyoming, Pennsylvania, June 1st, 1878. June 30th, 1880, he married Cora Josephine Knapp, of West Pittston, Pennsylvania. They have two children, Elizabeth and Karl. Since residing in Wyoming Dr. Knapp has been a member of both Borough Council and School Board, and is one of County Visitors of the State Board of Public Charities. He is a member of the D. K. E. Fraternity and P. M. of Wyoming Lodge No. 468, F. & A. M., also a member of Luzerne County Medical Society, Pennsylvania State Medical Society, American Medical Association, and a Fellow of the American Academy of Medicine. The Knapp and Hurlbut families have been connected with Wyoming Valley from an early date, the former becoming residents here in 1798, the latter in 1779. The first cording machine of which we have any record was owned and run by Col. Naphtali Hurlburt at Old Forge in 1805. Col. Hurlbut was also Sheriff of Luzerne County in 1825. His wife, Olive (Smith) Hurlbut, was daughter of Dr. William Hooker Smith, a respected practitioner of medicine in the valley for nearly fifty years and who, with James Sutton, built and operated a forge of 400 pounds of iron capacity in twelve hours, at the falls of the Lackawanna from ore procured from the surrounding hills, in 1789. George Knapp, in connection with Gould P. Parrish, built and operated two powder mills on Solomon's Creek and four mills on Wapwallopen Creek (now owned by the Duponts), with 300 kegs per day capacity, in the 50's. He also introduced the manufacture of bricks by machinery in Wilkes-Barre in the 60's. Zephaniah Knapp was a local botanist and horticulturist of some repute, and his son, Dr. Avery Knapp, of Pittston, is also a geologist and botanist of local repute, and chronicler of the doings of half a century ago.

George Landon Marcy, son of Rev. Nicholson B. Marcy, was born in Mehoopany, Pennsylvania, May 31, 1856. Educated in the public schools and Monroe Academy. Early life was spent on a farm. Taught school. Followed the trade of carpenter and painter and is now a contractor and builder at Dorranceton. Active in church work and takes an active part in temperance work. Married Miss M. U. Frear, of Beaumont, Pennsylvania, July 20, 1878.

Edward D. Schooley was born in 1864 in Monroe Township, Wyoming county, Pennsylvania. Went to school at the Monroe Academy, Beaumont. Taught school seven years. In 1882 came to Kingston and rented the D., L. & W. farm, which he has farmed since. Married in 1883 to Miss Mary Evans, of Wyoming county.

John J. McDonald was born in Edwardsville, Pennsylvania, March 6, 1870. Attended the public schools and Wyoming Seminary. Coal inspector for the Kingston Coal Company. Sale clerk. Coal inspector and weighmaster for the Delaware, Lackawanna and Western Railroad. In 1892 established with Thomas S. Lawless the business of furniture dealer and undertaking in Kingston. Purchased his partner's share in 1893 and continues the business.

WILLIAM E. DOKON was born in Mount Holly, New Jersey, in the year 1843, where he resided until the breaking out of the Rebellion. He was at that time nineteen years of age, and was serving an apprenticeship at the cabinet-making and undertaking business with the firm of Thomas F. Keeler & Son. He enlisted in the Twenty-Third New Jersey Infantry and was attached to the First New Jersey Brigade, Sixth Army Corps. His regiment was commanded by Colonel E. Bird Grubb, the present Minister to Spain. After serving out the time of enlistment, he came to Pennsylvania and located in Wilkes-Barre; worked at his trade as cabinet-maker with Blackman & Laning, also at the carpenter business. In 1871 he went to Plains, in the Company Store, on the river road from Wilkes-Barre to Pittston. After serving as book-keeper for four years with Amsbry & Company, Crane & Leonard and Tozer, Crane & Leonard, he started business for himself at Plains, in the furniture and undertaking business, where he was successful for ten years. During his residence at Plains he was always closely identified with the interests of the town. A member of the Methodist Episcopal Church, and for ten successive years, Superintendent of its Sunday-School. In 1883 he came to Wilkes-Barre, leased the store in the Commercial Block, 25 West Market street, where he remained eight years in the undertaking and music business. He is a member of the Grand Army of the Republic and was Commander of Conyngham Post of this city.

HENRY EVANS, born in Wales, January 6, 1857. Came with his parents to this county the same year. Was educated in the common schools. Worked in coal breakers and coal mines. Attended night school and graduated in Wyoming Commercial College. Elected County Commissioner in November, 1887, and re-elected November, 1890.

FRANK DEITRICK, born in Carbondale, Pennsylvania, April 19, 1867. Removed with his parents to Wilkes-Barre when thirteen years of age. Was educated at Carbondale public schools. Appointed Assistant City Clerk in 1880; served as such until January, 1887, when he was elected City Clerk, to fill vacancy caused by resignation of J. C. Bell, and has held that position since then.

WESLEY ELLSWORTH WOODRUFF was born in Salem, Wayne County, Pennsylvania, in 1865. Son of the Rev. J. O. Woodruff. Graduated at Wyoming Seminary in 1883 and Wesleyan University in the class of 1887; received a degree from Wesleyan in 1890 for a special course in history and political science. Served on the *Record of the Times* staff from 1887 until 1890, when he left the *Record* on account of night work, when he became City Editor of the *Evening Leader*. He was during his college days connected with the college publication, and has at various times written for the New York and Philadelphia papers. Mr. Woodruff is an honor to his profession, and has fine literary taste. His account of the Mud Run disaster was an event in journalism.

ROBERT HUTCHISON, born 1835 in Nova Scotia. Attended school at Minersville, Pennsylvania, having moved there in 1838. In 1847 moved to Hazleton, to Schuykill in 1850, to Dauphin County in 1852, and then to Plymouth Township. With his father and some other gentlemen sunk a shaft and put in the first mining pump and hoisted the first coal on the west side—1854. For twenty years he had been with the Delaware, Lackawanna and Western Coal Company at the Boston and Pittston mines as the Outside Superintendent. Was a member of the Kingston town council and was a Trustee of the Kingston Presbyterian Church. Died February 27, 1894.

HENRY WHITE DUNNING, son of Charles Sully Dunning, was born in Franklin. New York, September 11, 1858. Graduated from Williston Seminary. East Hampton, Massachusetts, 1878. In 1879 entered the freshman class of Princeton College, New Jersey; remained there for one year and was obliged to discontinue his studies on account of his father's illness. Began to read law in the office of William H. Lee in Honesdale, Pennsylvania, and continued his legal studies with Hubbard B. Payne, Esq., in Wilkes-Barre. Admitted to the Luzerne bar June 5, 1882. Assistant Superintendent of the First Presbyterian Sunday School; Recording Secretary of the Board of Managers of the Y. M. C. A.; Lecturer in the commercial department of Wyoming Seminary.

J. S. SANDERS, editor of the Wilkes-Barre *Telephone*, was born in Mahoning Township, near Danville, Pennsylvania, August 10, 1834. At the age of 19 he commenced to learn the printing business with Colonel Valentine Best, of Danville *Intelligencer*. After serving an apprenticeship he subsequently became the editor and publisher of the *Intelligencer*, which paper he conducted for three years. He afterwards purchased the Berwick *Gazette*, and published that paper until 1870, when he removed to Hazleton where he owned and published the *Sentinel* until 1879, when he moved to Plymouth and printed the Plymouth *Record* until 1884, when he became associated with Charles D. Linskill in the publication of Wilkes-Barre *Telephone*, with which journal he is still connected. Mr. Sanders was Postmaster at Berwick under the administration of President Johnson. He is connected with a number of the benevolent societies of this city and is at present a Grand Tustee of the Knights of the Golden Eagle of this state.

BUTLER DILLEY, born in Hanover 1834; educated in Wilkes-Barre; a printer; in the regular army; in the late war Quartermaster of the Eighth Pennsylvania Volunteers in the three months service; Captain of Company L, Twenty-third Regiment. Was Supervisor and is now Burgess of Kingston Borough.

CORNELIUS CRONIN was born in Bradford, Yorkshire, England; began his education in the Christian Brothers' School; went to Ireland at sixteen and attended the academies for six years; emigrated to America in his twenty-second year; served as mine clerk, school teacher, agent; for a number of years was in the office of the Kingston Coal Company; has contributed many articles on economical questions to the metropolitan press.

CYRUS STRAW, born in Hazleton, Luzerne county, Pennsylvania, October 1, 1837. Lived all his life in this county. Educated at Wyoming Seminary. Lived on a farm. Taught school. Been in the grain and lumber business and taken an active part in politics. Served in the War of the Rebellion, Company K. Eighty-First Pennsylvania Volunteers. Wounded at the battle of Antietam. Discharged for disability from wound, May, 1863. Elected Commissioner of Luzerne in 1885, for a period of three years. Always active in public school interests. At present a member of the firm of Phelps, Straw & Company, Hardware Merchants, Wilkes-Barre.

ROBERT P. ROBINSON, ex-Sheriff and Deputy Treasurer of Luzerne county, was born in Fairmount township, Luzerne county, Pennsylvania. Taught school and farmed until 1882, when he was appointed County Auditor by the Court; served three years, and as Clerk of the County Commissioners five years. Elected Sheriff of Luzerne county in 1886 by a plurality of 1292 votes—the first Republican Sheriff of Luzerne county.

SIDNEY ROBY MINER, son of Charles A. Miner, was born July 28, 1863. Graduated at the Wilkes-Barre Academy in the class of 1883; and passed the Harvard entrance examinations in the following fall. Took a post-graduate course at the Academy; went abroad for two months, and entered college in the fall of 1884. Graduated from Harvard in the class of 1888; in the fall of that year entered the Law School of the University of Pennsylvania; stayed one year. In June 1889, joined the Ninth Regiment, Company D, of which his brother, Asher, was captain, and served three years. In September, 1889, entered the Prothonotary's office as a clerk and remained till January, 1890, when he returned to the office of L. D. and R. C. Shoemaker, where he had registered as a student. On January 22, 1890, helped to found the Luzerne Law Club, and was its first Secretary. June 16, 1890, was admitted to the Bar of Luzerne County. On account of the death of Hon. L. D. Shoemaker, it became necessary to find new quarters. Moved May 1, 1891, into rooms 64 and 65 Coal Exchange Building.

S. L. HAGENBAUGH, born in Luzerne county, Pennsylvania. Educated at the public schools, and at an early age began farming. In 1861 he enlisted in the Seventh Pennsylvania Infantry, and was taken prisoner in May, 1864, and was in Andersonville and other Southern prisons for ten months. Mustered out of service in April, 1865. In 1868 he came to Wilkes-Barre, and in 1884 opened an art store in that city. He has the largest and the best trade in the county. He is a member of the Grand Army.

EDWARD GUNSTER was born in Scranton, Pennsylvania, November 8, 1860. Educated in the public and private schools and graduated from Nazareth Hall in 1876. Took a special course in accounting in New York city. Took charge of the books of several business houses in Wilkes-Barre, and in 1878 opened an office for type-writing, collecting, accounting and general office work, that has become the leading office in these lines in the State. His present offices are in the Coal Exchange, Wilkes-Barre, Pennsylvania.

JOSEPH J. McGINTY was born in Durham, England, forty-three years ago. He came, when a boy, to this country, and located with his parents near Hazleton, in this State, where he remained until he was elected to the office of Recorder of Deeds. In 1874 he was chosen School Director, and during one year of the term was Treasurer of the Board. He was elected Delegate to the Democratic State Convention which was held in Harrisburg in 1883, and was again sent by his fellow workingmen to represent them in the National Convention of the Knights of Labor at Hamilton, Canada, in 1885, and also at Cleveland, Ohio, in 1886. In 1876 he was elected Recorder of Deeds for his adopted county, by an overwhelming majority, and re-elected to the same office in 1889, when the rest of the Democratic ticket was defeated.

C. BEN JOHNSON was born in Philadelphia in 1846. Was educated at the public schools of that city. Served four years during the Civil War in the 104th Pennsylvania Volunteers and Seventh United States Veteran Volunteers. Entered journalism at the close of the War. Edited the organs of the Miners' Union 1868-75. Came to Wilkes-Barre in the latter year. Was Reading Clerk of the House of Representatives in 1883, and Secretary of the Board of Trade 1887-91. Member of the House of Representatives in the latter year. During the time not here accounted for, was on the editorial staff of the Wilkes-Barre Leader. Established the Wyoming Valley Sanitarium in 1893, is Secretary and General Manager of same.

WILLIAM BURNS DOW was born in Wilkes-Barre, Pennsylvania, January 12, 1850. Son of the late J. B. Dow, a teacher in the valley for half a century. The subject of this sketch followed the insurance buisness in Wilkes-Barre for twenty years, until five years ago, when he became proprietor of the City Steam Laundry, on West Market street, and at the same time having some dealing in the real estate and insurance business.

THOMAS SMITH, County Commissioner, was born in England. Came to this country in 1863. Followed mining for fifty years. Was an officer at different times in the Miners' Union. Elected as Commissioner of Luzerne county in 1890 and re-elected in 1893.

D. K. SPRY was born in Honesdale, Pennsylvania. Educated in the public schools, and served in the War of the Rebellion in the Pennsylvania Cavalry. Studied pharmacy with D. W. Wells and George Wells of Wilkes-Barre, Pennsylvania. Was for many years the leading druggist of Plymouth, and has been identified with nearly every interest of that place. He is a successful business man and deals largely in real estate. Holds stock in most of our large industries. He resides in Wilkes-Barre at the present time.

G. W. ZEIGLER was born in Lambertville, New Jersey, in 1855. Educated in that place. Entered the telegraph office of the Pennsylvania Railroad at Trenton, New Jersey; took charge of the distribution of the Company's coal for three divisions of that road, the Belvidere, New York and Amboy divisions; resigned after serving the Company for eleven years. In 1880 became proprietor of the Glenwood House at the Delaware Water Gap, one of the largest hotels in the country. In 1886 became proprietor of the Luzerne House in Wilkes-Barre, Pennsylvania, and under his management it has secured the largest commercial trade of any hotel in the city. Mr. Zeigler held the position of Volunteer Paymaster in the Ninth Regiment with the rank of Captain. He managed the Band Fair of the Ninth Regiment. A member of the Elks and Royal Society of Good Fellows and a Master Mason.

BOYD DODSON, M. D., born in Schuylkill County 1867. Graduated at Jefferson Medical College, Philadelphia, 1889.

MINER B. AUSTIN, of Wilkes-Barre, Pennsylvania, was born at Muhlenburg, Luzerne County, Pennsylvania, January 11, 1851. At an early age he evinced a decided talent for music and at once took up the study. He studied with private teachers of Wilkes-Barre and Scranton and at Wyoming Seminary where he also received his education. He came to Wilkes-Barre in October, 1868, and secured a position as clerk in the music store of Prof. L. Praetorius in which capacity he was employed about four years. He then took up the work of his chosen profession as teacher of music and his efforts have been crowned with a marked success. He was organist of the First Methodist Episcopal Church for fifteen years and filled the position with credit to himself and to the eminent satisfaction of that Church. He is a cornet player in the Ninth Regiment Band, of which he has been a member since its organization.

WILLIAM E. BENNETT, born in Jersey City, May 5, 1853; received a public school and academical education. Followed occupation of clerk, principally with Coal and Railroad Companies. Married Isadore, daughter of John M. Connor, in November, 1882; has three children—Bruce, Helen and Louise. Elected County Auditor in 1887; re-elected, 1890 and 1893, on Democratic ticket. Religion, Episcopalian.

JOHN SLOSSON HARDING, Esq., son of Hon. Garrick M. Harding, was born in Wilkes-Barre, Pennsylvania, 1859. Graduated from Yale College in 1880. Read law with his father and was admitted to the Luzerne County Bar 1882. In 1883 was appointed assistant District Attorney.

JAMES MAIDEN, JR., was born at Catasauqua, Pennsylvania, February 22, 1860. Educated in the public schools. Resides in Wilkes-Barre.

WILLIAM PENN ABBOTT, D. D., was born at Plains, Pa., December 31, 1838; educated in the Academy at West Chester and Wyoming Seminary; licensed to preach in 1860; entered the Wyoming Conference in 1863; joined the Troy Conference in 1865, located at Newburgh; in 1872 was stationed in New York City; served the Washington Street, St. Luke's and Thirteenth Street Churches. Died December 22, 1878. He was one of the great orators of the Methodist Episcopal Church.

CALVIN PARSONS, son of Hezekiah, was born at Laurel Run, April, 1815; educated in the valley; entered his father's fulling mill at eighteen and later in a saw mill; when he was twenty-one assumed control of his father's mill. Married 1837. Has filled the most important local offices; was prominent in temperance lodges and is an elder in the First Presbyterian Church of Wilkes-Barre; director and charter member of the People's Bank, and President of the Wyoming Monumental Association. Lives in his beautiful home at Parsons where he owns a large farm.

JUDGE DANIEL LA PORTE RHONE was born in Huntington township, Luzerne county, Pennsylvania, January 19, 1838; educated in the Dickinson Seminary, Williamsport, and Wyoming Seminary; studied law with Hon. Charles Denison; admitted to the Luzerne Bar in 1861; candidate for District Attorney in 1864; elected Judge of the Orphans' Court in 1874. Author of two standard works on Orphans' Court Practice. A writer and lecturer on literary, educational and economic subjects. One of the organizers of the Public Schools.

ISAAC TRIPP was born in Providence, Pennsylvania, September 7, 1817; came to Kingston in 1854 and occupied the farm now occupied by Frank Hehne; purchased his present property of one hundred and thirty-eight acres at Forty Fort. Married Mrs. Margaret Shoemaker February 17, 1840; after her death married Hannah Rodgers December 28, 1861. Mr. Tripp is a successful man.

PETER SHUPP was born in Plymouth, of German ancestry, 1820; educated in that place; a successful merchant and a prominent citizen; father of Charles.

HON. JOHN J. SHONK was born at Mount Hope, New Jersey, in 1815, of German ancestry; began life at hard work; in 1854 went into business as a coal operator and later as a lumberman and tanner. Served in the State Legislature for four years, elected in 1874; Hon. George W. Shonk is his son. Mr. Shonk has been a successful man.

F. L. HOLLISTER, D. D. S., was born in what is now Forrest Lake township, Susquehanna county, Pennsylvania, August 16, 1846; educated at the Montrose Academy and the Union School at Hamilton, New York; graduated from the Pennsylvania College of Dental Surgery in 1879; located in Tunkhannock, later in Wilkes-Barre, where he stands among the first in his profession. Married Miss Lillie Baker September 10, 1869. Member of the State and other Dental Associations.

DRAPER SMITH was born in Wyoming county, Pennsylvania, November 7, 1815; educated in the schools of that county. Came to Plymouth in 1832 and went into the employment of Gaylord & Reynolds; four years later went into partnership with Gaylord; in 1840 formed a partnership with Mr. Little, of Kingston; two years later engaged in the coal business; opened a store in Plymouth in 1847, which he conducted successfully for ten years, when Mr. Shupp became his partner, continuing until 1864, when Mr. Smith retired from active business life. President of the First National Bank of Plymouth for twenty years; President of the Light, Heat and Power Company and of the Water Company. One of Plymouth's successful men. Mrs. H. B. Payne is his daughter.

ALEXANDER FARNHAM, Esq., was born in Carbondale, Pennsylvania, January 12, 1834; educated at the Wyoming Seminary, at the Academy at Waverly, Pennsylvania, and the National Law School at Ballston Spa, New York; read law in the office of Fuller and Harding in Wilkes-Barre, and when he was twenty-one was admitted to the Luzerne Bar, 1855; District Attorney from 1874 to 1877; has declined political preferment; is President of the Bar Association of Luzerne county. Married Miss Augusta Dorrance July 18, 1865. He has no peer at the Luzerne Bar.

ASA RANDOLPH BRUNDAGE, Esq., was born at Conyngham, Pennsylvania, March 22, 1828; graduated from Centenary College, Mississippi, with honors; studied law with H. B. Wright; admitted to the Luzerne Bar in 1849; elected District Attorney in 1855; has served many times as a delegate to National and State conventions; an official member of the St. Stephen's Episcopal Church. Married Miss Francis B. Bulkely in 1853. Is a Democrat in politics.

ANDREW DERR was born in Northumberland county, Pennsylvania, May 29, 1853; graduated from Lafayette College in 1878 with the degree of A. B.; studied law with Hon. George W. Biddle in Philadelphia and in the University of Pennsylvania; was admitted to the Philadelphia Bar in 1878, and in the same year to the Luzerne Bar. In 1882 he entered the firm of Thompson Derr & Brothers, the leading insurance firm in this section. A director of the Miners' Savings Bank and has filled several offices of trust.

WILLIAM H. MARCY was born in Wilkes-Barre, October 1, 1836; educated in that city; followed carpenter work, later book-keeper for the Germania Coal Company; in 1869 went into the mercantile business. At the present time is in the mercantile and lumber business. One of the oldest members of Vulcan Lodge, No. 292, of Odd Fellows; member of Landmark Lodge, No. 442, Free and Accepted Masons.

JAMES R. SCOUTEN, Esq., was born in Bradford county, Pennsylvania, September 26, 1858; educated at Wyoming Seminary and other schools; graduated from the Law Department of the University of Michigan, October, 1884, with the degree of Bachelor of Law; began practice in Sullivan county; in 1886 located in Wilkes-Barre; admitted to the Luzerne Bar in 1887 and has been in active practice ever since. Married Miss Mercy E. Brunges October 20, 1891.

GEORGE T. DICKOVER was born in Wilkes-Barre, January 28, 1849; educated in that city; is a member of the firm of Dickover & Son, Brick Manufacturers; in 1873 became a partner with his father. Married Miss Francis Stocton April 28, 1883; has three children living. Is a Republican in politics.

ANDREW WILSON McALPIN was born in Wilkes-Barre, Pennsylvania, January 4, 1849; educated in the Wilkes-Barre Institute and the Moravian College, Bethlehem, Pennsylvania; clerked for John H. Swoyer, later shipping clerk for the Lehigh Valley Coal Company; for three years was connected with the Wilkes-Barre *Record of the Times*; since 1887 has been engaged in the real estate business. Married Miss Ida Phillips in 1879.

PATRICK HENRY CAMPBELL, Esq., was born in Scranton, Pennsylvania, November 24, 1843; educated in the public schools; served in the late war; then attended the Wyoming Seminary for three years; was a teacher and then principal of the Second District Schools in Wilkes-Barre. Studied law with D. L. Rhone; admitted to the Luzerne Bar in 1874; examiner in the Orphans' Court for a number of years. Married Miss Francis McDonald in 1874.

ANDREW JACKSON ELLSWORTH was born in Wyoming county, Pennsylvania, September 22, 1862; educated at Wyoming Seminary; at eighteen began teaching; taught in Wyoming county for four years, four years at Pringleville, this county, and was principal of the Dorranceton School two years. In 1891 connected himself with the Wyoming Valley Traction Company where he is now employed.

EDWARD RICHARDS was born in Wilkes-Barre, August 25, 1852; educated in the public schools; in 1890, with Eugene K. Fry, established a wall paper and paint store on South Main street, Wilkes-Barre. Mr. Richards has followed painting and paper hanging since 1869.

JAMES H. EVANS was born in South Wales, July 9, 1864; came to this country in 1870; educated in the public schools; lived in Johnstown, Wilkes-Barre, Terre Haute, Indiana; Edwardsville, and now in Kingston; learned the trade of boiler making; established his present mercantile business in 1886, in Edwardsville. Tax Collector, Auditor and Treasurer two terms each, of Edwardsville. Was a member of the Republican County Committee three years and its secretary one year. Married to Miss Maggie Waters in 1886.

THOMAS M. DULLARD was born in the county of Durham, England, of Irish parentage in 1854; came to this country in 1869 and settled in Plains and followed mining; took an active part in labor movements and held important offices in labor associations; in 1885 elected President of the M. and L. A. A. of Luzerne and Lackawanna counties; was the organizer of the K. of L.; Alderman of the sixteenth ward of Wilkes-Barre; in 1890 elected one of the Commissioners of Luzerne county and re-elected in 1893. Author of several popular songs. Won prizes at hand-ball. Married in 1889 to Miss Miriam Goerlity.

HERBERT Y. REESE was born in Bristol, England, of Welsh parentage, April 2, 1843; educated in England; at the age of twenty-five came from Wales to Johnstown, Pennsylvania, where he was employed as a clerk; came to Jermyn, Pennsylvania, and later to Wilkes-Barre, clerking in the company store; was located at Sugar Notch for several years. Has been for a number of years reporter and circulation manager on the Wilkes-Barre *Record of the Times*. Married Miss Isabella Moody in 1862. A member of a number of associations.

DARRYL LA PORT CREVELING, Esq., was born in Columbia county, Pennsylvania, October 7, 1869; educated in the New Columbus Academy and Wyoming Seminary; taught school; admitted to the Luzerne Bar in 1888. Married Miss Kate Hice in 1887.

GEORGE W. EDWARDS was born in Scranton, Pennsylvania, March 6, 1860; went to school in that city; moved to Plymouth, Pennsylvania, in 1866; to Kingston in 1873; has been in the employment of the Kingston Coal Company, and since 1887 has been outside superintendent of Breaker No. 2. Member of Knights of Pythias and Red Men. Was the first chief of the Edwards Fire Department. Is serving his second term as Councilman.

F. B. MYRES was born in Kingston, in 1845; educated in the Wyoming Seminary and at Cazenovia, New York. Is a successful farmer, owns a tract of valuable farming land and other valuable property. He is the son of Harriet and Madison Myres, who were of the old families. He married Miss Naomi Mott in 1869. Is a member of the Kingston Methodist Episcopal Church and a Prohibitionist in politics.

DAVID MILES was born in Merthyr, South Wales, in 1826; educated in his native town; came to the United States in 1861, located in Scranton and worked for the Delaware, Lackawanna & Western Railroad; came to Kingston in 1864. Superintendent of the blacksmith shop for the Delaware, Lackawanna & Western Railroad. Mrs. N. D. Safford, Mrs. Prothero, Sarah, assistant principal of the Kingston Public Schools, Mary and Edward, are his children. Charter member of the Masonic Lodge of Kingston.

REV. JOHN P. O'MALLY was born in County Mayo, Ireland, June 24, 1833; came to this country at the age of seventeen: entered the Jesuit College of St. Francis Xavier, New York City, and remained four years; studied three years at Emmitsburg, then entered the Theological and Philosophical Seminary at Philadelphia, and completed the four years course in two years. Ordained in 1865; served at St. James Church, Philadelphia, from 1865 to 1868; located at Athens, Pennsylvania, from 1868 to 1870; at Hawley, Pennsylvania, while there erected churches at White Mills, Milford, Lackawaxen and Hawley, where he resided from 1870 to 1891, when he came to Kingston.

BONIFACE HENRY BRODHUN was born in Germany, September 9, 1827; educated in that country; emigrated to the United States in 1849; located in Conyngham Valley, Pennsylvania; served in the Ninth Pennsylvania Volunteer Cavalry as a musician in the Regimental Band; after the war went to California and laid the brick work for many important buildings; returned to California the second time in 1873; in 1880 visited Germany to settle up the estate of his parents. Has a fine collection of gold and silver bearing quartz. Mr. Brodhun owns the property where he lives, on the corner of Main and Ross streets, Wilkes-Barre.

, JOHN S. McGROARTY, Esq., was born and educated in this valley. Has been teacher, editor, Treasurer of Luzerne county and now a member of the Luzerne Bar. He is well known as a literary man.

CONRAD LEE was born in Hanover township, Luzerne county, Pennsylvania, November 3, 1842; educated at Wyoming Seminary; taught school several terms; spent a number of years in Ohio, filling the position of foreman in a large firm; later a speculator in western cattle and mules. When he was twenty years of age was appointed outside Superintendent of the Avondale mines, where he remained twenty-one years. In 1874 became interested in the Wyoming Planing Mill and lumber business in Wilkes-Barre, formerly conducted by his father; since 1886 has been sole proprietor; is interested in other business enterprises and owner of valuable real estate. Married Miss Agnes Weir July 26, 1868.

A. A. STERLING was born at Meshoppen, Wyoming county, Pennsylvania; was educated at the State University of Wisconsin at Madison; was engaged in mercantile business at Meshoppen until 1872 when he accepted a position in the People's Bank of Wilkes-Barre; has been cashier of said bank for seventeen years.

BENJAMIN H. PRATT was born in Taunton, Massachusetts, August 16, 1834; graduated from Lafayette College in 1857; studied and practiced dentistry; located at Elmira and Bath, New York, until 1861, when failing health caused him to abandon his chosen profession; was principal of the Danville, Pennsylvania, Academy for three years; a member of the firm of Hall and Pratt for three years; city editor of the Scranton *Daily Times* four years; in 1887 became legislative reporter of the Scranton *Republican* and afterwards Wilkes-Barre manager with the Scranton *Republican* twelve years; in 1889 appointed Assistant Postmaster of Scranton; at the present time Wilkes-Barre manager of the Scranton *Republican* in Wilkes-Barre.

W. P. RYMAN, ESQ., was born in Dallas, Pennsylvania, August 23, 1847; attended the Wyoming Seminary and graduated from Cornell University in 1871; also took a post graduate course in law at the Harvard University Law School in 1871 and 1872; admitted to the Luzerne County Bar in 1873. Identified with several important business enterprises. Married December, 1879, to Miss Charlotte M. Rose.

WILLIAM T. ROBBINS was born in Washington, New Jersey, in 1838; educated in Brighton Academy and at the Academy at Princeton, New York; has been dispatcher and locomotive engineer, and is now in the employment of the Delaware, Lackawanna and Western Railroad Company. Married Miss Ella Soult in 1874.

SAMUEL GITTINS was born in England in 1860; educated in England and served seven years apprenticeship at the trade of painting and paper hanging; came to this country in 1883; located in Kingston, Pennsylvania; established his present business of wall paper and paints in 1888.

FRANK MORTON GARNEY was born in Kingston, Pennsylvania, April 6, 1870; educated in Wyoming Seminary and public schools; in 1887 entered the General Delivery Department of the Wilkes-Barre Postoffice; in 1889 assistant mailing clerk; later night clerk; now collector and distributor. Married Miss Margaret Mitchell in 1893.

JOHN S. LAMPMAN was born in Pittston, Pennsylvania, December 20, 1838; studied the profession of an oculist with his father; began practicing at Pleasant Valley; in 1870 moved to Wilkes-Barre where he has established an extensive practice and has brought into use remedies heretofore unknown. Married Miss Margaret Shales January, 25, 1872.

THE ANITA QUARTETTE. Of all the things of which Wyoming Valley is justly proud there is nothing that she takes greater pride in than the Anita Quartette. This quartette of sweet singers is composed of Wilkes-Barre gentlemen who are known throughout the State both as soloists and quartette singers. It was organized in July, 1893, and since that time they have appeared before the most critical audiences in the State. The quartette is made up as follows: J. C. Atkin, first tenor; A. C. Campbell, second tenor; W. A. O'Neill, first bass; J. P. Barns, second bass. Whenever the Anita Quartette is advertised to appear in concert the music-loving people never fail to attend, knowing full well that there is a treat in store for them.

GEORGE URQUHART was born in Wilkes-Barre in 1875; educated in Wyoming Seminary; graduated from Jefferson Medical College in 1850. Examining surgeon for the draft of 1861.

SAMUEL W. BOYD. If the old saying, "You can always tell the characteristics of a man by his writings," is true, then Editor S. W. Boyd of *The News-Dealer* must be both fearless and independent. He was born in Carbon county forty years ago, and in early life removed with his family to this city. He finally drifted to New York, where in business pursuits he accumulated considerable money. Returning to this city, he embarked in the grocery business, at the same time distinguishing himself in the political world as a leader in many hard fought campaigns. Elected to the office of Register of Wills of the county, he filled the important position with credit to himself and satisfaction to his constituents. Retiring from the office six years ago, he purchased, in conjunction with John J. Maloney, the *Daily* and *Sunday News-Dealer*, which under their management has rapidly risen to the front rank of Northeastern Pennsylvania journalism. Nature has eminently qualified Mr. Boyd for the journalistic world. Being a close student for many years, he possesses an unlimited supply of knowledge and information, and being a versatile writer, with a field peculiarly his own, and a commendable independence and fearlessness, his articles are easily recognized and widely read and quoted. Of late he has permitted his graceful pen to wander into the fields of poetry, and many rythmic flowers glistening with the dew-drops of genius is the result. The song charmingly entitled "I'll be Back Some Day to You," is from his versatile pen, and will no doubt achieve well merited popularity.

L. E. STEARNS was born in Ohio, October 2, 1845; removed from there with his parents when four years of age to Binghamton, New York, where he received a good common school education. At the age of nineteen he entered his father's photographic studio as a student, and made such rapid progress in the art that in a few years he was qualified to conduct successfully the large gallery in Wilkes-Barre that has borne his name for nearly twenty years. He is an elder in the First Presbyterian Church of this city. He has also been an active member of the Young Men's Christian Association since its organization in Wilkes-Barre, and served one year as President of the Association. Mr. Stearns's gallery is now located in the new and beautiful Osterhout Block, Public Squre and East Market street.

ANDREW T. McCLINTOCK, ESQ., was born in Northumberland, this State, February 2, 1810; educated in the public schools of that place and Kenyon College, Ohio; began his law studies with James Hepburn and completed them under Hon. George Woodward; was admitted to the Luzerne Bar in 1836, and became a partner of the latter; was appointed District Attorney in 1839. As Director of the Wyoming National Bank and President of Hollenback Cemetery Association, Director of Wilkes-Barre Hospital, President of the Wilkes-Barre Law and Library Association, member of the Wyoming Historical and Geological Society, Elder in the Presbyterian Church, he has served his generation. In 1870 Princeton College conferred upon him the degree of LL. D. He was the oldest member of the Luzerne Bar in active practice at the time of his death. His clientage included many of our large corporations. He died January 1, 1892.

RICHARD SHARP, an old and influential resident of the Valley. Director of the First National Bank, President of the Alden Coal Company, President of the Wyoming Manufacturing Company.

BENJAMIN GARDNER CARPENTER was born at Plains, July 2, 1827. In 1848 he became a partner of Theron Burnet in a store near where the Osterhout building now stands. The firm moved to North Franklin street, and from there to West Market street, and finally to the opposite side of the street, No. 57. Mr. Carpenter bought out Mr. Burnet and took in Mr. Emery. In 1873 they built the building now occupied by the firm. Mr. Carpenter purchased Mr. Emery's interest and took in A. H. Mulford and Frank Densmore. At Mr. Mulford's death, in 1875, Walter S. Carpenter, the eldest son of Mr. Carpenter, was taken in partnership. Mr. Carpenter was a Trustee of Wyoming Seminary and President of the Wilkes-Barre Water Company. He died November 11, 1889.

EDWARD P. DARLING, Esq., born in Berks county, November 10, 1831; educated at the New London Cross Roads Academy, and graduated from Amherst College in 1851; admitted to the Reading Bar in 1853 and to the Luzerne Bar in 1853. Died 1889. Mr. Darling was one of the foremost lawyers in Northeastern Pennsylvania. He was a partner with F. V. Rockafellow in banking, and Vice-President of the Wyoming National Bank, Miners' Savings Bank, and many other important offices.

WILLIAM PENN MINER was for many years the leading journalist in Wilkes-Barre and was the founder of the *Record of the Times*. He retired from active newspaper pursuits in 1876, after which time he lived in quiet retirement on the ancestral farm at Miner's Mills, engaged in pastoral and literary pursuits until his death in April, 1892. Mr. Miner was the son of the late Charles Miner, distinguished as a statesman, journalist and historian. Charles Miner was a pioneer in Wyoming, having come here in 1799 from Connecticut. He was associated here with his brother, Asher, in publishing the *Federalist*. In 1816 he sold out and went to West Chester, where he founded the *Village Record*. He served in the Legislature and in Congress. William P. Miner was educated for the law, and was admitted to the Luzerne Bar in 1841, he afterwards being elected Prothonotary and Clerk of the Courts on the Whig ticket. In 1853 he founded the *Record of the Times*, which he successfully conducted for more than a score of years. In 1873 he launched the daily edition of the *Record* and conducted it in person until its sale to a local syndicate, which in 1883 sold to the present proprietors, Messrs. Johnson & Powell. Mr. Miner was a life-long protectionist and his terse utterances on that subject have graced the columns of the *Record* from time to time. He was also fond of historical research. His son, William B. Miner, conducts a newspaper in Wisconsin.

J. BENNETT SMITH was born in Wilkes-Barre, July 8, 1834. Was connected with William Maffet on North Pennsylvania Survey, in 1853; also on North Branch Extension Canal with Mr. Maffet. Identified with survey and workings of the Lackawanna and Bloomsburg Railroad for a number of years, and several other enterprises in the valley. Afterwards with Lehigh Coal and Navigation Company as Soliciting Agent and Superintendent of Mines at Wanamie. For the last fourteen years connected with the Hazard Manufacturing Company of Wilkes-Barre, Pennsylvania.

ANDREW H. McCLINTOCK, Esq., son of A. T. McClintock, was born in Wilkes-Barre, Pennsylvania, December 12, 1852; educated at the College of New Jersey, at Princeton, and graduated in 1872. After his education he studied law with his father and J. V. Darling; admitted to the Luzerne Bar in 1876. Member of the Wyoming Historical and Geological Society, and Trustee of the Osterhout Free Library.

JOHN C. PHELPS, born in Granby, Connecticut, April 20, 1825; emigrated with parents to Pennsylvania in 1827; educated at the public schools of Dunlaff, Luzerne county, Pennsylvania, and at Harford Academy. Emigrated to New York at nineteen years of age, where he served as clerk in a wholesale grocery store for four years, afterward becoming a partner. Having been engaged in the wholesale grocery and hardware business, as a banker, and connected with several corporations as president, vice-president, secretary and treasurer, with many others as director—notably as Vice-President Lackawanna and Bloomsburg, President Dickson Manufacturing Company and Nanticoke Coal and Iron Company, Steuben Coal Company, Granby Coal Company, Wilkes-Barre Gas Company; Director of the Delaware, Lackawanna and Western Railroad Company, Parrish Coal Company, Amoora Coal Company, as well as other corporations of this and other States. Died July 14, 1892.

ISAAC P. HAND, ESQ., born in Berwick, Pennsylvania, April 5, 1843; prepared for college at Media, Pennsylvania; graduated from Lafayette in 1865. Served in the War of the Rebellion. Principal of Hyde Park School; Clerk of City Council of Scranton, Pennsylvania. Admitted to the Luzerne Bar in 1869. Secretary and Treasurer of the Wilkes-Barre Academy; Trustee of the Wilkes-Barre Female Institute and Lafayette College. Served as Chairman of the Republican County Committee.

JOHNSON R. COOLBAUGH, the subject of this sketch, is a native of Bradford county, this State. Spent the first sixteen years of his life on his father's farm. Early in life manifested a love for trade; came to Pittston and spent two years clerking; then came to Wilkes-Barre and secured a position with the late Andrew Kesler, where he remained two years. Taking the advice of Horace Greeley, to "go West, young man," went to Beloit, Wisconsin, remained there nearly four years, filling responsible positions with leading mercantile houses. In January, 1860, returned to Wilkes-Barre on a visit. Noting the old fogy manner of doing business here compared with the West, determined to establish an exclusive dry-goods business. Wilkes-Barre was at this time a borough of about four thousand people, bounded by the river, North, South and Canal streets. Among the leading merchants were Hon. Ziba Bennett, R. J. Flick, John B. Wood and Charles F. Reets. With little capital he determined that if honesty and enterprise could succeed he would. Continuing until the fall, and being desirous of enlarging the business, associated with him D. H. Frantz, and moved into the new store formerly occupied by Jonas Long. The war was now in progress, goods advancing in price, and their business proved a grand success, theirs becoming the leading dry-goods house. About 1868, Mr. Frantz retired, and Mr. Coolbaugh continued until 1872. Selling out to Mr. Bossler, he, with the late William M. Bennett, established the well known shoe house and continued with marked success until 1880. In the meantime, other business claiming his attention, he sold his interest to Mr. Walter. In 1872 formed the firm of Miller, Bertels & Coolbaugh, the object being real estate. From 1872 to 1883 was the trusted assistant to G. M. Miller, Tax Receiver. In 1878 bought out his partners in the real estate business, which he has continued until the present time with success. During the past twenty-five years Mr. Coolbaugh has done much to develop the city—Franklin street from Academy street down, Sullivan street, Dana Place, Church and Barney streets, were projected by him. He is the trusted agent of several large estates and enjoys the distinction of being the leading real estate dealer. Has never sought public office, excepting serving three years as Councilman-at-large. His has been a busy life, marked by strict integrity, reasonable success and good citizenship.

ROBERT C. SHOEMAKER, Esq., born in Kingston township, April 4, 1836; son of the Hon. Charles D. Shoemaker. Educatated at the Wyoming Seminary and graduated from Yale College in 1855. Read law with Andrew T. McClintock; admitted to the Luzerne Bar in 1869.

LYMAN H. BENNETT, Esq., was born in Harpersfield, Delaware county, New York, in 1845, and there resided (if we except his absence in the different years of his school life) until his arrival at the age of twenty-one. In 1866 he accepted a position as accountant in the United States Treasury Department at Washington, D. C., which he held until 1872. In the meantime he entered the law department of Columbia College, at that place, and there graduated. In 1872 he removed to Wilkes-Barre. In the same year he was admitted to practice in the Courts of this county, where he has since pursued his chosen profession of the law. For a number of years he has been a prominent member of the Luzerne Bar, and has enjoyed the confidence, not only of an important clientage, but of his brother attorneys, who, in a larger number of important contested cases than usually fall to the lot of any one lawyer, have mutually selected him to act in the capacity of both Judge and Jury, under the titles of Auditor, Referee, or Master in Chancery. He was the recent candidate of the minority—the Republican party in Luzerne county—for the office of Additional Law Judge, and although defeated at the polls, he received a flattering vote from the opposite political party. In 1874 he married Miss Ella Robbins, of Wilkes-Barre. Of this union two daughters, Anna and Lillian, were born in 1875 and 1879 respectively. The death of his eldest daughter, Anna, in 1888, left himself, his wife and one daughter, who constitute the present family circle.

EDWARD ALEXANDER NIVEN was born in Livingston county, New York, and raised in Buffalo. In 1856 he went to New York city, and entered the mercantile business in the wholesale hardware firm of which his uncle was a member. Commerce was not to his liking, and he quietly drifted into newspaper work. In 1861 he enlisted and served nearly two years in the Army of the Potomac, being taken prisoner at the battle of Savage's Station, June 29, 1862. He subsequently served in a battery of light artillery with Sherman's army, in the famous march to the sea. Returning to New York after the war, Mr. Niven went to work as a reporter, and served in that capacity for eight or nine years in that city. He afterwards traveled as a correspondent for several papers, and during his career as a newspaper man has worked on some of the most popular journals from Maine to California. Mr. Niven's great-grandfather, Daniel Niven, was a Captain of Engineers in the War of the Revolution, and raised a company at Newburgh, New York. He has written much in his time for magazines and weekly story papers, but newspaper work claimed his constant attention.

T. P. RYDER, formerly a teacher in the public schools; later in the Prothonotary's office, and at present on the editorial staff of the Wilkes-Barre *Record of the Times*. His productions have appeared in current literature and many of the leading metropolitan papers.

GEORGE CORONWAY was born in Liverpool, England, February 6, 1842. As a sailor crossed the Atlantic over fifty times; served in the commissary for the government at Harrisburg. Came to Wilkes-Barre twenty-six years ago and worked in the mines. Is now an Assistant Coal Shipper. His songs have been set to music by Dr. Joseph Parry (Gwilym Gwent), Prof. J. A. P. Price and others.

THERON G. OSBORNE, (Tom Allen), was born at Lake Wynola, Wyoming county, Pennsylvania. He was educated in the public schools and Wyoming Seminary. For several years he was engaged in newspaper work, the greater part of which was done on the *Wilkes-Barre Leader*. He is now principal of the public schools at Minooka. As a writer he is a master of the various forms of verse, has an extensive and well chosen vocabulary, and his inspiration is drawn from the living present and nature. His poems are delicate, refined, often subtle as well as strong. They are neither passionate nor sensational, but full of the warmth, richness and beauty of true poetic feeling.

LEWIS B. LANDMESSER, ESQ., was born in Hanover township, now the borough of Ashley, Luzerne county, Pennsylvania, March 5, 1850. He was educated at the Wilkes-Barre Institute, Hopkins Grammar School, New Haven, Connecticut, and at Yale College, graduating from the latter institution in the class of 1871. He is the son of Lewis Landmesser, who was among the earliest, most enterprising, and most successful of the German settlers of the valley, having emigrated in 1836 from Prussia, and who by continuous and well directed effort soon managed to place himself among the most prosperous and conspicuous citizens. The subject of our sketch, after graduation, spent a year in Germany attending lectures at Heidelberg and the University at Berlin, dividing the time equally between them. He then returned to Wilkes-Barre and entered the law office of Hon. L. D. Shoemaker as student at law. He subsequently read law with Hon. H. B. Payne and Hon. Stanley Woodward, and was admitted to the Luzerne County Bar April 5 1873. Mr. Landmesser has made a specialty of Orphans' Court practice, in which he has been very successful. He was for three years Examiner of the Orphans' Court, and in 1888, at the request of Hon. D. L. Rhone, Judge of the Orphans' Court, he revised and arranged the present Rules of the Orphans' Court. He is a Republican in politics; has always taken an active part in political affairs of the county, and was for three years Chairman of the Republican County Committee. He is also a prominent Mason, being Past Master of Lodge No. 61, F. & A. M., one of the oldest lodges in the State, having been constituted in 1794, and Past High Priest of Shekinah Chapter, No. 182, R. A. M. Appointed Postmaster of Wilkes-Barre in 1892.

HON. JOHN LYNCH was born in Providence, Rhode Island, in 1843; educated at Wyalusing and Wyoming Seminary; studied law under G. M. Harding; admitted to the Luzerne Bar in 1865. Was clerk for Sheriff S. H. Peterbaugh; elected Register of Wills in 1866; appointed Additional Law Judge in 1890 and elected in 1891 for a period of ten years.

G. M. REYNOLDS, the eldest son of William C. Reynolds, was born in Kingston borough; educated at Wyoming Seminary and Princeton; read law with Hon. Stanley Woodward, but never practiced. Was President of City Council for five years; for five years President of Board of Trade, and Colonel of the Ninth Regiment, National Guard of Pennsylvania, for six years.

FRANK EUGENE WRIGHT was born at Ridgebury, Pennsylvania, in 1863; educated at Wellsburg; farmed; came to Kingston in 1882. Learned the trade of blacksmith in Elmira, New York; worked at Bloomsburg, Williamsport and Shamokin. Returned to Kingston in 1888. Was Foreman and Treasurer of the Kingston Engine and Hose Company. Deals extensively in butter and eggs from Bradford county, also in general produce.

WILLIAM WALLACE LOOMIS was born in Lebanon, Connecticut, July 14, 1815. At an early age he came with his parents to Northmoreland, Wyoming county, and to Wilkes-Barre in the autumn of 1837. With the exception of N. Rutter, who came to Wilkes-Barre a year or two before, Mr. Loomis was the oldest resident of Wilkes-Barre. He was Burgess from 1855 to 1863, and Mayor from 1877 to 1881. In 1862 he was appointed by President Lincoln Election Commissioner of Pennsylvania, and visited the Union armies and held elections for President. Mr. Loomis was actively engaged in the harness and saddlery hardware business for forty-one years, and when his present brick store on West Market street was erected, it was judged one of the finest and towered highest of any business house in the city. Mr. Loomis was so well known and highly respected that further comment would be superfluous. Died May 2, 1894.

CHARLES FARMER INGHAM was born of English parents in Dublin, 1810, and came to the valley in 1823. He began life as a clerk; later taught school in the old Wilkes-Barre Academy, on the public square of Wilkes-Barre, Pennsylvania; attended lectures at the University of Pennsylvania; became a Civil Engineer; helped construct the North Branch Canal; surveyed for the Lehigh Coal and Navigation Company the famous Switchback at Mauch Chunk, and was employed by most of the large corporations in this part of the State. He assisted in the erection of Fort Sumter. The sewer system of this city was directed by him. The Geological and Historical Societies owe as much of their prosperity to him as any other man. Died January 18, 1890.

CHARLES MORGAN was born near Philadelphia in 1814, and came to Wilkes-Barre in 1839. In 1843 he entered into business with Elijah Kline, under the name of Kline & Morgan. They ran very successfully one of the numerous large shops of this locality engaged in the manufacture of boots and shoes. This was before machinery was introduced in the business, and all goods were made to the measure of the wearer. After the death of Mr. Kline, the business was conducted by Mr. Morgan, he having introduced the first machine-made goods ever brought to Wilkes-Barre. Since then the business has been radically changed, and now the shops so famous in the manufacture of hand-made boots and shoes are no more, but in their places are the modern shoe stores with plate-glass fronts with large stocks of machine and hand-made goods, brought by railroad from the manufacturing centers. Mr. Morgan brought his first ready-made boots and shoes from New Jersey by team, afterwards by canal, and later by railroad. Mr. Morgan's sons, J. T. and W. P., succeeded him in the year 1876.

GEORGE K. POWELL, ESQ., born at Penn Yan, New York, June 10, 1845; educated at Penn Yan Academy and Genesee College, Lima, New York; graduated in 1866. Was Professor of Latin and Greek at the Beaver College and Female Institute. Entered the United States navy and visited South America. Admitted to the Luzerne Bar in 1871.

WILLIAM LAFAYETTE RAEDER was born at Ransom, Pennsylvania, November 27, 1854; educated in select school and the West Pittston Seminary; prepared for college under the tutorship of Prof. W. J. Bruce; entered the Lehigh University in 1872, where he took the course of Civil Engineering. Studied law with E. P. and J. V. Darling, Esq., of Wilkes-Barre, and admitted to the Luzerne Bar in 1881. Was sergeant in the Ninth Regiment and is associated with important business enterprises. Married Miss Elizabeth Worrell February 17, 1885.

REUBEN JAY FLICK was born at Flicksville, Pennsylvania, July 10, 1816. He came to Wilkes-Barre in 1838, and engaged in mercantile trade. In 1870 he organized the People's Bank and was its active President until 1871, when the increasing cares of his many other interests compelled his re-ignation. Mr. Flick's ability, energy and integrity brought him success in all his undertakings and made him one of the most eminent and respected citizens of Wilkes-Barre. He was an incorporator of many of her leading industries and charitable institutions and their prominence and present success are largely due to his personal interest and business ability. At the time of his death, which occured December 18, 1890, Mr. Flick was a Director of the Wilkes-Barre Lace Company, Vulcan Iron Works, Electric Light Company, Wilkes-Barre Street Car and Iron Bridge Companies, Wyoming Valley Ice Company and others, and was a Trustee of the Home for Friendless, the City Hospital, the Female Institute of Wilkes-Barre, and of Lincoln University of Oxford, Pennsylvania.

REV. DAVID COPELAND, D. D., Principal of Wyoming Seminary, Kingston, Pennsylvania, from 1872 to 1882, was born in Braintree, Vermont, December 21, 1832, and was graduated from the Wesleyan University in 1855. In the same year he was engaged as Principal of the Monroe Academy, Henrietta, New York, and in 1866 as teacher of natural science and mathematics in Falley Seminary, Fulton, New York. He joined the Genesee Conference of the Methodist Episcopal Church in 1858, and was in the same year appointed Principal of the Springfield Academy, now Griffith Institute, New York. In 1865 he was transferred to the Cincinnati Conference, and was appointed President of the Hillsborough Female College, Ohio. In 1872 was appointed Principal of Wyoming Seminary, Kingston. Died, 1882, in Vermont.

GEORGE S. BENNETT was born in Wilkes-Barre, Pennsylvania, August 17, 1842; graduated from Wesleyan University in 1864. In 1864 went into the banking business with his father, Ziba Bennett, in Wilkes-Barre, Pennsylvania. Has been Director of the Wyoming National Bank and Secretary of the Board of Directors, member of the banking firm of Bennett, Phelps & Co., member of Town Council, Manager of the Wilkes-Barre Bridge Company, Manager of Wilkes-Barre Hospital, President of the Young Men's Christain Association, Trustee of Wyoming Seminary, Superintendent of the Sunday School of the First Methodist Episcopal Church and a member of that Church, Manager of the Hollenback Cemetery Association, member of the School Board and Secretary of the Luzerne County Bible Society, President of the Lace Works, Treasurer of the Sheldon Axle Company, Trustee of Wesleyan University, Middletown, Connecticut, and of Drew Theological Seminary, Madison, New Jersey; President of the Board of Trustees of Wyoming Seminary. After his education was completed, Mr. Bennett traveled in Europe. Married Ellen W. Nelson, daughter of Rev. Reuben Nelson, D. D., of Kingston, Pennsylvania.

JOHN CHRISTIAN WIEGAND was born in Laurel Run; educated in the public schools of Hazleton. Book-keeper in the Hazleton Savings Bank; in 1890 appointed teller of the Hazleton National Bank. Elected Prothonotary of Luzerne county in 1891. Married Miss Harriet Fetterman September 10, 1888.

EDWARD F. McGOVERN, Esq., was born in England, September 10, 1860; graduated from the Law Department of the University of Pennsylvania in 1886; admitted to the Luzerne Bar in 1887. Elected Alderman in the Second ward of Wilkes-Barre in 1881, for five years.

THE WILKES-BARRE LEADER.—From the handsome building at No. 7 North Main street, known as the Leader Building, erected especially for the purpose, three newspapers are issued—the *Daily Evening Leader*, the *Weekly Union-Leader* and the *Sunday Morning Leader* —the result of frequent consolidations and transfers of preceding publications, the oldest of them dating as far back as 1810. The building was erected by the late J. K. Bogert, by whose efforts and efficient management the publications were brought to a high standard of newspaper excellence, and the *Leader* continues under the proprietorship of E. F. Bogert, one of the best, as it is one of the oldest, Democratic papers in the State. The *Weekly Union-Leader* came into being through the merging of the plants of the *Leader* and the *Luzerne Union* in January, 1879, the *Leader* having been moved from Pittston in the fall of 1877, where it had been published by Messrs. E. A. Niven and C. H. Chamberlin, and the *Luzerne Union* being the only other Democratic newspaper at the county seat. The publishers of the consolidated journal were J. K. Bogert and George B. Kulp, Esq., who were the only stockholders of what was styled the Leader Publishing Company. J. K. Bogert in February, 1879, purchased Mr. Kulp's interest. In April, 1884, the present building was completed and occupied. The first issue of the daily was October 1, 1879, and the Sunday made its initial appearance in November, 1885, and although bearing the name of the *Leader* was a separate publication with E. F. Bogert and John S. McGroarty as editors and publishers. Mr. McGroarty, after a few months, retired from the partnership. Mr. J. K. Bogert died February 3, 1887. The *Leader* publications were under the control of the estate from then on until April 1, 1888, when they were purchased with all the appurtenances, by the brother of the deceased and present publisher and editor, E. F. Bogert. The *Leader's* circulation had increased so rapidly that improved press facilities were demanded, and in the spring of 1893 a new Goss Clipper perfecting press, with a capacity of 12,000 an hour, and with stereotyping outfit, was added to the already well-equipped plant, making it the most extensive and modernly fitted printing house in the county and placing it second to but few in the State. (For a more extended review see Nelson's 1893 History of Luzerne County, p. 599.)

JOSEPH KIRKENDALL BOGERT was born July 16, 1845, at New Columbus, Luzerne county, Pennsylvania; educated in the public schools and the Male and Female Academy of that place. Served in the late war in the Twenty-eighth Pennsylvania Militia and in the United States Signal Corps. After the war graduated with honor from Lewisburg (now Bucknell) University. Studied law with Hon. Caleb E. Wright and supported himself as correspondent for the Associated Press, the *Philadelphia Times*, *Scranton Times* and other papers. Was the first Deputy Clerk of the Orphans' Court of Luzerne county—1874; elected Register of Wills in 1875. In 1877, with George B. Kulp, Esq., purchased the *Luzerne Leader* and in 1879 they purchased the *Luzerne Union* and merged the two papers into the *Union-Leader*. Mr. Bogert became sole proprietor in 1880. Was chairman of the Democratic State Central Committee in 1884. Represented the Democratic party as delegate to State and National conventions. Appointed Postmaster of Wilkes-Barre in 1885. Died February 3, 1887. Married Miss Mary E. Patterson December 31, 1879. The family is of Dutch origin, Mr. Bogert's ancestors having been among the earliest emigrants from Holland to America. They settled in parts of New York, New Jersey and Pennsylvania, and many who bear the name have won distinction in professional and business life. Samuel, the elder Bogert, was a wheelwright and a respected citizen, but in moderate circumstances. He died at Wilkes-Barre, July 9, 1881, having attained the age of 68 years, and was survived

by his wife, Elizabeth Raton, who died in the same city seven years later, on August 5, 1888, aged 77. (For more extended biography see Nelson's 1893 History of Luzerne County, p. 724).

EDWARD FREAS BOGERT was born at New Columbus, Luzerne county, Pennsylvania, September 27, 1856. He attended the public schools and the Male and Female Academy of New Columbus, and for a short time was a student at the Keystone Academy, Factoryville. After quitting these institutions he worked in his father's wheelwright, blacksmith and paint shops, taking a hand in all departments of this work, and in the spring of 1878 leased a farm in the vicinity, which he personally superintended and worked until April 1, 1880. During a portion of the term of his brother, the late J. K. Bogert, as Register of Wills of Luzerne county, he fulfilled the duties of a clerk in that office, and on April 1, 1880, entered the business office of the *Leader*, shortly afterward assuming charge of its books. During J. K. Bogert's active service as Chairman of the Democratic State Committee in 1884, and from the time of J. K.'s appointment as Postmaster of Wilkes-Barre in July, 1885, the business management of the *Leader* was mainly in charge of the subject of this sketch. In February, 1887, J. K. Bogert died. E. F. Bogert managed the business for the estate until April 1, 1888, when he purchased the real estate and good will of the *Evening* and *Weekly Union-Leader*, and has ever since been the publisher and editor of the three papers—Daily, Weekly and Sunday—issued from its presses. This purchase was made at a time when Mr. Bogert's capital was very limited, but friends came to his assistance, and by the most careful economy, never once losing faith or becoming discouraged with his venture, he has succeeded in placing it among the fixed successful business institutions of the county. He has likewise effected a material enlargement of the plant, made additions to the building and greatly improved its interior appointments. It should be stated that the Sunday paper was not part of the property of the estate, but was an independent enterprise owned by E. F. Bogert, that became a fixed and paying concern almost from its start, in November, 1885. Mr. Bogert has been and is an active worker in the interests of the Democratic party, of which his paper is the official organ; an enthusiastic and untiring promoter of base ball and other athletic sports, having been the prime mover in establishing the new Athletic Park, and an advocate of all forms of municipal progress and improvement. Mr. Bogert holds an honorable discharge from Company D, Ninth Regiment, N. G. P., under date of December 1, 1886, having enlisted April 15, 1884, and is a member of the following fraternal organizations: Landmark Lodge, No. 442, F. & A. M.; Shekinah Chapter, No. 182, R. A. M., and Dieu le Veut Commandery, No. 45, K. T., of Wilkes-Barre, Pennsylvania; Lu Lu Temple, A. A. O. N. of M. S., of Philadelphia, Pennsylvania; Mount Horeb Council, No. 34, R. S. E. & S. M., of Plymouth, Pennsylvania; Keystone Consistory, 32°, Northern Masonic Jurisdiction, U. S. A., of Scranton, Pennsylvania; Wilkes-Barre Lodge, No. 109, B. P. O. Elks; Wilkes-Barre Council, No. 396, Royal Arcanum.

GEORGE B. KULP, ESQ., was born at Reamstown, Pennsylvania, February 11, 1839. Author of the "Families of Wyoming Valley"; editor of the *Luzerne Legal Register*. Married Miss Mary Elizabeth Stewart in 1864.

DR. D. J. J. MASON, born in Wales in 1855; educated in music at the Royal Academy for four years. Trinity College, Dublin, conferred the degree of Mus. Bach. upon him. Has composed many musical compositions and is the leader of music in this section.

CHARLES JONAS LONG, the oldest son of the late lamented and esteemed citizen, Jonas Long, was born in Philadelphia, Pennsylvania, May 3, 1859. After a brief residence in Philadelphia, his parents removed to Wilkes-Barre, Pennsylvania, where, in 1860, were laid the foundations of the present great dry goods establishment. At an early age he attended the Wilkes-Barre public schools and Wyoming Seminary at Kingston, Pennsylvania. Solicitous for the attainment of a liberal and higher education, he was sent to Philadelphia, where he entered the Philadelphia Central High School, after which, in a course of two years of private instruction and study under the celebrated teacher and author, Professor George Stuart of Philadelphia, he fitted himself for Yale College, New Haven, Connecticut, which he entered in 1878. After a classical course of four years, he graduated from Yale College in 1882. After graduation, his professional career, owing to his father's illness, merged into the cares of the growing and extensive dry goods business in which he is now engaged, associated with his mother and brothers. Although immersed in the pursuits of a large commercial business, yet he finds time to devote himself to the cultivation of literary work; and, in the liberal encouragement of local improvements, lends responsive voice and effort to enterprises that promise benefit to the city. His addresses are characterized by graceful thought and eloquent inspiration, particularly those before the Young Men's Hebrew Association, the Board of Trade, of which he is a Trustee, and before the mass meeting at Music Hall for Hospital endowment. He was President of the Young Men's Hebrew Association, is a member of Wyoming Historical Society, Yale Alumni Association of Northeastern Pennsylvania, Trustee of the Board of Trade, and numerous other societies of the community. His close observation, force of character, and genial disposition, fit him truly well for the development and success that so auspiciously heralds a useful career.

CHARLES DORRANCE was born January 4, 1805, at the old homestead, between Kingston and Forty Fort, Luzerne county, where he spent his life. His father, Benjamin Dorrance, was Sheriff of Luzerne county, County Commissioner, member of the Legislature, and the first President of the Wyoming Bank. Lieutenant-Colonel George Dorrance played a prominent part in the massacre of Wyoming and the early history of the valley. Colonel Dorrance, as he was called, was for many years the President of the Wyoming Bank, President of the Wilkes-Barre Bridge Company, one of the first members of the Wyoming Historical and Geological Society, President of the Luzerne Agricultural Society, &c. Mr. Dorrance died January 18, 1892.

ANDREW HUNLOCK, ESQ., born in Kingston, Pennsylvania; educated at Wyoming Seminary; read law with Lyman Hakes, Esq. One of the organizers and first President of the Anthracite Savings Bank. Trustee of Memorial Church.

LAWRENCE MYERS was born in Wilkes-Barre township October 22 1818; educated in Wilkes-Barre; opened a livery business in Wilkes-Barre. In 1850 opened a private Banking House called Myers' Exchange and Banking House, and dealt largely in real estate. Married Miss Eichelberger, of Virginia, for his first wife, and Miss Sarah Sharp, daughter of Jacob Sharp, of Dorranceton, for his second wife, who was the mother of his children.

JOHN MYERS, the father of Lawrence, was born at Forty Fort and married Miss Sarah Sharp, of Wilkes-Barre township. Was Justice of the Peace of Wilkes-Barre for nearly forty years. Opened Washington street from the canal to North street and Jackson street. Was a large real estate owner.

J. D. LACIAR was born in 1839 and when a boy worked in a printing office at Bethlehem. In 1860 became editor and publisher of the *Lehigh Daily Times*, a weekly newspaper, which he was conducting at Bethlehem when the war broke out. He entered the army as a Lieutenant in the One Hundred and Thirty-second Regiment, Pennsylvania Volunteer Infantry, and was promoted to a Captaincy in December, 1862, serving with that command until the expiration of its term of service. In 1864 he raised Company A, Two Hundred and Second Regiment, Pennsylvania Volunteers, in Carbon county, and served with that Regiment until the close of the war. After the surrender of Lee, he was sent to Pittsburg and placed in command of the District of the Monongahela, Department of Pennsylvania. He was wounded at the battle of Antietam, and also in a fight with Moseby's guerrillas near Rectortown, Virginia, in 1864. At the close of the Civil War he was tendered the appointment of Assistant Adjutant General with the rank of Captain in the regular army, but preferred civil life. After the war he located at Mauch Chunk and published the *Gazette* of that place for several years. From 1869 until 1876 he was connected with the Scranton *Republican* and again from 1884 to the present time, as editorial writer. He also served as an aid-de-camp on the staff of Gen. John F. Hartranft, with the rank of Colonel.

REUBEN MARCY was born in 1809 at Old Forge, Pennsylvania; spent his youth in Wilkes-Barre where he attended school and learned the carpenter trade; lived many years in Kingston where he died. He built the Wyoming Seminary in 1844 and rebuilt it after it was burned; also the boarding hall that was burned, the residence of Reuben Nelson, D. D., the First Methodist Episcopal Church, the old Presbyterian Church, the residence of Samuel Hoyt and many other buildings in Kingston and vicinity. There were three brothers who came here in the early days—Zebulon, Ebenezer and Able. The Marcy family is one of the historical families of the Valley.

HENRY WHITE DUNNING, son of Rev. Charles Seely Dunning, D. D., was born in Franklin, New York, September 11, 1858. Graduated from Williston Seminary, East Hampton, Massachusetts, 1878. In the fall of 1878 entered the freshman class of Princeton College, New Jersey. Began to read law in the office of William H. Lee, Esq., in Honesdale, Pennsylvania, and finished his legal studies with Hon. H. B. Payne, in Wilkes-Barre, Pennsylvania. Admitted to the Luzerne Bar June 5, 1882. Superintendent of the First Presbyterian Sunday School; Recording Secretary of the Board of Managers of the Young Men's Christian Association; Law Lecturer in the commercial department of Wyoming Seminary. Counsel to several corporations.

ALBERT WARREN BETTERLY was born in Schuylkill county, but with the exception of a year on the sea, has lived in Wilkes-Barre since childhood. He is the son of E. L. Betterly, M. D., one of the early physicians of this region. His education was secured in the public schools of Wilkes-Barre. Mr. Betterly has been on the *Leader* for nearly ten years, during which time he has filled every position connected with practical journalism of to-day. Shortly after leaving school he was the guest of W. W. Lee on the steam yacht "Climax" and visited many points of interest through Florida, West Indies and the Gulf of Mexico, including periods of some length spent at the Islands of Fernandina, Hayti, Cuba, Jamaica and the Bahamas.

GEORGE S. BURGAN was born in White Haven in 1857. Went to school in Philadelphia; learned his trade in Wilkes-Barre. At present Burgess of Miner's.

SAMUEL HADDOCK was born in 1814, in the Parish of Killyman, County Tyrone, Ireland; educated in his native place; was a professional gardener all his active life., Came to this country in 1853; located in Massachusetts until during the war; then went to Newport, Rhode Island; came to Kingston in 1893. Married in 1848 to Miss M. Gilpin. Mr. Haddock is the father of John C. Haddock, the coal operator. The late Samuel F., his son, who died in Boston in 1893, was born in 1855. There are five other children.

MICHAEL C. RUSSELL was born in Ireland, September 29, 1836; came to the United States in 1849; educated in Elmira, New York; came to Luzerne county in 1853. Was a locomotive engineer until 1877; then went into the mercantile business in Edwardsville. Elected Recorder of Deeds November, 1892, and assumed the duties of his office January, 1893. Married Elizabeth Keating December 19, 1863. Mr. Russell is an extensive real estate owner in Edwardsville.

MORGAN R. MORGANS was born in South Wales, June 24, 1848; educated in Wales. Came to America in 1867. Mine Foreman and Assistant Superintendent of the Lehigh and Wilkes-Barre Coal Company; in 1891 appointed General Superintendent. Married Miss Margaret Williams.

P. J. HIGGINS, M. D. Taught school; graduated from Bellevue Hospital Medical College, New York, in 1877; practiced medicine in Scranton. Located in Wilkes-Barre in 1881. Author of several serial stories published by the *New York Weekly* and other metropolitan papers.

W. H. CHAPIN was born in Huntington, Pennsylvania, in 1860; educated in the public schools. Learned the marble cutting trade in Berwick, Kingston, Pennsylvania, and Three Rivers, Michigan. Established a marble yard in Kingston in 1887, where he is still located. Married Miss Emma Johnson in 1886.

J. ANDREW BOYD, born 1856, at Buck Mountain, Carbon county, Pennsylvania. Went to public schools of Ashley and Wilkes-Barre. Married Miss Helen M. Joslin of Ashley. Resides in Ashley. Manager *Record* Job Printing Department. One of the Wyoming Valley writers.

# Wyoming Valley in the Nineteenth Century.

THE WORLD has a new face and a new spirit to-day. We love the old and deem it beautiful, yet we do not wish to reproduce it. The faces and the forms of the dead throw upon the mountain tops of the past a fading glory, nevertheless they only bring memories which have no part in our present or future existence. As we look back to the past it is golden with the full fragrance of youth and the charm that our imagination throws around the bygone. The past is a melody, growing fainter, and, like distant melodies, possesses the charm of mystery.

When the nineteenth century dawned the people were permanently settled. The Pennsylvania claimant had received compensation for the soil and the Yankee had become the legal owner of this fair valley.

They had outgrown to a great extent their intenseness and they were entering into possession of the liberty and privileges for which they had struggled and suffered so long.

The plowboy's whistle, the baying of hounds and the crack of the rifle were the only sounds to break the Sabbath-like stillness of nature. The valley was covered in most places with pine and oak, with the exception of the bottom lands, which were grown over with very tall rank grass.

The people spent much of their time in the green fields and quiet woods. They had more social intercourse and had more time to live than we have. They hated the English and they made the life of the Tory miserable. There were few old maids or bachelors, for the young man usually had a wife before he was of age. The problem of life was a simple sum. Land was very cheap; the neighbors would make a raising bee and put up a log cabin for the young couple; the old people would give them bedding and dishes; a few boards would make them stools and tables and they were settled for life. Two rooms and a loft they considered a commodious house. The spare chamber, parlor, library and kitchen were one room. The family would go outside while the guest retired. The children would sleep in the loft and would often find a foot of snow on the bed clothes on a winter's morning. The night wind's mournful music in the pines or the sweet melody of the rain on the roof were familiar sounds to them. The daily paper had not put the tongue into disuse. Gossiping, bragging, telling yarns and blowing on politics, with the glory of training day and the fourth of July oration occupied their leisure and gratified their vanity. The women would boil soap, talk about killing pigs and gossip about their neighbors. They wore stiff stays and hoops so large that they would be obliged to enter a door sideways like a crab.

The first departure from an agricultural life was the running of arks and rafts down to tide. The young man went out into the world and the old pastoral life was invaded. The opening of the canal made boatmen of many of the farmers and opened up a market for our coal. The first railroad in the valley was the "Underground Railroad."

Mr. Gildersleeve, a friend of the slaves, was ridden on a rail after being blacked by his democratic neighbors. Later a slave owner shot a slave as he was swimming the river. The

wounded man succeeded in getting to the shore, crawled upon the bank and lay there. The sight so wrought up the patriotic citizens that the southern gentlemen dare not afterwards hunt slaves in the valley. The northern rebel or Copperhead like the Tory traitor before him looked with contempt upon the man who was fighting for the preservation of the Union. Like the Tory they were largely represented by the aristocracy, if I may apply that title to an American citizen which we reserve for the landed aristocracy of Virginia and the lords of Europe. The Copperhead and the Democrat were the two ends of one party. The latter were patriots. When the call to arms rang through the valley like a trumpet blast, party lines were lost and all classes responded to the call to arms. The One Hundred and Forty-third Regiment was principally recruited from Luzerne county. Later there were several companies recruited and sent to the front. The first company that marched across the Kingston flats on their way to establish Camp Luzerne was Company A, commanded by Charles M. Conyngham and Lieutenant O. K. Moore. This was on July 29, 1862. Captain George N. Reichard and Lieutenant John C. Kropp started on the following day with about thirty recruits. This was Company C. Later Captain George E. Hoyt and Asher Gaylord arrived at the camp with twenty-five men each. George E. Hoyt was chosen Captain and a few days later was elected Lieutenant Colonel. A number of other companies came later from different parts of the county, making the muster roll on the thirtieth of August nearly one thousand men.

The ground on which the camp was established was given rent free with the use of the farm barn for storing tents and clothing, by the widow of Charles Bennet. Mrs. Bennet was known at camp as the "Mother of the Regiment." The Regiment broke camp November 7, 1862, and left Kingston in cattle cars during a severe snow storm.

The Regiment was engaged in the following battles: Chancellorsville, Gettysburg, Wilderness, Laurel Hill, Spottsylvania Court House, Cold Harbor, Bethesda Church, Petersburg, Weldon Railroad, Dabney's Mills and Hatch's Run. There were killed in action ninety-three, died of wounds ninety-six, died of diseases eighty-two, died in prison fifty-two, the total number of deaths three hundred and twenty; discharged prior to mustering out two hundred and sixty-eight; total wounded one hundred and ninety-nine; fifteen were never heard from. Among this number were Captain Gaylord and Timothy Powell who were supposed to have been blown to pieces by a shell; deserted one hundred and three, most of these came back to the Regiment when President Lincoln made the proclamation that all deserters who returned to the ranks would be pardoned. With the ninth company that was added to the Regiment it numbered all told fifteen hundred and seven. Six hundred men returned home at the close of the war. The Regiment suffered severely at Gettysburg, out of four hundred and sixty-five men the Regiment lost two hundred and fifty-three. E. L. Dana went out as Colonel of the Regiment and at the battle of Gettysburg when his superior officer was wounded he assumed command of the Brigade.

The Regiment erected a tablet at Gettysburg to mark the spot where they made what is called the "Glorious Stand," where the Regiment charged and saved their colors. The tablet represents Ben. Crippen, of Scranton, the standard bearer, who gave his life to save the colors of the Regiment. Colonel R. Bruce Ricketts commanded Battery F, First Pennsylvania Artillery, at Gettysburg and his bravery in saving his Battery made him one of the heroes of that battle. General Osborne made a splendid war record.

When the "Boys in Blue" returned they found an enemy more malignant than the gentleman aristocrat of the South, that menaced both life and property. This enemy was fresh from Europe. They marched through our streets to terrorize the public; they murdered their victims in the dark; they tied up the railroads and coal mines; they nailed a death notice on the door of the men who controlled public works; they controlled one of the political parties and insurrection paralyzed every interest. In 1877 the United States Government was called upon to protect us and seven thousand soldiers, eleven hundred of which were regulars, were sent into the valley. The tramp of armed men, the rifle and gatling gun, struck terror to these cut throats and anarchists and the mobs dispersed. Then the secret service ferreted out many of the murderers and they were hanged.

The change brought about by the war and the presence of a host of emigrants struck a spur into the old stock and rode ruthlessly over their standards and ideals. The mining of coal and the building of railroads made money plenty. Charles Parrish was the great leader in the industrial world and called into life great corporations.

To give an inventory of our industries or the history of their development is not my purpose. The prominent men of our past and those who are influential at the present time will be briefly noticed with other matter relative to our history and present development.

The later emigration represents three-fifths of our population. Nevertheless the soil is to-day as much the possession of the Yankee as any portion of the Nutmeg State. He owns and controls all but a small part of the wealth and industries of the valley and his standards and ideas are becoming supreme. Be not deceived. The old stock is the rock and the new comer the wave that breaks its foaming crest over it and falls into the trough of the sea.

We are in a stage of transition: the moulding forces and mellowing charms of Christianity, education and human intercourse are shaping into beauty our daily life, awakening our latent forces and hanging in our hearts a gracious light. The church is winning the youth to the moral side of religion, at least, by providing for his social nature; winning him by the personal touch of noble souls and helpful influences. The daily paper brings the thought of the world to nearly every home. The electric cars are making our population a unit and we are becoming cosmopolitan. As we grow wiser we become more practical, less emotional. Oratory has given place to the press; the individual is less potent and our accessions in mechanical lines are putting all men more on a level. Education and association are bringing about what we aspire to—unity. We have too much crude human nature and ignorance; a great deal of prosperity; we are submerged by the yellow Tiber of material well-being.

At the present time the people are twice as well off as they were forty years ago. The amount of education and general knowledge has doubled; we need twice as much to supply our wants; we get twice as much for our labor and for our money, and give less labor for our wages. The proportion of our church membership has increased more than fifty per cent. We can with propriety ask "If as a people we are to become mongrel"? It does not seriously disturb us as we are inclined to favor intermixing, regarding it as one of the economies of nature in perfecting the race. Doubtless the national distinctions will continue to show as marked as the colors of a rainbow.

The boast and desire of many Americans in the valley is to be identified as descendants of the Mayflower Pilgrims. But before we emblazon our heraldry to furnish a coat of

arms, let us be careful or we may run across a Penal Colonist. We delight to call ourselves Anglo-Saxons, but why should we? Were they not made slaves by the Normans
(French) and many of them driven to the mountain fastnesses of Wales? Why do we
deny our Norman blood? We ignore the fact that the Romans occupied Britain for four
centuries, longer than the Angles or Saxons and before them or the Normans. Are we not
the fellow citizens of Caesar and Napoleon? Do we not go back to the Tiber and the
Seine? Have we not the unconquerable and dominating spirit of the Romans? The
American is more a Roman than anything else.

The present population of the county is over two hundred thousand, mostly added in
the last ten years, which have centered in the vicinity of the mines. We are five hundred
and forty feet above the tide, and the height of our mountains ranges from seven to fifteen
hundred feet. We go down through one hundred feet of anthracite coal, separated into
fourteen well defined veins, and in some places the coal deposit is five miles wide. If you
wish to see the geological formation, look at the face of Campbell's Ledge.

The Susquehanna enters the valley through a magnificent gateway in the mountain at
the north side. After crossing the valley three times and traveling twenty miles it flows
out through the southern gateway. The valley is one vast plain reaching from mountain to
mountain, composed of drift, probably washed in this great synclinal when the Atlantic
poured in its tide. Its beauty can never be described; the pathetic history of its frontier
period cannot be written; its wealth cannot be computed nor its future foretold. It has
no ancient history. Two hundred years ago it was unknown to civilized man. Behind its
history stands the savage, and the sound of his receding footsteps finds a pathetic echo in
our hearts. He was not our enemy but our victim; we told him we were his friend but he
was too sagacious to put himself in our power or trust us. As long as the long grass grows
on the sandy bottom lands and the groves stand in their primitive beauty by the river's edge
the spirit of the savage will be there waiting for the vision of civilization to disappear.

This is one of the most famous valleys on the globe. An insignificant fight lasting less
than half an hour, where but a few hundred were engaged, so touched the heart of humanity
that it made it impossible for the mother country to continue the war. A poem gave it a
place in the imagination of mankind and stamped it there forever. Poetically, pathetically
and exquisitely beautiful, its mineral wealth has turned the footsteps of the poor and
oppressed of all lands to this valley. Our history is not made manifest in ancient ruins nor
crumbling towers; we are not the legatees of noble titles or of royal blood; we have but
few historical shrines and no graves of historical interest. No genius nor hero who has written his name on the pages of the world's history has honored us by being born in our midst.

Our forefathers built a beautiful monument at Wyoming over the bones of their unfor-
tunate ancestors. This shaft is chaste and elegant. This generation have as yet done
nothing to preserve and mark historical localities nor to perpetuate and proclaim any event
of our past history. It would become us to rear a few historical shrines where our pride at
least would be proclaimed. The spot of ground at Sturmerville where the massacre took
place should be marked by a tablet: the place where the men who fell there lay buried,
until they were removed to the monument plot, should be adorned by a column, and when
the Court House is removed from the centre of the Public Square it is to be hoped that a
statue may be placed there in honor of the "Boys in Blue." We of this age are not dis-
posed to erect ornamental monuments, for we are past the heroic and poetical period, our
hero worship has faded into practical wisdom.

We have a Monumental Association that on the third of July, each year, meets at the monument to echo echoes and build historical shrines in the July sunshine, while the location of the Fort at Forty Fort is not discernible and Queen Esther's Rock is marked only by a cow shed. The monuments this generation have built are of brick and mortar.

The statue of Reuben Nelson, D. D., the founder of Wyoming Seminary, does not adorn the grounds of that institution nor his bust the chapel, but in accord with modern sentiment Nelson Memorial Hall was erected to fill a double mission—a servant of the living and a monument to the dead. Nesbitt Science Hall, a gift to the Seminary, will make the name of Abram Nesbitt as well-known and honored in the twentieth century as it is in the nineteenth. The Osterhout Free Library and Historical Building, the Memorial Church, Harry Hillman Academy and the Memorial Hall of the Grand Army testify to the intelligence as well as the good taste and liberality of our citizens who have erected memorials.

The most economical and lasting monuments we have in the valley are the names given to the natural features, municipal divisions and geographical boundaries. These names when regarded collectively give us a brief history of the people. The Indian names possess beauty and individuality, stamping forever the only original poetry of this continent on this locality, and give our life a background of savage poetry. Our forefathers imported their names, which proclaim their English parentage. Kingston, Plymouth, Hanover and Troy suggest a British Province. The name of our county hints of our past relations to France. Nanticoke and Shawnee locate two Indian tribes. The name of our river and the valley possess as much beauty, character and poetry as any names in our language. The Indian names are responsible to a large degree for the Parnassian stamp which has given this valley to fame. All the names which were not borrowed or inherited by us either proclaim our lack of intelligence or taste. We have Gabtown, Whiskey Hill, Skunktown, Yellow Wash, Poke Hollow, Goose Island, Blindtown and the like. The descriptive names are Plains (which is a hill), Pittston, Ashley, Buttonwood, Pleasant Valley (that is neither pleasant nor a valley), Edwardsdale and Avondale, both mining towns built on a bare hillside. Our city perpetuates the names of two men of little interest to us; we spell it with a big B and a hyphen. For the rest of our names we have taken the surname of some citizen.

Our historical names are Zebulon Butler, who commanded the little band at the massacre; Frances Slocum, who was taken from her home in Wilkes-Barre by a band of Delaware Indians when but a child and spent her life among them, she is called "the Lost Sister of Wyoming"; George Catlin, the painter of the aborigines of America; Count Zinzendorf, an early Moravian missionary, and Queen Esther, a coarse, intemperate and brutal squaw from Tioga Point, who murdered the prisoners the night after the massacre in a dramatic manner; these have a place in our history. The name of Brant probably falsely is associated with the atrocities at Wyoming; then there is Butler, who commanded the British forces; and Campbell, the author of the once popular epic, "Gertrude of Wyoming"; for him it would be a nice exhibition of poetic sentiment and justice on our part if we should rear his statue in payment of the advertisement he gave us and the poetic luster he attached to Wyoming Valley. We are a little proud that Louis XIV put up at a hotel in Wilkes-Barre and that King James I made this classic valley over to the Council of Plymouth incidentally with a tract of land extending to the South Sea (Pacific) in 1620, and that Charles II, to liquidate an old debt he owed to the father of William Penn, gave to the im-

portunate William the same territory in 1681, all of which gives a background of royalty to our history. We have the satisfaction of laying on a King the responsibility of being obliged, after suffering untold miseries, to accept the Decree of Trenton, that gave the land to the hated Hessians who had hired themselves to the British to help conquer us and then had the effrontery to remain.

There are many names that the dust of years has not hidden on the pages of our local history. The most prominent private citizen of all our history was Matthias Hollenback. He was a monopolist, as he monopolized nearly all the business in northeastern Pennsylvania and central New York, and owned enough land if combined to make a State. The two great Judges, George W. Woodward and John N. Conyngham, stand fixed stars in our firmament. Hendrick B. Wright with his fine imposing figure and glowing oratory cannot be lost sight of. Father Hunt (Rev. Thomas P.), the great temperance lecturer of his day, with his long white beard and bent form demands our notice. Reuben Nelson, D. D., the founder of the Wyoming Seminary, we could not forget if we would. Our historians have made their fame secure.

No one at the present day is clamoring to be remembered in the future. It is a vain query to ask if any name among us will survive a century. If we have not served and hung a lamp in the hearts of mankind we should be forgotten.

The amount of wealth in the possession of the people of this valley is enormous. We do not know how many millionaires we have. John Welles Hollenback and Abram Nesbitt are millionaires, and Lawrence Myers, Charles A. Miner, W. L. Conyngham and Daniel Edwards reputed millionaires. The last two gentlemen, the first by selling coal and the second by mining, acquired their wealth. The very wealthy people of the valley are Thomas Ford, Ralph Lacoe and Scott Stark, of Pittston; George S. Bennett, Baker Hillman, Richard Sharpe, Thomas Atherton, Andrew Derr, W. D. Loomis, John G. Wood, Edward S. Loop, George C. Lewis, George Parrish, James Sutton, Robert Baur, Richard Walsh, Alexander VanHorn, S. L. Brown, Charles Farrish, Edward Welles, Andrew Hunlock, Nathaniel Rutter, Garrick M. Harding, A. J. Davis, William and H. H. Harvey, George Loveland, Sheldon and Benjamin Reynolds, E. W. Sturdevant, Marcus Smith, Charles D. Foster, Barney Burgunder, John C. Haddock, Morgan B. Williams, Charles Stegmaier, Mrs. A. T. McClintock, Mrs. John Phelps, Mrs. Samuel Turner, the Misses Bennett, Mrs. H. H. Derr, Mrs. Priscilla Bennett, Mrs. B. G. Carpenter, Miss Lucy Abbott, Mrs. Josiah Lewis, and the estates of H. B. Wright, Charles Dorrance, E. L. Dana, George W. Woodward, John Reichard, C. B. Price, Thomas Lazarus, Jonas Long, E. Maxwell, R. J. Flick, Reuben Downing, Richard Jones and Mrs. Emily Wright, all of Wilkes-Barre; Calvin Parsons, of Parsons; H. B. Plumb, of Plumbtown; Mrs. Frank Turner and George Davenport, of Plymouth; Mrs. Payne Pettebone and Robert T. Pettebone, of Wyoming; William Loveland, John D. Hoyt and Mrs. Samuel Hoyt, of Kingston, and many others.

This valley in the past was rich in noble men. The line has not died out. We have a goodly number left who are enjoying that beautiful pause between sunset and twilight that life takes as if to prolong its delights. Rev. E. Hazard Snowden, D. D., was born in 1799 and is sitting contentedly on the shores of time waiting to see the dawn of the twentieth century. Nathaniel Rutter was born in 1806, though slightly bent is strong, grand and vigorous. Calvin Parsons carries his splendid proportions with the grace of a young man, yet he was born in 1815. Draper Smith and John J. Shonk, of Plymouth, were born in

1815; Charles Morgan was born in 1814; Christian Brahl and Rev. Miner Swallow were born the same year; Frank Helme in 1816; Ira Tripp in 1817; Lawrence Myers and Lewis LeGrand in 1818; John B. Smith, John D. Hoyt and William Dickover in 1819; Squire Eno and George Parrish in 1820; William Loveland and John Sharp Pettibone in 1821; George Davenport in 1823; Rev. H. H. Welles, George Loveland, Rev. J. K. Peck and Edward S. Loop in 1824; Daniel E. Edwards, P. A. Reeves and Robert Baur in 1825; A. C. Laycock, John Welles Hollenback, Dr. J. B. Crawford and Simon Long in 1827; A. R. Brundage, Esq., in 1828; H. B. Plumb in 1829; Charles A. Miner, Garrick M. Harding and C. B. Sutton in 1830; Abram Nesbitt and Morgan B. Williams in 1831; Stanley Woodward in 1833; Isaac Long, George Reichard and J. Bennett Smith in 1834; E. H. Chase, Esq., in 1835; Rev. Theophilus Jones in 1810. The list if made complete would be a very long one.

We miss from our streets the many remarkable men who have passed away during the last few years. We look in vain on the streets of our city for face and form of Judge Dana, William P. Miner, Colonel Dorrance, L. D. Shoemaker, Dr. E. R. Mayer, A. T. McClintock, Reuben J. Flick, E. P. and J. Vaughn Darling, H. B. Payne, W. R. Maffet, C. F. Ingham, John C. Phelps, B. G. Carpenter, W. W. Loomis, Allen Dickson, General McCartney, and at this writing Charles M. Conyngham is lying dead at his home in Wilkes-Barre. The list if complete would show a line of men that we regard with affection and reverence.

Many of the old historic families are dying out, in this locality at least. Such as the Abbott, Bidlacks, Blackman, Dana, Dennison, Fell, Franklin, Gore, Hollenback, Inman, Jameson, Jenkins, Mallery, Pierce, Perkins, Ransom, Ross, Searles, Slocum, Stewart, Swetland, Tuttle and Wright. The most historic family of the valley is the Butler family. The great men of this family were Colonel Zebulon Butler, our greatest soldier, and General Lord Butler, one of the most prominent private citizens of our past history; E. G. Butler and C. E. Butler are descendants. The Dennison family shine on the pages of our history; the most famous name is Colonel Nathan Dennison, who commanded the left wing of the men who were slaughtered at the massacre; his marriage to Miss Sill was the first white marriage in the valley, in 1769; their son Lazarus is supposed to be the first white child born in this section; Colonel Dennison was one of the first Judges of the county. George, his son, served in the Legislature. The Dorrance family has stood as one of the first families of the valley; Colonel Benjamin Dorrance was in the fort when it surrendered, being but a lad; Lieutenant-Colonel George Dorrance was killed at the massacre; Rev. John Dorrance was pastor of the Presbyterian Church in Wilkes-Barre, many years; Colonel Charles Dorrance, of Dorranceton, was one of the foremost private citizens of Wyoming Valley, died 1892; the family is represented by his four sons and his daughter, Mrs. Sheldon Reynolds. The Hollenback family were the wealthiest in this part of the State; the famous head of this family in the valley was Matthias; he was in the massacre but escaped by swimming the river; his son, George M., inherited his father's wealth and his great genius for business. The Jenkins family begins with John Jenkins, who presided at the first meeting of the patriots to vote on striking for independence; he was a noted surveyor and his capture by the Indians makes one of the interesting narratives of our history; the late Steuben Jenkins, the historian, was a descendant. The Dana family in Wyoming fully maintained the prestige of that great name; Anderson Dana was a pioneer lawyer and an advocate of education and

religion; he fell in the massacre and his widow and children fled to Connecticut; Mrs. Dana carried her husband's papers in a pillow-case and thereby saved her title to the Dana estate; her son Anderson settled on the Dana estate and was a prominent man; the late Edmund L. Dana was his grandson; E. L. Dana served with distinction in the Mexican and civil wars; rose to the rank of General; was one of the Judges of our Court, and a cultured man. The Harding family were the first to yield their blood in the early struggles in the valley; two were killed in the Exeter massacre and four were members of Captain Durkee's company; Judge Garrick Harding represents the family. Major John Durkee was one of the forty settlers; Robert Durkee fell at the massacre; he was a captain in the Continental army and had resigned to come home to defend his family; the Durkee family were the founders of Wilkes-Barre and they denied themselves immortality by not baptising their offspring "Durkee." General Simon Spalding, made famous by the affair at Bound Brook, was also with General Sullivan in his raid on the Indians. The history of the Gore family is a tale of blood; the elder Gore was a magistrate under the Connecticut authority and was one of the old men left in the fort July third; in the battle were five sons and two sons-in-law and five of them were slain. The Pierce family furnished victims for the butchery at Wyoming; Ezekiel was a major. The Inman family is known to history mainly because Richard imbibed more whiskey than he could carry on the morning of July third and lived to save the life of Rufus Bennett by shooting an Indian that was chasing him; this family had four members killed by the Indians and in consequence the family became known as Indian hunters. The wealthy and influential Shoemaker family have given the valley a line of lawyers, legislators and worthy citizens; L. D. Shoemaker, Esq., lately deceased, ranked first at the Bar and as a representative of the people; Robert Shoemaker, Esq., and Dr. Levi, are conspicuous Shoemakers at the present day. Colonel Pickering was the most prominent man sent here by the Pennsylvania claimants and was kidnaped by the Yankees for arresting Colonel John Franklin. Two of the Ross family were slain at Wyoming; the family had a taste for military affairs and public life; the two famous names of the family are General William and William Sterling, his son; both were members of the State Senate; Edward Sterling Loop has the sword that the elder Ross was presented with by the Executive Council at Philadelphia; Doctor Ross of South Wilkes-Barre is the only male representative of the family left. The Bidlack family were soldiers, full of patriotism; James was captain and led his company to action while his father, who was an old man, was in command of a company of old men in the fort at Plymouth; the Rev. Benjamin Bidlack, of Kingston, made the fame of the family by singing the "Swaggering Man" to entertain his captors and swaggered himself over the fence. The Pettebone family are old settlers and soldiers; a large number of the descendants live at Forty Fort. Doctor William Hooker Smith was a very prominent early physician and also an author. The name of Stark is among the early settlers, and some of them were killed at the massacre; the Pittston and Plainsville branches are well and favorably known to this generation. Samuel Carey was a captive for six years with the Indians, having been captured after the massacre, on Wintermoot Island, and adopted by an Indian family who had lost a son. The Myers family has an honored place in our affections as well as in our history; Mrs. Myers, who was in the fort, furnished George Peck, the historian, with much matter for his history; B. F. Myers, of Kingston, represents the family. The Harvey family begins in our history with the name of Benjamin, who was an intimate friend of Zebulon Butler; the family has a creditable Revolutionary War record; they are an old

Plymouth family ; W. J. and H. H., of Wilkes-Barre, are wealthy and influential. John Abbott built the first house in Wilkes-Barre; he was killed by the Indians; the late William Penn Abbott, D. D., a descendant, was one of the most eloquent divines of the Methodist Episcopal Church; Miss Lacy, of Wilkes-Barre, remains to represent the family. Jameson was an old Hanover family; John was one of the two men shot by the Indians near the Hanover Green, in 1782. The Perkins family were great sufferers during the Revolution. The Swetland family were wealthy and influential—an old Wyoming family; Luke was a hero of the frontier times and published an account of his captivity among the Indians; Swetland Hall, Wyoming Seminary, was built by William. The Blackman family is an old Hanover family; Major Eleazer helped build the fort at Wilkes-Barre and was a brave soldier. The Marcy family of early days are known to us by the record of the sufferings of the wives of Zebulon and Ebenezer while flying from the valley after the battle ; one of the children died on the way and as there were no means to bury it the mother was obliged to cover it with leaves and go on and leave it ; the children of the late Reuben Marcy, of Kingston, represent the Marcy family in the valley. The Gaylords were numerous and of good repute; one branch settled in Plymouth. Lieutenant James Welles was one of the patriots who fell at Wyoming; the Welles family of this day is a synonym for all that is admirable ; Rev. Henry H., Edward, and John Welles Hollenback have no peers in the valley. The Church family were Kingston farmers and Nathaniel, John and Gideon were Revolutionary soldiers ; William E., of Kingston, is a descendant. One of the most intellectual and notable families of which we boast is the Johnson family; Ovid F. was Attorney General of Pennsylvania; Rev. Jacob was the first settled minister in Wilkes-Barre; Jacob drew up the articles of capitulation between the British and Americans in the Battle of Wyoming; Wesley was mainly instrumental in pushing to a successful completion the Wyoming Monument; Dr. F. C., of the *Record of the Times*, represents those splendid traits of character and intellect for which this family has been noted.

We regard these old families as representing more in themselves of worth and interest than the interest and dramatic incidents of their lives. They were formed before they came here and were not formed by the conditions that surrounded them here, but formed them. They had not been draught horses at home but a part of the most advanced people of modern times. They possessed what we lack more than anything else and that is character.

The old stock were Protestants. The Methodists formed the first class, at Hanover. This was the only one between Baltimore and Lake Ontario. The old Forty Fort Church was the first finished church edifice in Northeastern Pennsylvania. This valley was in the Oneida Conference. In 1834 the missionary collection for the entire conference was only eight hundred dollars. The collection from the valley was one dollar and nine cents from Kingston. There was a beautiful grove at the Forty Fort Church where the services were often held. The Presbyterian and the Methodist pulpits resounded with the orthodox abuse of each other and with politics.

There is but little friction between the different churches at the present time and little doctrine is preached. The Protestant churches are all in harmony. Sometimes a Protestant minister who is behind the good taste of the community will indulge in a coarse tirade against the Catholic church. The pulpit, as a friend of the working people, sometimes preaches a great deal of socialism and has done much to keep alive the hatred and mistrust of the employers of labor.

In the Catholics are the Irish population, which are about one-fifth, and the Huns and and Poles, which are one-fifth. One-half the Germans are communicants of that church. The Welsh represent about one-fifth and the Americans two-fifths, which are Protestants. The Germans have many Freethinkers among them and a large portion of the working class of the Americans are non-church-goers. The Poles and Huns go to church but they seem to separate morality and religion. All the churches are active in temperance work. In the Catholic church, or among the members of that church, are a number of temperance societies; the St. Aloysius is accredited with a membership of ten thousand young men in this diocese. The Irish nationalty is becoming the most temperate of all of the foreign population. The Protestant church has labored for the promotion of temperance and at no time has it done a greater work than at the present, in the care it is giving to the moral and social welfare of the youth. The church has tried several patent methods of temperance reform without the aid of religion. The temperance lecture was usually a loud advertisement for the liquor business. The Good Templar societies were not without their fruits. Then we had the woman's crusade or the pathetic sentimental movement, when woman's tears were applied to wash out the saloons. Then local option was tried, but the shoestring would not tie the lion. The last movement was an effort to realize the most dazzling dream of the nineteenth century, and that was Government control. A few are still chasing this rainbow.

The drink habit is considered disreputable as well as the selling of drink. The saloon where nothing but drink is sold is a modern institution in the valley. Drink was formerly sold in inns as an accompaniment to food and lodging, but the foreigner, agreeable to his taste, introduced these man traps wherever there were men and boys to be debauched. The Irishman like the early settler, drank whiskey, but the other emigrants drank beer and they have made it one of the staples of life. Beer has, to a great extent, become a substitute for whiskey, which is an advance. Twenty-five years ago our streets were full of drunken men, to-day you can spend a day in Wilkes-Barre on a holiday and see but few intoxicated men. The young man has other places than a saloon in which he may pass agreeably his leisure hours and he is coming in contact with influences that are lifting him above the associations of the bar room. The American population are more temperate than their forefathers, while the foreign population have made an advance in temperance, morality and intelligence such as the world has never before witnessed.

There are many interesting and beautiful points for the stranger to visit in this valley. The most imposing view is from Campbell's Ledge. The view from Prospect Rock on the mountain back of Wilkes-Barre is comprehensive; from Penobscot very picturesque. Point Lookout is very sightly. From Tilbury Knob near Nanticoke you may look down over a wild scene to the south. From the highest point on the Wilkes-Barre mountain you can view the scenery in every direction and the panorama is one of surpassing beauty. Away to the east may be seen Bald Mountain, the great peak of the Pocono, and the beautiful Blue range repeating itself in the distance. All our mountains are even, symmetrical and graceful. The view up the river from Forty Fort is the finest river view in the valley. Wintermute Island is to be seen; the plain where the massacre took place, the lower flat over which the few survivors fled and the heavy wooded river bank are spread before you; beyond, Campbell's Ledge stands grey and grim, while below the church steeples which betray the location of the old historic town of Wyoming, the Wyoming Monument is

visible. The great plain impresses one as a fitting scene for the great drama acted there. The scene is very primitive and the wooded banks are now probably nearly as they were when the terrified band of old men, women and children watched the red coats and the mob of savages coming down the flats after the fight.

Between Wilkes-Barre and Nanticoke, at the Red Tavern, is a view which combines into a scene, lavish with all the poetical and picturesque features of the valley, this composition is harmonious and complete. At this old tavern the aristocracy held their balls; here the runaway couple came to get married and the men who occasionally imbibed, came to go on a spree or have a quiet drunk.

Toby's Cave has no historical associations. Toby is only a name to us. The face of the cave is worn by the waves of the lake that filled this valley. A rock on the opposite side of Ross Hill on the same level shows similar water markings. It is inferred that these rocks indicate the shore line of the lake. The valley was probably drained by water washing out a channel at Nanticoke. There are several places on the Kingston mountain where, on the flat and exposed faces of the rocks, can be seen the markings of the flood that poured over the mountain. The scrapings of the glacier are found on the exposed ledges. The terminal moraine is to be found at Berwick. At Mill Creek, where excavations were made, sea shells were found deposited in large quantities. The bank on which East Pittston stands is a great gravel pile, washed in from the north. On the west side of the valley, at the base of the hill, is the bed of a river; the floor of the valley is broken in rolls. At the pond holes opposite Wilkes-Barre it is only thirty feet to the rock, while it is over two hundred feet to the rock on the Kingston flats. Twenty years ago the wild pigeons, ducks and geese flew over the valley in great numbers and the streams were filled with fish. The mine water has destroyed them and the only game left is a few muskrats, squirrels, rabbits and quail. Every one is on the hunt for a fortune and on the chase after the shy dollar.

The gorge back of Luzerne is worth visiting. At the Ice Cave you may find ice in August and see a beautiful waterfall. Back of Wyoming is Wolf's Den and below Kingston is Toby's Cave. River street is the pride of the citizens of Wilkes-Barre. The principal streets of Wilkes-Barre are too narrow to be effective and you feel that you are in an old country town.

Our Government Building is not our boast. We always send one of the boys to Congress who are fully occupied trying to shake down a postoffice. There are a number of fine business blocks. The church edifices of the city proclaim the devotion, wealth and good taste of the citizens.

The Court House is the old one made over several times. The city in the near future will be adorned with one worthy of this great county. If you go into the court room you will see the portraits of the distinguished Judges of the past. The most noticeable painting is that of the soldier-judge, Edmund L. Dana, painted by his son, the celebrated Charles Dana, of Paris. On the wall is a bust portrait of ex-judge Garrick M. Harding, the Boanerges of the Luzerne Bar. Judge Harding is an orator and is learned in the philosophy of the law. His presence is commanding and his address elegant. A painting of the most admirable man of our history, Judge John N. Conyngham, looks down with a face of a Roman senator. The powerful face of Judge George W. Woodward is represented by a crayon portrait. One gets the impression that this man was a tremendous intellectual force. His son Stanley graces the bench, clear headed, just and sociable. The portrait of Judge

Henry M. Hoyt, Governor of this Commonwealth, is of a very able man. The face of Judge Hendrick B. Wright shows remarkable individuality. The visitor should not fail to be in court when President Judge Charles E. Rice is on the bench, for he is second to no man in the commonwealth. He is not an orator and his only ambition is to see that justice is done. A very companionable man. As he was born in '46 he is yet a young man. We have noticed previously Judge John Lynch. To fail to meet the judge of the Orphans' Court, D. L. Rhone, is to defraud one's self. He has a noticeable face. He is Yankee, French and Dutch, and he has all the characteristics of the three nationalties emphasized. The bar is crowded with both brilliant and able men. Henry M. Palmer is a tremendous legal broadaxe and Alexander Farnham is by general consent the ideal man and lawyer at the Luzerne bar.

The most prominent men of the valley at the present time are: John Welles Hollenback, who built the Hollenback block, one of the finest structures in this part of the State; President and promoter of the new bridge; liberal contributor of Lafayette College and prominent in the financial interest in the valley. W. L. Conyngham, a prominent citizen. Abram Nesbitt, of Kingston; President of the Second National Bank; donator of Nesbitt Science Hall to the Wyoming Seminary. Judge Charles E. Rice; was candidate for the office of Orphans' Court Judge 1874; elected District Attorney 1876; elected Law Judge 1879; now President Judge; was on the bench when he was thirty-three years old. Judge Stanley Woodward; commanded a company in the late war; appointed Additional Law Judge 1879; elected 1880; re-elected 1890. Alexander Farnham, Esq.; elected District Attorney 1874; declined nomination for Judge and other important public offices; President of the Bar Association of Luzerne County. Charles A. Miner; served three terms in the Pennsylvania House of Representatives; represented the State as Honorary Commissioner at the World's Exhibition at Vienna, Austria; owner of Miner's mills. George S. Bennett; prominent in the industrial and financial interest of the valley; Superintendent of the Sunday school of the First M. E. Church for many years. Hon. Edwin S. Osborne; a distinguished officer in the civil war; Major-General of the third division of the National Guard for ten years; candidate for Law Judge 1874; served in Congress from 1884 to 1891. Lyman H. Bennett, Esq.; a prominent member of the Luzerne Bar; candidate for Law Judge. Hon. Garrick M. Harding; elected District Attorney 1858; elected President Judge 1870; resigned 1880; well known as a writer. Hon. George W. Shonk; elected to Congress 1890. S. L. Brown; prominent business man. Judge D. L. Rhone; was director of the public schools of Wilkes-Barre; elected District Attorney 1867; member of the Constitutional Convention from the Thirteenth District 1872; elected Orphans' Court Judge 1874, has filled that position to the present time; author of two standard legal works and many articles on miscellaneous subjects. Hon. Henry W. Palmer, Esq.; was Attorney-General under Gov. Hoyt; appointed 1878; probably the youngest man who ever held that position, (thirty-nine years), and one of the ablest bank directors; counsel for many large corporations and is interested in several large corporations; also author of a notable satirical production (Saxe's Pond). George R. Bedford, Esq.; a prominent lawyer and citizen. R. Bruce Ricketts; Colonel of Artillery; distinguished himself at the Battle of Gettysburg; Democratic candidate for Lieutenant-Governor 1886. Rev. L. L. Sprague, D. D.; President of Wyoming Seminary since 1882; has made that institution one of the first preparatory schools in the United States and has increased the valuation of the plant one half; it is now valued at a quarter

of a million dollars. Rev. T. C. Edwards, D. D.; one of the leading Welsh divines in the United States and the author of two valuable works on oratory. Hon. Daniel Edwards; a prominent coal operator; Presidential elector 1884. Agib Ricketts, Esq.; in 1862 Chief of police; 1880 independent Labor Reform candidate for Additional Law Judge; editor of a temperance paper. Andrew Hunlock, Esq.; was President of the Anthracite Savings Bank and is one of the wealthy men of the valley. Isaac P. Hand, Esq.; was Principal of the Hyde Park public schools (Scranton); was Secretary and presiding officer of the School Board of the Third District of Wilkes-Barre; was Chairman of the Republican County Committee. George K. Powell, Esq.; in U. S. Navy; was shipwrecked and experienced an earthquake in Southern Peru; is a prominent lawyer and active in church. E. Greenough Scott, Esq.; was nominated for Congress while he resided in Sunbury; candidate for President Judge of the Eighth Judicial District; was instructor of artillery at Fort Schuyler; wrote and published two legal works of great value. J. Bennett Smith; a prominent citizen. John A. Opp, Esq.; held the position of Judge Advocate with the rank of Major in National Guard of Pennsylvania and is prominent in the industries of Plymouth. F. M. Nichols; was appointed by the court District Attorney to fill the vacancy caused by the election of C. E. Rice to the bench; was candidate for nomination for that office; in 1882 was candidate for District Attorney; now the Mayor of Wilkes-Barre. John B. Reynolds; candidate for Congress and the father of the electric railroad in the valley and the organizer of the North street river bridge. John A. Gorman, Esq.; District Attorney. H. Baker Hillman; erected the Harry Hillman Academy. George B. Kulp; author of "Families of the Wyoming Valley;" editor of *Legal Register*. Charles Parrish; one of the leading coal and railroad men in the developing of these industries in the State; was President of the Lehigh and Wilkes Barre Coal Company; one of the organizers and first President of the First National Bank; President of the Hazard Manufacturing Company. Liddon Flick, Esq.; organizer and originator of the Wyoming Valley Trust Company and Grand Opera House. P. M. Carhart; Cashier of the First National Bank; prominent in church and Sunday school work. James M. Coughlin; Superintendent of the Wilkes-Barre public schools; Superintendent of the schools of Luzerne County for twelve years. Hon Morgan B. Williams; elected to the Senate 1884; candidate for nomination for Congress 1894. Hon. W. H. Hines; elected by the Labor Reform party to the State Legislature 1878; to the same office 1882; to the Senate 1884, and to Congress 1892, and nominated for the same office 1894. C. Ben Johnson; was Secretary of the Board of Trade; member of the House of Representatives 1891; well known as a writer and a public speaker. Rev. Henry L. Jones, M. A.; rector of St. Stephen's Church; one of the most cultured and eloquent ministers in the Episcopal Church. Rev. J. Richards Boyle, D. D.; captain in the civil war; pastor of the First M. E. Church; a prominent minister. Rev. F. B. Hodge, D. D.; pastor of the First Presbyterian; one of the leading ministers in the Presbyterian Church. Henry Blackman Plumb, Esq.; author of the "History of Hanover Township." Gustav Hahn, Esq.; is the only prominent German lawyer of the Luzerne Bar; was professor of modern languages at the Wyoming Seminary; was captain of Company K, Nineteenth Regiment, Pennsylvania Volunteers; appointed United States Commissioner 1864. D. L. O'Neill, Esq.; member of the State Legislature 1865; Councilman, Poor Director, candidate for Additional Law Judge 1874. Wm. S. McLean, Esq.; elected City Attorney 1875; delivered the master's oration at Lafayette College 1868; Democratic candidate for Judge 1879; president of the First National Bank; his father, Alexander, was a prominent coal operator. D. M. Jones, Esq.;

lawyer and poet; has published two volumes of his poems. John T. Lenahan, Esq.; candidate for District Attorney 1879. C. D. Foster; 1854 elected State Legislature; 1892 was the Republican nominee for Congress. Rev. Horace E. Hayden; historian and author. Ira M. Kirkendall; first Mayor of Wilkes-Barre. Henry A. Laycock, of Wyoming; has a brilliant war record; was appointed Colonel 1865. G. Mortimer Lewis, Esq.; one of the originators of the Electric Light Company and helped to bring about the combination of the street railways of the valley and originator of the Wilkes-Barre and Shawnee Bridge Company. Lieutenant-Colonel Eugene Beaumont; graduated from West Point; was made Assistant Adjutant-General after making a brilliant war record; received Jefferson Davis at Macon after his capture; commanded a battalion of troops at Palo Duro Canon; 1892 promoted Lieutenant-Colonel. Frederick Corss, M. D., of Kingston; lecturer on education and the natural sciences and a writer. John B. Crawford, M. D.; surgeon in the army during the civil war and served as president of the United States Pension Examining Board. Alfred Darte, Esq.; Lieutenant in the late war; elected District Attorney 1879; re-elected 1888; candidate for nomination for Law Judge 1891; is now the candidate for Orphans' Court Judge; (Rep). Harry A. Fuller, Esq.; a prominent lawyer, citizen and public speaker. Ralph D. LaCoe, of Pittston; collected and donated one of the largest and finest collection of fossil plants, etc., in the United States. Robert Baur; has published the *Waechter* since 1851; the oldest editor in this part of the State. John S. McGroarty, Esq.; published the first collection of Wyoming Valley poetry and is one of the poets of the valley; elected Treasurer of the county 1890. Dr. D. J. J. Mason; a noted musician and music composer; 1886 received the degree of Mus. Bac. at Trinity College, Dublin, and Doctor of Music in Toronto, Canada. Rev. Dr. N. G. Parke; a noted Presbyterian minister of Pittston, who has served a pastorate there of fifty years.

The Irish people were the first of the later emigrants in the valley. The most representative and notable man of that nationality among us is Wm. S. McLean, Esq., President of the First National Bank. John Lynch is Associate Judge, a man of strong convictions, with the courage to express them, and as a Judge, aims to be just. John T. Lenahan, Esq., is a leading criminal lawyer. He is naturally adapted to that branch of the law. He is true to his clients, versatile, self reliant and displays great physical and mental energy when pleading a case. James L. Lenahan stands second as a criminal lawyer. He is more argumentative and not so demonstrative as his brother; more of a student of books and less executive ability and more respect for the fine susceptibilities of others. P. A. O'Boyle, Esq., is an orator and a man of fine parts and never degrades the court by insulting witness. Hon. W. H. Hines is a young man of ability, whose success was made possible by the rise and reign of the short lived Greenback or Labor Party that advocated fiat money. John S. McGroarty, Esq., is talented and highly esteemed. T. P. Ryder is an active worker in temperance reforms and is a talented, exemplary young man. Dr. George Kirwan is a conspicuous member of the medical profession, as also are Drs. A. P. O'Malley and P. J. Higgins; E. F. McGovern, E. A. Lynch, D. L. O'Neill, all successful lawyers, Richard D. Walsh, vice president of the First National Bank; John M. Ward, G. P. Strome, Thomas Maloney; Roger McGarry, J. M. Bolan, Dan Hart, the playwright, Cornelius Cronin, of Kingston, who is noted for his mental accomplishments, are the most conspicuous representatives of the Irish people in the valley. The Irishman, we notice, has handed the pick and shovel over to the Hun and Pole and is leaving the Welshman to mine most of the coal, and is "doing well in this country."

The Welsh population is so large that this section is called the Wales of America. They are mostly miners. They are a nation of musicians, with literary and religious proclivity. They are as a people as intelligent citizens as we have among us, but not the most progressive. The first Welshman is Daniel Edwards, of Kingston, who, when he came over these mountains, had but a few cents in his pocket, could not speak English, and had not had any early advantages; began working as a laborer and is to-day one of the very wealthy and influential citizens of the valley. Rev. T. C. Edwards, D. D., of Kingston, is a man of varied talents and is recognized in this country and in Wales as a leader among the Welsh nationality. A high minded, cultivated and useful man. Rev. E. J. Morris, of Wilkes-Barre, is a highly cultured and talented man. Dr. R. Davis stands among the leading physicians. Dr. D. J. J. Mason is at the head as a musical scholar. Richard Williams is a tenor singer of note; he won the first prize at the World's Fair. Mrs. J. P. Thomas leads the female choir from the valley that received the second prize at the World's Fair; is the leading Welsh lady in music. David James is a successful teacher of music. Gwilym Gwent, who was a toiler in the mines, was one of the musical geniuses of this century. He composed glees which have given him to fame. D. M. Jones, Esq., is one of the leading Welsh poets of the country. Morgan B. Williams is a prominent Welshman. William T. Smith, George T. Morgan, Morgan R. Morgan, Morgan D. Rosser, James T. Davis and G. M. Williams are prominent Welshmen. Gwilym Edwards, of Kingston, is a rising man. Rev. Theophilus Jones is a very old man and has the distinction of being baptized by Carismas Evans. Rev. John P. Harris was with Mr. Jones, the pioneer minister in this section. There are many Welsh bards. The Welsh writers who write in English are D. M. Jones, who has published two volumes of his compositions; George Coronoway, whose productions strike a responsive chord in Welsh hearts. Rev. T. C. Edwards has published two volumes on Elocution. Rev. E. J. Morris has published two volumes, one on Theology and the other on miscellaneous subjects. W. L. Myles writes well and Frank Humphreys has issued a little book of his writings. Prof. W. George Powell, formerly of Kingston, but now of Scranton, is the most talented young Welshman in this part of the State. The late brilliant W. S. Powell was an occasional writer of verse. Rev. J. P. Harris wrote a successful drama. J. C. Powell is one of the editors and proprietors of *The Record of the Times.* The old Welsh ministers chant their sermons. The Welsh seem to have the impress of the poetry, music and solemnity of nature that seeks for expression.

The Germans are about one-tenth of the population of Wilkes-Barre, where most of them reside. In the legal profession Gustav Hahn stands quite alone. In the medical profession they have Drs. Sperling and Wagner. Robert Baur has been in the valley for fifty years and was an editor before his contemporaries in the valley were born. Frederick Theis is President of the Wyoming Valley Trust Company and a successful insurance agent; largely interested in local industries. Christian Brahl is a retired merchant, highly esteemed by his fellow townsmen. Anthony Voght, George Reichard and the Stegmaier family are well known. Fred Ahlborn, Philip Raeder, Philp Nachbar, Philip Steinhauer and Peter A. Kropp were but lately deceased.

The Scotch are quite numerous in Pittston and fill many important offices. The McColough, Hutchison, Waddell, Bryden, Dick, Scott and Graham are influential families. The Englishman is also found. There are but few French families. Ralph Lacoe, of Pittston, is a Frenchman, and also Col. J. D. Laciar, who has written the editorial for the

Scranton *Republican* for twenty years. These two men are distinguished citizens. Mr. Lacoe presented the Smithstonian Institute with one of the most complete collections of vegetable fosils ever made.

The Poles and Lithuanians are late comers. They are a progressive people and look down on the Hungarians. In a few years they will be an important factor in the political as well as in commercial life. Sylvester Paukztis, of Edwardsville, has in ten years made in the mercantile and other lines of business fifty thousand dollars and a number of his countrymen have done as well. The Hungarians are despised by the Poles. They are such a late importation into Europe that we may consider them Asiatics. These nationalties have brought to an end, for the present, strikes and the possibility of any successful attempt of the miner to control the mining interest.

The working man is ceasing to brawl "Down with monopolies," and we rarely hear that false claim made, that the "rich are getting richer and the poor poorer," for it is disproven by thousands of beautiful homes owned by working men that dot our valley, and the fact that only a few of our industries pay large dividends on the capital invested. Socialism has endeavored to strangle prosperity at its birth and all labor reform movements have tended to impoverish the working classes and have stood in the way of general prosperity.

The Jews are not numerous. Most of them are merchants in Wilkes-Barre. The first Jewish resident was Martin Long. The most notable family of that nationality among us is the Long family. There are four prominent Long families. The late Jonas Long and Isaac were brothers. The latter and the sons of the former are the first dry goods merchants in this part of the State. Marx and Simon are brothers and are also prominent merchants. These men were the architects of their fortunes. Other prominent families are the Burgunder, Rev. H. Rubin, the first rabbi in Wilkes-Barre; served thirty years and is succeeded by Israel Joseph; Joseph Coons, Abram Strauss, Isaac Livingston, F. Eisner, Henry Ansbacher, Galland, Levi. Hoffheimer and other families. The temple Baa'i B'rith is on South Washington street and their cemetery is in Hanover township.

There are more wealthy people in Wilkes-Barre and vicinity than in any city in the State, with the exception of Pitt-burg and Philadelphia. Kingston probably contains more wealth than any town of its size in the country. This county produces more anthracite coal than any county in the world. We mine about one million tons of coal each month and average about one million dollars in wages paid for mining. There are more than one hundred coal openings. The valuation of Wilkes-Barre property is over twenty-five million dollars and the number of registered voters in the city last year was nine thousand, five hundred and eighty-three. There are forty churches in the city. The M. E. Church property is valued at two hundred and seventy-five thousand dollars; the Presbyterian Church property three hundred and ninety-one thousand dollars; the Catholic Church property, three hundred and fifty-six thousand dollars; Protestant Episcopal, one hundred and eighteen thousand five hundred dollars; Jewish, twenty-six thousand; Congregational, twenty-nine thousand; Baptist, forty-three thousand five hundred; Lutheran, four hundred and thirty-five thousand; Reform, eighteen thousand; Evgangelical, fifteen thousand; the valuation of chuch property in the city is nearly one and a quarter million dollars. We have the largest wire rope and axle works in the world. And this valley is the home of many other great industries. Seven great railroads center here and every town and hamlet within fifteen miles is reached by the electric railroad, this system being

as large, if not the largest, in the world. The city has seventeen handsome school buildings, accommodating sixteen thousand pupils. Wilkes-Barre provides amusements for the population of the valley. The Grand Opera House and Music Hall between them give nearly forty entertainments every month during the amusement season, and at nearly every entertainment the house is crowded. Most of these entertainments aim not only to be highly amusing but are as good as the great mass of people who go to see them can appreciate, while many of them open up to the boy from the mine the world, revealing to him glimpses of society, human nature and the experiences of human life, such as he could not otherwise obtain. There are seven hundred and seventy licenses granted to sell strong drink in the county, and over one hundred in Wilkes-Barre. In the little borough of Edwardsville there are twenty-two saloons and but little accommodation for the entertainment of the traveling public. There is one thing that the moral people of this valley permit that is criminal, and that is to allow whiskey and rum to be sold as a beverage. It is bad enough to have beer and other lighter drinks sold over nearly eight hundred bars, but to let those who keep the groggeries sell strong drink is criminal. Our temperance reformers are trying to get into politics. This will be the next step that will be made, sooner or later, to stop the indiscriminate sale of intoxicants, when practical temperance reforms appear. The valley is the literary center of Northern Pennsylvania. The golden age of our local literature is behind us. Our greatest genius was Dr. J. T. Doyle, a man of great and varied talents. Mrs. Doyle is preparing a collection of his poetical writings for publication. In the writer's judgment, Mrs. Verona Coe Holmes, of West Pittston, has written the two most poetical productions of our local literature, i. e. "The Cricket" and "One Night." Theron G. Osborne has produced the greatest quantity of good poetry and W. George Powell is our finest critical writer. Professor Powell has lost his sight and is supposed to be permanently blind. Miss Edith Brower is the only local writer of national reputation.

Several years ago the poets of the valley often met together for an evening. The office of the lawyer-poet, D. M. Jones, was a favorite place to meet. The party usually consisted of Dr. Doyle, D. M. Jones, John S. McGroarty, E. A. Niven, Theron G. Osborne, T. P. Ryder and W. George Powell, the late Will Powell, Fred Williams and the writer, from the West Side. Dr. Doyle would occupy the easy chair and would lead the conversation; no one who has not listened to the Doctor under such circumstances knows what powers of expression and mental resources he possessed. The hours and conversation would fly. The air would be so thick with poetry, philosophy, wit, nonsense, smoke and mental friction as to nearly obscure Davy's (Mr. Jones) smoky lamp. The muses would be made to dance a breakdown and Pegasus would be driven at a breakneck pace. Will S. Monroe did considerable in drawing the attention of the public to the wealth and beauty of our local literature, as also did the *Wyoming Magazine*, published by the writer. It is well known that the valley has, for a hundred years, been a literary center. Our progenitors wrote unnumbered sonnets, ditties, lyrics, epics, couplets and epilogues, but hardly a line survives. The strong, noble prose writing in Charles Miner's history of the valley and other prose productions of the past proclaim of the merits of our early writers. The blind sister of Charles Miner was a poet. In the Historical Rooms is a little volume entitled "The Harp of the Beech Woods." The poems were written by a young married woman who lived in the beech woods. She was of a titled family of England. Her marriage displeased her parents and she came with her husband to this country. They built a little cabin, and away from all associations but her husband, nature, her thoughts and a harp, she spent her

life. The poems in this volume are redolent of the sweet odors of the pine, the pathos and poetry of nature and life. Marie M. Pursel and Juniata Salsbury are well-known writers. Charles D. Linskill published a book of travels and D. M. Jones, Esq., is our poet laureat.

Most of our early writers were bitten with the style of Pope. A lawyer, sea captain, surveyor, judge and legislator by the name of Abraham Bradly wrote and published a book that received a warm reception. The ladies of Wilkes-Barre gathered nearly the entire edition and burned them. They thought it had infidel proclivities. The most remarkable thing about this book was its title—it contained eighty-one words. The work was a philosophical retrospect of the universe. Two satires written within a few years made a sensation. The first one was a take-off by Dr. Doyle on a supper given to celebrate the nativity of Moore, a remarkable production. The other was by Hon. H. W. Palmer, entitled "Soxe's Pond," aimed at the cheap demagogy of some local politicians. The sensation created by the publication was all out of proportion to its literary merit or wit. There is no disposition at the present time to produce imaginative literature.

The literature may be languishing, art and oratory discounted, the legitimate drama trodden underfoot, the mind and the eye neglected, but the ear is charmed and the voice cultivated and the love of good music general. Our musical societies and vocalists are our pride. The music genius was Gwilym Gwent, a poor laborer in our mines, who wrote glees that have never been surpassed. The lovers of music are building him a monument. Richard Williams is one of the finest soloists in this country. There is a musical instrument in nearly every house in the valley. The Welsh and Germans take the lead. Most of the children of these nationalities are taught the notes before they have learned the alphabet.

Our politics for the last thirty years have been very intoxicating. The Americans are largely Republicans, the Irish Democrats, the Welsh Republicans. The Germans lean to the Democratic party. The Hebrews are about evenly divided. The Huns and Poles are like a foot ball and all are sovereign. In education the European population are in the crescent and their advancement toward the realization of New England ideals has no parallel in history. The acquisition of knowledge is raising up a barrier against the enemies of our institutions. Our method of reform is by the breeding out process. We are, by the enforcement of wise laws, education and the laws of health, making the repetition of the ignorance and degradation of the present impossible in the future. We have swung out the Cloth of Gold.

The newspaper has, with all its virtues, led us into the vicious habit of disjointed thinking. The millinery of sensationalism and the supremacy of mediocrity is proving fatal to high aims. Life itself is becoming the high school where men are learning to draw their inspiration. It is not books, but from original contact with men and practical life. Some look upon literary culture and ornamental branches of education as fatal to character and success in life. These intellectual bankrupts need to remember that nature's old soliloquy, "To let the flowers grow between the leaves of life," has not been repealed, and that ignorance is a species of immorality. If we are moles, life is ragged and monotonous and we are deceived and bullied by it, and fail to see that it is a pageant of beauty, we turn down Matthew Arnold's declaration that "We should know ourselves and the world and the best which has been thought and said." The reason why the Anglo-Saxon has been supreme

and will continue to be is because he is intellectually superior and the man who cannot see it is a blank. The long head and wide forehead will prevail: these play the magical wand that wind and unwind our destiny. There is a saying that the country is built up of the brain of an Irishman and the muscle of a German. Surely the Irish people have the faculty to assimilate all that will advance them. Unlike the Welsh, they do not let their language or nationality stand in their way, and consequently they soon blend into the mass. They are born politicians and make successful criminal lawyers. At the Luzerne Bar they represent about fifteen per cent. and in the other professions about the same proportion. Ignorance, viciousness and vulgarity is very rapidly diminishing. We are by natural processes decreasing ignorance and intemperance. A mastering force or law is at work and all that mars our civilization yields to it. As a mass our ideals are not high. Every day and public life we find rather chilly and not very cleansing. We lack the culture that broadens the understanding and enriches the heart. We practically deny that the sovereign good consists in greatness of soul. We are not proud of our individuality and do not resist the world's attempt to merge us into the mass. The youth is speechless because he has no base of knowledge, and culture and high standards are deemed as useless as a field full of daises. We stand condemned for our lack of spiritual aims and the unnecessary sacrifice we are making to material well being is giving us over to ignorance and vulgarity. Our stock of mediocrity is appalling and so is our standard. Our minds are constantly in a circle with nothing beyond. A little share of personal good and ephemeral objects suffice us. We need a Prometheus to animate our dead hearts and save us from intellectual bankruptcy and some agency to plow our very hearts up. Nevertheless, our streets are crowded with a great army of young men. They are the peers of any generation that has preceded them. They will be actors in the most enlightened period in the history of the world and will witness the greatest advance in mental, moral, social, mechanical lines, and material prosperity of any age. The borough limits are disappearing. The farms are becoming towns. We are fast becoming a great metropolis. All power is becoming so divided that the anarchy of a class, as in the past, or the supremacy of a party or nationality is out of the question. The owner will control his property. The wise and just minority will make the laws; the scoundrel and fool will fall together. There is a law working for righteousness that will prevail and everything that stands on any other foundation will fall. The one who turns his thoughts to the twentieth century will see the evidence of the coming of something more than material prosperity in the future. We have resembled a glass of beer—all foam and dregs. We are letting the dregs settle and the froth falls of its own weight. I will lay down my pen at this point. I have rambled in a discursive way over the great drama of human life in this valley during this century, with but a glance at a few of the multitude who have preceded us into eternity or are yet acting their part in the drama of life, and under what I have written will write *Ipse Dixit*.

Kingston, Pa., September 12, 1894.

# PRINCIPAL EVENTS NINETEENTH CENTURY.

Without hurry, without rest the century has nearly passed. Not even a memory remains of the great mass of humanity which has preceded us. The dead signify but little to us. Yet their thoughts have become our character and have fashioned our very countenance.

When the Nineteenth Century dawned George Washington had been in his grave but a few days, and Napoleon had just declared himself first Consul of France. John Adams, the Federalist, was President, and Thomas Jefferson, the anti-Federalist, was Vice President.

Momentous events were being launched upon the world and stupendous machinations were being evolved in the mind of that brilliant luminary that was shedding such a dazzling lustre while passing with lightning speed through the political firmament of Europe (Napoleon), before whose mighty sceptre monarchies and principalities vanished as manikins manipulated under the wand of an accomplished magician.

Every gentleman wore a queue, powdered hair and cocked hat. Buttons were scarce and expensive. The trousers were fastened with pegs or laces. Pork, beef, fish, potatoes and hominy (Indian meal) were the staple diet. There were no manufactures in the country and every housewife raised her own flax and made her own linen. Crockery plates were objected to because they dulled the knives and the pewter plater and mug were common. A gentleman bowing to a lady always scraped his foot on the ground. The center of population was Virginia, as it contained a fifth of the population of the country. The laborer worked from sun to sun and was glad to get two shillings. Nearly all manufactured articles were imported from England.

The population of this county was not quite thirteen hundred, and it then included what is now Wyoming, Bradford, Lackawanna and Susquehanna counties. The mail was carried by a man on foot and it came in once a direction and twice a month from two directions. The only postoffice was in Wilkes-Barre.

1807 the coal trade opened by shipping arks down the Susquehanna. 1808 Jesse Fell made an experiment of burning anthracite coal in a grate. During the same year the first brick building was erected in Wilkes-Barre. In that year the Wilkes-Barre Academy was incorporated and Wilkes-Barre became known as the educational centre of Eastern Pennsylvania and Southern New York. 1809 the old log house and the jail were converted into a school. 1810 the first bank was opened.

The first drama was acted here in the ball-room of the old Red Tavern, on the corner of Main street and Public Square; it was entitled "The Babes in the Woods." 1812 the church called the Old Ship Zion was completed. 1813 the Wyoming Matross, a volunteer company from Kingston, embarked on a raft from Toby's Eddy for the war. 1814 five companies went to the defence of Baltimore, which was threatened by the British.

The first bridge was built over the Susquehanna in 1818, at a cost of $44,000. In 1819 two piers were undermined and two reaches of the bridge were lost. 1824 this bridge was lifted from the piers by a hurricane and deposited on the ice.

In 1818 a fire engine was bought by the borough council, in Philadelphia, called the "Neptune."

During 1826 there was a great anti-Mason agitation caused by the alleged abduction of one William Morgan. 1830 the first canal boat came up the canal to Nanticoke. It was the "Wyoming" and was built at Shickshinny by Hon. John Koons. In 1834 the foundation of our common school system was laid. 1844 Wyoming Seminary was opened for students. In 1834 the first boat made a round trip by canal between Wilkes-Barre and Easton. 1855 the Lehigh Valley railroad was opened. In 1846 war was declared by our government against Mexico. About half of the men who went from this Valley never returned. There was a great reception given the troops when they reached the Valley after their discharge. E. L. Dana was the captain of the Wyoming Artillerists.

In 1849 over two thousand rafts floated past Wilkes-Barre. In 1852 a charter was granted for a railroad between Scranton and Bloomsburg. In 1856 the first train ran between Scranton and Kingston on the D., L. & W. R. R.

It was in 1858 the Historical Society was organized with E. L. Dana president. 1850 the Wilkes-Barre Library Association was organized. 1852 the first daily paper was published in Wilkes-Barre. 1859 the east side of the Square was destroyed by fire. In 1856 an effort was made to have the swamp in Public Square filled up. 1858 the Kingston Coal Company's colliery shipped coal for the first time.

Previous to 1845 every farmer in the Valley raised sheep, or rather, the sheep raised themselves, for they picked their living. In the winter the farmers fed them straw. 1835 a reaping machine was brought to the Valley.

1853 the corner-stone of the Wyoming Monument was laid with great pomp and ceremony. 1859 a fire burned the north side of the Square from the Luzerne House to Cahoon's hall.

The first war meeting was held in Wilkes-Barre in 1861, Hon. H. B. Wright presiding. In 1862 the One Hundred and Forty-third Regiment was organized, with E. L. Dana Colonel and George E. Hoyt Major. A reign of terror begun in 1862 by the discovery that an organization of desperadoes known as the Molly Maguires existed in the coal fields, who proposed to control local politics and corporations by terrorizing the public. During that year this society resisted the draft. Lee invaded this State and Governor Curtin called for fifty thousand men, and in 1863 the Governor issued a proclamation calling out the entire militia of the State. The navigation was destroyed on the Lehigh in 1862 by a great flood. The L. V. R. R. was opened from White Haven to Wilkes-Barre 1866. During the year 1867 both sides of West Market street was nearly consumed by fire. In 1865 the great flood occurred. It was thirty feet above low water mark. The old historians state that the great flood of 1786 was forty feet above low water mark; it does not seem possible.

The Fishing Creek rebellion broke out during 1864. Four companies of infantry and two of cavalry went back to Columbia County to repress the Copperheads and Democrats of that section who had congregated in the gorges of the mountain to resisist the draft.

The Avondale disaster was in 1869. The breaker burned, causing the death of one hundred and eight men and boys. 1871 Wilkes-Barre secured a paid fire department. The great riot at Scranton took place during this year.

1874. This year the great woman temperance crusade was inaugurated. Many acres of land over the Empire mines cave in and the steamboat Hendrick B. Wright put on the river were events of that year.

In 1877 what is known as the great strike occurred. From 1861 for several years currency became inflated and business acquired an abnormal activity that engendered reckless extravagance. Following these times was a period of reaction and to keep the price of labor up to war-time rates the miners struck and committed many acts of violence which ended in the calling of the United States troops to the Valley.

The Greenback party elected W. H. Stanton, Esq., for additional Law Judge in 1877; he resigned. The Wilkes-Barre Hospital was opened 1872.

1883 the steamer Susquehanna blows up on the river in front of the Valley House. The corner stone of the First M. E. church laid.

1885. An epidemic of typhus fever in Plymouth; 114 died out of the 1,150 sick.

1887. John Welles Hollenback donates five acres of land for the Hollenback cemetery. Opening of the Ninth Regiment Armory. Laying of the corner stone of Nelson Memorial Hall.

1888. An awful disaster on the Valley railroad at Mud Run, where fifty-five persons were killed outright and many who were hurt died afterward. The electric road began its existence in the valley this year.

1889. Osterhout Free Library opened. Red Nose Mike hanged. An epidemic of small pox in Nanticoke.

1890. August 19 a tornado swept over the valley, killing six persons, injuring thirty-five and causing damage to the amount of two hundred and forty thousand dollars.

1893. F. V. Rockafellow's bank failed.

1894. Nesbitt Science Hall opened. A cave-in at the Gaylord mine and thirteen men killed. The centennial anniversary of Lodge No. 61, F. and A. M., was held in Wilkes-Barre. The first Masonic Lodge in Wyoming Valley was organized when General Sullivan was in the valley. Then a traveling lodge was formed in the army, (1779) twelve years after the first settlement. Wilkes-Barre had then about one hundred taxable inhabitants. The first charter obtained 1794. When General Washington died the members of this lodge wore mouring for three months. Most of the notable men of the valley were Masons. Refreshments were served in the early days, inexpensive, with plenty of strong liquor. Wyoming Seminary observed its bi-centennial.

# HANOVER GREEN CEMETERY.

BY H. B. PLUMB, ESQ.

S. R. SMITH,

Dear Sir: In accordance with your desire I send you the inscriptions on the tombstones of the Hanover Green Cemetery as far as I have them. I put in brackets those dates of years that are not on the tombstones, but which ought to appear in order to make everything clear. Where I know the name of the wife, before marriage, I have inserted it in brackets also. I have also arranged the names in alphabetical order.　　　H. B. P.

Henry Ash, (b. 1794,) d. 1820, aged 26. Mary (Minnich) Ash, b. 1795, d. 1876, aged 81. Richard Ash, (son, b. 1816,) d. 1826, aged 10. John Ash, (son, b. 1817,) d. 1844, aged 27. Eliza Ash, (daughter, b. 1821, d. 1828, aged 7. Henry Ash was of German descent, probably a descendant of Nicholas Ash, who immigrated to Pennsylvania in 1754. Polly or Mary Minnich, the wife of Henry Ash, was the daughter of Henry Minnich, born probably in Northampton county, Pennsylvania, her father coming to Hanover in 1810. Henry Ash and all his children died young, of consumption. Mrs. Ash lived to be quite old, and died in Wilkes-Barre on South Main street, opposite LeGrand's blacksmith shop, where she owned a house and lived from about 1845.

Capt. Peleg Burritt, b. in Stratford, Conn., 1721, d. in Hanover 1789, (aged 68). Deborah Beardsley, wife, b. in Stratford, Conn., 1726, d. in Hanover 1802, (aged 76). Capt. Peleg Burritt was the third in descent from William Burritt, who was probably one among the first settlers of Stratford, Conn., in 1640, where he died in 1651. Capt. Peleg came to Hanover about 1773 or '74. He lived on the River Road on the lot adjoining Hanover Green Cemetery on the north, and died there. He was twice married. His first wife was Elizabeth Blackleach, and by her he had the Rev. Blackleach Burritt and Mabel Burritt, neither of whom ever came to Pennsylvania; by Deborah he had Gideon, who died in Hanover unmarried; Sarah, born 1750, died 1833, married, first, Cyprian Hibbard (who was killed in the Wyoming massacre July 3, 1778, leaving a child who married John Alexander) and second Matthias Hollenback, and lived and died in Wilkes-Barre, Pa.; Stephen, born about 1748, married Mary Keeler; and Mary, who married, first, Peter Hubbell; second, Capt. Woodruff. Stephen, who married Mary Keeler, had Joel, Stephen and Polly. Stephen, the son of Stephen, never married, and lived on the homestead adjoining the Hanover Green on the south. He must have been born about 1773, and died there about 1850. Joel, his brother, married Ruth Dilley and died about 1826; Polly, his sister, married Jonathan Dilley and had a large family of children, the youngest still living, Rev. Alexander B. Dilley. Now it seems a little strange that there are no other tombstones to any of the Burritts, while it is certain that Gideon and the two Stephens were buried here.

Rufus Bennett, (b. 1754,) d. 1842, aged 88. Martha (Bennett) Bennett, wife, (b. 1763,) d. 1852, aged 89. Sarah, (Bennett), wife of Darius Finch, (b. 1785), d. 1847, aged 62. Rufus Bennett was born in Connecticut; came to Wyoming Valley with his father and mother and grandfather and grandmother. I do not know their names, but Rufus was here previous to 1772, and an Isaac Bennett was among the original settlers according to the list of 1769, and he may be the father or grandfather of Rufus, who was then (1772) 18 years old. They lived in the lower part of Wilkes-Barre near the Hanover line. Rufus was a soldier in the Revolutionary War, was home at the time of the Wyoming battle, and appears to have been in the Hanover company, as he was not in the lower Wilkes-Barre company. He escaped death in the battle, and in the flight was running down the road toward Forty Fort and two Indians were close behind in chase of him with spear and tomahawk. Bennett had his gun with him, but it had been discharged and he had no time to reload it. Richard Inman had fallen out on the way up from Forty Fort to battle, and lay beside the road, but at this moment had awakened and was rubbing his eyes. Bennett saw him and called to him: "Inman, is your gun loaded?" "Yes." "Then shoot this Indian!" Inman shot the Indian in front and the other turned and ran back. This I heard my grandfather, Elisha Blackman, tell more than once or twice, but still it is only a recollection. According to my researches, he was one of the party that headed off the Indians on French Mountain, above Wyalusing, that had Roswell Franklin's wife and children prisoners, in April, 1782. Rufus Bennett was wounded in the fight there with the Indians. After pensions were granted in 1833, he drew a pension of eight dollars a month. He lived in Hanover in a house still standing, at Askam, where his land adjoined my grandfather's, with the cross road between them from the Back Road toward Middle Road. He died in Wilkes-Barre in 1842. His wife was a daughter of Ishmael Bennett, who had just lately married a second wife, the widow of Philip Weeks, who had been killed in the Wyoming massacre at the edge of the river. Weeks' land was in the neighborhood of the Gen. Sturdevant place on the River Road in the lower end of Wilkes-Barre. He must have been married about 1784. She was no relation to him before marriage, so far as I know. He began clearing the woods from his Hanover land in 1789. They had nine children that grew up and married. Sally, or Sarah, married Jared Marcy first, and second Darius Finch. She was the grandmother of the Marcys now living in Wilkes-Barre, Kingston and Ashley. William married Katy Teets and went West. Wells married Jane Fell. Miranda married George Gledhill. Selesta married Randall Stivers and Peter Fisher. Rockwell married ———— Fisher. Rufus H. married Harriet Laeder and went West. Ransom married Phoebe Smiley, and Elmer married ———— Beck. Elmer's father and mother died at his house in Wilkes-Barre, South Main street, nearly opposite Academy street.

Josiah Bennett, b. 1786, d. 1857, aged 71. Sarah (Taylor) Bennett, wife. (b. 1786,) d. 1858, aged 72. Nathan Bennett, (b. 1789,) d. 1872, aged 83. Ann Hoover, (wife of Nathan Bennett,) b. 1795, d. 1866, aged 71. Thomas Bennett, (b. 1782,) d. 1820, aged 38. Josiah Bennett was a son of Ishmael Bennett by the second wife, Abigail Beers, widow of Philip Weeks, born in Wilkes-Barre probably on the Weeks' place on River street, near where the Sturdevant house now stands; was brought up in Hanover, where his parents bought land on the Back Road now in Sugar Notch a half mile below No. 9 breaker. The old or first house stood on the north side of a creek that comes down from the mountain there. He married Sally or Sarah Taylor, of Lackawanna. He died in Hanover in his own house, a quarter of a mile below, or south of his father's house, near the stone bridge and little creek

now called Bennett's Creek; she died in Wilkes-Barre at the house of her youngest child, Silas W. Bennett, still living in Wilkes-Barre. They had Angelina, born 1808, still living in the West, who married Ashbel Ruggles; Luther, born 1810, was drowned by falling from a bridge he was assisting in building at Tunkhannock, unmarried; John Taylor Bennett, born 1811, still living in South Dakota, married Hannah Miller, and H. Shiner; Lydia, born 1813, still living in Kingston, Pa., (mother of S. R. Smith, married Robert Smith. J. Bennett Smith is also her son. Eliza, born 1815, still living in New York, married Solomon Newton; Polly, born 1817, died in Wisconsin, married Abram Smith, brother of Robert; Josiah, born 1819, died, lived on South Main street, Woodville, Wilkes-Barre, married Charlotte Smith; Samuel, born 1821, still living in South Dakota; I do not know his wife's name; Silas W., b. 1827, still living in Wilkes-Barre, married Margaret Moister. Nathan Bennett (born and died as the inscription says above) was a brother of Josiah, born in Hanover, married Ann Hoover, daughter of Henry Hoover, lived in Hanover till all his children were born, and about 1835 removed to Wilkes-Barre, where he was the lock tender on the canal until he grew too old. They had George W., born 1812, died 1884 at Ashley, married Jane Bevans; Polly, born 1813, married John A. Cary. She is still living at Ashley. Sarah, married Charles Drake; Daniel, dead, lived in Wilkes-Barre, married Emily Kite; Stewart, born 1829 or 30, died 1883, married Sally Ann Lynn. There may have been others who did not live. Thomas Bennett, died, the inscription says, 1820, aged 38. I do not know who he is. He was too old to be the son of Thomas Bennett, who was a half brother of Josiah and Nathan, and was born 1765, and married Mary Ann Espy and lived in Nanticoke and kept the tavern there.

Elisha Blackman, b. April 4, 1760, d. December 5, 1845, aged 86. Anna Hulbert, his wife, b. 1763, d. 1828, aged 65. Elisha Blackman was born in Lebanon, Conn. He was the son of Elisha Blackman and Lucy Polley, who was the son of Elisha Blackman and Susanna Higley, who was the son of Joseph Blackman and Elizabeth Church, who was the son of John Blackman and Mary Pond. This Elisha came with his father to Wilkes-Barre in 1772. His father was a cousin of the famous Governor Trumbull, of Connecticut, and young Elisha was living with the Governor at the time his father made preparations to remove to Wyoming Valley. The Blackman lot was the second lot on the west side of South Main street, below or south of Academy street. It was thirty-two rods wide and had thirty-two acres in it, so it must have reached 160 rods from Main street towards the river. Here his parents lived at the time of the Wyoming massacre, July 3, 1778, in which he, then 18 years old, fought and slew his Indian antagonist and escaped. After the massacre his father and mother and brothers Eleazer and Ichabod, younger than he, and his sisters Lucy and Lovina, older than he, returned to Connecticut. He returned from Stroudsburg with Captain Spalding in August, and after gathering in as much of the crops as remained undestroyed, and assisting in burying the remains of the dead killed at Wyoming in the battle and massacres, in October, he joined the army and served about two years in New York in Otsego county, about the head waters of the Susquehanna; then he enlisted for a year in a regiment on the Hudson, and was discharged at Peekskill. The money he was paid in on his discharge in 1782 though a "legal tender" was valueless and he had to walk and beg his way from Peekskill to his old home in Lebanon, Conn., except that on the way somewhere he came to a house where the proprietor knew him, and he said he owed a woman in Lebanon one dollar, and told him that he would let him have that dollar and he could use it on the way there, if he would promise to earn a dollar there and give it to her for him.

He promised and did it. He learned the trade of a tanner and currier, and he studied surveying, and in March, 1785, he and Eleazer and Ichabod came to Wilkes-Barre again and built a log house on the old place and went to keeping "bachelor's hall." Ichabod in 1786 married Elizabeth Franklin and the same year removed to Sheshequin, now Bradford county, where he lived and died, leaving three sons, Franklin, Elisha and Rev. David S. Blackman. Eleazer married Clara Hyde in 1787, and lived and died in Wilkes-Barre. He died in 1844. He left children: Lucy married Shepard Stearns, Minerva married Calvin Edwards, Melinda married Daniel Collings, Amanda married Thomas Gary, Julia married Edward Jones, Lovina married Richard Jones. Elisha, the eldest brother, married last. He married Anna Hurlbut, daughter of Deacon John Hurlbut, of Hanover. He removed to Hanover to the place where I now reside, and began clearing up a farm in the woods and built a house in 1791, and here he and his wife lived and died. They had ten children, six of whom grew up and married. Henry, born 1788, died 1843, married Sarah Bennett; Ebenezer, born 1791, died 1844, married Susan M. Stockbridge; Hurlbut, born 1794, died 1870, married Sarah Rollin; Elizabeth, born 1799, died ——, married Henry Boss; Elisha, born 1801, died 1872, married Amy Rollin; Julia Anna born 1806, died 1889, married Charles Plumb. All except Henry, or Harry, and Julia Anna went west, married, lived and died. The "west" in those early times—1815 to 1820—was Ohio.

Jacob Babb, b. May 3, 1776, in the town of Reading, d. September 25, 1821, aged 45 years, 24 days. I never knew this Babb. He came to Hanover about 1815 and bought land on the Middle Road near where Askam is now, just below or south of the Nanticoke creek, and his son, John Babb, owned it and lived there till 1838. I knew him and his family, though I was but eight years old when they all went west to Iowa. He—John, the son—married a Miller. They had Lydia, married Robert Downer; Elizabeth; Washington, married Elizabeth Coates; Miles, John, Jr., Susan, Mary Ann, and Abi. Some of these, the younger ones, are still alive, I hear. Downer had children about my age, say, born 1830. Abi was a couple of years older than I, born, say, 1827 or 8.

Ruggles Brush, (b. 1781), drowned 1800, aged 19. There was a Jonas Brush owned the place afterwards owned (bought of Brush, I believe) by George Koeher, the father of the George of my time, who was born 1763, died 1850. The elder George has no gravestone. Dr. Charles Streator bought the place of the elder or younger George Koeher, and built on the top of Hog Back Hill a house which in that age was a wonder of magnificence to the people. Streator sold it about 1837 and removed to Wilkes-Barre, where he was a druggist for many years and where he died. The main part of his house still stands, but all its glory has departed. Where Brush died or his family lived I never knew, but from the name of his son it would seem that he was in some way connected with the Ruggles family. I have heard that young Brush and a man named Tredway were drowned at Nanticoke Falls, along with Henry Line, but Line came to life again when he was got out of the water.

George Behee (b. 1788, d. 1846, aged 58. Elizabeth, wife, b. Feb. 26, 1789, d. Nov. 8, 1868, aged 79. Susan, daughter (b. 1830, d. 1865, aged 35. George Behee was of German descent and came from Northampton county, Pa., it is supposed, and settled first in Newport township. He traded his land in Newport with Ludwig Rummage for the mill in Hanover, near the Old Red Tavern, and lived there as early at least as 1818, as Elisha Blackman's account book has him there. I do not know what his wife's name was; they had George, married Susan Grover; Adam, married, first, Mary Ann Patterson, and

second, Susan A. Pryor, as I am informed. He still lives, 1893, in Wilkes-Barre and can answer for himself. Sally, married John Barney; Betsey, married Sidney Ide; John, married a Mrs. Fell; Polly, married Jacob Kline; Ellen, married James Butler. I do not know where any of them live except Adam, who must now be a very old man. The mill—Behee's mill—rotted down some forty years ago, but the mill-pond is there yet. Susan never married.

John Barney, b. 1800, d. 1881, (aged 81). Sarah (Behee) Barney, wife, b. 1809, d. 1882, (aged 73). John Barney, second, b. 1846, d. 1882, (aged 36). John C. Barney, (b. 1827), d. 1864, aged 37. Sarah Barney, wife, (b. 1827), d. 1863, aged 36. John Barney married Sally Behee (or Sarah, as the tombstone says). After the death of her father they lived at the homestead at Behee mill in Hanover, and there both of them and Mrs. Behee died. They had a number of children that I never knew. I knew Charles, of Plymouth, Pa., and the son John, the second, I think, who was the youngest son.

Susan Burrier, wife of Thomas Burrier, (b. 1802), d. 1833, aged 32. Thomas Burrier came here in 1810 from Northampton county, Pa.; he was born about 1798, married Susan Meyers, and died 1890, aged about 92. The above is the inscription on his wife's tombstone. He died in Ross township, I believe. He had a brother Samuel, who married Mary Edwards, and about 1846 removed to Wisconsin, and a brother Christian, who married a Courtright. They had Katy Ann, married William Rummage; William, went to Wisconsin; Priscilla, married George Kennedy; Susan, married Henry Gress.

Frederick Chrisman, (b. 1758), d. 1815, aged 57. This man built the Red Tavern in Hanover. He was of German descent, came to Hanover—probably from Northampton county, Pa.,—about 1788. After his death his widow married John Carey, of "Careytown," on River street, in Wilkes-Barre, below Academy street. Chrisman and she had eight children—Abram, Beshero, Rachel, Betsey, married Lazarus Stewart; Charles; Priscilla, married Lewis Mulison Horton; Harriet, Jesse, married Polly Hartzell. Abram Chrisman married —— ——, and had John, married Warner; Susan, born 1807, d. 1847, married George P. Steele; Katie, married John Long; Euphemia, married George Kocher. Jesse married, had children, started to move to the west in 1834, got as far as Pittsburg with a flat boat loaded with his family and goods and live stock, but there he was murdered and robbed. His family never came back here. His boat with its load was taken on a car at Hollidaysburg and carried over the mountain on the railroad to Johnstown.

Benjamin Carey, (b. 1763), d. 1830, aged 67. Comfort Carey, b. 1768, d. 1838, aged 70. The first Carey in Wyoming Valley was the father of these, named Eleazer, born in New England in 1718; came here 1769; his family came in 1772. The sons were John, born 1756, died 1844; Nathan, born 1754, married Jane Mann; Samuel, born 1759, married Theresa Gore; Benjamin, born 1763, married Mercy Abbott; Comfort, born 1768, married Hulda Weeks; Mehetable, married James Wright. John was a soldier in the Army of the Revolution in the company that did not get here in time to be in the battle of July 3, 1778. He lived and died in Wilkes-Barre on the River Road called Careytown, now, I believe, called Carey avenue. In his old age about 1816 he married as his second wife the widow of Frederick Chrisman. Nathan Carey was in the Wyoming battle and escaped the massacre. About 1798 he removed to Arkport, N. Y., where both he and his wife died and are buried. Samuel was also in the Wyoming battle and escaped the massacre, but was taken prisoner; and being young was adopted the same night by a squaw, whose son had been

killed in the battle. After some six years he was set free and came home, married and lived and died in Plains township, Pa. Benjamin married and settled in Hanover township in 1795, on the Middle Road, some sixty or seventy rods north of Hoover Hill school house. His children were Nathan, married Solly Ann Allen; Nancy, married Elijah Adams; Rachel, married Sira Landing; Elias, married Lettitia Smiley; Sarah, married Bateman Downing; Esther, married Darius Waters; Martha, married Peter Mensch; Benjamin, married Jane Smiley; Selesta, married Harvey Holgomb; John A. married Polly Bennett; Comfort married and settled in Hanover on the Back Road in what is now Ashley. His wife, Hulda, was a daughter of Philip Weeks, who was killed by the Indians July 3, 1778, on the bank of the river, after being taking prisoner on promise of his life. They had John, married Hannah Dickson; Benjamin, married Katy Askam; Daniel, married Lovina Dilley; Lucy, married Erastus Coswell; Lydia, married Jacob Worthing; George, died unmarried.

John Craver, (b. 1775), d. 1840, aged 64. Christiana Craver, wife, (b. 1786), d. 1839, aged 53. I do not know who these are, but I think they are the parents of Thomas Carpenter's wife, and the first wife of Peter Rinehimer, of Hanover, still living. Rinehimer called his first wife's name Graver, but Thomas Quick, of Wilkes-Barre, called Carpenter's wife Craver, and they were sisters; but Rinehimer was "Pennsylvania Dutch," and that made the difference in the name he gave. But the inscription is Craver.

Thomas Carpenter, b. 1798, d. 1874, (aged 76). Elizabeth Carpenter, wife, b. 1805, d. 1871, (aged 66). Thomas Carpenter was an Englishman and, as I understand it, came to America with Dr. Charles Streator, and lived with Streator as long as Streator lived on Hogback. After Streator left he lived there with —— Cox, who bought the Streator place, till about 1843, when he owned and lived in a little house in South Wilkes-Barre, across the street from Carlisle Gates' foundry, and was in Judge Conyngham's employment till his death.

Richard Dilley, d. about 1840. Mary Dilley, wife, d. about 1840. This Richard Dilley was the son of an older Richard, that came to Wyoming Valley about 1784, during the Pennamite and Yankee troubles after the Decree at Trenton which assigned this region to Pennsylvania, which troubles arose from the attempt of the Pennsylvania Government to drive out the Yankee settlers. He bought land in Hanover, and died here in 1799. His children were this Richard, who married Polly Voke; Susana; Adam; Jerusha; married Edward Inman; Prudence, married Edward Edgerton; Jonathan, married Polly Burritt; Mary, married David Richards; John F. went South; Ruth, married Joel Burritt; Nancy, married Nathan Wade. The above Richard, the eldest of these children, lived at Buttonwood, and his children were born there, and there he died; but the tombstone was put up long afterwards and only about the date of death (1840) was known. When he was born is not known, but as his daughter Susan was born 1788, it may be assumed he was born twenty-two years at least before that—1766. Jonathan had a son, Alexander, who became a Presbyterian minister, and is, I believe, still living. He has visited me twice when in Wilkes-Barre at church meetings of the clergy since 1879.

Susan Dilley, daughter of Richard and Mary Dilley, was born 1788, d. 1879, (aged 91). James Dilley, (b. 1792), d. 1862, aged 70. Margaret, (wife of James), b. 1797, (married May 19, 1815), d. 1877, (aged 80). Mary Brown, daughter of James and Margaret Dilley, (b. 1822), d. 1867, aged 45. Jesse Dilley, (b. 1794), d. 1852, aged 58. Hannah K. (Lueder), wife, b. 1801, d. 1878, aged 70. Jerusha Dilley, (b. 1796), d. 1853, aged 57. James married Margaret Campbell, a daughter of James Campbell and Margaret Stewart. Margaret

Stewart was a daughter of Captain Lazarus Stewart, who fell in the battle July 3, 1778, at Wyoming. James Dilley's children were William, married Catharine Butler; Richard; James, married Jane Cox; Stewart, married ——— Wertz; Charles; Alvah, married Mary C. Rinehimer; Harriet, married Charles Buel; Mary, married ——— Brown; Margaret, married ——— Howard; Ann, married William McCullough. Jesse Dilley and Hannah K. Lueder lived in Wilkes-Barre and had children: Sylvester, married Mary Ann Barkman; Anning, married Eliza Houpt; Lyman, died in the Mexican war; Charlotte, married Charles E. Lathrop; Urban, married Lydia Ann Webber or Weaver; Butler, married ——— Pettebone; Freidland; Monroe, married Joanna Marks; Mary, married Edwin H. Jones. There was a brother of James and Jesse called Dayton. He married Lorinda Marcy, daughter of Jared Marcy and Sarah Bennett. They had Richard, Ira, Loretta, Sarah, Mary Ellen and Avery Dilley. Avery died in the army in 1863.

  Sarah (Carey), wife of Bateman Downing, (b. 1797), d. 1864, aged 67. Burton Downing, son of Bateman, (b. 1815), d. 1841, aged 26. Sarah (Downing), wife of Levi Petty, (b. 1824), d. 1847, aged 23. Charles Denison Downing, son of Reuben, b. 1857, d. 1875, (aged 18). Bateman was the son of Reuben, married Sarah Carey, daughter of Benjamin, of Hanover; he had a brother Martin, married Laura Carey, of Plains; and brother Elias, married Jane Dana; and sisters, Sarepta, married Jonas Hartzell, of Buttonwood; Ann, married George Carey. Bateman bought out the heirs of Benjamin Carey and lived there till 1864. They had Burton, married Hannah Kriedler; Lydia Ann, married William Nagle; Reuben, married Nancy Miller; Sarah, married Levi Petty; Benjamin, married Caroline Holcomb. Burton died in 1841 and left one child, John C. Downing, long a resident of Wilkes-Barre, but last year he went to Washington, west of the Cascade range, and took a homestead claim as a soldier on Government land. Reuben died June 18, 1890, and left Burton and Martha L. living in Wilkes-Barre. Bateman went west in 1865 and died in Wisconsin in 1879.

  Edward Edgerton, (b. 1754), d. 1819, aged 65. Prudence Edgerton, wife (b. 1767), d. 1857, aged 90. Edgerton was born in Ireland, was the kind of Irish called in this country Scotch-Irish; came to America after he had learned the trade of flax hetcheling. He was in our Revolutionary War on the American side and was desperately wounded by having a bayonet thrust through his body at what is called the Massacre of Paoli; married Prudence Dilley, of New Jersey, lived on his farm behind the Hoover Hill school house, and died there in 1819. They had James; Mary; Jesse, married Jane Whipple; Ruth, married Anthony Wilkinson; Richard, married ——— Miller; Elijah, married Rebecca Nagle. Mrs. Edgerton lived at the homestead with one of her sons till she died, very old. The whole family went west about 1865.

  John Espy, b. 1779, d. 1843, (aged 64). Lovina Espy, wife, b. 1787, d. 1874, (aged 87). Anis, b. 1817, d. 1855, (aged 38). Espy was born in Hanover, was the son of George, married Lovina Inman, daughter of Edward Inman; lived on the middle road at or near what is now called Hanover Station on the Nanticoke branch of the Central R. R. of N. J. There he died, and about 1850 Mrs. Espy removed to her father's homestead on the River Road at or near the Buttonwood shaft, where she died. I do not know who "Anis" is. They had James, married Mary Miller; Fanny, married Abram Line; Lavina, married Peter D. Miller; Mary, married John R. Line; Priscilla, married Levi M. Miller; Edward; John, married Mary Taylor.

Ruluff Fisher (b. 1724), d. 1809, aged 85. Mary Fisher, wife, (b. 1725), d. 1830, aged 105 years, 5 months, 17 days. Jacob Fisher (son), b. 1771, d. 1852, (aged 81). Henry Fisher (son of Jacob), b. 1803, d. 1851, (aged 48). Abram Fisher (son of Henry), b. 1827, d. 1851, (aged 24). Ruluff Fisher was of Holland birth. He lived on the Middle Road or near it just north of the cross road from the Downing house to the Hanover Green. The house stood back west some thirty rods from the road. His wife, or widow, lived to be the oldest person that ever lived in Hanover, over 105 years. Their son, Jacob, built a house near the road, which still stands. He married an Adams, whose father owned the Knoch place before Knoch came there. Henry Fisher was his son; owned the hotel at South Wilkes-Barre, which he built in 1848, now, or lately, belonging to Jacob Kocher. Henry and his son, Abram, had a contract to build part of the North Branch canal in 1851, somewhere near Tunkhannock. The day before a pay-day they had prepared to pay the men and had the money with them near the place where they worked. They were both murdered and robbed that night and the house where they slept was burnt with their bodies in it. The rest of the Fisher family all went west about 1854 or '5. The children of Jacob were this Henry, married Mary Smiley; Clara, married Eleazer Marble; Susan, married Samuel Smiley; Polly, married John Mensch; Perry, married Rebecca Thomas; Margaret, married Joseph Steele; Jacob, married Harriet Inman; Giles, married Caroline Thomas; Sarah, married Charles Holcomb. I think their oldest son was Elijah. I do not know who he married.

John Frederick (b. 1782), d. 1854, aged 72. Eliza, daughter of Christian Frederick, b. 1815, d. 1871, (age 56). He came with his family to Hanover from Northampton county in 1821. His wife's name was Christiana Fogel. He lived in what is now called Ashley. His children were Isaac, born 1805, married Jane Hannis; Daniel, born 1807, married Christiana Steele; Joseph, born 1810, married Lovina Saum; Charles, born 1813, died 1886, married Susan M. Kreidler; William, b. 1815, wife not known. Daniel is still living at Ashley, and Joseph lives in Wilkes-Barre, near the Hanover line at Newtown, both very old men. Daniel died April 18, 1894. I do not know who Eliza is if not the daughter of John Frederick and Christiana, his wife.

Emily, wife of Solomon Fairchild, b. 1836, d. 1853, (aged 17). Nothing known of these Fairchilds by me.

Cornelius Garrison, b. 1756, d. 1825, aged 68. Mary, wife of Cornelius, (b. 1758), d. 1815, aged 57. Margaret, wife of Cornelius, b. 1782, d. 1827, aged 45. [John Garrison (son of Cornelius), (b. 1784), d. 1865, aged about 81?]. Catharine Garrison, wife of John, (b. 1784), d. 1854, aged 70. Sarah Garrison (daughter of Cornelius), (b. 1791), d. 1849, aged 58. Cornelius Garrison was a French soldier in our Revolutionary War; did not go back with the French; married in America; lived on the cross road between the Back Road at Sugar Notch and the Middle Road, now in Sugar Notch. His horses ran away, threw him out of the wagon going down the hill at the Preston place, forty or fifty rods south at the southern line of Ashley, and broke his neck. His children were Elizabeth, born 1782, died 1827, married John Saum; John, married Kate Mack; Mary, married John Robins; Jacob, married Rachel Rimer; Rachel, married William Stapleton; Nancy, never married; James, married Mary Wiggins.

John Garringer (b. 1785), d. 1836, aged 51. Mary Garringer, his wife, (b. 1787), d. 1868, aged 81. Daniel Garringer (son, b. 1826, d. 1858, aged 32. The Garringers came

to Hanover in 1810 from Northampton county, Pa.; lived on the River Road below—south of—the Red Tavern. His wife was Mary Magdalene Hess. They had Charles, born 1805, died 1888, married Elizabeth Leuder; Levi, born 1806, married Katy Reynard; Thomas, born 1807, never married; Eliza, born 1809, died 1850, married John Andrew or Andrus; Jesse, born 1812, died 1891, married Sarah Croop; John G., born 1814; Mary, born 1817, married John Klinker; David, born 1819; Susan, born 1822, married John Sutton; Isaac, born 1824; Daniel, born 1826, died 1858; Lucinda, born 1828, married William King; Aaron, born 1830, married —— Coolbaugh. Charles died in Nanticoke, and Jesse in Wilkes-Barre.

Henry George, b. 1797, d. 1849, aged 52. Catharine, wife of Henry George, b. 1801, d. 1878, aged 77. Isaiah George, b. 1831, d. 1875, aged 44. Henry George was of German descent; settled in Nanticoke when he was a young man; supposed to have come from Northampton county, Pa.; married Catharine Kocher, and died in Nanticoke. They had Elizabeth, married S. T. Puterbaugh; William, born 1822, died 1890, married Ann Croop; Hiram, married Amanda Gruver; Susan, married, first, Daniel Lazarus; second, A. M. Jefferies; John, married Serlina Robins; Adelaide, married Augustus Nybil; Samuel, married, first, Martha Vandermark; second, Hattie Totten, and died in 1890; Josephine, married Dr. William G. Robinson; Isaiah, born 1831, died 1875.

Amos G. Herrick, b. (1794), d. 1862, aged 68. Ruth, wife of Amos Herrick, (b. 1794), d. 1853, aged 59. Amos Herrick was of New England descent; his wife a daughter of Nathan Wade. They had Mary, Edward, Elizabeth, Daniel, Nathan, killed in battle in 1864 during the rebellion; Amos. The family lived in Hanover till 1860, when they removed to Newport township.

John Hoover, b. 1782, d. 1868, aged 84. Sarah, wife of John Hoover, (b. 1785), d. 1857, aged 72. John Hoover was of German or Holland descent; came to Hanover from New Jersey about 1790; married Sarah Sims. He had a brother, Henry, married Hannah Burgess; and Michael, married Asenath Burgess; and a sister, Hannah, married Silas Wiggins. His children were Polly, married John Rummage; Henry, married Elizabeth Sidmore; John; Michael, married Betsey Ann Custerd; Eliza, married Samuel Keithline; Jacob, married Susan Sorber. All gone west except Jacob.

Elijah Inman (b. 1718), d. 1804, aged 86. Susan Inman (wife, b. 1821), d. 1809, aged 88. Richard Inman (son, b. 1751), d. 1831, aged 80. John Inman (son, b. 1758), d. 1804, aged 46. Edward Inman (son), b. Nov. 23, 1763, d. Oct. 20, 1848, aged 84—10—27. Jerusha Inman (daughter), b. Feb. 10, 1766, d. Oct. 1, 1848, aged 80—7—21. Nathan Inman, son of Edward, (b. 1805), d. 1835, aged 32. Elizabeth (Inman) Stiles, b. 1801, d. 1851, (aged 50). Elijah Inman was of New England birth; was among the first settlers in Hanover and lived at Buttonwood on the west side of Solomon's creek; had seven sons. Four were in the Wyoming battle and massacre, July 3, 1778; two were killed; one died soon after from his exposure there, and one that was not in the battle was killed near home the same year. One—Richard—did not reach the battlefield, having fallen out on the way to it from the fort, but he shot and killed the Indian that was trying to kill Rufus Bennett in the flight from the defeat. Elijah's sons were Elijah, killed; Israel, killed; David, died from exposure and over heating; Isaac, killed near home the same winter, 1778; Richard escaped, married Hannah Spencer; John; Edward, married Jerusha Dilley. Richard had a large family—Israel, Isaac, Caleb, Richard, Walter, John, Parry, Mary,

Susan and Margaret. John, son of Elijah, married; had Hiram and Richard. Edward, son of Elijah, married Jerusha Dilley and had Lovina, married John Espy; Jemima, married John Turner; Susan, married John Whitney; Jerusha, married William Jackson; John E., married Mary Hannis; Elizabeth, married Stiles.

Samuel Jameson, b. 1777, d. 1843, aged 65. Hannah Jameson (wife), d. 1851. The Jameson family came to Hanover from Connecticut in 1776, and settled in Nanticoke. The eldest son, John, b. 1749, came in 1773 to Hanover; married Abigail Alden; was in the Wyoming massacre, but escaped death then, to be murdered by the Indians in the road at the Hanover Green cemetery in 1782. He was the father of this Samuel. He had brothers and sisters—Mary; William, b. 1751, was in the battle and massacre at Wyoming, July 3, 1778, and escaped but was killed by the Indians in Careytown in the same year, after the massacre; Robert, b. 1755, killed in the massacre; Elizabeth; Rosanna, married Elisha Harvey; Samuel; Hannah; Joseph; Alexander, born about 1761, married Elizabeth Stewart, daughter of Captain Lazarus; Agnes; Benjamin; Samuel, born 1777, son of John, married Hannah Hunlock and had Maria, born 1805; Eliza, born 1803; Ann, born 1806, married Anderson Dana and had two daughters who died without issue.

Conrad Knoch, b. 1759, d. 1828, aged 68. Conrad Knoch, Jr., (son), b. 1788, d. 1817, aged 29. Elizabeth Knoch (daughter), b. 1793, d. 1818, aged 25. Johannes Knoch (son), b. 1796, d. 1799, (aged 3). Peter Knoch (son), b. 1800, d. 1821, aged 21. Knoch came to Hanover about 1812. His wife died about 1835, the last of her family, and as I have no inscription I think there is no tombstone to her grave. According to their own story they were too poor in Germany to be permitted to marry, so they both applied to a ship's captain to carry them to America and sell them there for their passage. He did so, and when he sold them at public auction to the man who would take them for the shortest time and pay the cost of their passage he told the bidders he would like to sell both to one man, as they wished to marry. And so it was done, and they were married and worked out their pay. And afterwards they were so industrious and saving that they became "well-to-do" in the land; but their children all died with consumption. I believe there was a daughter or a son that married, had a child and died, and the child died in infancy, so the redemptioner's property went to his heirs in Germany. My mother said when they came to Hanover they had the finest team of horses, and wagon, she had ever seen.

Daniel Kreidler, (b. 1771), d. 1855, aged 84. George Kreidler, (b. 1776), d. 1855, aged 79. Margaret Kreidler, wife of George, d. 1856. Jonas Kreidler, (son of George), (b. 1803), d. 1828, aged 25. Daniel and George Kreidler, brothers, came to Hanover from Northampton county, Pa., in 1822. Daniel's wife was Catharine Hartzell, and George's was Margaret Hartzell. They both settled on Solomon's creek, where Ashley now is, and there they lived and died. Daniel's children were Elizabeth, married George Engle; Daniel, born 1800, married Margaret Boyer; Thomas, born 1802, married Mary Dill; Mary, born 1805, married Charles Hay; Rachel, born 1809, married Williston Preston; Susan M., born 1812, married Charles Frederick; Lovina, born 1818, married Simon Rinchimer. George had Margaret, married Henry Stroh; John, married Christiana Ransom; Catharine, married Nicholas Landmesser; Arthur; Hannah, married, first, Burton Downing; second, Reuben Keyser; Daniel, married Mary Haas.

George Kocher, (b. 1769), d. 1850, aged 81. Elizabeth, his wife, (b. 1770), d. 1850, aged 71. The first Kocher was the father of this George, and his name was George. He came

to Hanover about 1805 with a grown up family. His oldest son was the above George, married Elizabeth Rothermel; Henry; Mary, married Conrad Rinehimer; Sarah, married Philip Gross; Betsey, married —— Teeter. Henry lived in Hanover till about 1838, when he returned to Northampton county, from which they came. George, born 1769, had John, married Catharine Teeter; George, Jr., married Euphemia Crisman; Peter, married Eliza ——; Mary, married John Ash; Rose Ann, married Truman Decker; Lydia, married Samuel H. Puterbaugh; Susan, married Samuel H. Puterbaugh after her sister's death, and second, after Puterbaugh died, married Silas Alexander; Catharine, born 1801, died 1878, married Henry George. I do not have these in the order of birth.

Valentine Kizer, (b. 1769, d. 1847, aged 78. Anna Kizer (his wife), b. 1768, d. 1841, aged 73. Samuel Kizer, son, (b. 1817), d. 1839, aged 22. There is a puzzle here. Anna is called his wife on the tombstone, and yet Catharine Salome Saum was his wife, and she died in 1859, as their private register says. There is a mistake I cannot account for. Valentine had a son Christian, married Teena Merwine; John, married Frances Merwine; Charles, married Sally Gress; Peter.

Reuben Kizer, (b. 1815, d. 1872, aged 57. Hannah, wife of Reuben, b. 1818, d. 1879, aged 61. Reuben was the son of Christian, married Hannah Kreidler, widow of Burton Downing. Downing died in 1841, leaving one son, John C. Downing, now of the State of Washington, born in 1841.

Andrew Lee (b. 1739), d. 1821, aged 82. Priscilla Lee (wife), b. 1751, d. 1815, aged 64. Col. Washington Lee (son), b. 1786, d. 1871, aged 85. James S. Lee (son), b. 1789, d. 1851, aged 61. Andrew Lee (son of James), b. 1815, d. 1881, aged 67. Catharine Campbell (b. 1752), d. 1836, aged 84. Capt. Andrew Lee was a Revolutionary soldier; native of Lancaster county, Pa., (now Dauphin county); married Priscilla Espy, widow of James Stewart; came to Hanover to live in 1804, though he owned land here many years before that; lived and died in Nanticoke. His son, Washington Lee, born 1786, married Elizabeth Campbell (perhaps daughter of the above Catharine) and died without issue. James S., another son, married Martha Campbell. They had Andrew, born 1815, died 1882, married Sarah Jane Buckhout; Priscilla, born 1819, married Ziba Bennett; Washington, born 1821, died 1883, married Emily Thomas; Margaret, born 1825, died 1866, married Dr. James F. Doolittle; Mary, born 1829, died 1853, married Lewis C. Paine.

Conrad Lion, b. 1731, d. 1815, aged 84. Clarissa Lion (b. 1740), d. 1817, aged 77. Henry Line (b. 1783), d. 1849, aged 66. Anna Line (wife), b. 1787, d. 1862, aged 75. James Line (b. 1809), d. 1846, aged 37. Fanny, wife of Abram Line, b. 1813, d. 1846, aged 67. The Lines were of Holland descent and came to Hanover from New Jersey before the Revolutionary War; settled in Nanticoke. Conrad Line had Peter; John, married —— Harrison; Adrian; Conrad; Lena, married Nathaniel Worden; Henry, married Anna Sliker. Henry and Anna had Margaret, born 1807, married Samuel Peil; James, married Catharine Mill; Abram, married Fanny Espy; Elizabeth, married George Mill; Martha, married John Fairchild; Julia Ann, married James Beatty; Henry, married Eliza Ann Robins; Maria, married Jacob S. Robins; Catharine, married Daniel Raisley; Samuel, married Emma E. Butts.

Christian Lueder (b. 1769), d. 1832, aged 63. Mary M. Lueder (wife, b. 1776, d. 1852, aged 76. Lueder was a German by birth; married Mary Magdalene Ryswick in Northampton county, Pa. They had John, married Margaret Vandermark; Frederick, married

Mary Vandermark; Augustus, married Rose Ann Lutzey; Christian F., married Hannah Lutzey; Hannah K., married Jesse Dilley; Elizabeth, married Charles Garringer; Harriet, married Rufus Bennett, Jr.; Julia, married John Askam; Lydia, married Archibald Smiley; Mary, married Equilla Deeter. Mrs. Dilley died in Wilkes-Barre. She was the mother of Anning, Urban, Sylvester, Butler and Monroe Dilley. Garringer died in Nanticoke. Christian F. died in Hanover.

George Lazarus, b. 1761, d. 1844, aged 83. Mary (his wife), b. 1777, d. 1861, aged 84. Lazarus was of German descent; born in Northampton county, Pa.; married Mary Hartzell; removed to Hanover at Buttonwood in 1818. They had John, born 1796, died 1879, married Polly Drake; Elizabeth, born 1798, married Benjamin Stocker; Catharine, born 1800, died 1888, married Fritz Deterick; Sarah, born 1804, died 1892, married John Blanchard; George, born 1809, died 1882, married Margaret Barber; Mary, born 1812, married Asahel B. Blodgett; Thomas, born 1816, died 1888, married Rachel Miller. Thomas died in Hanover at the old homestead; has a fine monument in Hanover Green cemetery. John died in Wilkes-Barre. Catharine died in Wilkes-Barre, and all Wilkes-Barreans know her son, Miller H. Deterick, who was so many years the street car conductor to Kingston. George died in Pittston, Pa.; Sarah died at Port Blanchard; Mary still lives at Buttonwood, but she and her deceased husband have a fine monument in Hollenback cemetery.

George Learn, b. Aug. 21, 1781, d. Sept. 1, 1850, aged 69. Simon Learn (b. 1804), d. 1839, aged 35. Mary E. Learn, daughter of Charles, d. 1848, aged 1. George Learn was of German descent; born in Northampton county, Pa.; came to Hanover in 1810. His children were Simon; Levi, married Sarah Sterling; Louisa; Lee, married Hannah Hartzell; Heller, married Catharine Stocker; George P., married Naomi Keller; Michael; Charles; Adam, married Mary Line; William; Lydia, married William Askam; Mary Ann, married —— Gress. He lived on the Back Road when I was a little child on the farm that afterwards belonged to Col. H. B. Wright, now part of Warrior Run mines. He died on the River Road in Hanover close to the present Pennsylvania railroad, formerly where the canal crossed the road. His son, George P., lived there after him till about 1865, when he removed to a farm he bought a mile or so below Berwick, Pa. I do not know the name of Charles' wife.

Adam Laubaugh (b. 1778), d. 1853, aged 75. Catharine (his wife, b. 1782), d. 1853, aged 71. I know nothing about these.

Adam Lape, b. 1810, d. 1847, aged 37. Adam Lape was of German descent; born in Newport township, Pa.; married Elizabeth Croop; had Harriet, married Dr. Harry Hakes; William; Andrew; Alvin, married Amelia James; Francis S.; Dr. Allen A., married Frances E. Line, widow of William Lueder, and died 1884; Clara J. These all lived in Nanticoke except that Dr. Hakes lives in Wilkes-Barre.

John Mill (b. 1730), d. 1814, aged 84. John Mill, Jr., (b. 1765), d. 1840, aged 75. Peter Mill (b. 1800), d. 1871, aged 71. Wife of Peter Mill (b. 1800), d. 1848, aged 48. The Mills came to Hanover previous to 1796, as I learn from my grandfather's account books. The first John's wife is not known. The second John's wife was Catharine Klinker. It is not known whether the first John had any other family than John, Jr. They all lived in Nanticoke. John, Jr., had Mary, born 1797, d. 1890 in Wilkes-Barre, married Henry Anheuser; Peter, born 1800, married, first wife's name not known; second wife, Mary Keith-

line; George, died 1888, married Elizabeth Line; Solomon, married Mary Line; John, married Eliza Line; Catharine, married James Line.    Peter died in Nanticoke, Mary in Wilkes-Barre.   The others went west many years ago.

George Peter Minnich, b. 1764, d. 1826, aged 61.   Elizabeth Minnich (wife), b. 1752, d. 1824, aged 72.   Henry Minnich, b. Aug. 10, 1783, d. 1843, aged 60.   Anna Elizabeth (wife of Henry), b. 1781, d. 1828, aged 47.   Jonas Minnich (son of Henry), b. 1822, d. 1828 (aged 6).   William Henry, son of Henry, b. 1808, d. 1831, aged 23.   Abram Minnich, son of Henry, b. 1818, d. 1880, aged 62.   Mary Ann, wife of Abram, b. 1819, d. 1864, aged 45. George Peter, said to have been born in Germany, came to America when twenty years of age, settled in Northampton county, Pa.; married Elizabeth Rockel; came to Hanover about 1810; settled on the River Road north of the Dundee shaft.   They had Henry, born in Northampton county, married Anna Elizabeth Knaus; Sarah, married Lathridge Knaus; Elizabeth, born 1786, died 1821, married Henry Mack; Susan, married Jacob Rummage, Jr.; Catharine, married Conrad Rummage; Polly, married Henry Ash.   Henry bought the homestead of the heirs and lived there   Had Peter, married Katy Ann Downs; Julia, married Peter Andrew (or Andrus); Anthony, married Susan Young; Daniel, born 1814, died 1890, married Julia Ann Kocher; John, born 1817, married Julia ———; Abram, married Mary Ann Husselton; David, married Catharine Lester.   They all went west more than fifty years ago, except Daniel and Abram.   Perhaps John went in 1852 or '3.   Elizabeth, wife of Henry Mack (or Mock, as he was called here), was a daughter of George Peter Minnich.   She was born 1786, died 1821.   He married a second wife, and soon after traded his farm here to John Robinson for a farm in Susquehanna county, Pa., and removed there. His second wife was called, I think, Abby Bennett, but she was not of any Bennett family about here.

Barnet Miller, b. 1787, d. 1854, (aged 67).   Mary Miller (wife of), b. 1795, d. 1872, (aged 77).   Barnet Miller was of German descent; came to Hanover about 1834; settled on the River Road below the Dundee shaft.   They had Nancy, died 1893, married Reuben Downing; Mary, married James Espy; Peter D., married Lovina Espy; Levi, married Priscilla Espy; Andrew; ——— ———, the youngest daughter, (name not remembered), lived with her mother on corner of Middle Road and the Ashley cross road; there she married and there the mother died.

John George Nagle, b. 1746, d. 1823, aged 77.   Katy Nagle, wife of John George, (b. 1756), d. 1817, aged 61.   Christian Nagle, b. 1781, d. 1857, (aged 76).   Sarah Steckel (wife of Christian), b. 1789, d. 1871, (aged 82).   John Nagle, b. 1793, d. 1875, (aged 82).   Susan (Rymer, wife of John), b. 1795, d. 1869, (aged 74).   Joseph Nagle (son of John), b. 1830, d. 1831, aged 1.   John Nagle, Jr. (son of John), b. 1825, d. 1851, (aged 26).   Clarence, son of George M. Nagle, b. 1861, d. 1861.   Nagle was of German descent; came to Hanover about 1813 with a grown up family.   They had Frederick; Christian, married Sarah Steckel; Maria, married Christian Burrier; Elizabeth, married James Sterling; Catharine, married Isaac Derhammer; Mary; John, married Susan Rimer.   John Nagle died in Wilkes-Barre.   Christian had Rebecca, married Elijah Edgerton; William, married Lydia Ann Downing; Reuben, married Jane Davis; Daniel, married Sarah Stroh; Sarah, married Peter Petty; George, married Mary Rinehimer; Charles, born 1828, died 1891, married Mary Ann Custerd; Eliza, married William Watt.   John, born 1793, had Ephraim, married Sarah Edmonds; George M., married Sarah J. Fowler.   Christian Nagle or Der-

hammer owned the place on the Middle Road, where the Roman Catholic "Hanover cemetery" now is.

John Nyhart, b. 1799, d. 1849 (aged 50). Elizabeth (wife of John), b. 1799, d. 1856,
(aged 57). Nyhart was of German descent; came to Hanover about 1845 from Newport
township; was born in Monroe county, Pa. His son, Levi L., was a cripple from burns received in infancy. By industry and saving he acquired some property at Askam, where he
was long a Justice of the Peace, and died in 1892, aged about 68.

Josiah Pell (b. 1734), d. 1802, aged 68(?). Elizabeth (wife of Josiah Pell), b. 1756, d.
1802, aged 46. Samuel Pell, b. 1796, d. 1872, (aged 76). Margaret (wife of Samuel), b.
1807, d. 1881, (aged 74). Josiah Pell was an Englishman by birth, as I have heard my
grandfather say; came to Hanover before the Revolutionary War with a wife and family;
had a son Josiah the same age as my grandfather, (born 1760), who was in the Hanover
company in the Wyoming battle. July 3, 1778, and escaped. Josiah, senior, married a second wife, Elizabeth Jackson, of Newport township, and had Polly, born 1792, died 1860,
married John James; Samuel, married Margaret Line; Silas, born 1800, died 1836. Polly
and Samuel both died in the same house in Wilkes-Barre on South Main street. Polly
had no children. Josiah Pell, Jr., went off up the Susquehanna river into New York State
where so many of our Wyoming settlers went after the Revolutionary War. I have Josiah,
senior, marked on my notes made in the cemetery as sixty years of age, but I am quite sure
that is a mistake.

Benjamin F. Pfouts, b. 1709, d. 1874, (aged 65). Pfouts was born in Lycoming county,
Pa., married Mary Frances Sively and had George S., born 1842, married, first, Emma
Quick; second, Adella Eckroth. Mrs. Pfouts is still living on the old Sively homestead in
Hanover at Buttonwood, the same place settled in 1770 by Lieutenant Lazarus Stewart, Jr.,
who was slain in the Wyoming massacre, July 3, 1778, the grandfather of Mrs. Pfouts.

Jacob Rummage (b. 1767), d. 1835, aged 68. Jacob Rummage (b. 1792), d. 1858, aged
66. Susan Rummage (wife of Jacob), b. 1788, d. 1839, aged 51. Lazarus, son of Jacob,
(b. 1813), d. 1839, aged 26. Daughter of Jacob (b. 1817), d. 1819, aged 2. Jacob, son of
Jacob, (b. 1820), d. 1839, aged 19. John, son of Jacob, (b. 1821), d. 1837, aged 16. Chester,
son of Jacob, (b. 1824), d. 1844, aged 20. Mary E., daughter of Jacob, (b. 1828), d. 1844,
aged 16. Conrad, son of Conrad, (b. 1819), d. 1843, aged 24. Catharine, daughter of John,
(b. 1821), d. 1847, aged 26. Charles Rummage, d. 1854, aged 5. The Rummages were of
German descent; came to Hanover about 1809. Their children were nearly all born before
they came here. They were Conrad, born about 1766, married Katie Minnich; Jacob, born
1792, married Susan Minnich; Christine, born about 1794, died 1886, married Jacob Miller;
Polly, born 1796, married Jacob Shaffer; Sally, born 1801, died 1851, married Joseph Rinehimer; John, born 1804, married Polly Hoover. John died in Wisconsin. Jacob, born 1792,
and Susan had eight children, of whom all but two (William, married Katie Ann Burrier,
and Zebulon, married Harriet A. Price), died young. Conrad, born 1819, son of Conrad,
was killed by the accidental discharge of his rifle while hunting, in 1843. His wife was
Catharine Sauna.

Robert Robins (b. 1777), d. 1856, aged 79. Margaret Robins (his wife), b. 1783, d. 1850,
aged 67. Cornelius Robins, b. Feb. 10, 1805, d. Aug. 7, 1855, aged 50. Robert Robins
was a native of New Jersey; came to Wilkes-Barre or Hanover when a very young man,
and cleared up a farm called the Bennett lot in Wilkes-Barre township near Newtown or

Ashley, but returned to New Jersey in 1817 and lived there till 1837, when he came back to Hanover. His wife was Margaret Sharps. They had John, married Sarah Carter; Dr. Cornelius, born 1805, died 1855, never married; Elizabeth, married Philip Hortung; Jonathan, married Elizabeth Winters; Robert, married Helen Houpt; Isaac, married Margaret Keithline; Jacob, married Maria Line; William G., married, first, Margaret Albertson; second, Josephine George. They all removed to the west more than twenty years ago, except William G. Cornelius was the doctor and was killed by being thrown out of his carriage while making a professional visit in Wright township. The Robins farm was at the northern end of Nanticoke.

John Robins (b. 1785), d. 1831, aged 46. Mary Robins (wife), b. 1786, d. 1868, aged 82. John Robins was of a different family from Robert, but he also came from New Jersey. His wife was Mary Garrison. He owned the property where the Sugar Notch reservoir now is. They had Elizabeth, born 1806, married Lewis Whitlock; Mary, born 1808, died 1880; Cornelius, born 1810, married Hannah Wiggins; Abner, born 1812, died 1884, married Catharine Faustnach; Margaret, born 1814, married Nathan G. Howe; John G., born 1820, died 1855; James H., born 1822, married Harriet Monega; Elias, born 1826, died 1887, married, first, Mary A. Mill; second, Sarah Overton. Mrs. Robins lived some years at the homestead after her husband's death. Some one of the children got sick one night and she got up to attend to it, and as she stepped out of bed a copperhead snake bit her in the foot and when she stepped off of it she was bitten in the other foot. Yet she lighted a candle and hunted for the snake in the room and found it and killed it before she would let any of the children get up and go for the neighbors and a doctor. And yet she lived through it and lived to a good old age.

Lorenzo Ruggles, b. 1791, d. 1868 (aged 77). Polly Ruggles (his wife), b. 1798, d. 1832, (aged 43). Lovina Ruggles (b. 1810), d. 1817, aged 7. Ruggles was born in Hanover, lived on the Middle Road a hundred rods or so northeast of the Hoover Hill school house; died in Wilkes-Barre. His first wife was Polly Bennett, daughter of Ishmael Bennett, Sr. They had Almon; Alfred; Josiah, born 1816; Ziba; Catlin, born 1820, married Ruth Ann Edgerton; Lorenzo; Mary, married John Labar; Jane, born 1826, died 1889, married John Rimer; Paulina, born 1829, married Charles Whitesell.

David Richards (b. 1760), d. 1837, aged 77. Susan Richards (his wife, b. 1764), d. 1836, aged 72. William Richards (b. 1790), d. 1846, aged 56. L. Richards, b. 1791, d. 1851, (aged 60). H. Richards, b. 1799, d. 1851 (aged 52). Mary Richards (b. 1812), d. 1868, aged 56. There was a family of Richards lived in the lower part of Wilkes-Barre in the early times, but whether any of these are of that family I do not know. A David, of about this age, married Mary Dilley, daughter of the first Richard Dilley. So I cannot place these.

Joseph Rinehimer (b. 1792), d. 1846, aged 54. Sarah Rhinehimer (his wife, b. 1801), d. 1851, aged 50. Simon Rinehimer (b. 1818), d. 1857, aged 39. Joseph's wife was Sarah Rummage. They had Priscilla, married Solomon Freece; Mary, married George Nagle; Susan, married Charles A. Zeigler; A. Lanning, married Kate Bennett; Isaiah, born 1835, married Elizabeth Keithline; Jacob, born 1839; Zebulon, born 1846, died 1881. Simon, born 1818, married Lovina Kreidler and had John, married Alma E. Blodgett; Daniel, married Martha Bowman; Mary Catharine, married Alva Dilley; Sarah, married —— Stettler; Thomas, married Carrie Monia.

James Shafer (b. 1753), d. 1804, aged 52. I am unable to tell anything about this Shafer.

Joseph Steele, b. 1773, d. 1858, aged 84. Sarah Ransom Steele, b. 1784, d. 1851, aged 66. Susannah B., wife of G. P. Steele, b. 1807, d. 1847, aged 39. Joseph Steele was a son of Peter, born in Perry county, Pa., and in 1790 came to Hanover with his father's family. He lived at and kept the ferry near the Red Tavern. His wife was a daughter of Samuel Ransom, of Plymouth. They had George P., born 1801, died 1870, married, first, Susannah B. Crisman; second, Lydia Eldridge; Jane, married, first, Joseph M. Beek; second, Levi Adams; Chester, born 1805, died 1858, married Elizabeth Edwards; Joseph, born 1809, married Margaret Fisher; Sarah, born 1811, died 1881, married John Power; Olive, born 1820, married James B. Ramsey; John, born 1822; Charles, born 1824, married Miranda Myers; Margaret, born 1826, married Edwin F. Ferris.

John Saum (b. 1777), d. 1854, aged 77. Caroline Saum, wife of Christian, d. 1853, aged 48. John Saum was a son of Christian; came to Hanover with his father's family previous to 1796; married Elizabeth Garrison; lived on the Back Road adjoining the lower line of Ashley. They had David, born 1802, died 1854, married Mary Shireman; Elizabeth, born 1805, died 1860, married Jacob Rimer; Christian, born 1809, married Caroline Askam; Lovina, born 1813, died 1887, married Joseph Frederick; Joseph, born 1817, married Katy Bridinger; Catharine, born 1821, died 1847, married Conrad Rummage, Jr.; Mary, born 1824, married, first, Henry Shoemaker; second Abram Shoemaker.

Lazarus Stewart (b. 1781), d. 1839, aged 58. Elizabeth Stewart (wife), b. 1786, d. 1845, aged 59. Charles Stewart, d. 1854. This Lazarus was a son of James, brother of the captain. After his father died the widow married Captain Andrew Lee, of Nanticoke, and was the mother of Colonel Washington Lee, and James S. Lee. He lived and died in Wilkes-Barre. His wife was Elizabeth Crisman.

George Sively, b. 1789, d. 1854, aged 65. Frances Stewart, wife, b. 1777, d. 1855, aged 78. Stewart Sively, b. 1814, d. 1863, aged 49. Archibald Sively (b. 1824), d. 1880, aged 56. George Sively was born in Easton, Pa.; came to Hanover in 1809; married Fanny Stewart, only child of Lieutenant Lazarus Stewart, Jr., and had Stewart, born 1814, died 1863, and Mary F., born 1817, married Benjamin F. Plouts.

Sarah Thomas (b. 1746), died 1835, aged 89. Rebecca Thomas, b. 1774, d. 1849, aged 75. I do not know who Sarah Thomas is, but think she may be the mother of Freeman Thomas and Rebecca Thomas. I knew Freeman and his sister Rebecca. He had owned the cottage at the north side of Hanover Green cemetery, but I think he sold it to Barnet Miller and removed to Northumberland, Pa., when very old, and died there about 1854 or '5. Rebecca never married, but lived alone some forty rods south of the Red Tavern on the River Road. She had considerable property and Freeman Thomas administered on the estate, and there were two or three others besides himself to share in it, but I do not remember their names.

Joseph E. Vanlear, b. 1815, d. 1874 (aged 59). Vanlear lived in Wilkes-Barre and I do not know why he was buried here.

Joseph Wright (b. 1773), d. 1828, aged 55. Elizabeth Wright, wife of David, b. 1797, d. 1853, aged 56.

This list was made in 1883 for use in writing my History of Wyoming Valley and Hanover and there are many monuments and tombstones there now—1894—that have been erected since.   There are hundreds of burials there that have no tombstones to mark the graves, and there is no record of them unless the families kept a private register.

# INDEX.

www.ingramcontent.com/pod-product-compliance
Lightning Source LLC
Chambersburg PA
CBHW060540030726
47498CB00004B/1269